TRIALS

of

FIRE

and

REBIRTH

The Immortal Beings series is set in alternate fantasy world where magic is based on color. The main characters are all immortals; some are gods with mortal worshippers.

Chronologically, this is the third book, but it can be read first.

by Edith Pawlicki

Minerva

The Immortal Beings Series

Vows of Gold and Laughter

Loves of Shadow and Power

Trials of Fire and Rebirth

edithpawlicki.com

Trials

of

Fire

and

Rebirth

EDITH PAWLICKI

For Faith, who has challenged my assumptions since childhood.

Also for anyone who has ever felt uncomfortable in their own body. May you find your path to confidence and self-acceptance, if you haven't already.

Contents

EARTH

100,000 YEARS AFTER CREATION

This map shows the regions immortals use rather than the mortal nations of Earth. The only mortal creations drawn are their largest cities; other points of interest are immortal residences and magical sites made by immortal beings.

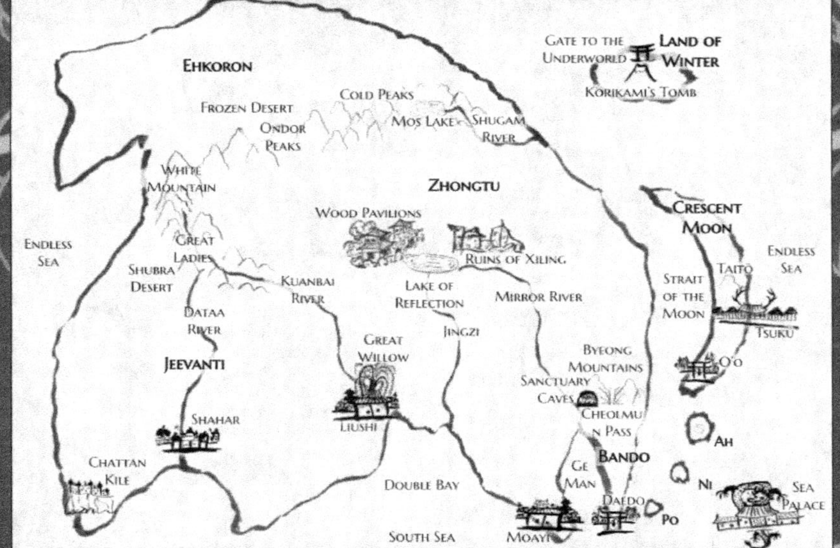

From the Ashes

3,000 *years ago*

AN NING woke with a gasp, a painful ragged breath that seemed to fill her lungs with air for the first time. A brilliantly blue sky blazed overhead, telling her nothing but *you're alive.*

Slowly she moved her fingers and felt something soft and powdery. She lifted her hands and found them streaked with ash.

She tried to remember where she was.

Who she was.

Both answers were equally elusive.

She pushed herself up, and, realizing she was naked, instinctively tried to cover her breasts.

But she didn't have any.

Confused, An Ning patted her flat chest. She had nipples,

but no breasts. Was she a child? Surely she was too large to be a child. She tried to remember a child—any child—but could not. She tried to remember what her chest was supposed to look like, and angry tears came to the corners of her eyes.

Why couldn't she remember anything?

She finally looked past her odd chest, down a smooth stomach, to a lumpy thing nestled on her thighs. Gasping in horror, An Ning tried to wipe the penis away, but it didn't move. She tugged it harder and was shocked to feel pain.

She released it.

That thing was hers. It was a part of her body.

Why would she have one of *those*? She didn't need it. Her body should be soft, smooth curves, not this flat, firm chest and extra appendage. Why didn't her body match her?

She started to shake and rubbed her arms, taking more of those ragged, almost painful breaths.

Impulsively, irrationally, she seized handfuls of the ash that surrounded her and wiped it all over her body, creating black streaks of soot that hardly covered her and yet made her feel better.

And then, inexplicably, the soot became cloth. She was robed in soft, streaky black trousers and a wraparound shirt. She rubbed her toes and gained a pair of shoes.

Then she practically collapsed back into the ash, for it felt as if she had run ten miles with a bag of rice over her shoulders.

Am I a god? she wondered.

Even though she was tired, she was vaguely aware that the energy she spent had not been physical, and she forced herself to stand. She surveyed her surroundings, and the tears spilled over.

What happened here?

There was nothing but black and gray ash stretching in all directions. No. That wasn't quite true. Blackened rocks pierced the powdery stuff here and there. Ruins.

It was a devastating sight, even if she had no idea what had been here before.

Enough to make her cry, but she could only wish she felt pure sorrow. Instead, she also felt a surge of satisfaction. A bitter delight, a cruel triumph.

What was wrong with her? Had she done this? This unending destruction?

If she were a god, what kind of god did something like this?

Not knowing what else to do, An Ning began walking.

IT took An Ning the better part of the day to cross the ash. The soft soot sucked at her feet, as if beseeching her not to leave, and the area was immense. She gradually realized that an entire city had burned; occasionally, she spotted temples and marketplaces in the ruins. There were no bones though—it was as if the city had been empty.

At the edge of the ash field, An Ning found the first signs of mortals. Thousands of them, huddled in clumps. They mourned together, shaking and crying, with lost, empty eyes.

As An Ning's gaze swept the crowd, it was pulled to a group of young ladies. Bright silks clung to their curves, sheer sleeves revealing the lines of their arms, and the upper slopes of their breasts exposed. Red paint made their lips pouty and full, and pink powder highlighted their cheekbones.

Courtesans. An Ning flinched at the word, and her eyes

skittered away from the group. What was wrong with her? Why did "courtesans" make her so uncomfortable? Courtesans... Despite having remembered the word, its meaning eluded her.

A moment later, as if hurt by An Ning's avoidance, one of the women cried out.

An Ning's eyes skittered back, just in time to see a black rock catch a courtesan on the shoulder.

"Whores!" yelled an angry voice. "You brought this ruin upon us!"

That voice scared An Ning, and she crossed her arms. She was momentarily disoriented when they folded against her ribs instead of atop her breasts.

But her personal confusion took second place to the real danger in front of her.

More stones were thrown, bringing the horrendous sound of rock bruising flesh. Blood rushed to An Ning's ears, making it hard to hear. She stepped between the courtesans and their assailants.

"What do you think you're doing?" she demanded.

Her voice was calm, confident, and throaty. An Ning couldn't quite believe it had come from her mouth.

Many of the bullies gaped at her in confusion, but one, an elderly woman, stepped forward with a snarl.

"This lot was condemned by the God of Destruction himself." She raised a hand over her eyes as she spoke and added, "Fate shield me from his gaze."

The God of Destruction. It must have been he who burned the city. An Ning was relieved to know it hadn't been her after all.

"If they were condemned, why are they here rather than burned to ash?" asked An Ning.

A young man puffed out his chest and said, "I heard the god speak to the Fourth Prince. He said Xiling must be cleansed because he and his men couldn't keep their robes tied!"

"What has that to do with these women?" said An Ning, though that word, *courtesans*, seemed to echo in her mind, and she felt scared. But she was scared *for* the women, not *of* them, she realized.

"Vile seducers," said the grandmother. "They seduced the noblemen and brought sin to our city—"

"You are confused," An Ning said. "Is a rabbit to blame for a hunter shooting it? Is a flower responsible for a little girl picking it? Is it the wine's fault when a man gets drunk?"

An Ning's heart had moved up into her throat, and she had to draw a slow breath before speaking again. "I know you are angry. You've lost your homes and all your possessions. You want someone to blame, a target for your anguish, but that's not right. Turn away now."

"Bullshit," said the young man. "Who do you think you are anyway?" and he chucked a black stone at An Ning, as did one of his cronies.

She imagined the stones rushing toward her exploding into fine black powder, becoming soft like the ubiquitous soot. But instead, one bruised her shoulder and the other cut her thigh. An Ning stumbled back and fell on her rump. It hurt.

An Ning was no longer afraid just for the courtesans, she was scared for herself. Had she imagined making her own clothes then? Was she not a god after all?

The angry mob surged closer, and An Ning found it hard

to breathe. Her arms once again wrapped around herself, trying to hold her clothes in place. She didn't want...

Her mind balked though, and she sat frozen, terrified of something she couldn't remember.

Before the mob reached her, another group ran between them and the courtesans.

"How dare you!" cried an elderly man who was brandishing a cane like a sword. "Attacking unarmed women because you're angry? This young man's right—the god kept those he wished to punish. No one here deserves your wrath. So do as he said and turn away!"

An Ning realized with some surprise that *she* was the "young man" being referenced. Her cheeks burned a little. Yet she found it easier to breathe. *Yes, I'm a young man.* Her shoulders eased back, and she looked up at their defenders. The old man with his cane seemed to be the leader, but the two dozen men and the handful of women with him had swords and leather armor.

Like most bullies, the harassers had no interest in confronting the strong. After a tense pause, the rock-throwers muttered apologies and slunk away.

Two courtesans wrapped their hands around An Ning's arms and helped her to her feet. An Ning met their eyes—one smiled and the other mouthed her thanks.

A third courtesan, a young woman with dark brown hair and big eyes, bowed to An Ning. "Thank you, sir, for stepping in." She turned to the elderly man and bowed again. "And you as well, Master Tianxu. I do not think they would have left without your reputation."

The courtesan then gestured to the rest of them. "And your

guards."

Master Tianxu grunted. "We've been planning a caravan for travel, Lady Guiying. I think you lot had best move on quickly. Why don't you come with us? And you as well, young man—what's your name?"

"An Ning." She cleared her throat. "Thank you, I would appreciate that."

THE difficulties of the next three weeks made An Ning ever more grateful that Master Tianxu had welcomed her into his caravan. Being late summer, it should have been an excellent time to travel. The roads were hard and dry, and most of the homesteads were reaping bountiful harvests, with plenty of surplus to sell to travelers.

However, the news of Xiling traveled before them, as if carried by the wind, and they were ostracized wherever they went. No one wanted to risk bringing the God of Destruction's gaze upon them by offering succor to the targets of his fury. There were a few who would make an exception for enough of Master Tianxu's gold, but he had lost most of his wealth in the fire, and there were many mouths to feed.

Some of his guards grumbled and talked of taking what they needed from the stingy homesteaders, but Master Tianxu whipped the one man who actually followed through. After the whipping, An Ning followed Guiying, the unofficial leader of the courtesans, to the river and asked her about it.

"Hmm." Guiying sat and removed her slippers before she spoke. "Master Tianxu is proud of his honor, and taking food by force, even if the farmers are greedy cowards, isn't honorable."

An Ning nodded and began removing her own clothes.

As Guiying waded into the river, she said, her voice soft and distracted, "He established the corps himself, as a young man, and made it successful by proving time and time again that his people could be trusted. Even Madame Azalea trusted him to guard us." She ducked under the water.

An Ning followed suit. When they both resurfaced, she asked, "Guard you from what? And who is Madame Azalea?"

"She owned the pleasure house where we worked. The Bloom-Laden Azalea. Madame Azalea was her working name, of course. People said she was a nobleman's bastard daughter. As for what they were guarding against...well, men who wanted to sample the goods without paying." Guiying splashed An Ning playfully then. "I suppose you don't understand that, do you? Do you like men?"

Guiying's comments about Madame Azalea made An Ning deeply uncomfortable, but the warm river water hitting her shoulder kept her from dwelling on it. She did her best to answer Guiying's question—after all, Guiying had been answering hers all week—but it didn't make much sense to her. "Like men? I like Master Tianxu and Hulk, but I don't like Hawker much."

Guiying snorted and started scrubbing her arms. "I meant generally." She bit her lip a moment then looked at An Ning more directly. "You've bathed with me several times—enough that most of the caravan thinks we're lovers, but you barely notice my body. So I thought you might be gay."

The word meant nothing to An Ning. "What is gay?"

Guiying rubbed her lower lip. "People who take the same

gender as lovers."

An Ning's eyes widened. "Is that what Shufen and Xia are? I saw them kissing, and I was surprised. I thought it was always a man and a woman."

"But you didn't consider taking me as a lover, did you?"

"Oh, but we're—" An Ning paused and looked down at her body again. She couldn't see her privates through the murky water, but her chest was a man's. She kept forgetting. She wasn't a woman. She just felt like one. "I'm sorry, I didn't think about it." She considered Guiying's first question, and realized the other woman was asking her if she liked male lovers. She mulled that over, then told Guiying. "I am not interested in any lover, male or female. It makes me a little uncomfortable when I see others touching. Is it bothersome if I follow you like this?"

"No," Guiying said. "I don't mind it. I kind of like that people think we're lovers because then they keep their distance. I didn't like working at the Bloom-Laden Azalea, and it's been a relief not to have any lovers since the fire."

"They made you take lovers," blurted An Ning. "that's horrid—and wrong!"

Guiying looked at her in surprise. "How are you so innocent? What was your life like before the fire?"

An Ning had avoided this question several times, but now she admitted, "I don't know. I don't remember anything before I woke in the ashes."

"Woke in the ashes? You mean—you were asleep while the city was burning? How..."

An Ning shrugged. "It was all very strange and confusing to me. I've been wanting to talk to someone about it, but I was afraid of how it must sound."

Guiying flapped her hand, inviting An Ning's confidences.

"I was lying in the ashes, completely naked, and I couldn't remember anything. Except my name. And I thought—" No, that was too strange to share. An Ning amended what she was going to say. "I thought I made my clothes out of the ashes!" She pointed to the pile of black cotton on the shore. "That was why I intervened when I saw those bullies throwing stones. I thought I could change the stones like I had the ash, but..." She laughed. "Isn't that crazy?"

But when she looked at Guiying, the other woman's eyes were glowing, and her hands clasped before her parted lips. "You're a god!"

An Ning blinked. "But—"

"You are a new god," Guiying insisted. "Anything can become a god. You must have risen from the ashes of Xiling!"

An Ning stirred the river water with her hand. "Anything can become a god? How do you know?"

"I'm done washing. Come on, let's dry off, and I'll recite How the Night God Fell in Love."

Guiying toweled herself briskly, and An Ning followed suit, not sure if Guiying had forgotten her offer. But then, her voice singsong, Guiying said:

> *Long ago, when the world was new and empty,*
>> *The Moon Goddess danced alone.*
> *Upon the cold ice of the North Sea, she twirled.*
> *She dipped and swayed like a hawk with its mate—*
>> *But no mate matched her.*
> *As the sun rose in the sky, she spun faster and faster,*
>> *and her shadow dwindled.*

But that same shadow could not bear to lose sight of her.
Just before it disappeared completely, it stretched up, up,
up, and became a being.
This was the Night God, and as the night embraces the
moon, so he embraced his Goddess.

An Ning waited a few moments after she stopped, but it seemed that was the end. "The shadow of the Moon Goddess is hardly 'anything,'" she protested. "I don't see why ash could become a god."

Guiying laughed. "So you want me to recite all twenty-four becoming stories that I've memorized? I like that one the best, that's why I chose it, but there are many others. Birds, flowers, deer, shadows, lightning, water—all these things have become deities. So why not ash?"

An Ning started plaiting her damp hair as she thought. "But I wasn't able to do anything with that rock they threw."

Guiying shrugged. "Well, I know tales of magic, but that doesn't mean I understand it. Have you tried to use any since?"

"No," said An Ning.

"Everyone's hungry," suggested Guiying. "You made ash into clothes; why don't you try making food?"

"I suppose it wouldn't hurt to try—say, if you think I'm a god, shouldn't you be..."

Guiying snorted. "Scared of you? Might as well fear a puppy. Besides, if you're a god, I'll be your head monk. We'll be lifelong friends—well, my life's length anyway. You'll live forever."

An Ning shook her head, not really believing Guiying's nonsense. But she let Guiying take her hand and pull her along through the woods.

When they reached the camp, Guiying led An Ning to a campfire. An Ning started to reach toward the coals, but Guiying pulled her back.

"Don't burn yourself! We had better use cool ash."

Perhaps half an hour later, Guiying presented An Ning with a cooking pot full of ash.

Knowing she must look a fool, and half-convinced that Guiying was mocking her, An Ning sifted her fingers through the dark ash. She let her mind wander, as she had when she clothed herself, imagining rice in her hands.

And suddenly Guiying shrieked.

An Ning stopped sifting the ash—no, the rice, for she had transformed it.

Guiying flung herself into the dirt, heedless of her recent bath.

"Divinity! Guide me, and I will pledge my life to you and your teachings!"

Guiying was a trained performer, and her voice was undoubtedly heard by their entire camp.

Soon everyone was crowded around them, and the black rice grains that An Ning had created were being passed around.

"It's rice alright," said Shufen excitedly, "but what a color! Thank you, thank you, divinity!"

Then Master Tianxu himself was kneeling before her. "Bringer of peace and prosperity!" He kowtowed three times, and An Ning winced to see dirt smudge his forehead. "Please, divinity, won't you make more?"

THE piercing, rapid ringing of a bell broke An Ning's

concentration, and she accidentally pricked her finger on a sharp thorn of her black climbing rose.

"Divinity? Are you alright?" asked Guiying. Not the same Guiying who An Ning had met outside Xiling two millennia ago—no, this was that Guiying's descendant, with sixty or seventy generations separating them. But because Guiying had been her first monk, it was a popular name among the locals. That simplified things for An Ning. Mortals were short-lived and prolific, and common names made it easier to address them correctly.

"I'm fine. That's not the temple bell." The massive temple bell rang low and long. "A travelling monk? Or a troubadour?"

Guiying sighed. "Divinity, I'm sure whoever it is will stay in the village for at least the night. But the rosewater—"

An Ning tsked. Unlike her ancestor, this Guiying was solemn and serious and always focused on her work. In fact, An Ning would go so far as to say she was boring. "Guiying, who is the god here?"

Guiying folded her hands and bowed her head.

Chuckling, An Ning led the way out of her manor and into the street.

"Oh, he's not a troubadour," she said.

"Then perhaps we could—"

An Ning waved her hand at Guiying. "Child, can't you see how agitated he is?"

In addition to ringing a bell with great enthusiasm, he was also shouting a psalm. "She has risen! As the Sun sets and the Moon wanes and the Night fades, glory in the brightness of the Threefold dawn! She has risen!"

An Ning strode down the road toward the monk, fast

enough that Guiying had to jog to keep up. An Ning explained, "Even though he's just a monk, he must have some interesting stories to tell! And he's wearing so many colors—whose monk could he possibly be? Do you think he follows multiple gods? Is that allowed?"

"I would think the god here would be better qualified to answer that." Guiying's arms were crossed.

"Don't sulk," An Ning chided her. She swore, if it wasn't for the fact that this family had been serving her for—well, for all of her existence, she would have sent *this* Guiying into the world to seek her fortune.

An Ning began running down the dirt road between the wide rice fields and caught the monk's sleeve.

It was an unusual patchwork of orange, red, yellow, and blue.

"Good monk," she asked, "how many gods do you serve, to wear four colors in your robes?"

The monk stopped and bowed his head. "Only one, young man, the most powerful of all, her divinity, the Threefold Goddess."

"The Threefold Goddess? Never heard of her."

The monk shook his head. "I should think not, for it is my sacred duty and my highest honor and greatest joy to bring word of her reign to all the corners of this Earth."

An Ning burst out laughing. Guiying at last caught up to them, panting and out of breath.

"Guiying," An Ning said, "I have found your soulmate. Come monk, please say all that again?"

The fussy fellow was all too happy to oblige, and An Ning struggled not to blame this Threefold Goddess for her long-winded monk. After all, An Ning would be frustrated if anyone judged her by Guiying.

An Ning held up a hand as the monk began to explain the Threefold Goddess was "the most beautiful flower, the most terrible fire, and the most favored child of the Sun."

"But what of the Sun? What was that you were saying about the Sun, and the Moon, and the Night?"

"They have died, young man."

Guiying exploded at this address. "Young man! The Peace Bringer is responsible for the prosperity of everyone within five leagues! He may not be as hoity-toity as your Three-faced—"

"Threefold!"

"—but he is divine! You will call him 'divinity.'"

The monk was briefly speechless, and then did kneel before An Ning to make his apologies (three times, naturally).

"Yes, yes, that's quite alright, did you say the Sun Emperor died? But immortals can't die!"

"Not just the Sun Emperor, divinity, but the Moon and Night deities as well. The new age will be ushered in by their children, the Threefold Goddess and the Love God."

"Love God? Don't you mean the God of Pleasure? And the Sun Emperor's daughter—why that must be the Goddess of Justice or the Goddess of Beauty."

"The Threefold Goddess was once called the Goddess of Beauty, as she hid her true power..."

The monk continued in this vein, leaving An Ning with more questions than answers. Whatever had happened in the Heavens, it was clear the Threefold Goddess had told a simplified tale to her monks.

"Well," An Ning said, after she realized they had drawn a large crowd, "Let no one say that Ningjingcun doesn't celebrate our new goddess. Tonight we will feast!"

The villagers cheered at her proclamation, while Guiying muttered, "But the roses..."

"Won't you stay and celebrate with us, monk?"

"I am always delighted, honored, and prepared to celebrate her divinity, the Goddess of Life, Death, and Beauty!" crowed the monk.

And celebrate he did. An Ning was relieved to find that he spoke more like a regular person once there was a bottle of rice wine in him.

"So what about the God of Destruction?" she asked, refilling the monk's cup. "Will he be imprisoned with the Goddess of Justice?"

The monk clapped his hands over his eyes. "Don't bring his gaze upon me!"

An Ning sighed. It was always so hard to get news of the God of Destruction. An Ning had always felt that the burning of Xiling had somehow created her, so she had been trying to learn more about this elusive deity for the past two millennia.

The few stories she had managed to collect about him said that he was closest to his full sister, the Goddess of Justice. If that goddess had been imprisoned for challenging her youngest sister's rule, then perhaps the God of Destruction was in trouble as well.

An Ning fidgeted in her seat, worried about a being she had never met—never even seen.

Idiot, she thought to herself. *You're just the patron god of a little village. None of this affects you anyway. It's not like any of these beings would ever talk to you!*

KARANA plied his oversized silk fan gently, putting some effort into maintaining a slight smile. He knew that many eyes were seeking his reaction to the wedding, undoubtedly eager to spot signs of conflict.

One would think they'd be more interested in the massive tiger that occupied half the pavilion or all the tiny peony-people that crowded the aisles, but no, instead they stared at the God of Destruction, wondering if he'd make a scene. Burn this pavilion like he'd burned Xiling perhaps, to avenge his elder sister.

And so he made an effort to look approvingly upon the two couples standing on daises, for if twenty-one millennia as the Sun Emperor's son had taught him anything, it was the importance of a flawless façade.

And the truth was, Karana saw no point in avenging his sister—she had earned her imprisonment—and he certainly did not covet his niece's position. Karana had never wanted to be a god, never mind the world's overlord.

He was relieved that Jin, his niece, had become the Threefold Goddess and that he was free to do as he pleased.

Sometimes it still seemed surreal to him. Even though it had been ten years since Jin had declared her dominion, ten years since his sister had been imprisoned in the Heavens, ten years since his father had died—

Well, ten years were nothing next to twenty-two millennia, so he was still adjusting. The past decade, he'd made a great show of attending every cursed event that Jin had organized, trying to show the doomsayers that they were on the same side.

But it was exhausting. Truthfully, he wasn't sure how he felt about recent events, and he wanted to get away from it all. If An Ning were still alive—

What a ridiculous thought. She'd be two thousand years dead, even if she hadn't been murdered. This wedding was making him maudlin.

He listened while his niece and her partner exchanged vows, and then as her best friend and his partner did. Only Jin with her sentimentality and extravagance would want such a double ceremony. And, perhaps, the three beings she roped into this circus.

At least it meant he only had to go to one celebration.

A few hours later, Karana was observing the feasting from the edge of the festivities, wagering with himself on whether that tiger was going to add some rarer meat to his dinner, in the form of the God of Festivals, when a hand clamped on his shoulder.

Karana turned and met brilliant gray eyes. The first immortal and, incredibly, Karana's new nephew-by-marriage.

"Hello, First. You didn't have to greet me. Besides my connection with Jin, I have nothing to recommend myself."

Bai ignored Karana's mocking, as he was wont to do. "Last month, the Cult of Alag Karana burned a Threefold monk at the stake."

"Yeesh, sounds unpleasant."

"Very," frowned Bai. "What are you going to do about it?"

Karana shrugged. "I don't see why I should do anything. Nothing to do with me."

Those intense gray eyes narrowed. "They worship you."

Karana snorted. "How can they worship me when I have no temples and collect no prayers?"

"The Cult is spreading lies. They are claiming that Jin murdered the Sun, Moon, and Night deities—"

"Well, she did kill the latter two."

"—and that if they burn her alive, the old gods will be reincarnated."

"I doubt anything could burn Jin. Her essence is flame."

Bai crossed his arms, and Karana supposed he should be grateful that the old being wasn't waving around the infamous Starlight Sword. "It's too late for you to choose to be a god or not. Since the cultists follow you, you are obliged to guide them."

Most beings would have to try to be this obnoxious, but it was a natural talent for Bai. For Jin's sake, Karana would tolerate it. And because he had no desire to be maimed by a pinky finger.

Raising his hands beseechingly, Karana said, "Do you really want to argue on your wedding day? How about I pour you some juice and we have a toast?"

"This is important, Karana," Bai insisted.

"Is it though? There's always going to be some crazy mortals who believe what they want, regardless of evidence or immortal guidance." Karana rolled his eyes and continued, "The so-called 'Cult of Alag Karana'—because, for the record, I have never encouraged them in the slightest way—has believed that burning the dead will lead to reincarnation for at least fifteen millennia. If they can weave such a fantasy out of nothing, what makes you think I can convince them Jin is good? It's not like they would recognize me. Or do you want me to burn all the offenders alive? Because I'm pretty sure Jin could do that more efficiently herself."

"It's not from nothing."

Karana blinked. "What?"

"You said they weaved the fantasy from nothing, but they didn't. All the immortal creatures that reincarnate do so by bursting into flame."

Karana rubbed his head. "Look, First, you're missing the forest for the trees. I have no standing with the cult, they just use my name. Jin's not actually in any danger from them. If you need something to worry about, I suggest you focus on Gu. He's full of anger and power."

Karana's gambit worked. Bai turned to look at his newly wedded wife. "I agree with you, but Jin can be ridiculously stubborn about certain things. Family is a blind spot for her."

"Why isn't he here, anyway?"

Bai lowered his voice. "We did invite him, through his mother. She asked to be excused. She wants to live in anonymity."

Karana mulled that over. "Freedom. That's what she always wanted. It should be a good life for Guleum, too. I can't blame them for avoiding us then. I wouldn't mind being forgotten."

"It's too late for you," said Bai. "You have to deal with the cult."

Karana almost said he was going to ignore the lunatics, but that would hardly convince Bai to go away. "If they so concern you, dear nephew, I will wander the Earth and observe exactly what mischief they are making."

Bai nodded once. "Thank you, Uncle."

Karana winced at the appellation, though he had invited it with that condescending nephew.

As Bai walked away, Karana figured that he could wander for a couple millennia before Bai nagged him again.

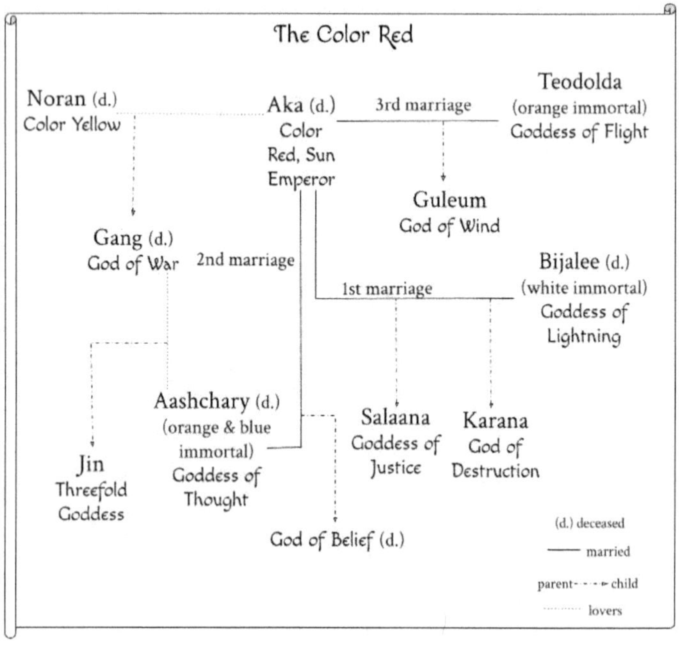

The Color Red

Noran (d.)
Color Yellow

Aka (d.)
Color
Red, Sun
Emperor

3rd marriage

Teodolda
(orange immortal)
Goddess of Flight

Guleum
God of Wind

Gang (d.)
God of War

2nd marriage

Bijalee (d.)
(white immortal)
Goddess of
Lightning

1st marriage

Aashchary (d.)
(orange & blue
immortal)
Goddess of
Thought

Salaana
Goddess of
Justice

Karana
God of
Destruction

Jin
Threefold
Goddess

God of Belief (d.)

(d.) deceased
——— married
parent- - - ► child
·········· lovers

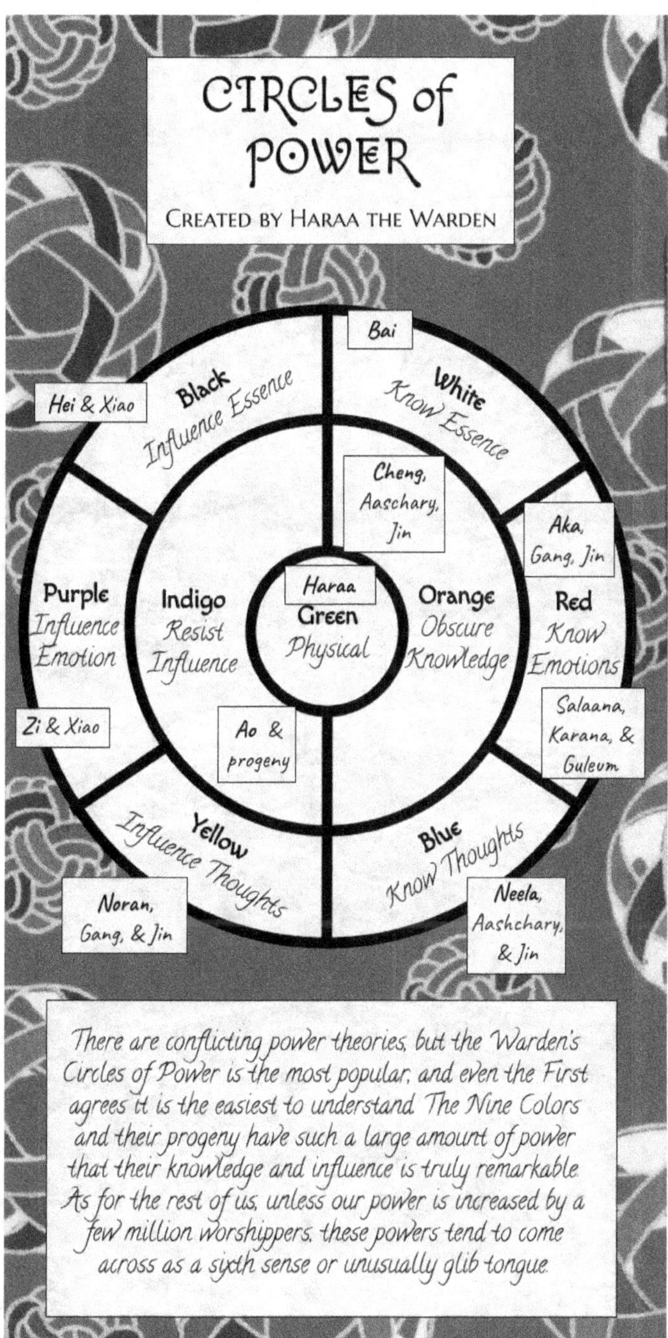

There are conflicting power theories, but the Warden's Circles of Power is the most popular, and even the First agrees it is the easiest to understand. The Nine Colors and their progeny have such a large amount of power that their knowledge and influence is truly remarkable. As for the rest of us, unless our power is increased by a few million worshippers, these powers tend to come across as a sixth sense or unusually glib tongue.

NINGJINGCUN

AND PEACE BRINGER MANOR

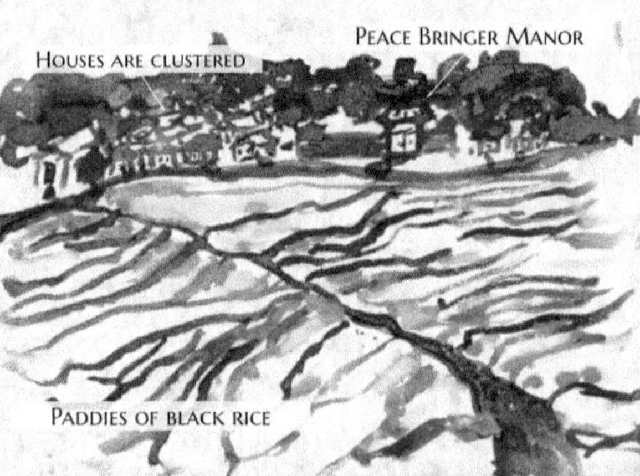

A small village in central Zhongtu, Ningjingcun has good harvests and little crime. The Peace Bringer is its patron god.

Destruction in a Village

Present Day

THE buzzing of the cicadas was so full and loud, it was hard to hear anything else. Karana didn't mind though—it wasn't as if he had anyone to talk with. In fact, the only sound the cicadas buried was the scuffing of Karana's soft soles on the narrow dirt path.

Summer was nearly over, but no one had informed the weather, for it was still unbearably hot and humid. The flooded rice paddies to either side of him didn't help with the humidity, but Karana rather liked them.

In nod to the heat, Karana had eschewed his usual black. Instead he was wearing red and white that he had shaped himself: a lightweight tunic and loose trousers underneath a sheer overrobe with wide sleeves to welcome the breeze.

He also carried a red parasol—without it, his makeup would be running in this heat.

He paused before a wooden column with engraved characters. Made from a thick trunk nearly twenty feet tall, it let travelers know they were entering Ningjingcun.

Karana's eyes lingered over that first character—he'd been hearing "Ning" everywhere the past few days. Not terribly surprising, he supposed, since it meant peace and that was a blessing most mortals were eager to collect, but it had left him feeling uneasy. He missed the days when hearing "Ning" brought him joy instead of guilt.

He could turn around and avoid the whole village.

But it was obviously a prosperous place—there was a large manor on a slight hill that overlooked the rice paddies—and it seemed this village's influence stretched far and wide. So he'd be travelling through its territory either way.

Still, he walked a little slower as he entered the village, casting his eyes left and right, seeking—

Seeking—

Seeking a phantom.

But then, knee deep in the rice paddies, he saw her. He knew that stance, that long black braid, and the way she straightened and stretched one hand toward the Heavens as she arched her back.

"An Ning!" he called in delight, before his delusion shattered.

It wasn't An Ning, of course. It wasn't even a woman, but an elegant young man who turned to face him.

AN NING was surprised to hear her name called—all the villagers addressed her as "divinity"—but she turned happily, for the voice brought a familiar exhilaration, just like burying one's nose in a rose and breathing deeply.

A tall, almost intimidating man stood twenty paces from her. He was dressed decadently, femininely, with the most gorgeous red overrobe she had ever seen and an oversized bamboo parasol. His lips were painted black, an unfamiliar but intriguing affectation, and they were curved into a smile of pure joy.

For a moment.

Then the smile disappeared, the man's expression shuttered, and he *was* intimidating, without qualification.

He shifted slightly, and she was suddenly desperately afraid that she would never see him again. An Ning reached for him.

She didn't know how it was possible, but in the next moment she seized his wrist for there was no longer any distance between them.

"Don't go," she begged, her voice oddly breathy.

And then she fainted.

ONE moment, the man stood in the rice paddy. The next, he was on the road, his large black eyes inches from Karana's own and his hand clutching Karana's wrist.

Shocked and *bewildered* were both understatements for Karana's reaction.

The man gasped out, "Don't go," and sagged forward.

Karana caught him against his chest. "Are you alright? Hello?"

The man's head lolled, his long braid falling against Karana's arm.

Concluding the fellow truly was unconscious, Karana shrank his parasol and tucked it into the wide belt at his waist.

Briefly Karana held him with two arms. Though this fellow was a stranger, it felt nice to embrace him, and Karana thought he'd better go visit someone soon. Not that he had many people whom he hugged—just his niece, and she didn't have much time for him anymore.

He looked up and down the road, searching for someone responsible for his armful. When no one appeared, Karana considered lying the stranger on the ground and teleporting away from this cursed village, but he wasn't quite detached enough to ignore the man's desperate plea.

Don't go.

What magic had the man used, to have moved next to Karana so quickly?

Karana's uncanny intuition suggested a teleport, but teleportation cost even the most powerful immortals a few minutes in between.

Still, this fellow was obviously an immortal, and Karana was curious about him. He wasn't too large—maybe a bit above average height, but only up to Karana's chin—and he was fairly lean. It would be difficult to cradle him, but Karana managed to get him onto his back.

He embarrassed himself by grunting as he hoisted the stranger higher and was forced to walk leaning forward so that the unconscious man didn't slip off.

"You should feel flattered," he told his burden. "You're the first being I've physically exerted myself for in, hmm, probably three thousand years."

Naturally, there was no reply. Should he take the man to the nearest house? Or maybe that manor he'd seen on the hill—after all, if the immortal was local, he'd live there.

His question was answered soon enough, as he was mobbed by villagers.

"Divinity!"

"Are you alright?"

"Divinity!"

They weren't addressing Karana, except for a monk in all black who demanded, "What did you do to his divinity?"

Karana turned and glared at the woman, letting the fire come into his red eyes.

"I stopped him from falling into the dirt. The young fool exhausted all his magic with one trick."

Even as Karana made up the explanation, he felt its rightness. He was hardly all-knowing like his nephew-in-law, but he had an instinctive understanding of the phenomena that he saw, the white inheritance from his long-deceased mother. He was suddenly sure that the man *had* teleported, putting absolutely everything he had into the short burst and so managing a shockingly fast teleport.

He must be strong-willed and flexibly minded. And desperate.

So mortified had Karana been by the name he had pulled out of the past that he had wanted to flee. But the man's frantic grip on Karana's wrist had shocked him into staying—for now.

Why exactly had a stranger been so determined to keep Karana around anyway?

AN NING sat up the moment she woke. Her heart was beating out of her chest, and the nape of her neck was damp with sweat.

"Don't go!" she proclaimed.

"I didn't," came the dry reply.

She whirled her head to find the tall man from earlier. Two brass lanterns had been lit—An Ning guessed it was evening—and by their light she could see that he hadn't just painted his lips black; he had also outlined his eyes. An Ning didn't know why she found that so sensual, but a frisson of awareness slid down her spine. She swallowed.

"Do you know me, young one?" the familiar stranger asked.

"I'm not young," she objected. "I'm three thousand years or more."

He laughed. "I stand corrected." He said that, but his tone belied his words. An Ning flushed.

"Well, how old are you then? You are an immortal, aren't you?

He cocked an eyebrow. "So you don't know me. I thought you must, and have something of import to discuss, to have teleported like that."

An Ning took a moment to process his words. Why had she wanted to speak to him so badly? Why did the thought he might leave alarm her?

"You called my name," she blurted.

He cocked his head. "Sorry?"

"You called my name. An Ning. Don't *you* know *me*?"

Those black lips parted, and a nervous tongue darted out to taste them.

He shook his head. "Is your name truly An Ning?"

"Yes. It's the only thing I knew when I came to be. But you recognized me..."

"Coincidence," he barked and turned his head away, showing An Ning his profile. His hair was swept back artfully from his face, and most of it was as dark as An Ning's own. However, she noticed now that the roots were lighter, red in fact, and for some reason the thought of him dying his hair made her smile. Her eyes traveled down his forehead, smooth and high, to strong, arched brows that had also been (she suspected) dyed black. He had a slim, patrician nose, those full black lips that had so intrigued her earlier, and a clean, defined jaw. His cinnamon skin was impossibly smooth, and An Ning suspected more artifice. The original Guiying had always looked far younger than she was due to her skill with the brush, and An Ning was able to recognize the signs. This man treated his face—and body, given the sheer red robe—as a piece of art for display.

Since he seemed disinclined to explain his remark, An Ning asked softly, "Coincidence?"

He lifted one shoulder in a nonchalant shrug. "From the back, I mistook you for another An Ning. It's a popular name." His lips quivered then, and An Ning knew that he had cared deeply about *his* An Ning. She was surprised when he added, lightly, "When you've as many millennia as I do, you'll find that doppelgangers are common. But my friend died long ago, and she was a woman."

An Ning flinched.

Her body was male, and she had more or less accustomed herself to being considered a man by others. She had never, not in three millennia, shared her disorientation with anyone, and she had even found beauty in this body that was stronger than most women's and had never failed her.

But when this immortal called her a man, it stung. She wanted him to see her as a woman, a beautiful woman.

Now that was a strange thought. She had never cared how others viewed her, for she looked upon physical intimacy with a mild disgust.

What about this stranger was making her reevaluate her choices?

"What's your name?" she asked.

"KARANA." He answered An Ning's question automatically.

Too late, he thought better of it. His shoulders stiffened, and his stomach knotted. Would An Ning recognize the name?

"Karana," An Ning repeated slowly, as if checking its flavor. "That's a Jeevantian name, isn't it?"

Karana nodded tightly. He supposed a little patron god like An Ning would only know his title, not his name. He hadn't given himself away. That was a relief, for if he was recognized as the God of Destruction, it would be too uncomfortable to stay, and Karana rather wanted to, despite the annoyance of An Ning's name.

"We're in my house," An Ning said after a moment, clearly surprised. "But how did we get here?"

"I carried you on my back," Karana said. "Your monk directed me."

"Xia? I'm surprised she left you alone with me. She thinks she's my mother, despite being only twenty years old."

"She's busy fulfilling that role," Karana said, "She went off to brew a nutritious stock."

An Ning's lips twisted. "That's unfortunate. She apprenticed under a witch doctor, and she makes awful herbal concoctions. I keep trying to explain that gods don't need them, but she worries about everything." An Ning swung his legs off the bed and tried to stand; Karana barely managed to catch him before he toppled to the floor.

"Oh—I say—" An Ning was fairly pale in complexion, and a slight flush appeared on his cheeks.

Karana lowered him to the bed, feeling rather motherly himself. "You've been unconscious for three and a half days. Your monk spoon fed you water." And so had Karana for that matter, but he wasn't going to admit it.

"Unless I miss my guess, you need both food and drink as often as any mortal does, so you feel weak."

An Ning gaped at him. "But—but why?"

"Well, it just depends on your original form. Although immortals don't die of old age, we still need whatever sustenance our parents or original form did."

"That's—I didn't know that, and it's interesting, but that's not what I was asking. Why was I unconscious for so long?"

Karana regrouped. "Oh. Well, because you exhausted your pool of power. With that teleportation stunt you pulled."

"What's teleportation?"

Karana snorted. But then he grew serious, for it was rather flattering that this young immortal had managed his first teleport simply to stop Karana from leaving.

"All immortals can teleport—disappear from one place and appear in another—but it takes a lot of magic. Someone with your power pool can only manage once a day, and I'd expect you to lose an hour or more between. But somehow you did it instantly and exhausted yourself."

"Oh." An Ning's gaze turned inward. "So that's why I faint."

Karana jerked his eyes to An Ning's. They were a deep black, the black of a warm summer night, and they were thoughtful at present.

"You've done that before? *Regularly*, even?"

"Well, sometimes creating things makes me faint," An Ning said with a crooked smile.

Karana stood up, abruptly angry. "Do you have any idea how vulnerable you make yourself? A being like you shouldn't be creating anything! What if someone attacks you while you've exhausted your power? Immortals can be killed, you know."

"Like the Sun, Moon, and Night deities," mused An Ning.

Karana reared back, before remembering that An Ning didn't know the Sun Emperor had been his father.

"I was shocked when I heard of their deaths," An Ning admitted. "I didn't know we could die before that. But wasn't it great magic that took their lives?"

Karana paced back and forth twice before he bit out, "Yes, but any mortal could slit your throat when you've rendered yourself powerless and unconscious."

An Ning burst into laughter, and Karana saw red.

"NO, please don't get angry," An Ning begged, realizing her laughter had offended her new friend.

Friend? Yes, friend. Perhaps her first since the original Guiying—the villagers and her subsequent monks looked upon her with too much reverence to be friends.

"I'm sorry, it's just such a preposterous notion. Me in danger? In this village? No one would hurt me here," she said confidently.

"Famous last words," groused Karana.

"No, really. When I faint, they bring me here and take care of me until I wake."

"No wonder your monk thinks you need a mother—you don't take care of yourself!" His brows were knit; he was still upset.

Upset that An Ning wasn't more careful.

The thought warmed her.

"It's safe here," she promised Karana. "This village was founded—"

A scream came from the village. It was muted by the walls of the manor, but it was definitely a scream.

She faltered. "Probably children are fighting..."

Then came another and another, accompanied by harsh barking.

An Ning leapt to her feet and once again was caught by Karana before she pitched forward.

"Thank you," she said, "I must check—"

"You must stay here," he ordered. "I will check."

He actually scooped her into his arms and deposited her back on the bed.

He pointed a long finger at her nose. "Stay," he ordered. Then he strode from the room.

WHEN had Karana been the type of fool that walked into

danger for a stranger? An Ning was ridiculously naïve, and for some reason he made Karana feel protective.

Which was too bad for An Ning—Karana's record when playing protector was quite poor. But An Ning was probably right about the lack of danger in this village, and this would be a small problem. He'd take care of it so that the younger immortal didn't drain his entire pool of power again—

Well, fate curse and mock him.

A pack of dogs were running through the village.

Dogs of blue and red fire that dripped sparks instead of spittle from their jaws.

Karana had never seen these particular immortal creatures before—in fact, he made it a habit to avoid immortal creatures and to know as little as possible about them—but it didn't take an expert to see they were insatiable monsters, eager to consume everything but the dirt beneath their feet. In fact, Karana could *feel* their endless hunger, a pain so intense that it drove them mad.

Some of the houses were ablaze, flames brushing the dark sky and painting the village a horrifying red. The air was so thick with screams and smoke that it should have been overwhelming, but it was hardly an unfamiliar scene to Karana. He ran his eyes over the houses, and realized their proximity meant soon all would be burning. A few villagers were filling buckets from the irrigation ditches and sloshing the muddy water against the worst fires and the firedogs themselves, but more were running in a panic, dragging flames along with them.

This crisis was beyond them, but still Karana hesitated. It wasn't his business if this village was burned to ground. He owed the people nothing—he had already helped An Ning, nursing him for three days after his collapse and explaining basic power rules.

Coward.

It was wise to be afraid. Immortal creatures were powerful, and Karana was unfamiliar with these. Maybe he wouldn't be able to defeat them.

Excuses. If you are too afraid to help, you should at least admit it before you run away.

Why had he told An Ning that he would help?

Well, so what? He hadn't made a vow. If he left now, he'd never see the fellow again, and no one would be shocked by his lack of valor.

Karana heard crying. A teenager was trying to reenter a burning house. Having too much experience with burning things, Karana could tell its collapse was imminent. Somebody was probably trapped inside.

A firedog bit the leg of one of the water throwers. The man screamed and caught on fire.

Karana slipped a miniature sheathed sword from his sash, growing it to full-size as he ran forward.

2

Peace Balances Destruction

ALTHOUGH the burning, screaming mortals were distracting, Karana suspected that there were more of them in danger *inside* the houses, so he focused on those fires.

Luckily, their flames were almost entirely red, and Karana could extinguish them through his will alone. The heart of the fires wouldn't obey him though, so he had to exert himself continuously to extinguish new red flames as they appeared. Still, the villagers were able to fight the fires more effectively now. As they went out, Karana could release his attention.

Now for the dogs.

He wasn't sure what would happen when he cut them—his niece had once told him about a massive ice wolf that continuously pulled its body back together—but luck seemed to be with him.

As his red sword halved the creatures, they burst into pillars of flame and disappeared.

But it was too soon to celebrate, for no sooner did he kill a firedog than another took its place.

How many of these creatures were there anyway?

Karana was an accomplished swordsman because his sister had insisted upon it, but he was soon at his limit. He couldn't stop moving, for there was always a new dog to meet his blade.

No, not a new dog.

The *same* dogs. Karana could feel their emotions, their bottomless hunger and increasing rage, as he slaughtered them over and over again.

These creatures were coming back to life?

He vaguely recalled someone telling him that some immortal creatures reincarnated. Fire creatures? Was that it?

Well, it seemed their "reincarnation" was instantaneous.

This was not sustainable. He had already used a lot of magic extinguishing the fires, but he had enough left for a teleport.

Should he leave?

He had to decide soon. Although the red flames of these beasts couldn't hurt him, their teeth could still shred his flesh and their blue flames felt cursed hot.

Everyone here will die if you run.

Won't they die even if you stay?

Karana had almost about decided to save himself when there was a wet thunk next to him. A dead chicken. The dogs were diverted. They pounced and started tearing it apart. Feathers and blood flew into the air, but other dogs caught and swallowed them.

Another chicken joined the first.

Confused, Karana looked around for the source, and found An Ning, looking like willpower alone held him up.

AN NING wasn't going to stay in her room when her village was in trouble just because a stranger told her to.

Even a stranger who could carry her in his arms and felt, well, not all that strange.

Xia arrived with a bowl of steaming broth.

"What's happening in the village?" An Ning asked, though she accepted the broth.

"I don't know, divinity. I heard the screams as well. But you need to—"

An Ning gulped the broth, only listening with half an ear as Xia reprimanded her. The bitter taste grounded An Ning, and as the heat spread through her body, she felt stronger and more present.

An Ning stood slowly, bracing herself with a bedpost. She tested her weight on her legs.

"Divinity..."

An Ning took a shaky step forward. "Something is wrong, Xia. Protecting this village is my purpose."

Xia slipped under An Ning's arm and braced her.

They were slow leaving the manor, and An Ning had to stop to use the outhouse. When they could finally see what was happening, An Ning thought she had stepped into a nightmare.

"What are those?" Xia asked, her voice strangled.

To An Ning, it looked like balls of fire were throwing

themselves on Karana. Karana himself was a blur of red as he cut the balls with a crimson sword.

"Immortal creatures." An Ning could figure that much out at least, but she had never seen these before. This was the Brown Griffin's territory, and it kept out most other immortal creatures. And An Ning bribed the griffin with plenty of meat, so that it would leave them alone.

"We need to help him," she told Xia.

"How?" Xia's fingers were digging into An Ning's arm.

One of the creatures broke off its attack on Karana to approach a villager. When the man hit it with a stick, An Ning saw that it looked like a dog. It ate the stick.

"They seem hungry," An Ning declared. "Let's get them something to eat, like we do with the griffin. Let's start with chickens—the ones from my coop."

Though An Ning was able and willing to do every chore needed to sustain herself, she was still a little dizzy and tired. Reluctantly, she let Xia catch and snap the chickens' necks. An Ning couldn't quite stop her hands from clenching and releasing compulsively. She grabbed the first chicken from Xia and started toward the gate, but Xia barked, "Why save two minutes if you're just going to fall down?"

An Ning scowled but she waited. In the end, she carried two chickens while Xia carried three and managed the doors.

When they emerged again, Karana was still keeping the firedogs occupied, but, to An Ning's eye, he wasn't moving as quickly as he had before. She ran closer—wobbled, technically—and threw one chicken into the fray.

Her gambit worked—at least six dogs turned away from the fight to tear apart the chicken. As they did so, the smell of chicken blood filled the air and the other dogs stopped to see what the source was.

An Ning threw another chicken, and Xia did as well. The creatures seemed more like dogs now than fireballs, though they ate with a wildness that was frightening.

"You're only delaying the inevitable." An Ning met Karana's eyes. His sword was pressing into the dirt, and he seemed to sag slightly.

"These things are insatiable—once they finish the chickens, they will attack again."

"Xia, get more meat," An Ning told her monk. Then she asked Karana, "Why aren't you taking advantage of their distraction?"

"It's pointless," he said. "They keep returning to life. Whether we extinguish them with water or if I cut them down, they come back moments later."

An Ning had never heard of such a thing, though myth said the Threefold Goddess could bring a being back to life—in exchange for another life. "How do you figure?"

"Same way I know they are hungry—I can feel what they feel."

An Ning's eyes widened. "Rice," she said abruptly, "we need to feed them the black rice."

"Black rice?" Karana echoed.

An Ning waved a hand at him impatiently, and with remarkable lightness, Karana leapt over the firedogs to her side. They hurried into her home, and An Ning led Karana to the store house. Five large bags of rice were stacked on top of each other. An Ning went to grab one, only for Karana to gently move her aside and lift two himself.

"Let yourself recover," he insisted.

An Ning was impatient. "The village is in danger! I don't have time—"

"As long as I'm here, you have time," Karana said, his tone brooking no argument.

An Ning whirled and hurried to the dogs. She glanced back once, but Karana was right behind her, despite the weight of the rice. Her heart beat faster—probably because this light jog felt like an exertion after three days of sleep.

"What are we doing with this anyway?" Karana asked.

"We're going to feed them."

"I had some of your local rice myself, and while it's delicious and unusually colored, I didn't think it was magic."

"But I am, and I made the rice. If the dogs are so wild because of their hunger, I will make this rice fill them."

Karana said nothing, but An Ning could feel his skepticism.

"Do you have a better idea for saving the village?" she asked.

"No," he grunted.

And then they reached the dogs, who were still eating. Some of the villagers must have thrown them food after seeing An Ning do so.

A few of them helped now, spreading the rice in a circle around the dogs.

An Ning buried her hands in the rice. Nutritious and rich in flavor, this rice had made Ningjingcun prosperous over the past millennia.

But these grains would be even more special. They would be filling; they would satiate the insatiable. An Ning poured her power and her will, her very essence, into the rice. This rice would tame the firedogs.

She held onto consciousness until she saw the first of the dogs eat a mouthful of the rice and fall asleep.

She tilted on her feet, only to be caught against a strange yet familiar chest.

"Is this thrilling for you?" Karana demanded, clearly angry once again.

An Ning tried to smile as the world faded away.

AN NING'S level of self-sacrifice was equivalent to idiocy.

He had only woken from a three-day sleep a few hours earlier, and he had already drained his entire pool of power. Karana had been forced to catch An Ning again as he fainted.

But fate was laughing, for An Ning's ridiculous stunt worked. The firedogs were sleeping, exuding contentment to Karana's magical senses. Karana shifted An Ning in his arms so that he could see his face.

An Ning had androgynous features—his brows were fine, his nose was round and low-bridged, and the lines of his face were soft. He looked youthful; well, he *was* youthful. A born immortal would still be a child. Spontaneous immortals—those who gained immortality by denying death through their will alone—appeared as adults immediately, but they were often ignorant and naïve. Like An Ning.

Karana's limbs were already aching from the fight, but he once again maneuvered An Ning onto his back.

The mortals mobbed him, seeking answers and guidance. Karana turned his burning gaze on them. "Talk to the monk," he said, and then started up the path to An Ning's manor.

He stopped after a few steps. Curse it, he hated being

responsible for anything.

"Leave the dogs," Karana told the crowd, "I'll come back for them."

Xia scurried after Karana, leaving the villagers' questions unanswered.

"Who are you?" She asked as Karana lowered An Ning onto his bed.

The question settled right between Karana's shoulder blades, a heavier weight by far than An Ning.

"And who are you to question me?" he said coldly.

Xia's lips were pale, and part of Karana felt guilty for having frightened her. She swallowed. "I'm someone who loves his divinity. You said you weren't a god..." Xia had tried to call him "divinity" while An Ning lay unconscious, and Karana had made it clear that neither she nor the villagers were allowed to do so, "...but you clearly have power. How-how can I trust you with his divinity?"

She raised her chin at the last, and her hands clenched, as if she were ready to go a few rounds, should Karana wish it.

Of course, if Karana did wish it, she'd be on fire right now.

Karana rubbed his brow. "Okay, you can call me 'divinity,' if it makes you comfortable. But don't worship me, and stop anyone in the village that you catch. You can't trust me with An Ning, of course, but you haven't got a choice. Don't you know that power is the only real law in this world?

"Now, I need to deal with those puppies."

Xia surprised him by smiling slightly. He might have imagined it, for the next moment she bowed her head, hiding her mouth, and knelt at An Ning's side.

Karana went out into night.

It was fully dark now, so Karana supposed the whole firedog fiasco had taken more than an hour. Some villagers had remained by the dogs despite Karana's admonishment to stay away, water-filled buckets at the ready. If the cursed things didn't reincarnate instantly, that might not have been a terrible idea.

As Karana stepped forward, the villagers stepped back. His order to Xia was obviously wishful thinking. These idiots were sure to worship him. The only way he could stop it would be to convince them he was powerless.

And given Karana's track record, any plan he came up with would probably backfire and convince the mortals he was more powerful than they believed now.

He did his best to ignore them as he held his hand just above the dog's fur. Well, not fur—the dog's fire?

He giggled, and the villagers backed further away.

The dog felt hot to Karana, but not unbearably so. The blue fire that he knew was inside them seemed to be fully enveloped by the red flames. Ideally, he would teleport these things far from here, but Karana had used enough power that he suspected if he teleported away, he wouldn't make it back tonight.

That would probably be fine. After all, everyone was clearly shocked by this invasion of immortal creatures, and Karana hadn't seen any others for the past two weeks. A farmer some miles back had told him that the area belonged to the Brown Griffin, who could be quite fearsome, but also kept nasty creatures like Xuezei and the Xiezhe away. An Ning would be asleep for three days, so it would be boring here anyway.

But that was also why Karana couldn't leave.

An Ning had made himself vulnerable—again—and these mortals might love him, but they could hardly protect him. How had these firedogs appeared anyway, deep in the griffin's territory?

Had someone brought them here? How? To what purpose?

He rubbed his forehead again. Probably he was being a paranoid old fool, but he wasn't going to teleport away tonight. If he returned to ruins...

He pushed those thoughts away. He wasn't responsible—couldn't be responsible—for all the actions of others. Guilt churned in his stomach anyway.

Karana scooped the first of the dogs into his arms and carried it up the hill to An Ning's manor. He was becoming a regular beast of burden, and the hill seemed a lot steeper now than when he had first laid eyes on it.

The mortals watched him carry all eight dogs up into the manor, their curiosity itching at Karana like mosquito bites. If he could have resolved this issue by swatting their eyes away, he would have.

When the firedogs were sleeping in An Ning's rear courtyard, Karana examined them.

This was really a task for his nephew-by-marriage, but Karana's more limited insight would serve.

An Ning had changed the essence of the rice to satisfy these creatures' hunger. And without that bottomless hunger driving them mad, they had fallen into a deep sleep, exhausted by the battle and—Karana suspected—their lives. He didn't think these creatures had ever rested before.

Poor things, what terrible lives those must have been. To have hunger constantly gnawing inside, so intensely that it was impossible to do anything but eat, or think about eating...

Karana felt angry as he thought about it. An Ning was just a minor god with a pittance of power. If he could help these creatures, why hadn't the Night God done this millennia ago? And after his death, his son should have!

Even Karana knew that was unfair. The Night God's son knew as little—no, less—about immortal creatures than Karana did. And the Night God himself had been a narrow-minded prick who cared only about himself and his wife. Karana didn't mourn their deaths at all.

He made himself focus on the present. When these things woke up, would they be hungry again? Not ravenous, for An Ning's magic had somehow taught the creatures to digest what they consumed, but yes, probably hungry.

Karana had never had a pet, but he was so old that it'd be stranger if he hadn't met some. So he fetched water and food bowls. He filled the water bowls with well water, and he filled the food bowls with more of An Ning's black rice. Did dogs usually eat rice?

Ah, no, that was a silly way to think about it. These might look and behave like dogs, but they were creatures of fire. They had obviously liked the rice. Probably they'd still like it, even uncharmed.

Then he went into the inner courtyard house. He stopped briefly at the door to An Ning's room, for it was slid open, and watched Xia in silence for a few minutes. She had covered An Ning with a silk blanket and was spoon feeding him something that smelled bitter. One of her herbal concoctions, Karana supposed.

"Where should I sleep?" he asked after a few minutes.

Karana had forgone sleep for the past three nights—strictly speaking, he didn't need it, but his power would refill faster if he gave himself over to oblivion. He had been tempted to take the couch in An Ning's room, but it was both too small and too presumptive for Karana.

Xia set down the bowl and walked to the door. She curtseyed once, and said, "Follow me, divinity."

All of the challenge had left her. It made no sense to Karana, but now that he was pigeonholed as an eccentric god, she was more comfortable with him.

She put him in a guest suite. It was quite clean and smelled of roses. He found them in a vase on the table, the fullness of their black velvet petals declaring they had been freshly cut. Xia must have prepared this room for him.

"A bath has been drawn for you, divinity, if you care for it." Xia indicated the bathhouse.

So ten minutes later, Karana was soaking in hot water that held yet more rose petals. He picked up one of the black petals.

He had never seen a rose of this hue before, but he liked it. Black was his favorite color.

This whole place felt like home in fact, more than anywhere had since—

No, he wasn't going to think about that right now. He wanted to relax.

Relax? When he had just decided to protect someone?

If he and Salaana were on speaking terms, that would have cracked her up.

It seemed even beings of destruction got lonely sometimes.

SOFT raindrops, pattering unevenly against the cobblestones in the side garden, woke An Ning. She opened her eyes and looked out the window, for someone had slid the rice paper frame to one side to let in a breeze as soft as the rain.

It was a gray morning, the kind that came after a hard night's rain, and left the air itself wet. Summer was finally conceding its rule to fall, and the sweet scent of rice ready to harvest was carried in by that breeze. Realizing her gambit with the firedogs must have paid off, An Ning smiled.

"Karana," she called softly, then stiffened with embarrassment. Over the centuries, she had become accustomed to the deep, assertive voice that had come with this body, but never had she heard it like this. Cloying, almost caressing. He'd think—

Reluctantly, An Ning turned her head to face him, but he wasn't in the room. She was relieved and then disappointed. How silly. It wasn't as if she expected him to simply sit by her side when she was unconscious. After all, they barely knew each other.

An Ning pushed herself up, and her red silk coverlet slid into her lap with a sensuous sigh.

Sensuous?

She didn't recognize herself today.

She looked around her bedroom and spotted a covered tray on a low table.

Carefully, she swung her legs off her bed and stood while bracing herself with the bedpost. Her lack of caution three days ago had been due to unusual circumstances; An Ning had fainted from exertion often enough that she knew to take it easy.

Beneath the woven tray cover was still warm chicken congee, pickled radishes, and water in a small pot. She made herself drink a cup of water first before attacking the congee. Thanks to her hunger, the rice tasted richer and more flavorful than usual, and she set an empty bowl down too quickly. She blushed when she saw the pickles, for they had slipped her mind. They were a little too sour and salty without the congee to temper them, but she ate them all anyway.

An Ning left the cover off the tray so that Xia would see she'd finished it as soon as she came to check and went to take care of her body's other pressing needs. When she exited the outhouse, Xia was hovering a discreet distance away (still too close for An Ning's liking).

"Divinity," Xia bowed.

"Yes, hello, Xia," An Ning washed her hands at the pump. "Where's Karana?"

"I put his divinity in the Pine Room," Xia said. "But, Divinity, perhaps a bath first?"

An Ning sniffed herself and winced. Well, she had been asleep for the better part of the last six days—no wonder she was a bit ripe. "Yes, a bath," she agreed.

Truthfully, An Ning wasn't feeling patient enough for a bath though. She scrubbed herself down using a wash basin but declined to have the tub filled for a soak. It was early in the day, and she liked evening baths better anyway.

Freshly dressed and smelling like roses, An Ning headed to the Pine Room. Her hand was posed to knock on the door frame when she faltered.

You don't need to be nervous, she scolded herself. It had been too long since she'd had a true friend, that was all.

She knocked twice and waited.

After a minute, she knocked again, more shyly this time. There was still no response. She hesitated, then opened the door a crack. She peered around it into the Pine Room—the empty Pine Room. The bed was bare at the far wall and bedding had been folded and piled at the door.

So he had left? And taken the time to clean up after himself, but not to say goodbye?

That bedding felt like a slap in the face. *Maybe he left while you were still asleep.*

She stepped in, looking for a note, but there was none.

An Ning's throat was tight, and she kept blinking. She had to get out of this room before she embarrassed herself.

She hurried from the room and barely stopped herself from bumping into Xia a few feet away.

"He's gone," An Ning told her and was glad of the steadiness of her voice.

"What? But I just told him that you were awake and would see him after your bath!"

Oh. Had she offended him in some way? He had been truly angry that she had overreached herself. Perhaps when she did it again, he had decided she wasn't worth his time. But then, why had he waited until today to leave? He seemed to be a drifter; maybe he merely wanted to use her room for a few days...

"Divinity, what are we going to do with them?"

An Ning realized that Xia had been talking, and she had missed half of it. Ah, well, Xia was used to An Ning getting lost in her musings.

"Them?"

"Those dogs. They seem tame enough, but the monks won't go near them. His divinity has been taking care of them. If he's gone…"

It hadn't occurred to An Ning that the dogs would still be around. "Where are they?"

"In the back courtyard." An Ning followed the wraparound portico of her inner courtyard to the doors at the rear. They were usually left open, but, in her eagerness to speak to Karana, she hadn't thought about the fact they were closed earlier. Obviously, that had been an oversight. She pushed both doors open simultaneously to Xia's belated warning. An Ning received an armful of fire, and a faceful of heat, as the overeager dog knocked her to the ground. Two more joined the first in licking her face.

It wasn't that unpleasant—An Ning liked it better than the slobber of real dogs—but it was rather disconcerting. She could see sparks dancing before her eyes—but it seemed that the fire of the dogs wouldn't hurt her if they didn't wish it.

Hesitantly An Ning stroked their fiery fur.

It was soft and clean, and while it felt a little warmer than a normal animal, it was rather nice on a chilly gray morning like this one.

An Ning forced the dogs to let her sit up.

She counted eight of them and thought fate was laughing at her. One—even two or three—of these creatures An Ning could work with. Now that they weren't mad with hunger, they seemed rather sweet. Trainable, even. But *eight*?

She wanted to talk to Karana again, not because he had felt like a friend, but because he knew so much more than she did. He might know what these creatures were or where they had come from and be able to bring them home.

And she was so cursed lonely. The first Guiying had told her that things became gods when they desperately wanted to continue to exist after their natural ending, and while An Ning *liked* life, she had not understood what could possibly have made her so desperate to stay alive until...

Until she saw Karana. There, she had admitted it. He felt special to her. Exciting. He had made her feel desperate.

An Ning didn't believe in nonsense like love at first sight, but she couldn't deny that she had felt something deep and primal when she saw Karana.

And now she was crying. The dogs lapped up her tears and nudged her hands with their noses, and An Ning found herself half sobbing, half laughing.

"I would cry, too, if I found these monsters in my back yard," came a dry voice. "Not that I have a back yard for them to be in."

An Ning lifted her head and found a tall blurry black blob at her right shoulder. She wiped away the tears, and the blob clarified into Karana, his lips quirked, and one eyebrow cocked.

An Ning said, "I thought you'd gone."

"So the tears were for me?" he asked.

She snorted and wiped her nose with the handkerchief he offered. "Of course not. I'm crying because of these cursed dogs, like you said."

He smiled, and she couldn't help but return it.

Bulgae, or Fire Dogs, are creatures of blue
and red and live exclusively in Bando. They
will consume everything in their path, but
they cannot cross water. Since they will
reincarnate almost instantly after death, it is
inadvisable to face them directly. Instead,
immerse yourself in water and wait for the
creatures to pass before coming out.

3

Firedogs and Fireworks

KARANA sat down next to An Ning on the wide wood steps leading to the rear courtyard and obligingly scratched one of the Bulgae's heads, and the tiny fur-like flames licked at his hand. The Bulgae wagged the fiery plume that passed for its tail.

"Where did you go?" An Ning asked, belying his claim that Karana had nothing to do with his tears.

"Ever heard of the Moon Deer?" Karana asked. He'd been impatient for An Ning to wake, but he had suddenly felt nervous and shy when Xia had informed Karana that An Ning would see him soon. He had teleported as soon as Xia had left, with the excuse of consulting the Moon Deer to learn what the firedogs were—and he got an answer, too. Bulgae. "He's got the most detailed records on the immortal creatures. I wanted to find out more about our new pests."

"Pets," corrected An Ning.

Karana shook his head in denial, but An Ning had already moved on, "What do you mean 'ours'?" His voice became high and fast. "Are you going to stay?"

Karana looked at the Bulgae, remembering how it had only taken him twenty minutes to return, which said something about where he really wanted to be. He said, too casually to his own ears, "I'll stay a few years. To teach you about magic and teleporting."

An Ning's smile turned his eyes into quarter moons, and Karana felt a nice warmth spread out from his belly. "That would be wonderful! Thank you!"

Karana wanted to... Well, pat An Ning's back or something. Instead, he scratched the Bulgae that was drooling—sparking?—all over him a little harder.

"So these fellows are called Bulgae, and they're native to Bando." He hesitated a moment, not sure whether or not he should share the next bit.

"And?" asked An Ning.

With a sigh, Karana added, "They're pretty much confined to Bando. Apparently, they never cross the Byeong Mountains, and they *can't* cross the sea. Since they're made of fire. So how did they get here?"

"Someone brought them," An Ning suggested.

"That's what I thought, too," he said, "but how and why? I mean, we barely managed to deal with them. If someone brought them and purposely released them in the village..."

"Do you have any enemies?"

"Me, the Peace Bringer?" An Ning smiled apologetically, inviting Karana to laugh at him, but Karana nodded.

"Seems unlikely, doesn't it?" He scratched one of the Bulgae on the side of its neck and its back leg started thumping against the ground.

Any attack was more likely directed at him than An Ning and Ningjingcun, but he didn't want to share that with his new friend. And though An Ning made Karana feel protective, his innovative solution to the Bulgae had shown that he wasn't as vulnerable as Karana had thought. Plus, as an immortal male, this An Ning was far less vulnerable than the other one.

Aloud, Karana said, "I could help you set up some basic defenses around the village and teach some martial arts."

"Martial arts? To me?"

"And the villagers, if they are interested. Why? You object?"

An Ning's expression looked strained—it definitely looked like he did object—but he said, "We would all be deeply grateful."

"I also wondered what you want to do with these things. I could teleport them back to Bando."

An Ning wrapped his arms protectively around the creatures as if Karana had suggested eating them.

"They're practically tame now! We can't abandon them in Bando."

Karana fought a laugh. "Well, I could see if any of my acquaintances are looking for a guard dog."

"Didn't you call them ours?" Those emotive eyes were pleading. "Can't we keep them?"

Ours. We. Karana felt the blood fill his cheeks, and he was grateful that his skin was dark enough to hide a flush. He was too old to be blushing.

He looked at Bulgae, and one of them licked his face.

"They'll be a lot of work, and your monks are ill-equipped to manage them." He hesitated and then said, "I suppose... If you were willing to import some caregivers... I know someone with a surplus of grandchildren that happen to have a useful skill when it comes to these puppies. What do you think? How would you feel about taking on disciples?"

"Disciples? Would anyone want to be my disciple? Maybe yours—"

"No. I've never had a disciple, and I don't intend on getting one now. But yes, I think the youths I have in mind would be happy to learn how you manage the village and your worshippers. If you're willing to lose one or two bedrooms to them..."

"Sure," An Ning grinned, with his usual easiness. "It's been a few hundred years since any of the local families lived with me, and the place is too empty."

Karana marveled at how different An Ning was from him. He was always suspicious of others and would certainly not accept strangers into his house.

Except you moved into a stranger's house. Is it really that different?

And the only thing Karana could think was that An Ning didn't *feel* like a stranger, despite the fact they had only met a week ago, and An Ning had been asleep for most of that time.

Karana cleared his throat and tried to convince himself that his face felt so hot because it was being licked by a tongue of flame.

"I'll go get them in a few days."

An Ning smiled and nodded.

A WEEK later, An Ning met her potential disciples. Karana listed their names and called them the Sea Dragon's granddaughters.

An Ning laughed. Because of course that had to be a joke.

But three sets of indigo eyes had blinked at her in confusion, identical expressions on their similar faces— expressions that said there was nothing funny about being the Sea Dragon's granddaughters.

The *Sea Dragon*, ruler of the oceans and the rivers, one of the oldest gods. Three of *his* granddaughters were standing in An Ning's inner courtyard, looking curiously at her black roses and her.

An Ning was mortified. And tongue-tied.

So she tripped over their names, which sounded unfamiliar to a being who had never travelled farther than fifty miles from Ningjingcun.

Karana repeated the names again, more slowly.

"Akemi." On the cusp of womanhood, she was only a little shorter than An Ning herself, with a pale oval face and indigo hair that hung loose to her bottom. She had bowed neatly to An Ning, and An Ning was aware her return bow was not nearly as elegant.

"Chika." She was holding Akemi's hand and so short and slight that An Ning took her for a child. However, she had smiled broadly and said she was the same age as Akemi – give or take ten years.

"And Miho." Miho was between her two cousins in height, and the plainest of the three, but her smile was also the kindest. She greeted An Ning in a soft voice and thanked her for inviting them.

That's right, An Ning reminded herself. *This is my home, and Sea Dragon or no Sea Dragon, they've come to be my disciples.*

She remembered Karana saying that they'd be glad to learn what she could teach. An Ning found her own smile and called three roses to her hand.

The girls' eyes widened in interest, and they accepted the roses with obvious pleasure.

"You are most welcome, and I thank you for your help with the dogs—the Bulgae. May I ask—how old are you, about?"

"We'll all be four thousand in less than four hundred years," said Miho.

"But that's older than I am!" An Ning snapped her mouth shut when she realized she was gaping. They looked like mortal teenagers.

"They are born immortals," Karana said, his voice lightly amused. "They won't be considered adults until their four thousandth birthday."

"Or five thousandth," said Chika with a pout. "Ojichan thinks that most people celebrate too early."

"And that's why you came with me! An Ning and I will consider you adults at four thousand."

Akemi snorted, surprising An Ning for she looked ethereal and it was a coarse sound. "We'd have come either way. At home, we each share a room with five other people, and Uncle Karana said that we could have our own here."

"Uncle?" Who was Karana anyway? For some reason, An Ning had thought he was a minor god like her, but An Ning couldn't go calling on the Sea Dragon for favors.

"Because his sister is married to our aunt," Miho said.

His sister? So he was a born immortal like these girls? Then he must be over five thousand years old. An Ning had many questions for him, but she didn't want to look ignorant in front of her new disciples. So she nodded, as if unsurprised, and said to the girls, "Why don't I show you your rooms, and then I can introduce you to the dogs?"

They nodded, and An Ning turned down the boardwalk to her left. Karana fell in step beside her; An Ning couldn't resist tracing his strong profile with her gaze. She flicked her eyes front when he started to look back at her.

"You are all sharing a suite," she explained to the girls. "My monks arranged it so that you can shut the doors and each have your own room, but for now—" she pushed open the pine doors to reveal a large room "—we left them open."

The three girls strode in boldly and began fussing over and praising both the painted screens and the vases that Xia had filled with late blooming flowers.

An Ning showed them how to divide the room into three with sliding screens, and from the excitement in the girls' eyes, she suspected this might be the last time the doors were open for a while. (Even if Chika and Akemi seemed attached at the hip).

Why are they so excited to have private rooms? She wondered in amusement. And then it turned to worry. *Aren't they too young for lovers?*

An Ning did not like the idea of policing the intimate lives of three girls on the edge of womanhood. *But if policing must be done, surely "Uncle" Karana...*

She hesitated. Fifty years or so ago, a girl in the village had married her aunt's husband's younger brother. It had been a little unusual, but not shocking...

What if Karana...

An Ning clapped her hands together and asked with forced cheerfulness, "Are you ready to meet the puppies?"

KARANA and An Ning stood back from the crowd of girls and dogs, letting the Sea Dragon's daughters get acquainted with the Bulgae. Karana was feeling quite satisfied with his own cleverness in recruiting the girls when An Ning cleared his throat—a little nervous?—and asked, "So your sister is married to a daughter of the Sea Dragon?"

Karana heard the unasked questions. *Who are you? How powerful are you? Why would you care about a village god like me?*

He didn't want to answer the first two, and he wasn't entirely sure about the last yet, so he stuck with the only one An Ning had articulated. "Yes. The Sea Dragon has thirteen children, and only a few of them are married to well-known immortals." That was true, and An Ning would assume his sister was a petty goddess.

Of course, she was actually the most famous of all the Sea Dragon's children-by-marriage. She had once been one of the most popular deities in the world, the Goddess of Justice. But then she had hatched a plot to kill the ruler of all immortal beings—their father, the Sun Emperor—and take the throne for herself.

And so for the past thousand years, she had been locked in a celestial prison, and her worshippers had forgotten her.

Karana wished his worshippers would forget *him*. But the Sundered Cult was still around—he had even met a couple of cultists a few weeks before he reached Ningjingcun, engaging in petty arson. He had used their own fire to scare them out of their wits, while not revealing himself, lest their obsession with him grow, but he still didn't understand why his nephew-by-marriage had a bug up his butt about some crazy mortals.

"Still," said An Ning, and Karana forced himself to focus, "you knowing the Sea Dragon seems so incredible to me. The farthest I've ever been from here is the Ruins of Xiling."

A knot settled between Karana's shoulder blades. Afraid that An Ning might want to talk about the ruins, he threw out a tidbit to distract him. "I am twenty-two millennia old. So I've met a lot of immortals and been to most places on this Earth." He shrugged. "You know, all these famous beings aren't as extraordinary as their legends make them out to be. The truth is, when you meet them, you realize they are as petty as you and me." He laughed suddenly and amended, "Well, as petty as me. You are far less petty than most of them."

An Ning flushed. He looked pretty with pink cheeks. Actually, even though Karana had never been attracted to a man before, he thought An Ning was very appealing. Beautiful, even. And he could tell that An Ning had some interest in him as well.

It had been a really long time since Karana had had a lover, and he'd never courted an immortal before, but he was thinking about it now.

But they should be friends first.

"Thank you," An Ning murmured. Then, "Why do you always put yourself down? The way you helped us was amazing."

"What, the way I chopped down some dogs over and over

until you came along with a lasting solution?"

An Ning's mouth worked, and then he laughed. "Forget I asked. Thanks for staying though."

"Mmmm."

"So, um, you said these girls had some special skill that would be useful with the Bulgae? Can they control fire like you?"

Karana laughed. "No. Rather the opposite. All—"

A shriek interrupted him, and Karana focused on the girls and the dogs to find Blue and Ember (An Ning had named all eight of the creatures) pulling on a rope that had three-foot-high flames.

An Ning started forward, but Karana grabbed his arm. "You'll see."

A moment later, water from the koi pond shot through the air and drenched the rope. Then it gathered itself back up and returned the pond with a splash.

An Ning gaped before saying weakly, "Perhaps we should rehome the fish."

SUMMER faded away—and good riddance, for Karana hated sweating—and autumn settled in with its bright moon. Although the Lover's Moon Festival had died with the Moon Goddess, an air of romance still clung to the upcoming Harvest Festival, to Karana's chagrin.

After the second time Akemi, Chika, and Miho had come home gossiping about the mortals they had seen cavorting under the moonlight, An Ning had decided that it was better for Karana and him to take the eight Bulgae for their evening walks.

So Karana held two leashes in both hands, and his arms were in danger of being pulled out of their sockets as the Bulgae sniffed with shocking pleasure at every suspicious pile they came across.

"People should clean up after their animals," Karana groused to An Ning. "This isn't sanitary."

"It's mostly oxen dung," An Ning replied with an amused smile. He didn't seem to mind the Bulgae pulling—or maybe they didn't pull so hard for him. At least three of them slept in An Ning's room each night, and the creatures seemed to agree that he was the one to whom they owed their allegiance. "It's the same as the manure we spread in the paddies."

Ember, the biggest of the Bulgae, made a play for one particularly fresh pile, and Karana hauled him back. The first time he walked them, he had let the creatures roll in the crap; after all, he had reasoned, they were made of fire, so wouldn't they just burn it off?

Turned out that burning oxen dung smelled awful and permeated everything. Xia had barely managed to exorcise the stench from the manor by burning massive quantities of sage.

"No," he said sternly to Ember. "Leave it."

Ember whined and somehow managed to look pathetic, despite the fact its flaming blue eyes threatened to burn the world.

"No," Karana said again, and pulled all four dogs to the opposite side of the path, where they couldn't reach the dung.

An Ning followed him, with far less resistance from his dogs.

A sudden pop in the air to Karana's right shocked him, and

he jerked his head up to see falling red sparks.

"Fireworks!" An Ning exclaimed. "I wonder where they got them..."

Another flower bloomed in the sky, not far from the first, lighting up the straw roof of the nearest home.

"And why they think it's a good idea to set them off by the houses!" Karana had actually invented fireworks some seventeen millennia ago, and he had seen about every way they could go wrong.

"I think they're at Old Zhao's place," An Ning said. "There's a shortcut ahead."

An Ning led them down a narrow path that cut between two paddies, though Ember stopped to lap at murky water, and then the other seven all had to taste it as well.

Karana held the dogs' leashes impatiently and hoped no mortals were using this particular path for their amorous adventures. He watched the fireworks uneasily. They were quite big.

"I can't remember the last time I saw fireworks," said An Ning. "They're beautiful."

Karana twisted toward An Ning, and his breath caught.

Thanks to that uncommonly bright moon—only two days short of being full—he could see An Ning's soft smile. His black eyes were lost in the dark, but his pale skin caught the moonlight, and he looked more beautiful than ever.

Karana opened his mouth to promise An Ning the best fireworks he'd ever seen, but snapped it shut, swallowing the words.

He didn't want to stay a few years.

He wanted to stay forever.

Which was stupid. With two dead parents, Karana knew that eternity was a lie. Even for immortals.

"Beautiful doesn't mean safe," Karana snarled, not sure if he was warning himself or An Ning. He hauled the dogs along before they finished lapping at the mud.

AN NING'S smile faded as Karana pulled Ember, Spark, Flare, and Blaze past her on the narrow path.

He was an odd one, that was for sure. Or maybe it was his age. An Ning sometimes lived in the past, and she was only three thousand years old. Karana had said he was *twenty thousand*, so perhaps the fireworks had reminded him of some past tragedy.

But for a moment, his teeth had flashed at her in the dark, and she had thought he was smiling. So she had been shocked to hear the anger in his voice.

"Come on, Blue, Red," she clicked her tongue. "Flame and Cinder. Let's go."

The four Bulgae obligingly let An Ning lead them down the path.

It was a gorgeous night, and An Ning was disappointed that Karana wasn't enjoying it with her. She hoped he wouldn't be too fierce with the mortals; they were just getting excited for the Harvest Festival, after all. Old Zhao's grandson must have come for a visit and brought the fireworks from the city where he worked. Maybe he had gotten married—now that would be cause for celebration!

"It's strange, I tell you, strange and wrong. And the worst part is, they think they're in charge of us. Women ought to know their place!"

The fireworks had stopped, and the too-loud voice carried across the paddies. An Ning recognized Old Zhao's grandson, but he was clearly a bit drunk and his bitterness unnerved her. Maybe he hadn't gotten married, but had come home to lick his wounds after a rejection?

Someone clicked their tongue. "His divinity has always had female monks, since saving the Lady Guiying outside of Xiling."

An Ning half-stumbled. They were talking about her monks? They thought Xia didn't know her place? It was true that she could be a little overbearing—look at the way she bossed An Ning—but An Ning wouldn't tolerate such nonsense. Xia did more for this village than anyone!

"That's another thing," said the grandson. "According to Meng, Xiling was burned for its sins. The God of Destruction—"

"Don't bring his gaze upon us!" barked Old Zhao.

The grandson scoffed. "No wonder you live in a town run by women, you old coward! Meng, tell Grandpa about Xiling!"

A new voice joined the others, and though An Ning knew it was a man, she imagined a Xuezei, for it was undoubtedly preying upon her people. "The whores of Xiling ruined the noblemen of the city, and so the Cleansing God purged it."

"Well, the monks of Ningjingcun aren't whores! His divinity is as chaste as a stone!"

"Is he?" asked that new voice. "I saw him walking with that man—the one that paints his face like a woman. Maybe the only reason he hasn't touched your women all these years is he has unnatural desires."

Old Zhao burst out laughing, but An Ning didn't find it

funny in the least. Her face was burning. What must Karana think?

"You can't have it both ways," said Old Zhao between his guffaws. "Are you trying to convince me his divinity is a hedonist who keeps lady monks for his sexual gratification or a pervert that takes male lovers?"

An Ning's feet had frozen to the ground. She didn't want to hear anything else, but she couldn't stop listening.

"I don't know, Old Zhao," said another voice, and the doubt in his voice made An Ning uncomfortable. "I saw those two gods looking at each other, and maybe they are lovers. What if his divinity brings the wrath of the Burner of Xiling down on us? I met a fellow the other day who wouldn't stay in town when he learned it was founded by refugees from the cursed city."

"Ignorance!" Old Zhao was truly angry now. An Ning wished she could share that healthy anger. Instead she felt sick. "Don't you ever let me hear you say that again, Yi Lin! This village has been the safest, most prosperous place to live for my whole life because of the Peace Bringer!"

"What about those firedogs?" argued Yi Lin. "Almost destroyed the whole town!"

"And the gods are the ones who stopped them!"

"But why are the dogs still here?" asked Meng, the stranger whose voice was both insidious and threatening. "Making pets of such devils—can you really believe your god brings peace?"

"This town will burn if you don't stop it," said another unknown man.

"How would we stop it?" asked Yi Lin, his voice fearful.

"Burn the monks," said Meng.

Karana thrust the leashes of the dogs at her, and An Ning took them automatically. Then Karana leapt into the air—he seemed to fly across the paddies to Old Zhao's house.

An Ning was speechless for a moment, but she took off at a run and the Bulgae were only too happy to oblige her whim.

"The truth doesn't need to be shouted to be heard," Karana was saying as An Ning peeled into the yard.

And then chaos broke loose.

KARANA was confused when An Ning froze on the dirt path. Surely he could hear the mortal bile that was spewing forth as clearly as Karana—didn't he want to stop it?

He peered at An Ning's face in the dark and decided his friend was shocked. He waited a few minutes for him to regain his composure, but instead An Ning seemed to crumple in on himself, his shoulders hunching and his focus on the ground. He seemed to have forgotten that Karana was next to him.

When one of the mortals said that An Ning's monks should be burned, Karana decided that was enough. He pushed all the leashes into An Ning's hand and "flew" across the rice paddies. Really, he was moving his red robes through the air and they were pulling him along for the ride. His sister had taught him to do it this way to intimidate mortals.

He touched down in the circle of men. He met each of their eyes, letting them see the fire that burned within him. It was easy to see who was a local—these bowed or even kowtowed, while the outsiders leaned forward eagerly, their lips parting as if they were aroused.

They wanted a fight.

"Why are you bringing hate into a peaceful village?" Karana demanded.

"We are bringing truth!" The man who shouted was well-muscled with many scars on his face and his bare arms. Karana could feel his excitement, his lust for destruction. He was a Sundered Cultist; Karana was sure of it.

Karana struggled for calm. "The truth doesn't need to be shouted to be heard," he said. Those who knew him would realize the quiet of his voice meant they should tread very, very carefully.

But no one had taught the Bulgae that.

The eight of them burst into the yard, barking their heads off and lunging at the men.

No, not at the men. At the outsiders.

They were furious, full of anger, as they had been the first time Karana had encountered them. But this time the anger was from fear and resentment rather than hunger.

These men brought the Bulgae here. The cult must be using the Bulgae to burn down villages.

How'd they manage that? And why this village?

The answer came to Karana, though he didn't want to know it.

After the Sun God's death, the Sundered Cult had viewed the Threefold Goddess as a murderer and their enemy. But there was nothing a bunch of mortals could do against the supreme ruler of the world, and so their anger had found other outlets. Several hundred years ago, they had started capturing minor goddesses and burning them at the stake.

But it was hard to kill a goddess—even the weakest ones could usually manage a single teleport to save their lives—and the cultists often settled for monks.

And it was uncommon for a deity to have only female monks; An Ning's quirk must have provoked the cult.

So they really were here for the Peace Bringer rather than the God of Destruction.

"It was you who brought the firedogs here," Karana declared, for the villagers benefit. "It is you who seek to burn this village!"

The cult leader, who had been trying to hold the Bulgae off with a stick, suddenly laughed.

"We will burn this village even if we burn with it! For we shall be reborn in fiery glory when the ancient gods return!"

"Rebirthed in flames!" screamed the five outsiders. And they lit more fireworks—ones that were strapped onto their chests.

They were going to kill themselves to destroy the village.

An Ning's Lie and Karana's Sorrow

IT was depressingly easy for Karana to contain the resulting explosions. The only things that went up in flames were the cultists themselves, and Karana at least wouldn't mourn them. In fact, he made them burn hotter and faster, so that they would be rid of them sooner.

So he was a little surprised when, after the flames snuffed out, one of the villagers let out a keening wail.

An Ning ran forward, knocking Karana aside, and wrapped his arms around the old man. "Old Zhao!" he said.

"My grandson!" gasped the man.

"I know, I know," said An Ning, and Karana realized the god was crying. "I'm sorry, I'm so sorry."

Old Zhao shook his head and cried harder. "How will I face my daughter in the Sea of Souls? How will I tell her that I taught her son wrongly and so he died such an ignominious death?"

An Ning rocked Old Zhao back and forth, like a mother soothing her child.

Even as Karana told himself he couldn't worry about every mortal sorrow, he replayed the scene. He shouldn't have been surprised that the cultists were prepared to kill themselves. This whole evening could have gone better if he had been a little more cautious.

And...

The way that Old Zhao blamed himself for his grandson's misdeeds.

I taught her son wrongly.

"You cannot control what another believes," Karana offered, trying to comfort himself. He was not responsible for the cult. He hadn't taught them at all, never mind "wrongly!"

"Yes, Old Zhao, it's not your fault," several of the other villagers mumbled, and hands reached out to pat Old Zhao's back.

After a moment, Old Zhao pulled out of An Ning's arms. Still on his knees, he bowed. First to An Ning, his god, then Karana, then the rest of the villagers.

"Thank you, divinities, for your kind words, and my neighbors, for your forgiveness. But I do not shirk my responsibilities." He twisted toward An Ning again. "Divinity, I must undertake a pilgrimage to atone for my grandson. Will you make sure my fields are taken care of while I am gone?"

An Ning stood and pulled Old Zhao to his feet.

An Ning bowed to his own worshipper, and Karana felt tears prick his eyes. He blinked rapidly—smeared kohl was the worst.

"Of course, Old Zhao," said An Ning. "You must do as your conscience bids you. Your field and home will be kept ready for your return."

"Thank you," he bowed again, and then the old man disappeared into the house.

An Ning turned to the other men who lingered in the yard. "This has been a dramatic evening. My friend and I saw that there were fireworks dangerously close to the houses, so we came to investigate. I know all of you were simply visiting your neighbors and enjoying the novelty of fireworks brought by visitors.

"Tomorrow we will hold a service to send these men's confused souls on to the Sea properly. But tonight, I think it best if we all return to our homes and reflect on this sorrow. If any of you wish to ask me questions tomorrow, I will gladly hear them."

An Ning took one step before one of them men stepped forward. "Divinity—why do you only accept women as monks?"

An Ning hesitated. "I'll accept anyone who asks to be my monk. No man ever has."

The villager looked dumbfounded. "May—may I enter your service, divinity?"

"Yes, of course, Yi Lin." An Ning laid a hand on Yi Lin's head, and a moment later he dropped to his knees to kowtow. "Report to Xia in the morning," An Ning added.

FIRST the Bulgae, now this. Of course, if what Karana said

were true, both things were one and the same.

An Ning shuddered as she and Karana brought the Bulgae home—everyone gave them a wide berth, for somehow the dramatic events in Old Zhao's yard had spread throughout the village.

"Are you alright?" asked Karana calmly.

An Ning eyed him uneasily. She had questions for him—he seemed to know more about the Sundered than she did—but something more immediate worried her. She blurted, "What nonsense those cultists were saying! As if I'd be interested in you. I'm celibate. Have been my whole life."

Oh, fate mock her, what on Earth was she saying? *As if I'd be interested in you.* The words rang so patently false to An Ning's ears—and were they offensive? But she remembered what Old Zhao had said—*a pervert who lusts after men*—and she couldn't find it in herself to soften her words.

Karana stiffened—she *had* offended him. "I'm so relieved," his voice dripped sarcasm. "I wasn't looking forward to breaking your heart."

"Well, good then." An Ning said. She wasn't going to cry. How ridiculous. She had only known Karana for what, a month? And sex was gross. Messy and violent. Being friends was the best way. She had never wanted a lover and never would.

KARANA took a bath before bed, trying to forget the disgust and terror that had emanated from An Ning as he made his feelings clear.

Karana shouldn't have been so shocked. Of all the regions

of Earth, Zhongtu was by far the most sexually restrictive. Some ten-odd millennia ago, Karana's father had performed a miracle just east of here and, with his usual lack of reflection, had declared the purpose of sex was to allow a husband and wife to have children. That idea had led many Zhongtuese to condemn any other kind of relations, despite the Moon and Night deities and, eventually, the Love God's attempts to teach otherwise. And An Ning had never been anywhere besides here. So Karana had been stupid to forget that he'd probably object to a romantic relationship between men.

Karana curled up into a ball so that he submerged his head in the hot water. He held his breath until it grew uncomfortable—unlike some immortals, he needed air, though he barely needed to eat.

When he came back up, he said aloud, "It's not as if you need a lover. You've been alone more often than not."

Karana had had nine lovers in his whole life. Each one had been a mortal woman, and so even summing all of the time he had committed to someone was less than half a millennium.

He still felt disappointed though.

That night, his bed felt uncomfortable. At first, he was too hot, but when he threw off his blanket, he shivered. Karana gritted his teeth and drifted into an uneasy sleep.

SHAANTI was leaning forward, the tip of her tongue visible at the corner of her mouth, as she tried to hold her gnarled hands steady. Her kohl brush tickled as it slid over Karana's eyelid, and he struggled not to giggle.

Shaanti pulled back and laughed. "There. Your eyes look

twice the size now. Not that they needed to look bigger." She sighed. "Your eyes have always been lovely."

Karana blushed at her words before leaning forward and pressing his lips against hers. "I love you. You know that, right?"

The next moment, Shaanti was stretched out on a funeral pyre, her hands folded across her belly. Shaking with rage, Karana leaned forward and kissed each of her closed eyelids, not caring that the kohl there would turn his lips black.

Not caring? No, he was glad that it did. The sorrow and rage inside him were so great that it should be writ on his face for the world to see. Or at least his treacherous monks.

"Who did this?" he roared at them. Twenty men who claimed to follow him, but they had poisoned his first monk.

Shaanti. Whom he had loved, though he had never told her. Why hadn't he told her?

The cowards knelt before him, wringing their hands, and smacking their heads into the dirt. Karana didn't care. They were violent, cruel, and selfish. There would be no forgiveness here.

He would burn all of them alive.

Even the boys.

Even the boys?

They were crying, their faces so distorted that it broke his heart. The youngest was only four years old, far too young to be condemned. Even if it had been he who brought the poisoned tea to Shaanti.

I must. It's the only way...

Red flame surged up around him, and screams of agony lashed his ears.

Karana stayed hard, determined to end this here and now.

If he showed mercy—

No, he wouldn't! He wouldn't make that mistake again!

Karana sat upright in the dark, sweat drenching his robes. He was gasping for breath. It had been a dream. A nightmare, twisted from his memories.

He pressed his hands hard against his eyes, trying to drive the dream and the memories away. Stubbornly, both stayed, churning inside until it was hard to remember what had really passed.

After a moment, he jumped from the bed and flung open the doors of his room. It was barely dawn, the haze of red and pink just outlining An Ning's roof.

He needed to get out of here. He strode across the inner courtyard to the gate that led to the entrance. He pushed it out of his way, as he had his doors, and moments later he was running down the dirt roads of Ningjingcun, past the quiet paddies with their full, dark fronds of rice ripe for harvest.

Karana almost set them on fire, to expel the destruction inside, but some part of him realized he'd feel worse after. He kept running until he was out of town, past the massive wooden pillar. He could have teleported of course, but the running helped. The slap of his bare feet against the hard packed dirt—

Oh, fate laughs. He had forgotten his shoes. He pictured himself for a moment. Bare feet streaked with dirt. Crumpled robes. His sweat had dried as he ran through the chill morning air, but he stunk.

He must look like a madman.

Maybe he *was* a madman. He sat down and hid his face in his hands. It was so early that probably no one would see him cry. When he finished, he would teleport back to An Ning's manor, and no one need know—

An arm wrapped around Karana, and he was being rocked, just like Old Zhao had been last night.

And by the same motherly being.

"DO you want to talk about it?" An Ning asked.

She had trouble sleeping last night, so when Karana had started slamming doors and gates in the wee hours, she had come immediately to attention. Part of her had felt presumptive running after him when he took off through the village, but...

But he mattered to her. She was afraid he might be leaving, even though he had brought his nieces to her and had promised to stay for a few years. An Ning didn't know Karana that well yet, but she had already figured out that he was impulsive.

When he had collapsed on the ground and started crying, an internal voice had whispered that she should turn away so as to not embarrass him.

She had ignored it for she couldn't ignore Karana.

But Karana was clearly mortified, and An Ning expected him to tell her to mind her own business.

"When I first came to be," An Ning said, looking across the paddies as if they were more interesting than Karana's tear-streaked face, "I had nightmares regularly. I tried to keep them to myself, but they got worse. Finally Guiying—she was my first monk—made me tell her about them. And then they got better. The more you avoid your fears, the more frightening they become. But if you look them straight in the eye, you might discover that slavering wolf is just a little puppy."

Karana snorted. "Or maybe you'll discover it's the Korikami, and you're an idiot for looking back."

An Ning looked at him and grinned. "Or that," she agreed. "Maybe I could have chosen a better metaphor."

Karana didn't reply immediately, and An Ning thought she had indeed presumed too much.

"The Sundered are my fault," he said suddenly, leaving her speechless. She hadn't known what was bothering him, but she would never have guessed that.

He continued on, speaking a little too fast, as if now that the dam had broken, the reservoir of sorrow couldn't be held back.

"My sister wanted me to get worshippers as soon as possible, so she established a mortal temple for me when I was only a teenager. No one wanted to be a monk for a scrawny teenage boy who didn't look remotely god-like, except for Shaanti."

He laughed—a sad sound. "In retrospect, she was a scrawny teenage girl, and she probably had a crush on me. I certainly felt in love with her, but we were kids, and then she was an old woman while I was still a teenager so... But when I look back on it, I know I loved her, and I hope she knew it, too."

Karana, despite the fact that An Ning was aware of how tall and strong he was, seemed painfully vulnerable. And An Ning felt jealous of a long dead mortal—she pushed that away and focused on the man in her arms. He needed her right now, even if they'd never be lovers.

"Shaanti was a good organizer, and she recruited a dozen

and then a hundred monks. I wasn't that interested in them; I didn't want to be a god, but I went to the temple as often as I could to see Shaanti. The second and third monks were jealous that I spent so much time with her. They believed that Shaanti was deliberately limiting access to me, their god.

"And then..."

When it seemed he had forgotten to speak, An Ning whispered, "What happened?"

"I was trying to be closer to Shaanti. There was a big gulf between us, you know, and I wanted to be closer to her. So I asked her to help me dress in her sari and to paint my eyes like she did hers. Actually, almost everyone in that region of Jeevanti painted their eyes with kohl, so that shouldn't have been a problem, but for some reason, me dressed in a sari was deeply offensive to the other monks."

Karana looked her straight in the eyes then, and his mouth twisted cynically. "I suppose it bothers you, too. You have strict ideas about what men and women are supposed to do, don't you?"

That observation hurt—because it was true. It made An Ning feel like she had somehow betrayed Karana—or herself. She shrugged, her arm still wrapped around him. "I'm young and ignorant, or so you've been telling me."

She must have succeeded in keeping her voice light and mocking, for Karana burst out laughing. "Very good," he told her.

He sighed suddenly, and those dark red eyes, which she had lit with amusement, darkened abruptly. "Anyway, they killed her."

Obviously, Karana had been upset about something, but An

Ning had been in no way prepared for this. Her stomach dropped. "I—your other monks killed your first monk? Because you wore a sari? I—I'm so sorry."

Karana shook his head. "It wasn't the sari, not really. It was the jealousy. The sari was an excuse."

"What did you do?"

"Burned them alive."

An Ning went stiff. "All—all of them?"

"Unfortunately, no," Karana replied, his voice so dark and threatening that it terrified An Ning. "I let the children go. And they started the Cult of Alag Karana." He hesitated. "Alag Karana means 'Sundered.' So you see, the Sundered are my fault."

An Ning swallowed. She knew that something was wrong with Karana's reasoning, but she was so shaken up that it was hard for her to pinpoint what. "I don't think you should regret sparing children."

Yes, that was it. Karana was basically saying that he had made a mistake in not burning the children with the other monks. That was not his mistake—actually, without more details, An Ning wasn't totally sure what his mistake had been, but she didn't think mercy was ever a mistake.

"Those children," Karana went on, coldly, "are the reason that a few thousand women have been burned at the stake, all in the name of reincarnating a selfish old man."

He pulled away from her suddenly and stood up. He stalked a few feet away.

An Ning came to her feet more slowly. She forced herself to think through his story. "I wasn't there, so I can't judge, but if you made a mistake, it was in abandoning the children. In not teaching them right from wrong."

Karana whirled on her, absolutely furious, fire dancing between his fingers, and An Ning was terrified. She stumbled backward and tripped. She flung up an arm to protect herself, a useless gesture.

She was expecting to feel flames along her skin—to become once more the ash she had been—but nothing happened.

Hesitantly, she dropped her arm and met Karana's gaze.

Fire no longer danced among his fingertips. He looked devastated, not angry.

"I have made a lot of mistakes in my life," he told her, "but I'm not a monster. If that's how you see me—"

"No!" An Ning shouted. She jumped to her feet and grabbed his arm. "I'm sorry, I've always startled easily, and the flames scared me. But I know you're a good being. And you can't go. You promised me a few years of magic lessons." She forced a smile.

Karana didn't smile back. His solemnity was frightening. But after a few minutes too long, he nodded. "I won't leave while you want me to stay."

Revels and Revelations

30 years later

AN NING was nervous, understandably so. Hosting thirty guests was quite an undertaking, but when they were both strangers *and* members of one of the most famous families in the world—well, who wouldn't be nervous?

The Sea Clan would be descending on Ningjingcun for Miho's adulthood ceremony in two days.

Chika had been training the Bulgae to do tricks, which An Ning didn't doubt would be satisfactory, while Karana was managing the decorations. He had an excellent sense for such things, so An Ning wasn't worried about that either.

But An Ning and Akemi were organizing the feast, and Akemi had just told her the Sea Dragon would expect fish.

"Fresh water fish?" An Ning asked doubtfully.

Akemi snickered and shook her head. "It had better be sashimi," she said, "though some roasted eel could supplement that."

"Akemi," An Ning said, "no one around here makes sashimi."

An Ning herself had only had sashimi once—Akemi, Miho, and Chika had fetched some from the Crescent Moon when they learned An Ning had never had it. That had been ten years ago, and An Ning had hated it. The way the dark red fish cubes had mushed in her mouth, so that An Ning couldn't forget that she was eating a creature's flesh. That salty bubble-egg that Akemi had sworn was a delicacy. Worst of all, that horrid radish paste that Chika had tricked her into eating.

"And we don't have the ingredients," An Ning went on. "What are we going to do, teleport buckets of raw seafood here?"

"Exactly," said Akemi. "As well as a chef, I think. Ojichan wouldn't be satisfied with what amateurs could produce."

An Ning narrowed her eyes and stared at Akemi intently. "Are you teasing me? Is this a prank?"

Akemi and Chika loved pranks—especially Chika. Miho was the only one of An Ning's disciples whose words could be taken at face value.

Akemi's eyes crinkled in amusement. "No, I am wholly sincere. Fate trick me if I am not. If you want to make a good impression on Ojichan, you need to serve sashimi."

"But you said he rarely comes this far inland. Some local specialties—"

Akemi shook her head. "Not a good idea. Ojichan has very set opinions about what is best, and he is *not* open-minded.

My guess is he's already criticizing you for letting Miho have her ceremony so soon. I strongly suggest you should get the sashimi."

An Ning threw up her hands in surrender. "Fine. But that means *you* had better get the sashimi and I will be your assistant. Because if I'm in charge..."

Akemi laughed. "But of course."

Just then there was a tremendous splash, as if five large buckets had all been emptied simultaneously. An Ning and Akemi both turned to the sound.

Karana was a statue, his hands flexed as if they'd like to strangle something. He was also dripping—even from across the courtyard, An Ning could tell his makeup was running, giving his face a grayish cast. An Ning lifted her skirts and ran across the stepping stones. She slipped as she approached, for the rocks were slick around him, and Karana finally moved in order to stop her fall. They whirled together once before he set her upright.

Slightly breathless, An Ning asked, "What happened?"

Chika had her hands clasped before her, her eyes wide and innocent. Which meant she knew she was in the wrong.

"I was worried that it might rain tonight, so it was too early to put up the paper streamers, but Uncle Karana said his ribbons would hold up to any soaking, so I wanted to test them."

Karana lifted his hands and wiped his cheeks—it didn't help, instead smearing the thick kohl even more.

"The streamers are waterproof," and his voice was so dry that An Ning was surprised it didn't evaporate the water right off of him, "as you can see." And indeed, the vibrantly red streamers, edged with silver, looked perfect, despite the water dripping off of them. "I, however, am not."

Given Karana's calm, An Ning's anger seemed foolish, but it was undeniable. Chika and Akemi both were always trying to provoke Karana into losing his temper—why on Earth they wanted to, An Ning had no idea. Chika said she was curious to see what would happen. And yet, Karana never seemed to. In fact, it had been nearly thirty years since An Ning had ever seen him express any strong emotion—not since the incident with the Sundered, and that had been sorrow more than anger.

An Ning loved Karana's calmness; she didn't understand why Chika and Akemi couldn't just be grateful for it. But whenever she pressed them about their provocations, they would turn evasive.

"Chika, you'll be responsible for the household washing next week."

For a girl who could control water, it wasn't a harsh punishment, but Chika hated laundry. She also did a terrible job with it, so An Ning added, "And if you don't do it up to Xia's standards, you'll be doing the dishes too."

Xia was now a grandmother, and if she had been fussy as a young woman, she was a genuine tyrant of late.

Chika pressed her lips together. "Sorry, Uncle Karana."

Karana seemed more amused than anything, his lips quirking up. "Actually, if I could make my kohl as waterproof as the streamers, I wouldn't begrudge a drenching on a day like today."

It *was* hot and drier than usual.

An Ning looked at Karana's face, covered with damp black smudges. "Perhaps..." she said and wrapped her hands around his face.

She froze as soon as her fingers touched his cheeks, surprised by her own boldness. His cheeks were cool, thanks to the water, and impressively smooth. An Ning wanted to stroke them.

Luckily, she met Karana's eyes and saw his shock and discomfort before she made a fool of herself. She focused on the kohl.

Karana realized what she was doing, and his hands wrapped around her wrists. "Don't make yourself faint!" he scolded. "I can wash my face—"

An Ning tsked. "This is nothing. Don't insult me." And it was. Moments later, the kohl was back in place.

"You'll need oil or soap to remove it now," she warned him. He released her wrists, and she dropped her hands. A little slowly maybe, for she liked touching him too much.

Karana touched his face lightly, his eyes on her, as if he was suspicious that she still might faint.

That intense look made her breathless again. So An Ning turned to Akemi. "We should go now, don't you think?"

"Where are you going?" asked Karana.

"To Hirohama," answered Akemi. "I convinced An Ning to serve sashimi."

"Ah," Karana nodded. "That's good." He met An Ning's eyes and smiled. "I know you hate it, but the Sea Dragon will be impressed."

An Ning forced a smile in return. She was still angry at Chika, and her tummy was all fluttery.

About an hour later, An Ning and Akemi reappeared in an unfamiliar city. Unfamiliar in more ways than one—the air was sharp with salt, and An Ning could hear... A storm? Yes, it sounded like a terrible storm, when the wind blows the rain so hard that it slaps the side of the house. But the sky was clear.

"What's that noise?" An Ning asked.

Akemi tilted her head in confusion. "What noise?"

An Ning waved in the general direction of the roar. "That—crashing sound."

Akemi still looked at her blankly for a few moments, then her whole face lit up, her mouth curving into a wide smile and her dark eyes quirking into half-moons. "Come with me," she said, catching An Ning's wrist and pulling her along.

The last time Akemi had caught her wrist like this, Ember had gotten into An Ning's flower garden and eaten the heads of half the roses, so she couldn't quite quell the trepidation that started rising in her, but Akemi didn't pull her far.

"That noise," she declared grandly, "is the sea!"

An Ning's breath caught. A troubadour had once described the sea as being like the rice fields of Ningjingcun, but blue as far as the eye could see.

That wasn't right at all!

It was more like a sky, a turbulent, stormy sky, that stretched across the land. An Ning looked up again, at the sky that was as cloudless and calm as one she had seen when she first awoke, and almost wished that it *was* a stormy day. Would the sea and the sky then be like reflections of each other, both roiling gray-blue?

"An Ning!" said Akemi, breaking her reverie. "Don't cry! Are you alright?"

An Ning closed her eyes in embarrassment. She wiped the

tears from her cheeks. "I was having a moment." She smiled to lighten her words. "Until you ruined it."

"Oh." Akemi flushed. "Sorry."

An Ning shook her head with a small sigh. "It's not important. Why don't you lead on to this chef and his fish?"

Akemi nodded reluctantly, and, shortly after, they hired Hirohama's best sushi chef. He cried (from happiness, An Ning hoped) when he learned he was to serve the Sea Dragon. An Ning was impressed with Akemi's efficiency, so when the young immortal said there was one more thing she wanted to do, An Ning was happy to oblige.

"You'll like this better than the ocean!" Akemi said, pulling An Ning though narrow streets.

But when they turned the last corner, An Ning was horrified.

The street was full of *courtesans*, that cursed word that had never sat easily in An Ning's mind, even after seventy years of friendship with the first Guiying. They were uncomfortably beautiful, their faces painted white and their lips painted red, with the most colorful silks that An Ning had ever seen wrapping their slim figures like gifts. They even had massive bows on their backs, to make the comparison blatant.

Did Akemi think she would like *this*? She who was famously celibate and had remained prim and proper the entire time she had been Akemi's teacher? Did Akemi think that An Ning regretted her choices? An Ning felt offended. Hurt. *Devastated.*

As if Akemi not only didn't know An Ning but wouldn't like her if she did.

Akemi was watching her in puzzlement. "An Ning?" she

said uncertainly. "I don't want to interrupt another moment, but this time I really think you are upset?"

"I don't want... I would never hire..."

Akemi brows remained knit for a few seconds more, before rising to her hairline. "Oh! Oh, no! That's not why I brought you here. Besides, this street isn't where you—" Akemi blushed. "These are stores! I wanted to buy you a kimono! To impress the Sea Dragon."

"Oh." That was better—but not much. An Ning did love the clothes the women—were they not courtesans?—were wearing, but seeing such prettiness reminded her that she was not a woman but a man.

And then Akemi shocked An Ning. In a wonderful way.

She grabbed one of the beautiful women's wrists and said, "Excuse me, sir, but what shop do you favor? I think your tailor would suit my friend."

And the *man* smiled back at Akemi, though his vivid red lips didn't actually move. "Lady Sashiko's, with the purple noren." He gestured with his parasol—he did not *point*, that would have been too vulgar for such a being, but somehow he conveyed the direction with a delicacy that An Ning envied.

As he moved away, An Ning murmured to Akemi. "That was a man? So—so, if I was to dress like that, the Sea Dragon..."

An Ning met Akemi's eyes. They were full of smiles and secrets, and An Ning suddenly thought that Akemi *knew*. Somehow, she understood that An Ning was a woman. Or, if that were too strong to say, she knew that An Ning wanted to dress femininely, to look beautiful. An Ning swallowed twice and blinked rapidly.

Akemi wrapped her hand around An Ning's wrist and led

her halfway down the street into a store with rich purple curtains in its door.

And then they stepped into a wonderland.

KARANA was reiterating the safety instruction for the various chemical compounds he had procured for Chika when she laid a hand on his arm and said, "I've got this."

He couldn't blame her, for he had given them at least ten times already.

"Why are you so nervous anyway?" she asked.

Karana snorted. "Nervous? With my face and powers? Don't be ridiculous."

Chika stuck her tongue out at him, but almost immediately pulled it back in and looked around her. She'd been more careful the past two days, ever since An Ning had assigned her laundry duty for dumping water on Karana.

Karana chuckled and told her, "An Ning's still getting ready."

Chika's shoulders relaxed. "It is ridiculous that you are nervous, but you are."

Karana wanted to dismiss her observation again, but he wasn't even convincing himself. Anxiety was bubbling through him, making him queasy. Maybe it was An Ning's nerves rubbing off on him? It was hardly a secret that An Ning was worried about impressing his disciples' family.

But that wasn't it. Karana cared about An Ning—he was Karana's friend, after all—but the gnawing worry in his belly was more personal.

What if someone tells An Ning who I am?

After thirty years, An Ning still didn't know Karana was the God of Destruction—the son of the former Sun Emperor and the uncle of the Threefold Goddess. And while at first it had felt like a little secret, it now seemed like a big one, for An Ning had once told Karana that he was fascinated by the God of Destruction. Karana had learned that he had formed from the ashes of Xiling, and so considered the god a creator of sorts. Karana had been puzzled, for he was sure An Ning needed to eat and sleep, and ash didn't have to do either, but more than that, he had been horrified. If An Ning learned Karana had burned Xiling, would he think of Karana as his creator? Or, worse, his *father*?

The idea made Karana shudder.

Chika, Akemi, and Miho knew, of course, that they were not to mention Karana's title.

He asked Chika now, "Are you *sure* that no one will...you know, call me...?"

Chika rolled her eyes. "Everybody knows you hate your title. None of them ever call you that, do they? They are more likely to slip up if you mention it. Wait, is *that* what you're so nervous about?" She started laughing.

Karana was searching for a scathing setdown when An Ning called, "What's so funny?"

Chika abruptly stopped laughing, undoubtedly fearful of being given latrine cleaning duty if An Ning found she was mocking Karana again.

Karana smirked at her, before turning to An Ning with a lazy smile, ready to distract him.

But he forgot his words. An Ning wore a lavender kimono with orange and white butterflies embroidered on it. A wide green obi cinched his waist, and he was slightly turned, revealing the generous folds that billowed at his back.

Most notably, An Ning was beaming. He clearly approved of his own appearance, and Karana both loved and hated Akemi in that moment.

Loved because he had realized that Akemi must have taken An Ning to a seamstress in Hirohama and thus fulfilled one of An Ning's dreams. An Ning, like the villagers in Ningjingcun, tended have rigid views about gender, but there were times when his yearning for elaborate, feminine attire was painfully clear. And yet Karana had never managed to convince him to try anything besides the practical, masculine robes he always wore. So Akemi was to be commended and thanked.

However—and Karana didn't think this was jealousy that Akemi had succeeded where he had failed, but maybe there was a little of that, too—he was certain that Akemi hadn't explained that this manner of dress was adopted by men who were sexually available to everyone. Karana, of course, believed that any clothes could be adopted without the customs that usually accompanied them, but wearing such robes to host the Sea Dragon's family without knowing what they implied?

Karana was sure that *someone* would try to seduce An Ning, and he was equally sure that An Ning wasn't prepared for that possibility. An Ning chose celibacy, and any hint of sexuality tended to make him fold up on himself.

And so Karana hated Akemi for being irresponsible.

And now, what was Karana to do? Should he warn An Ning about the assumptions those robes would bring? But how devastating, if An Ning was then too embarrassed to wear them.

Perhaps it would be better to stay by An Ning's side and dissuade any admirers who grew too bold.

Of course, then they would assume Karana and An Ning were lovers.

That thought made Karana happy, though he knew he should be ashamed of himself for wanting something that An Ning had clearly denounced.

And yet, in the same way An Ning's love of feminine frills sometimes came through, there were moments where Karana thought An Ning also wanted him, he was just too afraid to admit it.

And so even Karana didn't know if he was being selfish or kind when he approached An Ning and said the kimono suited him.

However, the way An Ning's full lips curved and revealed his perfect teeth told Karana he'd made the right choice. One way or another.

RED lanterns were strung around the perimeter of the courtyard and overhead, giving a gentle rosy cast to An Ning's face as he toasted Miho. From the way he fisted his hands behind his back, Karana could tell An Ning was nervous, but he doubted anyone else realized. Instead, they would be caught up in An Ning's wide, sweet smile and sincere love for Miho—like Karana himself.

Reluctantly, he dragged his gaze from the speech's maker to its subject. Miho was definitely flushed, both from wine and embarrassment, and looked almost red in the rosy light. When she met Karana's eyes, he gave her a smile and wink. Miho grinned and swung her face back to An Ning.

An Ning told two more stories—both totally wholesome praise of Miho's sincerity and thoughtfulness—and though the Sea Dragon clan was too refined to cheer, Karana could tell they were pleased. Chika took the makeshift stage then, as well as one of the Bulgae. Honestly, Karana wasn't positive which dog it was, but An Ning briefly squeezed Karana's arm in excitement.

"Oh, look at Ember's flames! How did she do that?"

Chika had asked Karana for help, that's how. There were certain compounds that, when burned, produced flames of unusual colors. Chika had coated Ember in the ones Karana had procured, and now it was edged in violet and green. It was pretty, but Karana's eyes were drawn to An Ning, who had withdrawn his hand as quickly as he had placed it.

Karana could see the reflection of the colorful flames in his friend's dark eyes. As he watched, An Ning's lips curled into an open-mouth smile, and his eyes crinkled with joy.

Karana's whole body felt tight, like a giant hand was squeezing him. Seeking distraction, he used his chopsticks to select a wafer-thin slice of a pale fish. It melted in his mouth and tasted faintly of the ocean, but Karana would have preferred deep fried pastries and grilled chicken.

He drank his soup, which was at least warm, if too thin for his taste. Now, a nice thick dal...

An Ning squealed in excitement, and Karana looked at him from the corner of his eyes.

And noticed he wasn't the only one. Miho's brother was raking An Ning with his eyes, and a smile that Karana didn't like in the least was playing on his lips.

Well.

The boy would be disappointed, that was for sure.

But an hour later, when the Bulgae show was replaced by a quartet of Sea Dragon grandchildren, the impudent youth asked An Ning to dance, and An Ning said *yes*. Karana had to clasp his hand in his lap to stifle the flames that danced on his palms.

Yes? *Yes*? Karana had once asked An Ning to dance during the Harvest Moon festival, ten or so years ago, and An Ning had told him gently that men didn't dance together! Apparently, he just hadn't wanted to dance with Karana.

Chika slid into An Ning's empty seat.

"Ask him yourself."

Karana whirled on her, eyes narrowed to slits.

Chika shrugged. "Or have some sake instead." She poured Karana and herself cups, and after a tense pause, Karana deigned to click them together before gulping his.

"An Ning doesn't dance with other men," Karana said through gritted teeth.

Chika widened her eyes in faux innocence. "An Ning follows the expected social mores. Akemi and I explained to him how the customs of the Crescent Moon vary from Zhongtu." She leaned forward conspiratorially. "But we didn't do it for our cousins' benefit. We did it for yours."

Karana stared at her a beat, took in her sly smirk, then filled both their sake cups again.

"What nonsense are you on about?" he asked—quietly, in case anyone was listening.

Chika rolled her eyes. "Uncle Karana!" she huffed.

He was unmoved.

"Look," she said, "I love An Ning. But you have to admit, he's a little closed-minded. It's obvious he's in love with you, he just has strange ideas about what's appropriate between men."

Karana ran his finger around the rim of his sake cup. "Why do you say it's obvious?" His lips begrudged the words, and they came out barely coherent.

Chika understood though. "You constantly keep each other company. You share food. He laughs at your terrible jokes."

"The same might be said about you and me," Karana said dryly.

"I don't laugh at your jokes," said Chika, "and I look at you like the boring uncle you are. An Ning looks at you like you are the most beautiful being in the world."

Could Chika be right? But An Ning said he wanted only friendship. Should Karana press him? Did he dare?

THE whole evening was magical, and not just because the Bulgae were jumping through spinning rings of water or because impossibly colored flames dazzled An Ning's eyes.

The air itself smelled like the ocean that An Ning had seen in Hirohama. It wasn't the piles of sushi, that had been displayed to resemble dragons, but seemed to emanate from the Sea Dragon clan themselves. An Ning had heard the Sea Dragon formed from sea water and now she believed it, though the ocean she'd seen looked more gray than indigo.

At her side, Karana looked more handsome than ever. It had been a few years since he'd last dyed his hair, exposing a good hand's length of the most glorious crimson that An Ning had ever seen. She had carefully said nothing to Karana, for fear that it would prompt him to dye it, but tonight she realized he was very aware of the red, for he had his hair braided and ornamented to highlight the contrast between it and the coal black of his lower locks. His eyes were elongated, as usual, by kohl, but he had added something to it—a powder, she supposed, that caught the light and shimmered. The same shimmer highlighted his slashing cheekbones, and his plump lips were a deep, sensual red.

His face was a credit to skill rather than magic, but he still seemed otherworldly.

He wore white robes tonight, with black vines painstakingly worked all over—An Ning knew it had taken a seamstress in the village the better part of a year to satisfy Karana on that front, but the results were worth it. His shoulders were impossibly broad, and a dark red belt worked with silver outlined his narrow hips.

He seemed larger than life, partly perhaps because all of the sea clan was quite short—An Ning thought she was the tallest being present after Karana, who had a good head on her.

And he sat a tinge closer than she was used to—close enough that she smelled cinnamon and his arm sometimes brushed her when he moved. He wasn't deliberately crowding her; the table was a little too full.

But a tiny little voice wished that it *was* on purpose.

The way they sat, at the head of the table next to Miho, they seemed like a couple.

Oh, fate, was she drunk? She had limited herself to amazake, the less potent and far sweeter brew of the evening, but she could feel the flush of her cheeks. Maybe she needed a little space—she could go check on the Bulgae. Chika had put them back in the courtyard, where An Ning was sure they were fine, but it would be a plausible excuse.

A man, youthful in appearance with a fine beard, paused at An Ning's other side, practically wedging himself in between An Ning and Miho.

"Oh!" exclaimed Miho in surprise. "An Ning, this is my brother. Kensuke."

"I so appreciate your kindness toward my little sister," Kensuke said, his eyes quirking into a smile. "Won't you let me thank you with a dance?"

An Ning was pretty sure her flush spread. Akemi and Chika had told her that young men were apt to dance together and warned her it would be rude to refuse anyone who asked, but she was still a little surprised.

"Yes, of course," she said, though she hadn't consciously formed the reply. "My pleasure."

Karana made a strange noise, and An Ning glanced at him. His face was serene and unreadable. Kensuke took An Ning's hand and tugged her around the table to the courtyard that had been prepared for dancing.

An Ning looked at the hand clutching hers. His palm was slightly smaller than her own, but pleasantly warm.

What would it be like to hold Karana's hand?

Kensuke released her hand as a steady drumbeat started. And then he was spinning to notes of three flutes, and An Ning was following as best as she was able. Actually, she would have been totally lost if Miho hadn't given her a brief dance lesson yesterday.

Soon it felt natural, and An Ning loved the way the large

bow on her back seemed to tug her along to the music. She felt graceful—elegant—feminine.

And that was wonderful, even if she'd have to return to herself tomorrow.

Kensuke was replaced by another young man whose name An Ning didn't catch, but he looked so similar to Chika that An Ning wondered if he were her brother.

An Ning danced more clumsily—or perhaps her partner wasn't as able to compensate for her inexperience—and she kept bumping into his hand. She was embarrassed, but he grinned at her, so she tried to keep up and not dwell on her mistakes.

And then—

FOUR more shots of the potent rice wine, and Karana decided he did dare dance with An Ning. He absolutely dared. Especially since An Ning was now dancing with Chika's brother, and the fellow's hands were wandering where they shouldn't.

It was surprisingly easy to move through the dancing crowd of indigo kimonos—maybe the flames that occasionally flared on his shoulders helped—and then Karana caught An Ning as he spun away from his dance partner.

BROAD hands spanned her waist, so hot that they scorched her. And that was no exaggeration—flames were flickering all over Karana, including at his fingertips.

As An Ning met his eyes, she knew she ought to be scared,

but instead she was thrilled. The flames faded, but the heat in his eyes remained. An Ning soon discovered that Karana was the best dance partner yet, even though this style was unique to the Sea Dragon's family, or so she'd been told. Of course, Karana had known them for thousands of years, and he was quite athletic...

Maybe too athletic! He spun faster, and An Ning was vaguely aware that the other dancers moved to give them space. She felt like she was on the verge of losing control, but she never quite did. It was headier than the amazake earlier, and she felt hotter than ever—entirely Karana's fault, she was sure.

She didn't think they were following the dance that Miho had taught her anymore—she was sure of it when Karana caught her by the waist and twirled her through the air. An Ning arched her back by instinct, one hand flung above her head. They froze like that a moment, and An Ning almost remembered something. Sunlight filtering through rainbow scarves, hot hands on her hips—

No, that last part was not her memory, it was happening! The Sea Clan clapped, and Karana let her slide to the ground, his hands burning paths along her ribs. It was a miracle that she didn't melt!

They stepped off the dance floor then, and Karana pushed some amazake into her hands. She gulped at it gratefully, for Karana's fire seemed to be inside of her.

AN NING seemed dazed, and Karana far preferred that to his smiling at every cursed grandson of the Sea Dragon. He kept him at his side with the occasional light caress to his hand or arm—something he half-expected An Ning to object to, but instead he kept smiling at Karana's touch.

The smiles of the Sea Dragon clan were far more knowing, but thankfully An Ning seemed oblivious to them. Finally, far later than Karana wished, the lot of them teleported away.

An Ning didn't seem to fully realize their guests had left – his eyes were still glued to Karana. Karana wrapped a hand around An Ning's elbow and walked him to his room.

"It was a beautiful night, wasn't it? Magical." An Ning seemed slightly breathless and didn't open the door.

Karana hesitated, then swung the door open and escorted An Ning inside.

"Beautiful. Magical." Karana agreed. An Ning was beaming up at him, so Karana placed a hand on either side of his face. An Ning's smile didn't falter, and his eyes continued to shine.

Karana leaned forward and kissed him, right on the lips.

KARANA'S hands were warm against An Ning's cheeks, but pleasantly so. The fire on them had subsided, leaving a soothing warmth, like heated massage stones.

She knew she was acting a little strangely, but she didn't care. She didn't want Karana to leave yet, so she wouldn't pull away first. Instead, she looked directly into those red eyes and wished he could understand how safe he made her feel. Like nothing in this world could possibly go wrong.

Karana leaned forward and kissed her softly. Cinnamon and flame, love and strength. An Ning knew she was quivering—there was a little part of her that understood Karana was asking her to be his lover. That little part thought that she should pull away, that she should remind him that she didn't like kissing.

But it was Karana. Karana who spent hours fixing his hair and makeup but was the first one in the mill pond when the little mortal boy fell in last year. Karana who huffed that mortal birthdays were tedious but made a custom present for each of An Ning's monks every year. Karana who was tall and scary and had a burning sword but who touched her like she was a flower just budding and never raised his voice.

An Ning kissed him back, and something wonderful and elusive unfurled in her chest. Only this—forever.

But then Karana's hands wrapped around her arms and slid down to encircle her wrists.

Holding her in place, so she couldn't escape. She pulled and screamed, but they were too strong—if anyone was listening, they didn't care.

An Ning tugged her hands, and Karana released them. He started to pull back, but she wrapped her arms around his neck and held him close. His hands slid up her back and her unease hid itself in unknown recesses of her mind.

She liked the way their chests pressed together, as if they were merging into a new, single being. Karana lifted her suddenly and pressed her against a pillar. She was pinned between the hard wood and the almost as hard Karana. His hips leaned into hers, their erections grinding against each other.

An Ning slapped him as hard as she could and kneed him in the groin.

Karana fell backward, clutching his privates, and An Ning fell to the ground, landing painfully on her bottom.

THE floor smacked his shoulder, but Karana was more focused on the nausea-inducing pain shooting from his groin into his gut.

He knew he had only himself to blame. The one time it had come up, An Ning had stated unequivocally that he had no interest in a sexual relationship and he had said nothing over the years to counter that. But Karana had kissed him anyway, and when An Ning had seemed to enjoy it, he had gone further.

Karana was so ashamed that he wanted to die—or at least, disappear.

So he did.

Danger and Despair

KARANA reappeared in what was once his residence, some thousand odd years ago. He was sprawled on the ground, one hand thrown behind him for support, exactly as he'd fallen in An Ning's room.

He rehashed the embarrassing scene once again. They'd been kissing, and Karana had *thought* An Ning was enjoying it. There'd been a moment of uncertainty, when An Ning had pulled his hands away, but then he started kissing Karana more passionately than before. Even now, despite the pain in his privates, Karana still felt vaguely aroused by that ardor. So what had happened? What had gone wrong?

Karana let his arm relax at last, so he was fully supine in the dirt. Above him the stars offered no answers. Karana stuck his tongue out at them, annoyed that they should be so indifferent.

Tears started then; Karana flung an arm over his face to hide from no one.

He wished—oh, how he wished—there was someone to hide from.

KARANA was gone. After a moment, An Ning crawled over the pine boards that had been revealed by his disappearance and stroked them softly.

What was wrong with her? Why had she done that?

The answer came too quickly and was the more upsetting for it.

She had been disgusted by her own erection and fearful of Karana feeling it. She had felt alluring tonight, both desired and desiring. But that evidence of her desire... She couldn't abide it. The fact Karana could almost felt worse. What if he wanted a man, not a woman?

Why couldn't she convince herself that she was a man?

The villagers called her a god, her disciples called her uncle, and strangers addressed her as sir. This, this stupid delusion that she was a woman—a goddess, an aunt, a lady—was so embarrassing that she had never admitted it to anyone! She knew that Karana was attracted to her as a man—and she, a man, was attracted back. Chika, Akemi, and Miho all knew. They had each, in their own way, expressed their approval. Chika had told An Ning about the Bandoan prince who had married one of his generals. Miho had said that customs were different around the world, and all love was equal. And Akemi had bought her this kimono, for even if its like had been worn by men, An Ning had always understood its meaning. This beautiful, effeminate garment was meant to attract and hold the male gaze. And she had worn it, gone along with the fantasy, because she had adored it and because she had wanted to attract Karana's gaze. Why was she so ashamed of that? Why had she panicked and attacked him? Why couldn't she follow through with her desires?

An Ning realized she was crying. She swiped at her eyes, but it was no good. A keening escaped her. Like she was dying, but it was her dream that was gone.

Oh, what melodrama! There were—there were people starving in the world! People who didn't have a safe place to sleep, who were separated from their families by wars that had nothing to do with them! How dare An Ning cry because she had a penis?

Those thoughts made the tears come faster and harder, wracking her body.

It took An Ning a few minutes to realize she wasn't shaking solely from sorrow. Someone's hands were helping. She forced herself to look up, to focus on their face, hoping against hope that Karana had returned.

But it was Xia.

A terrified Xia. An Ning patted Xia's arm awkwardly, trying to reassure the monk that she was alright.

But Xia wasn't worried about An Ning. "Divinity, please, you must come! They'll die!"

It was surely a different person who stood, who addressed Xia calmly and said, "Slow down. Who is going to die?"

The words tumbled from Xia helter-skelter, but An Ning soon understood that a merchant caravan, on its way to Ningjingcun for trade, had been attacked and its women kidnapped.

An Ning went for the Bulgae first, and their happy barking summoned her three disciples. An Ning was reluctant to let the three of them come with her—she was supposed to be their protector after all—but the truth was they were far better in a fight than An Ning herself.

"Where's Uncle Karana?" Miho asked. She was still flushed with triumph and alcohol from the party, though she seemed sober enough, and she was wearing work clothes rather than the elaborate kimono of earlier. She had her tessen, a metal fan whose ribs were like knives, at her waist.

"He—he had to leave."

All three disciples froze and looked at An Ning in disbelief.

"He left? Went for a walk?" asked Chika. She had gone one step further than Miho and donned leather armor that Karana had made her. He'd offered to make some for all of them, but only Chika had accepted. Chika's long and short swords were visible over both of her shoulders—she was certainly the fiercest of the four of them.

"No," An Ning managed. "He had to teleport because— because he remembered something." She felt itchy all over, but on the inside of her skin. It had been a long time since she had found her body so unbearable.

Before the silence could stretch, she strode to the manor's door, and they all hurried after her.

But Akemi still asked, as they entered into the darkness of the fields, "Why would he go now? If he were here—"

"He didn't know there'd be a crisis!" snapped An Ning.

It was easy to see the caravan in the dark, for about five white lanterns dangled from hands around it. As they approached, An Ning saw the wagons were meant to be pulled by horses, but they had obviously been pulled by the men themselves, most of whom were bleeding.

Some of the villagers should collect the animal carcasses tonight—the Brown Griffin would appreciate them, but the village wouldn't get the credit if he found them himself tomorrow.

"Fate curse it, what's taking so long?" demanded an elderly man who was shaking so hard that he didn't notice An Ning approaching. His old clothes belied his wealth, for An Ning recognized him as Master Lu, who she'd first met as a young boy when his grandfather had established this trade route.

She forgave him his anger, instead reaching out a hand to steady him. "Master Lu, my monk said bandits attacked your caravan?"

"They weren't bandits," Lu practically spat, wrapping his fear in anger, "They were Sundered!"

SUNLIGHT woke Karana, and, when he opened his eyes, the brightness made them water.

He didn't remember falling asleep, but based on the stiffness of his back, he had been for several hours. He rose with a groan and stretched as he looked around.

It was hard to believe that the rampaging flora around him had once been an orderly garden or that the chunks of stone had formed a wall taller than Karana. Of his old residence, there was no sign.

This whole place had once been home to a thousand or more immortals—the Sun Emperor's court. Karana hadn't exactly liked it, no more than he had liked being the Sun Emperor's son, but it had felt like home. He supposed that was why he returned to the ruins now, when he felt he had nowhere else to go.

With no clear purpose in mind, Karana began wandering through the ruins. He paused at the crumbling outer wall of his former residence, surprised that in places he could still see the chaotic red and white swirls that had decorated it. He touched one swirl gently, for it reminded him of the past.

I wonder if...

And then he was climbing the once impenetrable wall of his father's inner court, stumbling over crevices left by a meandering stream, and breaking through the branches of the maples that had taken over the garden.

And there it was—a monument to the Sun Emperor's first wife. Karana's mother.

It was barely visible beneath thickly leafed, overgrown vines, but he began pulling at them and they came free surprisingly easily. Soon sunlight gleamed on the dark red jasper and white quartz inclusions. It was magically formed, of course, by Salaana, and mimicked the patterns on Karana's wall. Salaana had insisted on making it herself, though their father offered to do it—at that time, both Salaana and Karana had blamed him for her death.

Her suicide.

Karana knelt and traced the characters of her name. *Lightning.*

Mortals thought it so terrifying—such a magnificent force of nature—but the truth was, lightning was elusive and brief. Not sustainable.

A thin white line that was invisible when the sun shone.

20,000 *years ago*

"WHY don't you come outside? The weather is fine." Although Karana couldn't see the speaker, he knew it was Father—a firm, deep voice that was worthy of the ruler of the Heavens.

There was no response that Karana could hear. He shuffled his feet, and Salaana took his hand. The two of them were waiting outside Mother's hall.

They were dressed in silks heavy with embroidery; red with silver, of course, and the metal thread chafed Karana's skin. He had asked if he couldn't wear plain black robes like the Night God but, according to Salaana, that would upset Father. Karana hadn't mentioned it again because Father was scary when he was upset.

"I'm sure there's a whole pile of presents waiting for you in the hall," Salaana said. As if presents mattered.

Well. Some new toys *would* be nice. One year, the God of Festivals had given Karana a wind-up bird that flew.

Father's voice came again, louder this time, tinged with impatience—maybe even anger.

"Bijalee! It's the boy's birthday!"

Still no response, and Karana squeezed Salaana's hand harder.

He didn't want to cry. He wasn't crying.

Salaana knelt, so that she could look straight in his eyes, and she smiled at him. As if he weren't crying, as if Father weren't yelling, and as if Mother...

"Mother might need help getting dressed," Salaana said. Salaana often took care of Mother, playing the parent when Mother couldn't. "I'm going to check."

Salaana pulled open the rice paper door carefully, slipped inside, and shut it firmly behind her.

Karana didn't know why she bothered. Mother wouldn't be visible from the front hall anyway, but he knew what he'd see if she was.

She'd be lying on her bed, her eyes open, maybe tears on her cheeks, ignoring the world. Sometimes she lay like that for months at a time, not eating. She didn't need to, having once been lightning.

And then she'd suddenly perk up and take Salaana and him on wild trips to Jeevanti where they'd dance in the street as if they were mortal children. There'd be color and music and laughter, and Mother would constantly be pushing sweets on them, until Karana's stomach ached.

Then she'd get tired and disappear. Salaana would teleport the two of them back to court, and they'd find Mother back in her bed.

That was the cycle. That was how it always was.

Truthfully, Karana was almost glad it was his quiet mother this birthday. The wild one sometimes scared him—she was too noisy, too excited, too pushy. Even when they were having fun, she was apt to do things like throwing him in a pond and jumping in after, though they were fully dressed. Karana hated the wildness.

He liked quiet things, gentle smiles, and careful games.

The door to the hall banged shut.

Karana jumped and found Father standing there, a faint

smoke drifting off his shoulders, as if he might combust from pure anger at any moment.

And Karana knew he was angry, though Father smiled at him. "Well! Your sister has chased me out! Says I'm—" He cut off his words with a too-hearty laugh. "Your mother is feeling poorly. But that's no reason to stop the party! A boy only turns two thousand once, after all!"

And Father scooped Karana up in a hug, as if he thought Karana was still a baby.

Karana squirmed free, and Father set him down. "Guess you're too big to be carried, eh?"

Karana hunched his shoulders, and the two of them set off down the long garden path towards the Sun Hall.

The whole garden reminded Karana of fire, all red and gold—not silver like Karana's robes. Even though Father was red and Mother was white. Karana had an older brother, and Salaana said the gold was for *his* dead mother.

Karana wondered if Father had loved that dead woman, as he didn't love Mother.

He knew he shouldn't poke. He was scared of Father when he was angry. But the words churned around and around in Karana's stomach until Karana vomited them up.

"Why do you keep all this garish gold? She's dead."

His father froze, one foot suspended in the air, his face so still that it was almost funny.

Karana giggled, even though almost funny was not funny at all.

The foot set down.

"What did you say?"

"Sh-she's dead! Mother is the empress! It should be silver,

not gold!"

Father's hand wrapped around Karana's upper arm, squeezing painfully, and Karana knew that he'd been wrong. He was still a baby after all.

Father shook him. Karana felt like his brain was bouncing in his skull like beans in a rattle.

"You think your mother has the power to build this?" Father's hand swept over the garden. Father snorted, his lip curled.

Karana felt like he'd been slapped, and he once again told himself not to cry.

"Even if she didn't lay in bed every day, pitying herself, she doesn't have half that power that Noran had!" Suddenly, Father's face went blank. He let go of Karana's arm.

"I'm sorry," he said, but he didn't sound sorry. He still sounded angry, though he wasn't yelling anymore.

He knelt and tried to wipe Karana's eyes.

Karana jerked away, screaming, "I hate you!"

And then he took off like an arrow, lest Father grab him again.

There was no way Karana was going to that stupid party.

Present Day

KARANA swiped at his eyes fiercely. He shouldn't dwell on the past. Mother was dead, Father was dead, and Salaana was imprisoned.

For no less a reason than plotting Father's death. But even that would have been forgiven if she could have let go of her anger.

And that was the worst cursed part, because Karana missed her. Technically he could visit. He could teleport to her prison in the sky, not far from these ruins, and he could stay as long as he wanted.

But she wouldn't welcome him—not unless he was willing to be consumed by the same anger that she was. That bitter hatred for their niece. Karana rubbed his eyes. He wanted to talk to Salaana so badly now that it hurt. She at least knew what romantic love was, having been with her wife for over five thousand years.

What he really needed was someone who understood how to love a man, and Salaana couldn't help him there.

Karana had never thought it would be different than loving a woman, but clearly An Ning disagreed. He needed someone who understood love and sex and relationships.

A love god.

And Karana blushed because he actually knew the one and only Love God quite well. It galled him, to go begging advice from a youth that he'd watched grow up, but...

Karana could let go of a little pride for An Ning. He would go see Xiao.

FATE *smiles after all*, An Ning thought. Anytime the Sundered came up, Karana wallowed in guilt for a week—although their mission would be easier with Karana, An Ning was glad to spare him the anguish.

"There's no time to lose then," she declared. "We need at least one of you to lead us to the site of the ambush. The dogs will track the cultists from there."

With the Bulgae lighting their way, they moved quickly, running across the dirt roads of Ningjingcun. The road broadened, as they left the town itself behind, and after about an hour, the caravanner who was guiding them slowed to a walk.

It wasn't as if they could have missed the spot though—An Ning could smell blood and horse from here.

Her eyes skittered over the beasts, noting the arrows in their side. *We really should have accepted that armor from Karana.*

An Ning's disciples seemed less shaken than she was; they immediately knelt and got the Bulgae sniffing for the cultists.

An Ning didn't know what they smelled—she didn't have Karana's uncanny communion with the creatures—but suddenly Ember let out a long, mournful howl, followed by Blaze and Flare, and then the other five Bulgae. Moments later, all eight of them were off, running far faster than they had thus far, An Ning's disciples barely keeping their feet on the ground and their hands on the leashes. An Ning managed the pace, but the villagers and caravanner who had come soon fell behind. Perhaps that was for the best though—there was danger ahead. This was work for immortals.

Her disciples tried a few times to pull the Bulgae up, to slow them down so they could converse, but they were as untamable as that long ago night in Ningjingcun. Wild, terrifying, demonic. So through brush and over rocks they all scrambled, knowing that if they lost the Bulgae they might also lose their chance to save the mortal women.

The night was dark—there'd only been a sliver of a moon earlier and storm clouds now covered it. An Ning shivered. A storm would make it harder to control the Bulgae, as they feared rain, though they simply reincarnated after being snuffed out.

A storm would also make it harder to find the women—if they were still whole enough to be found.

An Ning pushed forward through the chill, heavy air, begging fate to be kind.

She might have been too afraid to keep going if it weren't for her disciples to either side of her. They were more excited than scared—perhaps they were less concerned by the fate of mortals than An Ning was or maybe they didn't understand what the cultists would do to the women. After all, the cult had no way to reach a palace under the sea, and Karana had kept all cult activity out of Ningjingcun since they had come.

Suddenly the Bulgae, who'd been silent after that first tortured howl, began to bark, and An Ning smelled what so excited them: smoke. She saw the flames next, and they were bigger than she expected, far larger than any torch. The Bulgae became more frenzied as they ran forward, but even so it took An Ning too long to realize that she was in fact seeing more of their kind—but these were caged.

AS Karana stood on the threshold to the Tower on the Horizon, the sea sparkled around him, sunlight setting a thousand tiny fires on the gentle waves. Despite being made of obsidian and amethyst, the tower looked like a waterfall stretching above him, for the light bounced off the waves to dance along its long sides so that the stone seemed to stream down.

Such a tall edifice might have been intimidating—and if Karana thought about the power that kept it floating on the sea, it certainly was—but its entrances stood open, so Karana could see the flowering courtyard beyond. The sweet smell of grapes drifted out to challenge the salt of the sea for dominance. Music and laughter could be heard from the never-ending party that Xiao and his wife hosted—it was a nice place to be, if one liked other beings. Which Karana didn't, for the most part.

He had already checked his appearance before he teleported, so he knew his makeup was flawless and his hair as perfect as it could be when he had ten inches of roots showing. He kept meaning to dye it, but it hadn't seemed important in Ningjingcun—a lapse he regretted now.

Karana strode into the gorgeous garden and ignored the way the revelers who lay about fell silent at the sight of him. That was nothing new; it meant that he'd been recognized as the God of Destruction.

Sure enough, a tall, gawky man that Karana recognized as Xiao's first disciple appeared at his side.

"Divinity," he said with a bow, "might I show you to a private room?"

Karana smiled lazily. "Don't I suit the garden?"

"You are an ornament wherever you stand, divinity," the man said smoothly, though Karana could feel his amusement, "and deserve to be as comfortable as possible. I'm sure these gawkers must be burdensome, and yet as long as your beauty is dazzling them, how can our guests look away?"

Karana snorted and indicated that the disciple should lead on.

He was soon seated in a wide room with woven bamboo mats, a low table set with flowers, and plump floor cushions.

Karana arranged himself on one of these, and more disciples of the Love God offered him a variety of juices and rice crackers.

"Of course one must sample the grape when visiting the Tower," Karana said. "I'm surprised you offer anything else."

The elderly disciple smiled. "His divinity teaches us that all preference is subjective. There is no right or wrong when it comes to pleasing oneself."

Karana arched a brow. "And when can I see his divinity?"

The disciple's smile widened. "He's already been informed of your arrival. I'm sure he will attend to you as soon as he is able."

Sure enough, Karana was just draining the sweet-as-honey juice when a cheerful voice called his name.

"How long has it been?" asked Xiao, the Love God, as he strode into the room. "A hundred years?"

Karana stood and was surprised, for the millionth time, when he realized Xiao was taller than him. It was rare that Karana encountered anyone taller than himself, and he tended to think of Xiao as a child around waist height rather than the man he'd become.

"Probably closer to five hundred," Karana admitted.

"That's right," Xiao agreed. "At the Meeting Grounds, when Jin and Bai announced they were expecting. Those were great fireworks."

Xiao had never figured out how to make fireworks of his own, and he made no secret of how much he enjoyed Karana's.

"I'll be sure to leave you some when I leave," Karana said,

and he was rewarded by Xiao's famous dimples.

They settled on the cushions around the table as the love disciples left. Karana could feel Xiao's curiosity, and he knew it was his moment to speak—and he shouldn't waste Xiao's time, as he was a very busy god—but despite having wished for someone to talk to, Karana suddenly found he didn't know where to begin.

"I've been living in central Zhongtu," Karana blurted, "a small village of rice farmers, mostly."

Xiao nodded. "Beautiful country there."

"The rice is unusual because it's black."

"Oh?" said Xiao.

"The local god made it. From ashes. He's a funny fellow. Not powerful, but I've seen him perform miracles because he pours his whole being into everything he does." And Karana described how An Ning had tamed the Bulgae. "You should go to Bando and see if you can't do that for the rest of them," Karana told Xiao, speaking to the boy he'd once held on his lap rather than the second-most powerful being in existence.

"That's an excellent suggestion," Xiao said diplomatically and then paused. "That's why you're visiting—concern for the Bulgae?"

"No," Karana said. "That happened thirty years ago now."

Xiao rubbed his finger against his lips before saying, gently, "I know people think I can read minds, but I can't really."

Karana laughed once, before silencing himself, embarrassed by the explosion of sound. "I know." He turned his head, too uncomfortable to meet Xiao's eyes. "I'm in love with him."

Xiao was quiet. Then, "The god who made the rice?"

"Yes."

"Well, congratulations. No wonder you are looking so young—I told you that love does wonders for the complexion. Or maybe it's the fact your eyebrows aren't dyed."

Karana ignored that. "I've never loved a man before."

"Who have you loved?" Xiao asked. "I've never heard any rumors about you."

"Mortal women," Karana admitted. "Nine times I've been in love. And they were all very similar. But An Ning..."

"He doesn't fit your usual type?"

Karana wished he had a fan to hide his face behind, and he pulled a red silk handkerchief out of his pocket to make one with magic.

Xiao waited patiently.

After he had cooled his cheeks with the fan, Karana said, "He does. He's exactly my type. He's quiet and gentle and self-sacrificing to a fault. I couldn't care less if he's a man or woman or a Xuezei. He's the being I want to be with. But he does."

"He does what?" asked Xiao.

"He cares! About us both being men."

"So he doesn't like you romantically?"

"He does though—I think. I'm pretty sure. But he doesn't..." And something clarified in Karana's mind. "I think he likes me romantically, but not sexually. But isn't that the same thing?"

Xiao tugged his chin. "Often, but not always. Some people separate the two—sex without romance, romance without sex. Some people feel sexually attracted to just about everyone, others to just about no one. Does this god have other sexual partners?"

"No," Karana said immediately. "Never. He's a virgin."

"Perhaps he's asexual. Doesn't want to have sex at all. But he could still love you and want you as a partner."

"Really?"

"Yes. Does that bother you though? You obviously would like to have sex."

Karana waved his fan more vigorously. "I don't know how you have conversations like this all the time."

Xiao laughed. "It's only one aspect of love. And beings are fascinating. I like understanding them."

Karana sighed, "I want An Ning to be comfortable. But it is frustrating."

"You could find other partners, you know. Romance with An Ning, sex with others."

Karana grimaced. "No."

Xiao chuckled. He reached out a hand and stopped Karana's rapid fan waving. "There're other possibilities. About your lover, I mean. If you're right, and he's uncomfortable with same-gender relationships, he might be repressing his sexuality. It would be easier for me to talk to him directly, but if he's too shy...I have a book that would help. I'll find it."

Karana nodded, still too embarrassed to meet Xiao's eyes. "I'll make you the firecrackers while I wait. We probably need a little space anyway. And it's not like there's anything happening in Ningjingcun that needs me to attend to it."

AN NING, Chika, Akemi, and Miho managed to pull the Bulgae to a halt when they reached an oak copse, the trees hiding them fairly well in the dark. If it weren't for the Bulgae glowing dark red like the last embers of a fire, they'd be invisible.

Unfortunately, the cultists' camp was equally difficult to see. The captive Bulgae were on the edge of the camp, and their cages seemed to be made of flame themselves, with the way they flickered in the Bulgae's light. An Ning could just make out one more cage, a little past the Bulgae. It seemed larger and filled with dark shadows—she suspected it held the women. As for the cultists themselves—well, perhaps they were sleeping. It was, after all, the wee hours of the morning. An Ning saw no sign of movement, besides the Bulgae stirring in their cages.

The captive Bulgae weren't merely restless sleepers though—they had been woken by the barks of their fellows and returned them with interest. That desperate, mindless baying could not be ignored, even from the deepest sleep, and the men leapt up yelling. They were angry—no doubt at being awakened after what must have been a hard day's march for them—and they milled around the cages. An Ning realized their aim when the Bulgae vanished from her sight—they had thrown water on them, extinguishing both them and their howls.

But those buckets didn't silence her Bulgae and neither could her disciples. The twenty-odd cultists turned in surprise toward the woods.

By the time their Bulgae reappeared in the cages and resumed barking, the cultists had their bows out and strung.

An Ning was superfluous now—it was Karana who had practiced the martial arts with her disciples. Even without his guidance, they rushed into action. They unclipped the Bulgae's leashes, and the eight of them surged forward.

An Ning winced as they left the tree line, for they were terribly exposed, but as Chika had trained them, the Bulgae leapt in the air when the first volley came and snatched the arrows in their fiery jaws, so only harmless ash fell to the ground.

"Don't worry, sensei," Akemi said to An Ning, "in the end, they're just mortals. If you're scared, the three of us can handle this on our own."

An Ning stiffened because she *was* scared. Almost senselessly so. It was as if she could feel violence radiating from the men, though they were more thirty feet away.

But if she, a god, felt like this, how must the mortal women feel?

These men intended to kill them, to burn them alive. That's what cultists did with the women they captured.

And so when her disciples ran forward, trusting the Bulgae to protect them from the arrows, An Ning went too, half-stumbling over the rocks and roots beneath her feet.

The wild Bulgae were released from their cages, and An Ning hoped they would turn on their captors, but they charged forward to fight with their fellows.

The wild barking drowned out all other noise, so it took An Ning a moment to understand why the wild Bulgae had chosen to fight strangers rather than the cultists, and then she couldn't quite believe what she was seeing. At the creatures' backs was a wall of rain, a torrential downpour that would put all of them out.

The hairs rose on the back of An Ning's neck, even as she shouted to Akemi, Miho, and Chika. That rain was dangerous to the Bulgae, but in their hands it would become a thousand daggers to turn against the cultists. But no sooner had they seized the drops than a fierce wind blew the clouds away, the rain fleeing with unnatural speed.

Her disciples weren't unnerved by the odd weather though—they simply flew over the fighting Bulgae, landing among the cultists and forcing them back with their rapid blades.

An Ning suddenly realized her own foolishness—her disciples had pulled themselves through the air by their indigo robes. Karana had taught her to do it too, but between her lavender kimono and green obi, there was nothing for her to grasp magically.

Instead, An Ning ran on her own two feet, awkwardly weaving through the fighters. Luckily, Ember turned back for her and cleared a path through the other Bulgae. Then she was running past the empty cages, until she practically collapsed against the larger cage. She wrapped her fingers around the thin metal bars as she struggled to catch her breath. As she'd suspected, it was full of the women from the caravan. They screamed and called her divinity, but An Ning barely acknowledged them. Kneeling, she examined the latch of gleaming red metal. It was locked securely, but An Ning didn't see how.

And then something smashed into the back of her head.

She fell to the ground and looked up at Karana, red fire dancing on his arms to reveal his patrician nose and a cruelly twisted mouth.

She tried to speak his name, tried to understand what was happening but it was beyond her.

He opened the cage and shoved her into it, snarling

something that she couldn't make sense of.

How was Karana here? And why was he helping the cultists?

He must have a plan...

An Ning struggled to rise—she only managed it because two women grabbed her by her arms. One was an old mortal whom An Ning vaguely recognized as Madam Lu, the caravan leader's wife. She was visibly distressed, and her hands were covered in blood.

There was a scream, and An Ning turned to see Karana pull a sword free from Akemi's body. Akemi crumpled to the ground like a rag doll. He swung his flaming sword at Miho, and it looked to An Ning like he took off half her face. An Ning tried to rise, to get out of the cage to help, but the mortal women held her back. Or maybe they were holding her up— nothing made sense anymore.

Chika and Miho disappeared as that terrible flaming sword was descending once more.

Akemi didn't teleport though—she stayed in a heap on the ground, and the man ripped her kimono.

"Cursed whore!" he shouted and kicked the body. Only then did An Ning realize he wasn't Karana.

"Forget the Bulgae," he shouted to the men. "Pack up. We leave within the hour."

The God of Destruction

HOME at last, Karana returned straight to his room and hid Xiao's pillow book underneath his pillow. He stared a moment at the book's black silk binding, which blended surprisingly well with the black silk of his pillow before cringing at the triteness of it. He took it out, shifted his weight back and forth as he scanned the room, and then lifted the heavy straw mattress and set the book under.

He had better make a box for it, that could be opened only by him.

It wouldn't be so bad, he supposed, if the girls found it. They'd giggle, but they were old enough to learn about such things and probably already had from their mothers.

But if An Ning or one of his monks saw the book!

Even Karana had been a little shocked by the improbable flexibility and large phalluses depicted in the drawings—An

Ning would probably kick Karana out of the manor if he saw them.

He had to go apologize to An Ning. He steeled himself and left his room. To his shock, he found the Bulgae wandering in the main courtyard, while Xia and two other monks tried to shoo them into the back.

"Xia?" asked Karana. "What's going on? Why aren't the disciples taking care of the Bulgae?"

"The dogs came home alone," Xia wailed, turning on Karana. "And where have you been?"

Karana didn't have a chance to answer though—Chika suddenly appeared in the middle of the courtyard.

She was wearing the red leather armor that Karana had made her, blood and soot smeared over her face.

THAT first night was a blur to An Ning, thanks to her bleeding head. Madam Lu bandaged it and all the women took turns keeping her awake, for Madam Lu believed that sleeping with a head wound was a good way to never wake up again.

At any rate, the whole night felt surreal and terrifying to An Ning. Akemi had been left where she had fallen, and the red metal cage had started floating, seemingly of its own accord. She had half convinced herself that it was all a terrible dream—after all, there was no way that Akemi had died—but then the sun rose, and the terrible god announced they'd take a break for food. The cage dropped to the ground, rattling An Ning's already aching head, and the cultists all sat and pulled out dried meats from their pouches. An Ning felt too nauseous to eat herself, not that anyone offered the prisoners food anyway.

The god did come over after a few minutes and looked An Ning up and down with narrowed eyes. Once again, she was reminded of Karana, though Karana had never looked so merciless.

"You're a man," he said, derisively, "playing at being a woman. Cursed Crescent Mooners. What were the four of you doing here?"

An Ning didn't know what to say. Part of her wondered if this conversation was really happening, though it didn't seem like the sort of thing that she would imagine.

He reached into the cage and grabbed the back of her kimono. Instinctively, An Ning tried to pull away, but he didn't seem to care about her. Instead he tore violently at her new kimono. An Ning cried out—partially in surprise, but also in pain for the new, strong fabric dug into her before giving out. She couldn't help but remember that it had been a gift from Akemi, and the terrible rip that exposed her back, one arm, and half her chest felt like a rip in her heart. Flustered, An Ning clumsily held up the front, trying to cover her nipple. Her assailant didn't seem to register her response, he simply gave a cursory examination of her back.

An Ning hated him. Her eyes felt tingly, but she was too dehydrated for tears.

"That girl who died had a Sea Dragon tattoo on her back, but you don't."

The world spun. "Akemi's dead?"

Karana had told her immortals could die, but she'd never witnessed it. Never known one who had. Her throat swelled now, and An Ning started shaking all over. Akemi was her disciple. An Ning was responsible for her safety.

And what about Miho? She had just had her adulthood ceremony! An Ning had seen blood pouring over Miho's face before she and Chika disappeared.

An Ning crumpled on herself, and she felt Madam Lu wrap an arm around her.

Where had Chika and Miho gone? Home?

No, the Wood Pavilions, she thought, though it was more hope than certainty. An Ning had heard of its miraculous healers; maybe Chika had brought her cousin there, and they were both okay.

And maybe the god was lying about Akemi. Maybe Chika had returned for her cousin, and even now, Akemi was being tended to as well. The thought calmed An Ning, and she was able to breathe again.

The man's hand suddenly shot through the bars of the cage to grab An Ning's throat. An Ning clawed ineffectually at his wrist.

"Who are you? What were you doing here?" he demanded again.

Two of the younger women shot forward and tried to help. Their cries of divinity did the trick, for the god released her after a moment.

"You know this god?" he asked them.

"He's the Peace Bringer," said Madam Lu, "the patron of Ningjingcun."

"But you are wearing Crescent Moon robes," he argued, "And why was that Sea Dragon girl with you? What ties do you have to the Sea Clan?"

He's scared of the Sea Dragon, An Ning thought. She

remembered how unnerved she had been when Karana had first brought three granddaughters of the Sea Dragon to her village, and *she* hadn't done anything to offend him. No one but the Threefold Goddess and the Love God would dare annoy the Sea Dragon. Could she use his reputation to win their freedom?

"Yes," An Ning said. "They are granddaughters of the Sea Dragon—I hosted the whole family last night. They will definitely come to avenge Akemi." The words rang true, and An Ning realized that Chika might indeed have gone to fetch her family. "If you let us go—"

He strode away, as if she no longer existed, and went to confer with one of the cultists. After a few minutes, he glanced back at them and gestured. Their prison and the empty Bulgae cages rose into the air again—*he* had done it. He must have some affinity with the strange red metal.

An Ning shivered. He was surely more powerful than Karana. Was there no hope for them?

An Ning stiffened her spine. She was a god. She had to be strong for the mortal women whom she had wanted to save.

"Hey," she shouted. "We need water and food."

He glanced back, scoffed, and pulled the empty cages to him.

"Who are you?" she asked, not expecting a reply.

"The God of Destruction," said the cultist nearest her, an unholy light in his eyes. "Who will purge the Earth with his heavenly fire so that the Sun Emperor can rule once more."

Maybe it was the wooziness from her head wound, but An Ning felt those words like a slap.

After a lifetime believing she owed something to this god,

she finally understood why no mortal mentioned his name without covering their eyes and begging fate to keep his gaze from them.

Legend had claimed that he had burned Xiling on a whim, in a fit of pique, but An Ning had remembered the way he had killed the nobles of the city and spared the courtesans and believed that he was enacting justice. A terrible, harsh justice, yes, but justice nonetheless. She believed that she had been born from a noble act.

But this god was filled with anger, malice, and cruelty.

The god disappeared shortly after, the empty cages going with him.

The cultists tied ropes to their prison and began hauling it through the air. An Ning realized it was easier than pulling a wheeled conveyance, but it still slowed the men down.

I scared him away—he doesn't want to be here if any of the Sea Clan shows up, but he doesn't mind sacrificing the mortals who follow him.

Or maybe they were the ones that didn't mind. The cultists began to sing, a low chanting that seemed to vibrate deep in An Ning's bones.

> *Bring forth the heavenly fire,*
> *The flames of eternal life.*
> *Burn us to ash to live forever,*
> *And our light will never die.*
> *The immortal blaze will save us*
> *From drowning in the Sea of Souls.*
> *Seared by the gaze of Destruction,*
> *We can see the infinite life.*
> *We will die to live forever.*

Living 'til the end of time.

The song was endless in its contradictions, and yet the pure belief in their voices was terrifying.

They were afraid of death, and so they deluded themselves that—what, being burned alive would let them live forever?

Was that how they justified burning the women?

Did they think that the women would live forever, too?

But An Ning thought the cult hated women.

She shook her head. There was no point in trying to understand; they were completely crazy. They had a reality that they wanted to believe and so they were ignoring all evidence to the contrary. A poison from within, there was no external cure for self-delusion.

You know that better than most, whispered a hostile voice inside of her.

But my delusion is only about me—I'm not hurting anyone to pursue it, she told the voice.

It made no reply, and An Ning decided her head hurt too much to debate objective truth with herself.

The day grew hot as the sun moved across the sky, and with nary a breeze, the air in the cage felt heavy and stagnant. The terrain was rough and overgrown; An Ning supposed that floating spared them bumping and jostling, but she couldn't find it in her to be grateful. She dozed off, despite the women's concerns about her head. When she woke, they had stopped again, in an unfamiliar forest, though this time the cage remained suspended and there was no sign of the God of Destruction. An Ning stretched—even though her back was sore from sleeping in a cage, her head felt much better.

A cultist offered them a water flask, though no food, and a

few sips helped An Ning a great deal. She then passed the flask on, for it was clear that all the captives had to share it.

She asked the cultist who'd given them the flask, "Where are you bringing us?"

He opened his mouth, but then glanced toward another man and closed it. An Ning sighed. No easy answers here. She could *possibly* teleport away from here, but how could she leave the women? Even injured, she could feel the way they looked at her. If she disappeared, they would despair. She had to find a way to leave with them, and yet she knew she wouldn't be able to teleport them. She had tried to carry people and things with her before, but the clothes on her back were all she could manage.

Time stretched interminable, and it felt like hours that they dangled in their cage, watching the cultists eat, yet all too soon the cultists rose to their feet and began hauling the cage again. An Ning might not know where they were going, but she was sure she didn't want to get there.

And soon An Ning regretted those measly sips of water. She had to pee, badly.

She asked to stop, but the cultist ignored her.

Madam Lu placed a hand on her arm and said, cheeks red and eyes lowered, "They've never let us out."

"But—" An Ning protested. Miserable faces met her gaze.

"It doesn't smell like..."

"They dump water on us, to wash us," said Madam Lu's granddaughter.

And sure enough, the reek of urine grew overpowering, as the women—and then An Ning—lost control of their bladders, one by one.

SILENT tears shone on Chika's cheeks as she told Karana what had happened, but her voice was alarmingly steady as she recounted the night before.

"He cut Akemi from here to here," she dragged her fingers from her left shoulder to her right hip, "and she fell. Everything just sort of spilled out. His sword was like yours."

Karana's red sword had been made from pure power—such artifacts were indestructible. Karana's older brother, the God of War, had smithed dozens of golden weapons in this way. Karana had only ever made his own sword—where had another come from? Or perhaps Chika was mistaken, for the events were surely blurred by emotion, despite her matter-of-fact tone.

"He sliced Akemi like she was a rag doll. I tried to help her, but Miho said—" Chika stuttered to a halt. Karana knew the words that had defeated her: *Akemi's dead.*

Chika continued on, leaving them unsaid. "He struck at Miho next, and the blade caught her here." Chika covered the left half of her face. "There was so much blood. I didn't want to leave Akemi or An Ning, but I was afraid, if we stayed, that Miho... like Akemi..." Chika swallowed. "I took Miho to the Wood Pavilions."

"You were right to save Miho—and yourself," Karana said, though the words felt like a lie. "You said An Ning ran to the women..."

Chika nodded. "Miho said he was caged, but I didn't see." She squeezed her own wrist so tightly that her veins popped on the back of her hand.

Karana's own fists clenched as well. *He's a god,* Karana reassured himself. *If things were desperate enough, he'd teleport to safety... Maybe.*

"Miho will be alright at the pavilions for the foreseeable future?" Karana asked.

Chika nodded. "She agreed to wait until someone fetched her home."

"Then we'll go after An Ning and the mortal women first."

Karana took both of them to the site of Akemi's death. There was no sign of her—the whole vicinity was nothing but gray ash.

"The wild Bulgae must have consumed her," he told Chika.

She flung her arm over her face, and her whole body shook. Then she yelled, "I will kill that man!"

Karana fought not to hunch his shoulders. "We will find them, kill him and the cultists, and rescue An Ning and the women."

Chika swiped at her eyes. "Can you track them?"

"Yes." Karana's sixth sense made that easy. The Bulgae had turned all physical signs of the cultists' passing to ash, but Karana could feel where they had headed.

He and Chika set off to the west, and they escaped the ash in less than a mile. They weren't far from Ningjingcun and the endless rice paddies, but this land was wild and lush. They were about halfway between the Mirror River and the Jingzi—small streams crisscrossed the rolling terrain, and the brush was dense. The cultists had traumatized the undergrowth with their passing, making them easy to follow, but unfortunately, easy did not mean fast.

Karana and Chika were doing their best to run, but thick

roots and jutting rocks mocked their efforts. Karana briefly entertained the idea of flying both of them after the cultists, but he dismissed it.

That would drain his power, and it wasn't just the cultists he had to deal with. There was also the red immortal who had killed Akemi.

He glanced at Chika.

Karana was relatively unaffected by Akemi's death. Oh, he felt sad and guilty—if he hadn't left, she'd still be alive—but after the death of his parents, his brother, and the imprisonment of Salaana, and all of his mortal lovers...

Well, death didn't quite affect him the way it should. He had boxed his feelings for Akemi and thrown them away, leaving a little hollow spot in his chest, but otherwise he was fine.

Chika didn't have that experience to call on. Her face was set, her shoulders tauter than a bowstring, even as she ran, and Karana wondered if she would break down.

Not until after they'd killed the red immortal, he decided. Right now, her vengeance was driving her. He believed he could rely on her, although he'd have to be sure to protect her when they eventually reached the cultists. In this state, she was likely to be reckless.

Karana didn't need sleep and the smallest amount of water and food would keep him going, but Chika needed regular meals and sleep, for her heritage included several animals.

Each time they stopped, Karana agonized that the cultists would reach their destination—and commit their murders— before he could catch them.

He thought of leaving Chika behind, but that wouldn't

guarantee his success.

If only he knew where they were headed, then he'd be able to cut them off.

AFTER a day of dragging the women and their cage through the air, the cultists were tired and sulky.

An Ning watched them impatiently—they had to sleep sometime. And though she hadn't come up with any potential escape plan, she could at least make food and knives for the women. But she didn't dare do it while the cultists were watching—they would take both away.

But though the cultists were tired, it seemed their frustration was the more pressing issue. Two of them approached the apparent leader and started talking at him. An Ning listened, but she couldn't understand what they were on about.

"We're all bored. We need a little fun tonight, to remember why we do this."

The leader, a tall, thickset man, scowled. "That's not why we do this. Our purpose is to resurrect the Sun God, so that he may drive the darkness out of the world."

"Seems to me that we could drive out a little darkness tonight. If you don't do something, the men are going to brawl."

The leader shook his head again. "His divinity doesn't like it."

"He ain't here." The man leaned forward. "And you and I both know he left us because he expected trouble. If we're putting our lives on the line, we better get something that makes it worth it."

The leader looked at the cage.

"You can't kill her. She must die by fire in Xiling."

An Ning suddenly knew what their "fun" was.

She could remember hands, pinning her wrists down, and more hands at her ankles. And body after body—

No! That never happened!

The leader produced a glinting red cube that matched the metal of the cage. A key.

Moving faster than she had in days, An Ning wrapped her hair around the bars of the door. She pushed her will through the braid, and it became a chain, locking the cage a second way. For they were safer inside than out.

And then An Ning fainted.

WHEN An Ning awoke again, not much had changed.

Madam Lu told her it had been another three days, and they had crossed the Mirror River. An Ning realized they must be close to the ruins of Xiling—she hadn't seen them since she'd awoken in their ash.

Close to Xiling meant close to their deaths. That night, when the men slept, An Ning turned most of her hair to food. The women were all weak with hunger—if they were about to fight for their lives, they needed any strength she could give them. She used some women's hair—all but Madam Lu's, whose had gone silver with age—to make knives. It was better than nothing—at least they could kill themselves rather than be burned alive.

And then, though it was probably pointless, she ripped her kimono and used her last remaining drops of power to turn a few strands of hair to ink.

She wrote the characters for Xiling, and then held the scrap to the wind. It tugged the little bit of lavender silk from her fingers, and An Ning begged fate to be kind.

ON the sixth morning, Karana and Chika found a stroke of luck.

Well, not luck—a note. From An Ning. It was a scrap of her brand-new kimono, caught on a broken tree branch so that it almost stabbed Karana in the eye. There were two characters inked on it, and they read Xiling.

Why that name should be more ominous than the kidnapping itself, Karana didn't know, but his heart sank.

"We should teleport there directly," he told Chika.

She hesitated. "But—"

"I know," he told her. "I share all of your doubts. But if they are headed to Xiling—and I can't think why An Ning would write this if they weren't—they will make it there before we can. We have to go there now."

Chika's eyes were full of unshed tears, but there was nothing but hate on her face as she nodded.

"PLEASE, wake up!"

It wasn't the piteous cry that broke through An Ning's haze of sleep though, but the vigorous shaking of her shoulder.

She rubbed her eyes. Had they reached Xiling?

She hadn't quite passed out last night from making food and her little note, but her pool of power had been left dry.

She had warned Madam Lu and the other women that they must let her sleep as long as possible before waking her, so that she might have enough power to do something—though she didn't know what—when the cultists tried to burn them.

What she saw was overwhelming.

They were in a field of golden grass that stretched in every direction. The only thing that broke the field were three tall pillars, each as red as blood and glinting in the sunlight. At the bottom of each pillar was a wide circle of—of—of bones and ash. These were the pillars the cult used for their sacrifices, and the remnants of past women were piled at their bases.

But it was worse than that.

Three women were bound to two of the pillars. One old, one young, and one middle-aged. The third pillar was empty, and the cultists who had hauled An Ning and the caravan women stood between them and it, arguing.

"No, the cage won't be hurt by a little fire! It was made by his divinity!"

"I'm not so worried about the cage, as the numbers. It's supposed to be three, and there are four women inside. Not to mention—"

"There's a man, too. What if burning him steals the salvation of Xin Min?"

Although she was still disorientated, An Ning was able to piece everything together.

Three of her cage mates were supposed to be tied to the third pillar—was the fourth a *spare* sacrifice?—but they hadn't been able to break the chain of her hair.

And as for salvation—well, she'd wondered why the cultists would burn wicked women if they thought death by fire brought eternal life. They must burn the women and one man, supposedly granting the man his reincarnation.

It would be the most ridiculous thing she had ever heard if it wasn't so horrifying—and if the cultists didn't believe it so wholly. For unwavering belief makes even nonsense dangerous.

"Well, we can't burn the others without them," said the man who'd argued for the indestructible nature of the cages. "We have to burn three sets at once."

"I know that!" snapped the one who didn't want Xin Min to lose his reward.

"Okay, I've got it," said the third. "We kill one of the women so there's only three, and Xin Min will have to wait until the next sacrifice."

"You bestow eternal life upon a nonbeliever?" hissed the second. "We should kill him, too! He's a pervert who dresses like a woman anyway."

"But he's still a man," argued the first.

An Ning giggled hysterically. She couldn't help it. They were upset because they thought they were giving her eternal life by *burning her alive*. All they'd be doing would be wasting her eternal life because she was an immortal!

But it seemed that as frustrated as his comrades were by the decision, they were going to follow it.

They started hauling the cage over to the pillar.

An Ning had been wrong about the inside of the cage being safer than the outside.

Madam Lu's granddaughter began to cry.

"Wait!" said An Ning. "I'll break the chain!"

Then at least they could fight.

The men hesitated and started arguing again, this time in

whispers so An Ning couldn't hear.

She began to plead with them, even as she urged the women near her to ready their knives.

But all of what she was saying became moot, as the cage exploded around her.

KARANA and Chika appeared in a golden grass field.

It's so peaceful.

When he thought of Xiling, he actually remembered the city of wood and stone, with its sprawling marketplaces and busy temples.

And the last time he had seen it, it had been nothing but red flame.

He turned in a slow circle. The city had been roughly thirty square miles when Karana had burned it, so the plain stretched as far as the eye could see.

"Where are they?" Chika demanded.

Karana glanced at her. Her eyes were scanning the grasslands as restlessly as his own, and her arms were wrapped around herself in a parody of a hug. Karana almost offered a real hug to ease her worries—Akemi dead, Miho lying in a bed at the Wood Pavilions, and An Ning lost in this field with Sundered Cultists.

But he felt so guilty that he couldn't. It seemed so long ago that he had kissed An Ning and teleported away in shame. The fact that he'd been drinking juice with the Love God while Akemi was already dead!

He didn't deserve the comfort a hug would grant him—and he couldn't imagine Chika would find it very reassuring herself.

"What if you are wrong?" Chika's eyes were darting over the grass.

"Why would the cultists come to Xiling?" Chika asked. "I thought mortals were scared of this place because—" she hesitated, but went on, "you burnt it to the ground. You know, they always ward themselves from your gaze."

Karana was also scanning the area and answered without considering his words carefully.

"The cult worships me," he said, "so they tend to seek out places of destruction. This is probably a massive temple to them."

"The cult worships you?" Chika echoed. "But then—do you get power from them?" Her voice sounded odd, and Karana glanced at her.

He didn't collect power from any worshippers—prayer collectors and incense and such were needed to do that—but it hardly seemed like the right time to go into details. "Let's talk about this later," he replied.

Chika punched him in the arm, and Karana stiffened. That had hurt. "You knew the cult was using this place for their sacrifices and you did nothing?"

"Chika, I can't be everywhere—"

"This is only a week's journey from our home!" she screamed. "You could have been here! But you were too busy playing house in Ningjingcun to care! And now Akemi is dead!"

Karana locked his jaw to keep from yelling at her. He didn't like losing his temper—it was when he was truly angry that his similarity to his parents was revealed. He was frightening, just like his father had been, and he was uncontrollable, like his mother during her bursts of energy.

"An Ning will be so upset when he hears that you've been ignoring this!"

Karana hauled Chika close, forgetting that they were supposed to be looking for signs of cultists. Their faces inches apart, Karana hissed, "Don't tell him."

Chika flushed, and when she spoke again, her voice was quavering. "Oh, so you know you're in the wrong, then? Could have fooled me!"

Karana's hand tightened involuntarily in Chika's lapels, and she flinched. Karana released her and she stumbled back.

Part of him screamed that he should apologize now and explain that he *had* stopped dozens of killings from the cult, he'd just been a little complacent for the past thirty years.

Playing house in Ningjingcun.

His temper was bubbling over, like porridge that kept spilling over the side of the pot even after the fire was put out. He couldn't speak because he was so angry that words tangled up inside of him.

Chika ran at him, tears and snot streaming down her face, as she screamed, "It's your fault that those women were kidnapped—your fault that An Ning is imprisoned—your fault Akemi is dead!" The words practically choked her.

Somewhere, under the red mist that was filling his vision, Karana knew that Chika was in pain and lashing out. In a few weeks—or a few years—she would apologize for these words and admit it wasn't his fault after all.

But she wouldn't be right. It was his fault.

Playing house.

He wasn't just Karana. He wasn't a little patron god with a mere drop of magic.

In Ningjingcun.

He didn't get to live in a tiny village, growing rice and celebrating the mortal festivals.

He was Sundered by Sunlight, the third child of the Sun Emperor, one of four surviving descendants of Red.

He was the God of Destruction.

Using Chika's red armor and his own robes, he pulled them into the sky. If they went high enough, they should be able to see the cultists' base.

He scoured the field.

There. Four miles to his left.

Cultists. Women. An Ning.

Then the world turned to flame.

THE bars of the cage buried themselves in the cultists' bodies. They fell to the ground even as An Ning and the women did. Then the cultists burst into flames that shot higher than the metal pillars to which they had tied the women.

A man-shaped flame hung above them, and a voice of splintering wood and overheated coals howled, "I will give you the fiery death you seek!"

An Ning was so shocked that she couldn't move, but then two strong arms hauled her to her feet.

The arms belonged to Chika, though never had An Ning seen her fiercest disciple in such a state. Though Chika was short and slight, she was as tough as old leather. But today she was shaking and crying like a toddler who had lost her mother.

An Ning stroked Chika's hair, trying to make sense of it all.

She alternated between making shushing noises and asking Chika what was happening. Finally an answer came, though it took An Ning a moment to understand the panicked words.

"You were right. I should never have tested his temper!"

"Whose temper?" An Ning asked in bewilderment.

The reply made no sense.

"The God of Destruction's."

Confessions

"THE God of Destruction?" An Ning echoed in horror. "He's here?" She looked toward the man-shaped inferno that had descended to the ground. "That's him?"

As she watched, cultists fell into the grass, kowtowing before their god moments before he incinerated them.

An Ning didn't understand why he was burning his own worshippers—even if it was what they seemed to want—but she wouldn't sit by and watch as he torched the helpless women tied to the stakes, even if it meant being incinerated herself.

She pushed herself free of Chika and struggled to her feet. She managed one wobbly step before hiking her kimono to run. The long golden grass sliced at her legs, and a cold internal voice—probably the one that was always harassing her—muttered that they were lucky he hadn't set the plain ablaze.

As she reached him, only yards from the women tied to the stakes, An Ning screamed, "No, please! Don't kill them!"

And she wrapped her arms around the living flame.

KARANA extinguished the flames on his skin as soon as he felt An Ning wrap his arms around his shoulders, but it wasn't soon enough to avoid burning An Ning.

He wasn't sure how he knew it was An Ning, unless it was because he was the only being Karana knew who'd hug an inferno to save strangers.

He turned and caught An Ning, then lifted the slighter man in his arms. Angry red welts and sickly yellow blisters were rising all over An Ning's bare skin; his kimono, which had been badly torn, was now singed as well. It was hard to remember how An Ning had looked in all his finery at Miho's adulthood ceremony, and Karana's heart lurched with guilt.

An Ning was staring at him in bewilderment. "Karana," he choked out, "I thought you were the God of Destruction."

Taking a deep breath, Karana said, "I am."

AN NING was so surprised to see Karana's beloved face—even if his eyes remained flame—that she couldn't tell up from down. Luckily, she didn't need to, for he cradled her in his arms. Although it hurt to do so, she wrapped her arms around his neck in relief. She would have cried in relief as well if she weren't still too dehydrated to summon tears.

"Oh, Karana!" she gasped, "I thought you were the God of

Destruction!"

Her relief shifted to confusion when he replied, "I am."

An Ning decided that she was hallucinating then. The cultist must have already tied them to the stake and set them ablaze—that would explain the pain she was in.

She was glad that Karana's was the last face she'd see, though she wished he'd smile instead of glower at her.

Karana was still talking some sort of nonsense, but An Ning was having trouble listening. It wasn't until he set her on the ground and Chika pulled her in between that An Ning realized she might not be dreaming after all.

DIMLY, Karana realized he was getting cold, and he flicked the tepid bathwater with his finger. How long had he been sitting here anyway? The green copper tub around him made him think he was at the Wood Pavilions, where Miho was and where he had sent Chika with An Ning. But he didn't remember arriving, nor did he remember getting into the bath.

In fact, everything after he lost his temper at the ruins of Xiling had taken on a surreal, dreamlike quality, and Karana wasn't sure if it had all really happened.

He remembered incinerating a few dozen cultists, accidentally burning An Ning and sending him with Chika for healing, and then sending the women home on flying ships made from the large red metal stakes.

Those stakes and the cages the cultists had used were the strangest part of the whole afternoon. They had felt familiar, as if they had been made from the red magic of Karana's family. But why would any of them make such horrors?

Unless Salaana had used them for executions before Karana had burned Xiling. Karana didn't remember them specifically, but she had burned arsonists at the stake and Karana would expect her creations to have withstood his destruction for her will had always been stronger than his own.

But he had found it easy enough to remake them—he still couldn't quite believe he'd set them sailing on the wind. Well. Maybe it had been a fever dream. He wouldn't believe any of it truly happened until he checked with Chika. Or...

"Feeling better?" Karana jerked his head up and gaped.

An Ning was kneeling by the bath, his hands folded placidly on the rim of the tub. He was wearing a shy smile, his pale pink lips slightly curled up at the corners and his large, dark eyes practically glowing with love. He'd never intruded on Karana's bath time before, not in thirty years.

Oh, fate, he was delusional.

An Ning cocked his head, and Karana's mouth went dry, imagining what might happen next. Then An Ning's hand darted out, and he tweaked Karana's nose.

Karana roared in surprise and leapt to his feet, sending bath water splashing out of the tub.

A large green cloth landed on his head. Karana pulled it off his face and realized An Ning had thrown a towel at him.

He stepped out of the tub and wrapped it around his waist.

He looked at An Ning and found the other man's cheeks ruddy with embarrassment. An Ning was also darting shy glances at Karana's chest.

Belatedly, Karana thought he should have tied to the towel higher, but it was too late now.

He expected An Ning to run from the room, but instead

the other man asked, "Are the women alright?"

"Hardly. I suspect they'll be traumatized for the rest of their lives. I did send them home though. At least, I think I did," Karana said.

"You think?" An Ning asked, his brows lifting.

"Well, I remember sending them home, and I felt them arrive, but I also remember you covered in burns."

An Ning lifted one hand to cup his own cheek, and Karana had to resist the urge to cup the other. He wanted to make sure the skin was as smooth and healthy as it looked.

"The Warden healed me," An Ning said, his voice full of awe. "She slathered some clear jelly all over, put her hand on my shoulders, and, as you see, I'm good as new. The first time I've experienced the true power of a Color." Then his shoulders stiffened. "That's not true, is it? Chika told me... Those pillars of fire. That's the power of a Color too, isn't it?"

There were thousands of immortals, some born like Karana, others spontaneous like An Ning, but there were only Nine Colors. Each Color had a pool of power a thousand times greater than any other immortal—at least, before mortal worship was considered. Haraa the Warden, and the greatest healer in the world, was the Color Green. And Karana's father, the Sun Emperor, had been the Color Red. Now that power was shared among his surviving progeny.

"Yes," Karana admitted.

An Ning shook his head. "I don't understand why you stayed in Ningjingcun all these years. My life must seem so inconsequential to you."

"An Ning, nothing about you is inconsequential to me."

At last An Ning lifted his eyes to Karana's, something shy

and tentative lurking in those dark depths. "What do you mean?" he asked.

Karana laughed sharply. "What do I mean? I mean, I fell in love with you the moment I saw you in that rice field, when you lifted your hand to the sky, before I knew your name. I know you don't want a romantic relationship—I'm sorry for—for what happened after—before I left—"

An Ning was shaking his head again, and Karana knew he'd gone too far. He would no longer be welcome in Ningjingcun.

"Don't be sorry, please," said An Ning. "I love you, too. Since you first called my name, before you knew it was my name. I know it makes no sense—there's no reason or rationality behind it—but that's the way I felt, from the beginning. I do want a romantic relationship with you. I do want..." An Ning stepped forward, and, going up on his tiptoes, he pressed his closed lips against Karana's briefly. "I'm sorry I slapped you—kicked you." His cheeks were even redder than before. "But it wasn't you at all, you know. It was me. I was embarrassed. I, hmm." An Ning heaved a huge sigh. "I was embarrassed by my body."

Shyness?

"You're beautiful," Karana said. And then, wondering if An Ning would object to that word being applied to a man, amended, "I mean, you're handsome. And fit and attractive. You shouldn't be embarrassed by your body."

"Yes. Well. It's not female." An Ning's cheeks were so hot that Karana wondered if they would burst into fire the Karana was wont.

"I don't mind," Karana said, still not understanding what was making An Ning so self-conscious.

"I know that." An Ning was staring at the ground now, his elegant fingers twisting together. "I mind. I mean, I wish my body were female. Isn't that ridiculous?" He laughed, and it was a heartbreaking sound.

Karana half-lifted a hand to comfort An Ning but couldn't quite find the courage to touch him. "It's not ridiculous. But please explain. You want to be female to be with me? Or—" and suddenly Karana was sure that he was right, just as he sometimes knew the essence of the things, "—you wish you were female because your male body feels wrong to you?"

"The latter," and An Ning bit his lip.

No, her lip. An Ning bit her lip.

Karana thought for a moment. "Let me get dressed, then I have a story to tell you."

AN NING adjusted her dark green robe and sat on the edge of the pavilion's wraparound porch to wait for Karana. The chirrup of crickets rose all around her, but An Ning didn't find their soft song soothing. She swung her legs as they dangled, nervous energy that almost drove her back to her feet.

She hadn't intended on confessing her innermost feelings to Karana—she had intended to talk to him about other things.

Akemi's funeral for one—An Ning flinched at the thought. After the Warden had healed her, she had a long talk with Chika and Miho. They had agreed that all of them would go to the Sea Palace tomorrow to tell the whole story to the family. Chika wanted to go today, but she was the only one who could manage. Well, Miho might have the strength but—

The Warden had done her best for Miho, and her cheek

was as smooth as Akemi's own. However, Miho's right eye had been totally destroyed. Because of that, An Ning wasn't sure how clearly Miho had processed her cousin's death.

But when she had seen Karana, looking so sad and lost, she hadn't been able to bring up her disciples. She knew it would just add to his burden.

And now he wanted to tell her a story—well, she would listen. He obviously needed to clear his mind.

An Ning didn't hear Karana approach or sit down, but suddenly his warm hand was covering her own. Impulsively, she interleaved their fingers, ivory and cinnamon skin creating a crisscross pattern.

Impulsively, An Ning said, "I can't believe I'm holding the hand of the God of Destruction."

"I promised you a story," Karana said in a rush. "Let me see..."

While Karana gathered his thoughts, An Ning studied his expression, and she abruptly understood that as accepting as Karana was of her keeping a secret, he did not extend that same courtesy to himself. He was ashamed that she had discovered his identity this way. Chika had apologized to her an hour ago for not telling her that Karana was the God of Destruction earlier, explaining that Karana had forbidden her to do so.

"But you are my sensei, not him," Chika had added. "We shouldn't have kept it from you."

It did make An Ning feel a little sad. It was a lie after all, when she thought of how many times she had spoken of the God of Destruction before them and wondered about him. But she had lied too, hadn't she? She had never revealed the truth in her heart, and if her unease with her physical body was her secret, then Karana's unease with his title was his.

"The sun rose quickly the day Daichin was born," Karana intoned, "As if it knew a great hero had come and it was eager to meet him."

An Ning sat back in surprise. Karana had said he'd recite the story for her, but she had expected him to paraphrase it. Instead, his voice had taken on the singsong quality of a wandering minstrel, and she was certain these words were recorded somewhere.

"Daichin grew tall and strong under the sun's benevolent gaze, and by the time he was five years old, he could lift his father's sword.

"But by the time he was twelve, Daichin was forbidden that sword, for he was born into the Eagle Tribe of Ehkoron, and they did not allow girls to wield swords.

"For Daichin, though he screamed and protested, had the body of a woman. He bound his hair in a warrior's knot, and he refused women's skirts, but his mother slapped him and braided his hair, and his father paddled him and pulled a dress over his head."

An Ning found her eyes closing to hide the tears in them. She didn't know Daichin, who was surely long dead, but she hurt for him.

"When he was sixteen, Daichin caught the eye of the Bear Tribe's chief. He thought Daichin a beautiful maiden, and he offered his parents thirty furs as a bride price.

"The night before the wedding, Daichin did not cry though his heart was breaking. He lay awake in the dark, trying to reconcile himself to being a wife and mother who could never swing a sword again.

"He knew such a life would be the death of him.

"As if it knew how Daichin mourned, the sun rose slowly that morning, and in the dark hours of the dawn, Daichin slipped from his parent's tent, stealing his brother's sword as he left.

"All alone, but at last able to live as himself, Daichin travelled the world. His sword seemed to become one with his arm, and together they defended the weak, struck down the villainous, and brought light to the dark corners of the world.

"One day, Daichin came to a small village in the Great Ladies. The village was quiet and peaceful, and so Daichin thought he would eat and leave, for this place seemed to have no need for such as him.

"But Daichin was wrong, for no sooner had he received a meal than a flock of Dalagoi descended upon the village.

"Long serpentine necks, fangs the length of a man's hand, and wickedly curved talons, the creatures would make short work of such a village. And though Daichin was but one man, he lifted his sword and dove into battle.

"He thought he would greet his death, but the sun was shining brightly to illuminate Daichin's bravery, and that glinting sun caught the eye of a bird flying high in the heavens.

"But this was no ordinary bird—with feathers like fire, it was the Threefold Goddess herself.

"When she saw Daichin's sword flashing in the sunlight, she also saw the Dalagoi. The Threefold Goddess felt no fear, of course, for there is no being nor creature in this world that she cannot overcome.

"She dove through the sky, fire falling from her wings, and

the Dalagoi burned.

"Only Daichin was left unharmed amidst their ashes, sword still glinting.

"When the Threefold Goddess landed before him, she became a woman, the most beautiful woman there has ever been or ever will be.

"'Speak, brave warrior, and ask a boon of me,' said the goddess.

"'Oh, most divine one,' cried Daichin, falling to his knees, 'I am but a humble fighter who has done naught to deserve such kindness.'

"'Do you doubt my judgment?' asked the goddess. 'Bravery and skill such as yours is rare and will be rewarded. Ask your favor.'

"Again Daichin shook his head. 'The only boon I would ask is impossible. I wish my body matched my soul—that others would see me as a man, as I see myself.'

"The goddess laughed, and Daichin turned red, thinking she mocked him. But the goddess said, 'Do I not make bodies from flowers? To change a female body male—why, that is far easier!'"

An Ning's eyes opened in surprise, and she looked back at Karana. Although his fingers were still interlaced with hers, he didn't seem aware of her. He was focused on the story that he was weaving.

"And she laid her hands upon Daichin's shoulders. Daichin felt a terrible fire rush over his skin, and he screamed, fearful that changing his female body male would be the death of him.

"But then the goddess stepped back, and the sun shone brighter than ever. For at last Daichin's true self was visible for all to see—he was no longer only a man at heart, but a man in every way.

"And Daichin cried in gratitude and swore to follow the goddess for eternity. In truth, he was so determined to do so that when his natural mortal death came to him, he ascended to immortality and became the God of Swordmanship.

"But that is tale for another day."

An Ning was pressing her hand against her lips when Karana stopped. He blinked once, as if returning to the world. Then he leaned forward and wiped An Ning's cheek. She was surprised to see his fingers glinting with moisture, for she hadn't realized the tears had fallen.

"But is that true?" she asked.

Karana nodded. "I've met Daichin. Nice fellow, though not much of a thinker."

Could there be a way to change her body? She wanted it more than anything. Even more than she wanted Karana.

"But—" she protested and was embarrassed by the faintness of her voice, "but I haven't done anything to earn a boon from the Threefold Goddess!"

Karana laughed. "Did you forget? She's my niece!"

"That's right," An Ning murmured, as another idea occurred to her. "But—if she could make my body female— could she regrow an eye?"

WOOD PAVILIONS

The Wood Pavilions, home to Haraa the Warden, are in central Zhongtu on the Lake of Reflection. All are welcome, and there is only one rule: do not damage the plants.

Mourning an Immortal

"AN eye?" Karana echoed, and then double checked, even though he had just seen that An Ning had both of hers. "Who's missing an eye?"

An Ning flushed, "Miho." She stood and tugged him to his feet. "Come on, you need to see her."

"Miho lost her eye?" He followed An Ning. "Chika said she'd left her here, but I hadn't realized..." *Fate has always made my bad decisions worse*, he thought resignedly.

"Jin could regrow an eye, I am sure." He wanted to ask An Ning what she thought of the story of Daichin, but he realized it wasn't the right time. An Ning was too busy thinking of others to think of herself. She wasn't selfish like he was. She would probably want to check on Ningjingcun and all the mortal women they had sent home before they petitioned Jin...

And hold a funeral for Akemi.

"An Ning, has Chika told her family…"

"Not yet," An Ning replied, a little brusquely, and Karana knew she was trying to keep her emotion at bay, "I told her that we'd all go together."

"The Sea Dragon might try to punish us."

An Ning stopped short, her eyes widening. "Well. We did fail."

Karana snorted. "I failed. There was nothing you could have done. But I'm not going to let that old man take a bite out of my hide."

An Ning wrapped her arms around her body. "Are you stronger than the Sea Dragon?"

Karana hesitated. "Well, he has worshippers, and I don't, but I'm not an easy target either."

An Ning laughed out loud. "No—I didn't think you were." Then she frowned. "Don't the cultists worship you? Why don't you get power from them?"

Karana hated that she knew that, though he had admitted it himself. "I would need prayer collectors. Besides, they don't really worship the God of Destruction anymore."

An Ning chewed on her lower lip. "Yes, they do. There was an immortal among them—he called himself the God of Destruction, and they were worshipping him."

Karana stopped short and caught An Ning's arm. "What? What did he look like?"

An Ning's pale cheeks turned pink, and Karana wondered what was embarrassing her.

"Well," she said, "I think he might have been trying to imitate you. He had dark red hair, and he was about your height. Slim, with red eyes and a thin nose."

Red hair? Red eyes?

Some of Karana's fear must have shown on his face, for An Ning asked, "What's wrong?"

Karana shook his head and forced himself to start walking again. "Miho and Chika will be waiting," he said aloud.

But his mind was churning.

Only the Nine Colors and their progeny were so tightly tied to a color that it manifested in their hair and their eyes.

Of course, someone who was masquerading as the God of Destruction might have found some way to color both... Karana had been dying his own hair black for over fifteen millennia, but the mosaic of him in his first temple showed his natural red hair. Maybe that was the explanation.

He remembered those red cages, and the red stakes, made by familiar power.

Most of his family was dead; Salaana was imprisoned. Jin obviously wouldn't help the cult...

Karana tried to remember the last time he saw his youngest half-brother.

Probably when his niece declared herself the Threefold Goddess, donning the mantle of authority for immortals and mortals alike.

Guleum had only been a teenager then. Scrawny, with red hair and eyes, shorter than Karana by head. He and Karana's stepmother had just... Well, quietly disappeared. Hadn't Bai said they *wanted* to be forgotten?

Karana's stepmother had never hidden her unhappiness as the Sun Emperor's wife; it had been obvious to everyone that she would rather have been a nobody on Earth, without duties or expectations.

Since Guleum hadn't come to any family gatherings since, Karana had assumed that he had followed his mother into obscurity.

If he hadn't, it was a problem. Because while the Sundered Cult couldn't truly challenge the gods, Guleum could. He was as powerful as Karana. Maybe more so if he were worshipped by the cult.

Karana wasn't sure why he didn't tell this to An Ning, but he cringed from the idea. He had already messed up so much—if he told An Ning that his brother was the one who had kidnapped her, who was burning mortal women alive...

Let him investigate a little more first.

He forced himself to focus on the present: An Ning at his side, her generous mouth downturned at the edges, her strong black brows slightly knit.

Karana reached out and took her hand in his for the second time that day. Hers was a little smaller than his own, but she interwove their fingers and glanced at him in surprise.

Karana found a slight smile for her, and she smiled back, her brow relaxing even as her hand tightened on his.

"This is your first time at the Wood Pavilions, isn't it?" he asked her.

"Yes," she admitted. "I have heard many stories, but it is so beautiful." She closed her eyes briefly. "So many different birds!"

She was referring to the calls that echoed around them: sweet warbling to short chirps. Despite hosting a few hundred immortal beings under its famous copper-roofs, the Wood Pavilions were dense with wildlife.

Karana looked around for the birds, but they were well-hidden among the greenery. The trees were tall and thick, a mix of evergreen and deciduous. The gravel path they followed wended its way among them haphazardly—but it would be unwise to cut a more direct path through the underbrush. If a visitor damaged any of the plants here, Haraa would appear and kill them. That was why she was called Haraa the Warden and not Haraa the Healer—she held dominion of the physical bodies of all organisms, and she could end a life as easily as she could save one. The air smelled sweet and summery, but the shade of the trees made the path pleasantly cool. Karana suddenly wished that he had brought An Ning here earlier. There were so many wonders of this world that he wanted to show her; the only reason he hadn't was he had feared her discovering his true identity.

"An Ning," he began before he realized what he was saying, "did Chika tell you how I neglected the Sundered?"

An Ning cocked her head. "What do you mean?"

Karana expelled a breath that he hadn't realized he was holding. "You already know the Sundered originated from the worshippers I spared when—when my head monk died. Now you know that they believe they worship me still. Furthermore, the Knowing God charged me with dealing with them a thousand years ago. Until I settled in Ningjingcun, that was more or less what I was doing. I wandered the Earth, dealing with the Sundered when I came across them. But..."

An Ning squeezed his hand again. "But you haven't been doing that while you lived in Ningjingcun, so you feel guilty for all those women being captured."

"He should feel guilty," came Chika's voice from just ahead. "And it's not just that—Akemi's death and Miho's eye are his fault, too."

Karana looked forward and met Chika's eyes.

She was nervous—after his display at Xiling, who wouldn't be?—but she couldn't quite resist being an adolescent.

"Yes," Karana agreed.

Softly, An Ning said, "That's not fair, Chika."

Chika whirled and stalked into the pavilion at her back.

"Miho's inside," An Ning said, peering up at him anxiously. "You know it's not your fault, don't you?"

Karana was pretty sure that his attempt at a smile looked more like a grimace, for An Ning's face clouded. He pulled his hand free and strode into the pavilion.

Chika was pacing inside the door, but she ran up the stairs when Karana entered. Miho stood next to an open window, her eyes closed as she enjoyed the summer breeze on her face.

She turned at the sound of Chika's footsteps on the stairs, and Karana realized he was wrong. Her eyes hadn't been closed—it was simply that the one closest to him was permanently shut. Her eyelid was depressed, for the socket beneath was empty.

Karana swallowed.

He wanted to leave; he really did. He thought it might kill him to have to apologize to Miho.

An Ning entered the small pavilion behind him, and Karana stepped forward.

"I'm sorry, Miho," he said.

She nodded, then shook her head. "Not your fault. I heard what Chika said to you. I don't agree."

Karana shrugged.

"Miho," An Ning said, "do you want to petition the

Threefold Goddess for your eye? Karana told me—"

But Miho started laughing.

"What a waste of power!" she declared. "If I was going to beg a boon of the most powerful being in world, I assure you that I could think of something better than that."

Chika reappeared on the stairs, tripping over her own feet in her eagerness—Karana flew to her and caught her. She pulled out of his arms as she demanded, "Are you really going to ask a boon of the Threefold Goddess? We could ask her to resurrect Akemi!"

Miho's laughter abruptly cut off.

Karana forced himself to say, lightly, for the heavier the topic the more lightly one must speak, "It costs a life to resurrect one lost. Did you have a sacrifice in mind?"

Chika declared, "Her murderer! The Threefold Goddess often restores those who have been murdered with the lives of their killers!"

Karana nodded. "That is true—but we don't have her killer at hand."

"Then I will hunt him down!" yelled Chika.

Miho grabbed her cousin's hand and squeezed. "If you could have overpowered him, you would have when he was striking me. Instead, we barely managed to teleport to safety in time."

Chika stood up. Not quite meeting Karana's eyes, though it was clear to whom she spoke, she said, "But you could do it! You must be more powerful than he is."

Karana wasn't so sure—not if the murderer was his younger brother.

And—even if he had the capability—could he kill another

half-brother?

9,000 *years ago*

A SCREAM, like nothing he had ever heard.

Karana's father and eldest brother had both been seated, awaiting the empress's return with the newest addition to the Sun family. Both of them leapt to their feet at the scream, his brother's hand going to his belt, where his sword would hang if they were anywhere but the Empress's Hall. Not that he needed a sword to be dangerous—Karana's oldest brother was the God of War. He was twice as wide as Karana himself, if not quite as tall, and he had gold eyes with a thick orange beard and top knot that made him look unsettlingly leonine.

Karana remained seated and looked to his sister for guidance.

Salaana wasn't bothered by the scream—if anything, her face flushed with triumph.

Karana looked down at his hands. Had his stepmother already discovered the baby was deaf and blind? He hadn't thought it would be obvious so soon. After all, weren't all newborns a little unfocused in their gazes? Not that Karana had spent much time around babies.

His stepmother ran into the room. She had a curved knife in each hand, and she ran unhesitatingly at Karana's father.

It was his brother who stepped forward though, catching her wrists and forcing her to drop the knives.

"You murdered him!" she screamed. "You murdered my baby!"

Suddenly unable to breathe, Karana looked at Salaana for clarification. The magic Karana had used, a poison of the blood, shouldn't have been lethal.

Salaana's mouth had formed a soft "oh" of surprise, and she looked gray instead of her normal red-brown. She looked back at Karana, searching for answers of her own, and Karana suddenly realized their plan had gone wrong.

Salaana rose swiftly. "This is fate. For having the gall to name the baby the God of Belief. Who do you think you are, to put your son above us?"

Karana's stepmother stopped fighting her way toward the Sun Emperor and turned on Salaana.

"You witch! Have you ice instead of a heart? You killed my baby!"

"No," said Karana's brother. "If Salaana did it, she would be proclaiming her justice to the world." Those golden eyes met Karana's, and Karana flinched away.

He knows.

Karana's stepmother turned toward his brother again. "Then who did it?"

She followed his gaze, and blue fire rose on her arms. The God of War dropped his grip, and Karana realized she was going to kill him.

His heart was in his throat, but he didn't run. He had killed her baby. His half-brother.

The Sun Emperor stepped between them.

"You will not touch my son," he roared.

Karana could feel the heat of their competing flames on his face, but he closed his eyes, unable to look.

So he was shocked when a hand grabbed his collar roughly.

"Fate curse you, Karana, get out of here!"

Karana tried to run, but his brother didn't let go of his collar.

"Not the room, idiot—the palace! Don't let me see you for ten thousand years!"

Karana couldn't usually teleport within his father's compound, but it seemed the Sun Emperor agreed with the God of War. He felt no resistance as he teleported out of the palace.

Present Day

AN NING didn't like the look on Karana's face as he nodded and agreed to Chika's accusation. She couldn't tell what he was thinking, but she knew it wasn't good.

"I might be able to overpower him. But even if I catch him, and Jin agrees to resurrect Akemi, she'll be mortal, Chika."

Chika stood there for a few minutes longer, and then tears started leaking down her face. She whirled to run away once again, but An Ning ran forward and caught her in a hug.

Chika sobbed in An Ning's arms so fiercely it felt like An Ning's own heart was crying.

After a moment, Miho joined them and stroked her cousin's hair. "We need to go see Ojichan," said Miho. "We need to hold the funeral."

An Ning looked at Karana, but his eyes were fixed on the ground. She sighed and said, "I also need to check on Ningjingcun—we've already been away over a week."

Finally Karana looked at her. "Yes—and I need go to the

smaller villages to check on the other women. But Miho, if you want to go to the Sea Palace now, I will accompany you and Chika first. An Ning and I should be able to join you tonight."

An Ning almost protested. She felt like she had abandoned her village, but Akemi had been her disciple. And Chika and Miho still were.

"If you don't want to follow me any longer—"

"Don't be stupid," said Chika, and Miho clucked her tongue in disapproval (at Chika's language or An Ning's suggestion, it was hard to say). "I'm mad at Uncle Karana, not you."

Chika pulled back. "I'll go with you to the Sea Palace, to tell my aunt what happened, but then I am going to the Immortal Grounds, even if you all won't come with me. I am going to petition the Threefold Goddess, regardless of what anyone says!"

An Ning squeezed her hand. "I'll come with you. I want to petition the Threefold Goddess myself."

She glanced at Karana—his face was somber, but he lifted one corner of his lips for her.

KARANA had prepared himself for the Sea Dragon's roaring, but he hadn't been ready for the Sea Queen's tears.

The Sea Palace was like any grand Crescent Moon estate except for its improbable location on the ocean floor. Instead of sky, water of darkest indigo stretched overhead. The palace was lit by iridescent lamps, but it was still quite dark, as if the air itself was colored by the sea.

It was home to the hundred-odd members of the Sea

Clan—about half were the Sea Dragon's family, the others sworn retainers. All of them were now gathered in front garden, crowded in between the twisty pines and the over-sized rhododendrons.

An Ning was pressed close to his side, and her eyes were as leaky as the Sea Queen's. Karana himself felt like an emotionless monster. He had been fond of Akemi, but he just couldn't...

He just couldn't care. If he cared, he might do something violent and dangerous. After all, the last time someone he truly loved had died, he had burned Xiling. Instead he kept his emotions numb, and let his eyes roam the crowd.

They settled on Ao, the Sea Dragon, and the Color Indigo. The Sea Dragon reminded Karana of his father, though he was far shorter and bearded. His aggressive use of indigo in all that surrounded him was like Karana's father and red. And Karana could feel the Sea Dragon's sorrow, though his face was harsh and angry. That was like his father, too.

It was funny that they had never gotten along—Karana had never even been to the Sea Palace before his father's collapse—but then again, maybe the two old men had been *too* similar. Both were narcissists who craved power and lots of progeny. Karana's father had undoubtedly been the winner of the former contest and the Sea Dragon the winner of the latter. Each must have resented the other bitterly.

Only two of the Sea Dragon's thirteen children were missing; the eldest, who was trapped with Karana's sister, and the seventh, who had married the Love God. She was not welcome here, not ever.

Karana would never disown one of his children. Not that

there was much chance of him ever having any...

He glanced at An Ning.

If An Ning became a woman, that would be a possibility.

Tears pricked Karana's eyes, and he felt horribly guilty that they were for the idea of a child instead of Akemi.

An Ning's hand slipped into his and squeezed. Karana knew he shouldn't let her comfort him, but he reasoned that she was seeking comfort too and that he shouldn't pull away.

Lots of people had been talking, telling stories that Karana tried to tune out, lest they open that little box where he had stored Akemi, but when Chika cleared her throat, Karana focused on her. Surely she wouldn't...

She would.

"Akemi shouldn't have died," she declared. "I will petition the Threefold Goddess myself to bring her back to life."

"You will do no such thing," commanded the Sea Dragon.

"Even if she's mortal—"

The Sea Dragon's hand cut through the air, though he might have been cutting Chika's throat, so effectively did the motion silence her. "No member of my family will ever petition the Threefold Goddess! We will owe her nothing!"

The Sea Dragon despised the Threefold Goddess for she called his disowned daughter "friend." He wasn't so foolish as to antagonize the most powerful being in the world, but Karana wasn't surprised that he was unwilling to ask her for anything.

Chika turned bright red. "I don't care what you say. Uncle Karana and my sensei are going to petition her, and I'm going with them. Akemi is more important than your stupid pride!"

The Sea Dragon's face darkened, his dark brown skin

gaining a purple tinge. He stepped forward as if to hit Chika.

Karana stepped between them.

The Sea Dragon tilted his face up and then up some more, until his dark indigo eyes met Karana's own.

They were both silent, and Karana wondered if the Sea Dragon could really turn into a dragon like legend said.

An Ning might think Karana's martial skills prodigious, but Karana knew better. It would be bad if the Sea Dragon started a fight.

But the Sea Dragon didn't move, and Karana realized that he didn't want to fight. Karana just needed to offer the old being a way out that didn't hurt his pride.

Karana bowed to the Sea Dragon—deeply, from the waist— and apologized on Chika's behalf.

"Please, my lord," he said, "An Ning and I consider Chika a member of our household. Any actions she takes reflect on us, not you. It's not so strange for one of my nieces to ask a favor of another."

Karana usually didn't like to remind the Sea Dragon that the Threefold Goddess was his niece, but it served to mollify the ancient being in this case.

The Sea Dragon nodded as Karana unfolded himself and asked, "Why do you visit the—your niece?"

Karana hesitated. This was An Ning's private matter, after all, and the outcome was still uncertain.

To his shock, An Ning stepped forward as well, to his side.

"I AM the one who wishes to petition the goddess, my lord," An Ning said, though her heart was in her throat.

She wasn't sure why she wasn't letting Karana handle this—she trusted he would come up with a reasonable excuse after all—but she suddenly had to say her hope aloud. She wanted everyone to know; after the scene she had seen in Hirohama, and even that nasty red immortal's reaction to "Crescent Mooners," An Ning trusted this was a safe place to do so. If she couldn't say it here, how would she tell her villagers?

"I wish her to make my body female." The words felt uncomfortably loud (had she shouted them?) and yet a massive weight moved off her chest. Maybe that's why the words had come out so forcefully—she wasn't used to being able to breathe so deeply.

Despite her hopes, An Ning braced herself for laughter. For ridicule.

Instead, the Sea Dragon, who was a terrifying being despite being no higher than her shoulder, nodded as if she said she wanted rice for dinner.

Well, he did live on the bottom of the ocean, so she supposed he was used to miracles.

"Good luck," he told her. Then after a moment, "I spoke with my granddaughter at your home. She told me how happy she was in your village; how much she admired you. Thank you for taking care of her. I suppose you are one of those rare beings who deserves to be happy and content."

Tears escaped the corner of his eyes, only to be caught be the crevices of his face.

An Ning's own tears dripped freely, and she stepped forward to hug him.

"I'm so sorry I didn't keep her safe," she said, "I don't know if the goddess will agree to restore Akemi but..."

He patted her on the back and said, so quietly that she suspected it was for her ears only, "There are always stronger beings who will overwhelm us."

That surprised An Ning—who could overwhelm the Sea Dragon?

She released the hug and felt the weight of a hundred eyes. Thinking they were focused on their patriarch, she stepped back.

But the eyes followed.

She looked at Karana in confusion.

Even he was gaping at her. Then his expression softened, and one side of his mouth quirked up.

"I suppose you are ready to see the Threefold Goddess now. If you are brave enough to hug the Sea Dragon, I imagine nothing scares you."

The Knowing God

NEVER in her life had An Ning been surrounded by this many immortals. In fact, never had she been surrounded by this many people—three weeks ago, Hirohama had impressed her with its crowds. But here, despite the endless sky overhead, she could barely breathe. Perfume and sweat assaulted her nose, and so many different voices assailed her ears that An Ning could barely listen to Karana.

When they left the Sea Palace, Chika had argued for teleporting directly to the Immortal Grounds, but it hadn't made sense. Miho had wanted to go home, and An Ning had needed to check in with Xia—what if their requests took longer than expected? So it had been a week before Karana brought the two of them to the Grounds.

An Ning had heard of them—wandering monks often told stories of the Immortal Grounds, an endless garden that hung in the Heavens, made by the Threefold Goddess and the Love God from a vibrant sunrise.

Karana had assured her that the grounds were finite, but they certainly seemed endless to An Ning. And the crowd seemed endless too. In fact, she could hardly see the famed gardens.

Beings dressed in every hue and fabric, representing every culture and locale in the world, mingled and shifted around her. Like a sea of immortals.

Chika pressed closer to An Ning, probably subconsciously. An Ning followed suit and pressed closer to Karana, very aware of what she was doing.

Karana was dumbstruck. "I've never seen it like this. I mean sure, there's always plenty of immortals who want Jin's help, but this must be five—no, ten times as many as I've seen before."

"Ah. Well, she is the most important being in the world." An Ning touched her hair self-consciously; she was wearing hair ornaments for the first time in her life. Butterflies, that Karana had given her, and she worried they looked ridiculous. They were the type of thing a young lady would wear, and her simple black silk robes made her masculine body obvious. But she really liked those ornaments. And they kept her now awkwardly short hair out of her eyes—not that she regretted using it for the women. But she didn't think she'd ever wear a color besides black again, now that she'd experienced firsthand how convenient it was to have her own color on hand for emergencies.

Karana focused on her, and An Ning knew he could see how overwhelmed she was.

His large hand settled on her shoulder, and he gave a reassuring squeeze. "Don't worry—we won't have to wait for this crowd to disperse. I'll find one of the Colorful Disciples and let them know we're here."

An Ning grabbed Karana's hand, even as Chika grabbed hers. An Ning glanced at Chika and found her disciple's lips pressed tight and her eyes wide. It was hard to believe that Chika could be frightened of anything, but she obviously was.

An Ning looked back at Karana. "I think we should all stay together."

Karana looked like he might object for a moment, but he said, "Okay."

It was a testament to the sheer size of the crowd that they didn't part before Karana. An Ning had assumed most wouldn't recognize him, but he was still a tall, muscular immortal with a vaguely menacing air and a long red sword at his waist. There were many immortals who took in his red hair and eyes with blanched faces—these made some effort to push backward, but they were met by neighboring bodies. They settled for awkward head bobs to express their apologies. Karana didn't seem to notice them.

Finally he found what he was seeking: a plump immortal wearing an ombre sari and a hassled expression.

"Excuse me," said Karana, "I need to speak to Jin. The Threefold Goddess."

"You and the rest of the folks here," she snapped.

"I'm her uncle," Karana said coldly.

"And there are five hundred petitioners ahead of you. Find a booth and take a number. You'll be summoned." She pointed to the left, where An Ning could make out a colorful awning.

"Are you really her uncle?" asked an immortal of middling height and wide waist.

KARANA wanted to ignore the impudent immortal who questioned his identity, but he also wanted to know the cause of this madhouse.

"Yes. What's going on? Why are there booths?"

The chubby immortal shrugged. "I'd think you'd know better than me, but someone said the goddess isn't feeling well, so the petitions are being narrowed down by her disciples first."

"Not feeling well?" he echoed.

"She's pregnant," said a female immortal. "Why don't you try growing a baby for a thousand years and see how you feel?"

Karana felt her aggression was excessive, but he nodded mildly. "That's right—she's six or seven hundred years along now."

It had been a while since Karana had seen a pregnant immortal, but he remembered his stepmothers' pregnancies well enough. He supposed Jin must be spending most of her time at home, but he was loath to go to the White Mountain. The reason he'd come here in the first place still stood—he wanted to avoid Jin's husband.

Karana sighed and turned to An Ning and Chika. They were pressed close together and looking at him expectantly.

"We'd better take a number."

The Colorful Disciple at the booth handed them a flat piece of wood with the characters for beauty, life, and death carved on it—the elements that gave Jin the title "Threefold."

"The characters will glow when it's your turn," the disciple explained. "And your number will appear here. That tells you which disciple to speak to. The matching number hangs over their tables in the pavilion."

Karana turned the bit of blonde wood over in his hands. "Is there a distance restriction on this?"

"No," said the monk, "but you have five minutes to present yourself once the characters start glowing."

Which would make it hard to teleport in time—certainly impossible for the majority of this crowd.

"Alright. Thank you," Karana said, though he didn't feel grateful. This seemed like one of the most obnoxious systems ever invented. He looked around the crowd again and said to An Ning and Chika, "I don't want to risk a teleport, but I could at least pull us out of this crowd."

"So we dangle above them held by our blood?" Chika snorted. "No, thank you."

"I kind of like the crowd," admitted An Ning. "It's overwhelming—"

"—and gross and sweaty—" put in Chika.

"—but it's fun to see all the different immortals."

Chika rolled her eyes.

Karana felt bad for her, but he also didn't have much patience for her new attitude. She was the one who had decided to stick with them, after all.

"Do you want to see the rest of the Immortal Grounds, then?" he asked An Ning.

She smiled and nodded.

Karana could not help but smile back as he looked at her.

An Ning's hair was far shorter after her kidnapping—she told Karana that she made most of it into food for the women, and Karana had wanted to punch something as he imagined her unconscious and vulnerable in that cursed red cage. However, she also had little silver butterflies in her hair to hold it back, and they suited her perfectly. Karana had made them himself, though he hadn't told her that. He hadn't wanted to pressure her into wearing them if she didn't want to, and she would definitely feel obligated if she knew.

Despite the butterflies, An Ning still looked like a man—the simpler robes of Ningjingcun didn't soften her lean musculature like the kimono had.

"Chika," said Karana, "can you pull yourself up?"

"Of course—" she started to say, but Karana didn't listen to the rest. He wrapped his arm around An Ning's waist and pulled them up into the air.

She gasped in surprised and wrapped one arm around his neck. Several members of the crowd gawked at them—Karana wondered if anyone was remembering the way his sister and her Light Hands had flown through the air—but he kept his own attention on An Ning. He had to go pretty high, probably forty feet, before they could see the edges of the Immortal Grounds.

"See," Karana murmured against An Ning's ear, "I told you they didn't stretch forever."

"I believed you," she replied, and Karana smirked when her voice came out slightly breathless.

"Do you mind?" demanded Chika.

"Not at all," said Karana, but An Ning turned bright red. Karana pulled his sword from its sheath and floated it beneath An Ning's feet. Once she had her balance, Karana pulled back so that they weren't blatantly canoodling.

"What's that?" An Ning pointed to white walls that were about twenty feet high. The whole area within them was strikingly empty when compared to the rest of the grounds.

"That must be Bai's school. Or will be, I suppose. I don't think it's finished yet," Karana said.

"His school?" echoed Chika, trying hard not to sound curious. She went so far as to cross her arms in front of her chest and slouch—no mean feat when one was floating in the air.

Karana stopped a smile. The only thing worse than an adolescent was one who thought they were being mocked. "Yes, he says that any qualified immortal will be allowed to enroll and learn to optimize their power."

"From him? The Knowing God?" Chika asked.

"I think so—and some other instructors."

"What's the cost of admission?"

Karana raised a brow. Was Chika interested in going to such a school? "Five hundred years of patrolling for immortal creatures."

"What? That's ridiculous," said Chika. "That's basically slavery. High-risk slavery. Who would be stupid enough to do that?"

Karana couldn't quite swallow a laugh. "I think Bai's saying that after going to his school, it will be safe, but I'm hardly going to sign up."

Chika was shaking her head.

"You already deal with immortal creatures when you meet them anyway," said An Ning, and her hand tightened on his.

Karana's heart flipped. He met her eyes. She thought too well of him—he had only actively protected other beings from immortal creatures since moving to Ningjingcun. And that was more for An Ning's sake than theirs.

Chika snorted contemptuously, as if she could hear his thoughts. But she couldn't—her indigo nature let her resist other magic, not read minds.

Still, Karana stuck his tongue out at her.

ALTHOUGH the Immortal Grounds were beautiful and would fascinate her any other time, An Ning couldn't stop looking at the carved tag that hung from Karana's waist. She didn't want to miss it when it started to glow.

She did her best to listen to Karana and Chika's conversation, and occasionally managed a contribution, but mostly she watched those three characters: beauty, life, and death. It was strange—she had known that those were the aspects of the Goddess, but seeing the character for death, like two blades slashing at each other, beneath the delicate and elaborate one for beauty had unsettled her.

Sometimes Karana was frightening—what was his niece like?

And then the characters came ablaze, ghostly flames dancing from them.

"Oh, oh, oh!" said An Ning, like an idiot.

Chika clapped her hands. "Let's go!" She dove like an osprey toward the tall pavilion—if An Ning were one of the Colorful Disciples waiting there, she'd probably hide.

Karana chuckled and pulled her after Chika at a more sedate pace. An Ning squeezed his hand, and he said, "We've plenty of time."

"I know!" she said and then laughed as well. "Do you really think—will she…"

Karana turned to smile at her, his red eyes crinkling at the corners in a way that made the rest of the world fall away.

An Ning smiled back.

FATE mock them, but Karana despised bureaucracy. He knew it was necessary. What else could be done with a thousand-odd immortals all clamoring for attention?

But he was this close to setting the Colorful Disciple in front of him on fire.

"I don't think these constitute as the kind of noble cause, delicate situation, or desperate need that would allow you to bring your petition to the next level."

"My cousin is dead! What's more desperate than that?" demanded Chika.

"Currently dying, about to cause other deaths, or in danger of dying are all classified as more desperate, important, and pressing."

"Can you stop with the threes already?" said Chika.

"I don't know what you are implying, referencing, or describing."

Maybe Karana *should* set him on fire. Just this one disciple. Surely Jin wouldn't miss this fellow.

Karana pushed An Ning and Chika aside and leaned so close to the disciple that their noses nearly touched. "In danger of dying? Causing other deaths? Currently dying? I can arrange all three of those for you." He let flames engulf his hands and he reached for the disciples' robes.

The man squeaked—like a mouse—and jumped three feet back.

"Are—are you the God of Destruction?"

Karana's eyes narrowed to slits. "Yes."

"Ah, well there is a special dispensation, exception—I mean, you can go right in!" He bowed his head and held his arms out toward the door behind him. He was trembling.

It took Karana a moment to understand the fellow, and then he smiled broadly, though the disciple didn't seem the least reassured.

"I'm glad you can stop saying everything in triplicate when the situation calls for it," he said as he passed, Chika and An Ning at his heels.

And then they were in a throne room of sorts, with massive murals of immortal creatures and beings getting along improbably well, with a golden dais in the middle.

Only, instead of his friendly and generous niece waiting for them, her cursed know-it-all husband was sitting there.

Bai's eyes locked with Karana's, and then he was on his feet.

THE white-haired man was quite a bit shorter than Karana— closer to her own height, An Ning thought—but he absolutely dominated the room. Even the way he was walking toward them—every movement so controlled, so intentional, and yet somehow so threatening that the butterflies in An Ning's hair seemed to take up residence in her stomach.

This was obviously not the Threefold Goddess—could it be the Knowing God?

There was certainly something in his gaze, as he swept it

boldly over all three of them before settling it on Karana, that left An Ning feeling exposed. Despite herself, she crossed her arms to cover her chest.

"So you finally showed up," the man...snarled? No, that was too emotive, yet he had almost snarled. "Those cursed cultists burned Tiguna Temple ten years ago. I told you to deal with them. What have you been doing? Sunbathing in the South Sea?"

"You need me to protect your temples?" Karana didn't look afraid exactly, but his back was so tense that An Ning's ached just seeing it. "I need to talk to Jin."

The man stopped and one brow arched superciliously. "Of course you are here to beg a favor, not to accept your duties."

Karana hunched, like a child who'd been scolded. "I'm sorry about Tiguna. I have been a little distracted these past few decades. But—"

"Jin's not here. She isn't up to these sessions right now."

Karana sighed. "Well, it's unfortunate, but I suppose we'll have to wait until the baby is born then. That's what, two more centuries?"

"Nearly three," said the Knowing God, and An Ning pressed a hand to her own abdomen. She couldn't imagine growing a child for a thousand years. Not that she could— unless...

"And you'll be stuck here, dealing with all the petitioners? I'm sorry about that—"

The Knowing God held his palm up, silencing Karana. "Just tell me why you're here."

Karana glanced first at An Ning and then at Chika.

An Ning inclined her head to Chika, who was already

stepping forward regardless. "My cousin was murdered. I want her resurrected."

The Knowing God looked at her with interest. "You're one of Ao's? And your cousin?"

Ao—An Ning thought that was the Sea Dragon's name. At any rate, Chika nodded.

The Knowing God nodded slowly. "I will see if Jin is up to it. But where's the soul?"

Chika, usually so fearless, bit her lip. "Her soul?"

"You haven't fetched it yet? Confirmed that she wants to be resurrected?"

"I—uh—"

The Knowing God's expression was quickly becoming bored and impatient. "You must collect the soul yourself from the Sea of Souls. You must also capture the murderer for justice. Then, assuming the soul wishes it, we will create a new body and sacrifice the murderer to resurrect your cousin."

"But isn't the Sea of Souls in the Underworld?"

"So?"

Chika's dark tan mottled from the blood rushing to her face. "So I will go find it." She swallowed once—An Ning couldn't blame her. There were enough tales of horror about the Underworld—and the fact many immortal creatures still roamed there—to dissuade her from going. But if Chika went than An Ning would, too.

"I will go with you, Chika."

Chika's face evened, and she nodded once.

The Knowing God was ready to be done with them. "If that's all—"

"Bai, what if the murderer is Guleum?"

An Ning thought the Knowing God stopped breathing at Karana's question. The pause stretched long before he said, "Is he?"

"I didn't witness the murder," Karana admitted, "but the immortal was impersonating me. From the artifacts left behind... I think it must be him."

"Jin will be reluctant to kill family." The Knowing God shook his head. "But I will convince her. It should have been done years ago." His expression darkened. "Karana—"

"I will deal with Gu if Jin won't. As you say, it is better done." Karana's jaw locked though, and An Ning's heart hurt, even as she tried to decipher this conversation.

If "Guleum" was the Threefold Goddess's family, wasn't he Karana's family too?

An Ning remembered how much he had looked like Karana. They could easily have been brothers.

She felt cold.

"This is more pressing than I realized," declared the Knowing God. "If that's all, you should be on your way."

And, despite everything else seeming way more important than her personal delusion, An Ning couldn't bear the idea of losing her only chance to escape it.

An Ning blurted, "I want to become a woman."

The Knowing God had barely acknowledged her earlier, but he examined her now as if she were an unfamiliar bug. A mild curiosity that would most likely result in her being squashed beneath his heel. And then it came, a single word that ground her into the floor. "Impossible."

"Why?" It came out more whimper than word, and An Ning chastised herself. *You didn't even know of this possibility a week ago! Don't you dare cry.*

The Knowing God frowned. "How can you become what you already are?"

An Ning blinked. That wasn't what she expected him to say—and she didn't understand what it meant.

"Don't be obtuse, Bai! Her body!" barked Karana. An Ning glanced at him and saw his clenched fist. Realizing how bad it would be if Karana struck the Knowing God, she grabbed his wrist. Karana's fingers uncurled, though the tension didn't leave his arm. In a slightly more moderate tone, Karana said, "She wants her body to be female."

"Then why did she choose a male one when she ascended?"

"I didn't choose anything," argued An Ning.

"Of course you did. Every spontaneous immortal chooses their form when they ascend. You were a mortal woman, but when you became immortal, you chose a male form."

The tears were still tickling the back of her throat, but anger was rising too. Her voice was harsh and perhaps too loud as she said, "I was ash, not a woman. I would have remembered if I were a woman."

Would she have though? When she first came to be...

If she really had been a woman, why had she chosen to be male?

She wouldn't have! There was no way!

But she also felt strangely afraid. As if maybe, just maybe, the Knowing God was right.

AN NING had been a woman? Not ash? A woman in Xiling...named An Ning.

No, it wasn't possible.

Well, it was possible, but then...

If An Ning really was that An Ning, the other An Ning...

Had Karana burned her alive?

On top of everything else, he had *burned her alive*?

11

The Other An Ning

3,000 *years ago*

THE last time that Karana visited Xiling, maybe two-hundred years ago, it had been a prosperous market town. Now though—well, no wonder immortals were calling it the capital of Zhongtu. The buildings were mostly two stories, and Karana had seen several that were more. The market was confined to one third of the city; there was also a pleasure district, a manufacturing quarter, shanties for the poor, and mansions for the wealthy.

Karana paused before a store whose pillars were carved with the symbol for beauty—maybe they worshipped Jin. She had only established her first temples in the past few decades and would enjoy seeing what her worshippers sold. He mounted the wide wooden steps and ducked between the pink curtains that kept the dust of the street out of the shop.

Inside were magnificent embroideries—hyper-realistic flowers, birds, and fruits, all depicted in vibrant silk threads. Karana grinned; Jin would love any one of these. He stepped closer to examine a woman sitting in a garden beside a peacock. It reminded him of Jin's dead mother—would that make it a depressing present or a thoughtful one?

He was still debating when he became aware of a mortal all but pressed against his arm, studying the same embroidery.

He turned, half-planning some ironic observation, until he saw her. Then coherent speech was impossible.

She was tiny—the top of her head was only just higher than Karana's elbow—and her skin was that rare porcelain that Zhongtu nobles all wanted though Karana thought it looked sickly.

Had thought it looked sickly—before he'd seen her.

Her hair was a raven's wing, her eyes wide and dark, her face a heart. Everything cliché yet perfect. Her tiny bow lips curled into a sweet smile as he looked at her, and Karana almost recognized her, though they'd never met before.

"Hello, sir," she said shyly, her eyelashes fluttering. "I saw you admiring the peacock and thought you might have questions."

Was she flirting with him?

She was a baby; he'd guess three and a half millennia—no, she was mortal, so sixteen or seventeen years old. Shouldn't he look ridiculously old and intimidating to her?

And if she was so foolish as to find old and intimidating attractive, Karana should not indulge her. He cleared his throat.

And said, "It's stunning; I thought my sister might like it.

May I ask about the artisan? She likes to know such things."

Fate laugh at him. He was as foolish as she was. But this feeling, the what-if that was dancing through his veins—he couldn't ignore it.

Her smile widened, and she started reciting the artist's history with increasing animation, her fine-boned hand touching his sleeve for a moment. She seemed to realize her own daring with alarm, for blood stained her pale cheeks.

They spoke for over an hour, but only one thing that she told him was important: her name was An Ning.

Karana whispered it to himself as he slipped between the shop's curtains into the street, the wrapped embroidery under his arm—Jin would like it.

Once a week for the next year, Karana returned to see An Ning. Stars sparkled in her eyes every time she saw him, and her hand rested on his arm with increasing frequency. Karana wanted to take her as his lover, but she was too young—she had turned seventeen a few months after their first meeting.

And then the unthinkable happened.

Karana wasn't the only one admiring her womanly figure and sweet disposition; a wealthy young nobleman had also done so.

An Ning went so far as to hold both his hands, her eyes wide and her cheeks ghostly white, as she told him.

"My father is excited because of how this will help my family," she said. Her eyes said, *But I'm not.*

"After the wedding, I won't be here anymore," she continued, and her eyes wondered, *Will you miss me?*

"I told my father I wasn't ready to marry, but he said a filial daughter would smile and keep silent." Her eyes pleaded him for help.

Karana took a deep breath. He wasn't equipped to deal with this situation—but neither was she. When all was said and done, she was only seventeen years old.

He squeezed her fingers gently. "If you want to run away, I'll help you," he told her.

Her face fell, and she tugged her hands from his. "I couldn't leave my family. I had hoped..." She shook her head, her eyes almost closed so that her lashes made dark half-moons against her cheeks. "I like you," she whispered. "I had thought that you..."

He touched her chin lightly, tilting it back up. "I like you, too. I'll give you anything you want. Do you want me to ask your father for your hand in marriage?" He had married mortals before. It was dangerous for them—most times, it seemed that someone found them and targeted them—but if that's what she wanted, he would do it.

She looked briefly hopeful before biting her lip. "My father won't approve. He badly wants this marriage—and the nobleman might ruin my family if we embarrass him." A single tear ran down her cheek, and suddenly she rose up on her tiptoes, her hands tugged his neck down, and she kissed him.

She pulled back and never had her eyes looked bigger or darker. "I want—I want to be alone with you, just once."

Karana wasn't sure that was a good idea. Scratch that— Karana was sure that was a *bad* idea. She was too young.

And yet, he wanted it as well. It had been so long—a thousand years, give or take—and that simple kiss had set him ablaze.

Even if she didn't want to marry him—even if she put her

filial piety above her own desires—surely they could have one night. Karana would make sure, as he always had with his mortal lovers, that no child would result from the union.

He stepped back, careful not to touch her.

"Are you sure that's what you want?"

She nodded.

"Will you be alone in your room tonight?"

An Ning nodded, her expression serious and determined. "Yes, after sunset. But our manor is guarded—how will you...?"

Karana smiled and chucked An Ning under the chin. "Wait and see."

Karana spent the rest of the long summer day walking the streets of Xiling, buying anything he thought An Ning might like. Pink peonies from this vendor; candied hawthorn berries from that one. Time seemed to stretch interminable, but finally the sun fell beneath the horizon and Karana teleported to her room.

She was waiting for him, dressed in a beautiful pink robe with small white plum blossoms scattered across it—the embroidery looked so real that Karana was surprised when they stayed affixed to the cloth as she moved. Well, her family did work with the best artisans, and this was clearly a special outfit.

"How did you do that?" she asked, her eyes wide.

He couldn't help himself—he had barely touched her over the past year, but now he picked her up and swung her around.

"I'm a god," he told her.

An Ning's lips parted in surprise.

"Does that change things?" he asked her softly. "Will you run away with me now?"

She shook her head. "I couldn't be a god's wife!" she told him. She bit her lip. "But—if you truly want me?"

"More than anything."

He kissed her, and she tasted like lemongrass and mint. Her after dinner tea, he supposed.

Her hands slid into his hair, and for once Karana didn't care if it was messed up. His hands twisted in the buttery soft silk of her robes even as he teleported them from her room to his at the Sun Palace.

She didn't notice that they had slipped through time and space, simply pulling herself closer to him so that her chest mashed against his.

The thrill and folly of youth.

After he grew uncomfortably hot, he set her on his bed and undid the silk knots on his shoulder.

Her lips were parted again, her breath panting, and her lids heavy. As she watched him unrobe, her tongue darted out once to touch her upper lip.

When he was down to his long silk underpants, Karana sat on the bed beside her. Karana could feel her passion, her longing for him, so he didn't waste time asking if she was sure again. Instead, he collected her hands in his. "An Ning, you must tell me what you like and what you dislike."

Those heavy lids rose. "I don't know what I like! I haven't done this before!" Karana saw that she was surprised and perhaps a tinge offended.

He cradled her cheek. "I know that. I mean tonight—there is no moment where we can't stop. There's nothing you can't say to me. Your pleasure—your comfort—is my first priority."

She stared at him, and Karana wondered what thoughts

were running behind those dark eyes.

How he wished they had more time—he had wanted to court her, to woo her, but he had thought to wait until she was at least twenty.

She smiled suddenly then and said, "I want to be wearing less clothes."

Urgent lips, trembling fingers, sharp inhalations, and sweet moans. Everything was fast and slow at the same time, a pounding need overwhelming them both even as time stretched endlessly for mere moments.

How could it be so perfect between them, as if they'd made love a thousand times before?

Karana didn't know, but they spiraled to completion together and lay replete in a tangle of limbs.

An Ning smiled at him, her dark hair a halo around her head, and Karana thought his heart would beat out of his chest. He kissed her temple and called her, "My peace."

She slept, but he did not. He would not waste a single moment of this night, and when she woke in the morning, he pleaded with her to stay with him. She refused twice though, insisting she had to obey her father's wishes, and the third time Karana asked she grew angry.

"You said there was nothing I could not say—no moment it was too late to stop! Or was that only last night?" her eyes flashed.

So Karana brought her home. But she grabbed his arm before he left. "The wedding isn't for a month. Until then..."

"I will come every night, and if you wish to come with me, I will show you the wonders of the world."

And so they had a stolen month. Karana made love to An

Ning beneath the red camellias in southern Zhongtu; he taught her to swim in the warm Strait of the Moon. They danced in streets of Shahar and kissed on Po, where the air was as sweet as honey.

Every night, he suggested she stay with him forever, and every morning she asked to return to her family. And then it was the day of her wedding. Karana went away, as far as he could get, and stood in the cold North Sea, letting it freeze his ardor and numb his mind.

He stood there for two days.

On the second evening, he realized he had made a mistake. She was seventeen—why on Earth would he trust her judgment? Not that he wanted to violate her autonomy, but...

Giving up eighty years of happiness because she wanted to please her father?

Karana was a *god*! No one could please her father more than he could! He would bring the old man more gold than a mortal could conceive; he would create rubies so large that An Ning's husband would be crushed beneath their weight.

Not that he would crush the man—unless he had been mean to An Ning. Then no power on Earth could save him.

Still dripping with cold saltwater, Karana teleported to the noble husband's house to claim his love.

The first servant that Karana spoke to tried to send him away; Karana let flames dance on his arms and the man covered his eyes. Trying to hide himself from Karana's gaze, stupid though it was.

Babbling with a fear that Karana didn't understand, the servant led Karana to a room filled with men.

Men and An Ning.

They were hurting her, violating her body in ways that Karana couldn't have imagined.

The world turned red, and the men turned to ash.

But that didn't heal An Ning's bruises, nor stop her weeping.

Karana was afraid to touch her, though he covered her body with his outer robe. She coughed blood.

"I will take you to Haraa," he told her. "She will heal you."

"No!" she cried. "I can't!"

She was hysterical. Karana tried to calm her, but even his hand on her shoulder seemed to cause her pain. So he didn't touch her, instead standing at her side.

"Please," she begged him over and over, "I want everything to end."

"Yes," he finally told her, "I will destroy everything."

Never mind that he had already incinerated her rapists—her cursed husband hadn't been among them. Karana would destroy everyone who believed it was okay to ever treat another being this way.

When she fell still, beaten to death, Karana wrapped her in a fiery embrace.

For the ninth time in his life, he felt like his heart had been removed. Nine names passed through his mind. Shaanti, Amalgan, Heping, Santi, Chain, Heiwa, Pyeonghwa, Santiphaph, and An Ning. *Please don't leave me*, he begged her silently, as he had begged each of them. But they all had left.

Nine times he had loved, nine times he had lost. But never had it hurt as badly as this. Never had he wanted to burn the entire world to ash.

And he would begin with this manor.

Fire consumed everything, everyone in his path.

At first, Karana couldn't hear the shouting, the crying, the desperate begging.

There was nothing but anger, sorrow, and flame.

But then.

There was a child. A girl. She was shaking and crying, and Karana saw her.

Somehow, miraculously, as he had with the child monks at his temple, he found the sanity to spare her. Because, despite his promise to An Ning, he couldn't kill a little girl.

He told her to run, to flee Xiling. Her presence allowed him to recover himself enough that he started sorting through the mortals in the city. Those who were more kind than cruel, those that lacked the malice to inflict pain on others just to satisfy themselves, he spared.

When the city stopped burning, and every cursed rapist, misogynist, and chauvinistic prick had been cremated, Karana went home.

He sat on the floor where he arrived. He couldn't be bothered to find a proper seat.

Moments later, two red-robed disciples entered the room. They bowed nervously, flinching backward when Karana looked at them.

"Divinity," said one, "your father asks you to attend him in the Sun Pagoda."

Karana managed to shrug one shoulder—even that felt like too much effort—and remained where he was.

There was a long pause, and then the disciple took a step closer.

"Divinity?"

"No," said Karana. His voice sounded terrible. A croak really. He'd breathed in too much smoke.

"No, you won't go to the pagoda?"

Karana's eyes slid to the man's face. The disciple blanched; he and his fellow ran from the room. Karana flopped onto the floor.

And then his father, the Sun Emperor himself, was standing over him. Karana blinked once. He couldn't remember the last time his father had entered his residence—maybe he never had.

"Karana," his name was said softly, as if his father was afraid of breaking it, "why did you burn Xiling?"

Karana almost didn't answer. But then, "Because I wanted to."

His father's face blurred. Actually, the whole world looked blurry.

Maybe his father would kill him. Surely many immortals were upset. Probably several had lived in the city. The capital of Zhongtu, they had called it.

"You wanted to kill ten thousand mortals?"

"Yes," said Karana. And he waited for the Sun Emperor's punishment. Yearned for it.

But his father said, "I'm sorry."

Karana realized it was tears that were blurring the world. "For what?"

His father shrugged. "For whatever made you want to kill them all."

Karana looked away again. It seemed like he wasn't going to die today after all.

As much as he wanted to.

Separate Paths

Present Day

PROVING what a cold prick he was, Bai said to An Ning, "I have no time to waste on people who argue against facts."

Karana wanted to slug him, but he couldn't help but process what Bai was saying.

Facts. He was saying that An Ning really had been a woman from Xiling, and Karana felt ill.

Why would she have wanted—on a subconscious level, on impulse—to become a man?

Maybe because she had been afraid of assault. Maybe because having witnessed the violence of men, she had been too afraid to be a woman.

No, she isn't An Ning.

She was. Karana knew it. Had always known it. He had

recognized her that first day.

Forget why she "chose" the form that she did. Why did she even choose to live? She was begging to die. And was it her wounds or the fire that killed her?

He couldn't very well ask her, could he?

Bai turned to Karana. "Deal with Guleum. Capture him alive, and I will convince Jin to resurrect Ao's granddaughter."

Even though An Ning was still holding his wrist, Karana almost punched Bai anyway. Bai claimed to be made from stone, and sometimes Karana thought his heart still was. But Karana knew Bai was just a convenient target for his anger. Fate curse it, he wanted to hit something—anything—to escape his own shame.

And even more than he wanted to smack Bai, he wanted to ask him a question. The cursed Knowing God—he could be the biggest prick in the world, and everyone would still lick his boots for that absolute certainty he dangled before them.

Gently, for he could see those long-ago bruises on her, though (as far as he knew) no one had ever beaten this body, Karana tugged An Ning's hand from his wrist.

"Chika, would you please walk your sensei outside? I need to speak to my nephew for a moment."

An Ning's eyes widened—she looked hurt.

Her face wavered before him, becoming heart-shaped instead of oval, though those large black eyes stayed exactly the same.

Why hadn't he seen it earlier? Because he hadn't wanted to. If she was the seventeen-year-old mortal that he had failed so badly, how could he pretend he had the right to court her again?

Chika stepped around him and gave him a fierce, angry look as only she could. She linked her arm with An Ning's. The two of them bowed to Bai as one and walked from the room. Karana knew her obedience was thanks to Bai's consequence, not his.

He focused on their feelings, using the sometimes-overwhelming power that he had inherited from his father, to make sure they were out of earshot. When he could no longer feel their confusion and stress, Karana stepped closer to Bai.

"If you wish me to track Gu, will you assign a Heavenly Guard to escort Chika and An Ning in the Underworld? Neither of them is a real warrior."

Bai pursed his lips, then nodded. "I know who to send. He's been to the Underworld before to visit the souls of mortal relatives. The God of Swordsmanship."

Karana was surprised. He hadn't realized Bai could be thoughtful.

"And?" demanded Bai. "You didn't send them away just to say that."

Karana took a deep breath. "I need to know everything you could read about An Ning."

Bai's brows cocked. "And why would I tell you that? Seems like it's her business, not yours."

"She's from Xiling."

Still Bai said nothing.

"She woke among the ashes of Xiling. I incinerated that city; there's no way a mortal could have survived the fire."

Bai's expression softened minutely. Karana hadn't known it could. Bai said, "You think you murdered her." He frowned. "Her soul came from a mortal woman." He hesitated. "She might have been the ashes of a mortal woman."

Karana waited.

"It's rare, but I have seen souls linger by their corpses. In one case, it eventually ascended to immortality. I postulated that, while strong-willed enough to become immortal, it couldn't decide whether or not it wanted to. If your friend was having trouble choosing between life and death, she might have lingered and changed her own ashes into an immortal being."

Karana found himself crying.

To his shock, Bai wrapped his arms around Karana and patted him on the back. The made-from-stone Knowing God was hugging him, comforting him.

Karana actually laughed—a strangled, tortured sound, but a laugh nonetheless.

Bai stepped back quickly, with an offended scowl.

"Why did she want to live?" Karana asked quickly.

But the moment was over. "I know neither her thoughts nor her emotions," barked Bai. "Ask her yourself."

Karana wanted to, but he knew An Ning remembered nothing of her mortal life.

And maybe it was better that way.

THE trill of crickets drifted in through An Ning's open window. They sounded like the crickets that she had heard a week ago at the Wood Pavilions; the pavilions had felt like a different world, and it was strange to realize they were only about a week's walk away.

Miho, Chika, Xia, Xia's chosen successor, and Karana were

all seated in her suite. Although they'd had a formal meal earlier, a steaming cup of broth was also in An Ning's hands. Xia had practically been shoving food down An Ning's throat since her return—she often eyed An Ning anxiously as well, sure that she was about to wither away ever since she had learned the cultists had starved An Ning when they kidnapped her. An Ning wasn't happy with Miho for telling her; there were some things Xia was better off not knowing.

An Ning had insisted she was too full to eat another bite, and thus the broth, which Xia argued consisted of sips, not bites. An Ning forced herself to take one, and Karana snorted.

She tried to meet his eyes, but he looked away. He had been strange ever since seeing the Knowing God. Maybe, though he said it didn't matter, he was disappointed that her body was unchanged. He had rushed to assure her that it didn't matter what Bai said, he was sure that Jin would help her, though they might have to wait until she gave birth.

An Ning wasn't positive if he were reassuring himself as well and that made her sad. Now that he knew how strange she felt in her body, was he repelled by it? They hadn't kissed since the Wood Pavilion, and they hadn't held hands. In fact, Karana hadn't touched her since teleporting Chika and her home.

Chika had been updating her cousin on everything they'd been told by the Knowing God. She now said, "So you'll stay here, Miho, while we capture the prick—"

"Language!" hissed Miho.

"—that killed Akemi." Chika stuck her tongue out, not the least repentant for her word choice. Remembering how he had kicked Akemi's corpse, An Ning also felt the slur was appropriate, though she had never used such a word herself.

"No," said Karana, surprising An Ning, for she had heard him use worse language. But that wasn't his objection. "You and An Ning will go to the Sea of Souls to find Akemi's soul. I will capture him myself."

"You don't know what he looks like," objected Chika.

An Ning was also shocked. She had assumed they would all stay together... Wasn't the Underworld dangerous?

Karana asked, without looking at her, "An Ning, would you close the shutters?"

She obliged, and he closed his eyes.

Moments later, light flowed up from his palm, a soft red haze with fine white lines. The light coalesced into a youth. "Is this what he looked like?"

His nose was narrow and sharp, his lips thin. He was gangly, with a head that looked too big for his scrawny neck.

"Similar," said An Ning, "though that being looks too young. He should be a little more filled out. Taller maybe, too."

She thought back to the exchange between Karana and the Knowing God about "Guleum."

"Is he your brother?" she blurted.

"Yes," admitted Karana. "My younger half-brother. His mother was the last empress." The image on his hand grew slightly and thickened. "He is the one who cursed the late Sun Emperor," Karana also said, then looked surprised by his own words.

"He killed the emperor?" asked Miho in shock. "But then—why didn't the Threefold Goddess kill him? Or imprison him, like she did with Aunt Salaana?"

An Ning leaned forward to catch Karana's answer.

Karana sighed. "Because it was Salaana who goaded him into doing it. She took the full blame. Gu was only three thousand and some years old."

It was Xia who said, "A murderer's a murderer, no matter the age. Besides, our Peace Bringer is only three thousand years old!" She then flushed and added, "Begging your pardon, divinity."

Karana shook his head. "No pardon needed. I agree that Guleum should have faced stronger repercussions for his actions. And now it seems he's been using the cult for some time...

"Anyway, he must be found and stopped as soon as possible. Bai was clear enough about that. But there's no reason to delay finding Akemi."

"Isn't the Underworld dangerous?" blurted An Ning.

"I can handle it," said Chika, puffing her chest and slapping it once. "And we can bring the Bulgae—"

"The Bulgae should stay here," said Miho, "to protect the village—"

They started arguing. An Ning rose and touched both their shoulders.

Her disciples fell silent and looked up at her.

"Most of the Bulgae should remain here. Ember will come with us."

"Ember can't, nor can the other Bulgae," said Karana. "The Sea of Souls would extinguish them. However, the God of Swordsmanship will accompany you."

An Ning turned to Karana in surprise. "The God of Swordsmanship?" That title sounded familiar, but she couldn't think of a temple to any such deity. Where had she heard that title?

"Yes," said Karana, "I asked Bai for an escort before we left. Daichin should be here tomorrow."

Daichin? That was the man who had been born in a female body. The mortal that the Threefold Goddess had transformed, and who had ascended to immortality.

Karana's eyes darted toward her, *almost* meeting her own. "You might have questions for him."

Questions? Yes, she had a scroll full!

"That was thoughtful of you," she said.

Karana cleared his throat. "Actually, it was Bai who thought of it." Karana rubbed his hands together, before adding in a rush. "He's not as bad as he seems. He means well. And my niece loves him."

An Ning was confused. Why did Karana care what she thought of the Knowing God? Her opinion hardly affected the two most famous gods in the world.

Then she realized.

They're his family. He wants me to like his family. But didn't that mean he liked her? Why was he keeping his distance then? Why wouldn't he look at her?

SOONER than An Ning liked, she was standing in the central courtyard of her manor, holding one of Chika's hands while Daichin held the other. Although there was something unsettled between her and Karana, she was following his plan without objection.

Daichin was a short man, smaller than An Ning, though he still loomed over the tiny Chika. He had a thick brown beard with flaring ends that An Ning vaguely associated with statues of the late God of War; maybe he did that on purpose, since their vocation was similar. He had been nothing but polite, and Chika in turn had been refreshingly respectful to him, but An Ning still wished that Karana was coming with them. When all was said and done, Daichin was a stranger.

She had tried to talk to Karana last night—not to object, just to see what was worrying him and to say good-bye.

She had asked him if he was frustrated by the outcome of their petition.

Karana had frozen. He still hadn't met her eyes, but he had taken her hand in his and squeezed it. "Only in that I thought you were."

"But you've been avoiding me."

He had nodded once, briefly. "Not because of you. Because I'm disappointed in myself."

An Ning had tsked. "I wish you'd stop blaming yourself for what happened with the cult! The Knowing God expects perfection, but you're one being after all! That's why you are chasing down your—Guleum—on your own, isn't it? To make amends for not doing it earlier. But—"

Karana had held a hand to her lips, silencing them.

"An Ning, don't worry about me. I can handle Gu. This is what I should do. And maybe it will help me feel a little less guilty."

"You shouldn't feel guilty."

"But I do anyway," he had murmured.

An Ning had flung herself so hard at his chest that he had taken a step back. Though his arms had remained tense, she had felt comforted when they wrapped around her.

"I love you," she had reminded him.

"I don't know why," Karana had said.

She had poked him in the ribs.

"But I love you too."

She had gone to kiss him then, but he had turned his cheek.

He had turned back almost immediately. "It isn't because of your body. It's me—I feel so guilty that..."

"You don't have to explain," she had said, though she didn't mean it. She wanted his explanation.

An Ning hadn't slept well, despite lecturing herself multiple times that she should take advantage of her bed since who knew what they'd be sleeping on tomorrow.

Now she squeezed Chika's hand and looked toward Karana one last time.

He smiled for her, but it was obviously forced. His red eyes were darker than usual, and he wore only his kohl and his lip paint.

Without creams and powders to smooth his face, he looked older and more tired. Sadness seemed to cling to him.

An Ning opened her mouth to say goodbye one last time, but Chika pulled her between.

They reemerged almost an hour later by a beautiful, brilliantly blue lake. An Ning had never been here before, but she knew it was Ah Lake, on an island of the same name.

Yesterday, she had learned that while it was impossible to teleport into the Underworld from Earth, there were certain entrances on Earth that *usually* led to certain sites in the Underworld. Apparently, the entrance in the middle of this lake generally brought one to the Sea of Souls. Annoyingly, the entrance was at the bottom of the lake, not the side.

An Ning wasn't a strong swimmer, and she had a large pack on her back filled with food, but Chika had said they wouldn't be swimming. An Ning glanced at Daichin—he wouldn't have been able to swim, between the metal plates on his chest and the twin swords on his back.

"Stay close to me," Chika ordered. She seemed an appropriate companion to Daichin, in her red armor and her short and long swords also sheathed on her back. An Ning had a stave in her hand and was also wearing newly made armor, but she felt like a fraud. She wasn't at ease with the accoutrements of battle like they were.

Still An Ning fell in beside Daichin, who gave her a reassuring smile as they followed Chika.

The water parted in front of them and closed behind them. At first, it looked like their feet were simply driving the water away, but about ten paces from shore, it became clear that the water was arching away from them in a perfect sphere. Another thirty paces and the water closed over their heads, completing the bubble.

An Ning found herself looking up, watching as the sun slowly became harder and harder to see through the water.

"You're amazing," she told Chika.

"I know," Chika replied, and An Ning could hear the smile in her voice.

"This is quite fascinating," agreed Daichin. "I have seen the Love God's Heart do something similar, but I have never been inside such a bubble personally. She's your aunt, isn't she?" That last was directed to Chika.

An Ning was surprised—she had never heard that before, and Chika went stiff.

"The Love God's Heart—she has no connection to my family."

Daichin was startled. "But—I've seen her tattoo. On her back..."

"She has no connection to my family," Chika repeated, and she glanced at An Ning over her right shoulder, a plea for help.

An Ning cleared her throat awkwardly. Despite having questions for Daichin, she had barely managed to speak to him since he arrived in Ningjingcun. Despite his friendly manner, An Ning felt he was a deity above her touch.

But this conversation was clearly making Chika uncomfortable, and An Ning didn't want to see what would happen if she lost control of the water around them.

"Divinity," An Ning addressed Daichin, "May I ask how long you've been the God of Swordsmanship? You used to be a mortal, isn't that right?"

He laughed, a clear tenor that suited his open face. "Oh, call me Daichin. And I'll call you An Ning." His brown beard rippled with a smirk. "How long have I been a god? Not quite a thousand years. I used to know exactly, but somewhere between two hundred and thirty-four and two hundred and fifty, I lost track! But Jin tells me that my ascension is recorded in the books, so we can be sure to celebrate the thousandth year. I guess immortals all round time that way. And yourself?"

"About three thousand years, give or take," said An Ning. "I don't think the day of my ascension is recorded anywhere."

"That's right," said Chika, "You don't know when your birthday is, do you?"

"Well, no."

"That's too bad," said Daichin. "Perhaps we could estimate

it. Was there any major event near your ascension?"

"Hmm, I don't know. The burning of Xiling..."

"Oh, that was in early summer! I'm sure that someone has written the exact date. The Moon Deer if no one else—he keeps extravagant records. You witnessed the burning? Do you know how many days old you were?"

"I—I was born from it. I mean, I was ashes in Xiling."

Daichin looked at her in confusion. "Oh—I had heard—" he cleared his throat.

An Ning realized that the Knowing God must have told him that she'd been a mortal woman. She blushed, realizing that he knew exactly why he'd been asked to escort them. Her shyness had been obvious to him, while she had thought her secret was just that: secret.

"You heard that I was a mortal woman," she said, trying to sound nonchalant.

He nodded once.

"I suppose maybe I was, but I always thought I had formed from ash in Xiling. I woke in it, naked, with no memory of the past."

"Wait, did Uncle Karana *kill* you?" Chika asked.

"What?" An Ning was completely taken aback. "Of course he didn't!"

"No, think about it!" Chika insisted. "You were a mortal living in Xiling; you woke in the ash. Uncle Karana destroyed the city and burned at least ten thousand mortals alive. Doesn't that mean he killed you when you were a mortal? It's possible to ascend after death—from your ashes instead of from your body. One of Ojichan's retainers did that. He drowned, but his soul stuck around and then his bloated body was remade into an immortal one. He loves to tell the story—Drowned Hiro, we call him."

An Ning was speechless.

She wanted to object, but... Could this be why Karana had been behaving so strangely? Because after seeing the Knowing God, he realized he had killed her?

That was a horrible thought.

And then, swift on its heels, *Could he have met me when I was alive? Does he know what my life was like?*

An Ning remembered leaving the city, and the citizens who tried to kill the courtesans. Master Tianxu had said that the God of Destruction had killed everyone he condemned; had he killed *only* those he condemned?

Was it possible that his strange behavior, the distance he'd been keeping, wasn't because he felt guilty for killing An Ning, but because he knew some horrible sin that she had committed as a mortal?

An Ning suddenly felt like there wasn't enough air in the bubble, though both Daichin and Chika still seemed fine.

"If so, fate is mocking us, don't you think?" Somehow An Ning kept her voice light.

"Fate does have a strange sense of humor," agreed Daichin.

As An Ning put one foot in front of the other, she thrust her worries away. This wasn't the time to agonize over Karana. She had a mission: help Chika find Akemi's soul.

And it would be good to know Daichin better.

So with a determined cheerfulness, she relayed how she and the other refugees from Xiling established Ningjingcun. From him, there were stories of Ehkoron and the Ondor Peaks, places she had never heard of in her life.

For the third time in recent days, she decided that she should travel more. There were so many places that she hadn't been.

And finally, Daichin told of how the Threefold Goddess transformed his body to suit his soul. An Ning had already heard it from Karana of course, but she listened intently, as did Chika.

"When you became immortal," asked Chika, and An Ning knew that she was also remembering the Knowing God's words, "do you remember choosing your body? I never made such a choice, of course, being born immortal, and An Ning doesn't remember it at all."

"It's a little hard to describe," Daichin said. "I wouldn't have said it was a choice—it wasn't like I was weighing all the options. But yes, I could feel my needs and wants shaping my body. I am a little taller and definitely more muscular than I was as a mortal. And my face changed a little as well—people always used to comment on how pretty I was, and I didn't like it, so I suppose I made myself plainer."

"That's fascinating," said Chika.

An Ning didn't find it fascinating. She found the idea of her wants and needs giving her *this* body troubling. Over the years, she had found it useful. It was strong and had done everything she had asked of it. However, when she met Karana, all those feelings that had so haunted her the first few decades of her life had come back. She had so wanted her body to be curved and feminine—shorter too, perhaps. And not once, in three thousand years, had she thought of herself as a man. She knew she was a woman, regardless of her genitals or her chest.

"I've never grown a beard," she suddenly said, surprising

herself. She was looking at the bushy growth on Daichin's chin. "I don't mean I didn't choose to—I meant I can't. I've never shaved. My chin doesn't grow hair."

The thought was strangely comforting. There were many men in Zhongtu with little facial hair, but as far as An Ning knew, most of them shaved at least sometimes. The fact that she had chosen not to, even though she made the rest of her body male, seemed to tell An Ning that the woman she had been wasn't totally committed to being a man.

Why on Earth would she have wanted to be one at all though?

"There it is," said Chika, trying to sound unimpressed, though her excitement leaked through.

An Ning and Daichin both looked over her head to find the entrance to the Underworld. A tear in reality, rainbows shimmered over its surface like the pearlescent inside of a clam. Magic, made visible.

Despite knowing what—vaguely—was on the other side, An Ning felt a tremendous desire to step forward and touch that shifting iridescence. To fall into its light.

Because the call was so great, An Ning's favorite little voice cautioned her to run away, to let Chika continue alone. Nothing that alluring could be good.

But Daichin stepped forward, and Chika tugged An Ning after.

"Here's to adventure," cheered Daichin, his voice full of laughter as he touched the portal. Chika hesitated a moment, and An Ning collected her hand in her own.

They nodded at each other and stepped into the fluid iridescence together.

A Timeline of Karana's Life

Years in Millennia after Creation

79	*Karana is born to the Sun Emperor and the Goddess of Lightning. He is named the God of Destruction.*
82	*Karana gains his first mortal worshippers. By the end of the millennia, the Sun Emperor seals the Underworld with all immortal creatures locked inside.*
87	*Karana meets Amalgan, the Khan's daughter.*
89	*Karana meets Heping, the gardener.*
91	*Karana's mother dies. His father marries the Goddess of Thought.*
92	*The Goddess of Thought's son dies in infancy, and Karana is banished from the Sun Palace.*
93	*Karana meets Santi, the mother.*
94	*Karana meets Chain, the singer.*
95	*Karana meets Heiwa, the warrior.*
96	*Karana meets Pyeonghwa, the pilgrim. The future Threefold Goddess is born.*
97	*The Goddess of Thought dies and Karana is allowed to return to the Sun Palace. Karana meets Stantiphaph, the queen.*
98	*Karana burns Xiling. An Ning awakes in the ashes.*
100	*Tales 1 & 2 of the Immortal Beings.*
101	*Karana enters Ningjingcun.*

The Queen and the Pyre

"SO where will you go?" Miho asked Karana. "Can you find the God of Wind through your blood tie?"

Chika, An Ning, and Daichin had disappeared together. Karana knew that it would take nearly an hour for the three of them to reach Ah Lake. Chika had access to a wide pool of magic, being of the Sea Dragon clan—not many immortals could teleport two others—but she still had to share that power with fifty-odd relatives.

There wasn't anything he could do for them now—and it was kind of a relief. He already missed An Ning and had to resist the urge to follow her, but he also needed space. To sort through his feelings. Or what he could allow himself to feel.

He turned to Miho and her question. "The God of Wind? I haven't heard that name in a long time. He was never canonized, you know."

Even immortals who were named deities at their birth didn't establish temples until they reached adulthood. Guleum had been called the God of Wind by other immortals before Jin's ascension, but he never had any mortal worshippers.

Maybe that was why he'd been attracted to Karana's.

"I can't find him that way. As far as I know, blood ties can only be used for tracking along direct lines. Parent to child.

"However, the cultists were using the Ruins of Xiling for their rites, and Gu was using my name. It seems likely that they might be taking advantage of other sites that I created over the years. I'll start there and a lead will turn up, sooner or later. Hopefully sooner—I'd like to find him before Chika and An Ning return."

"When do you think they'll return?" Miho asked. Xia, who had been hanging in the shadows, leaned forward at the question. Karana nodded to her in acknowledgment.

"Unfortunately, I don't know. The entrance I suggested is *supposed* to lead to the Sea of Souls, but the Underworld shifts and changes. Depending on where they come out, they might have months of travel ahead of them. If they're unlucky enough, they might have to return to the Earth to restock their rations and try again."

Xia sighed, and Karana smiled at her sympathetically.

He looked back at Miho, and then impulsively combed his fingers through his hair. He handed her a strand that had come away.

"If there's an emergency, use this to find me."

Her eyes widened, and Miho accepted it reverently.

"Thank you, Uncle." She folded her fingers over it and bowed. "Take care. Sensei won't be the only one who'd be sad if something happened to you."

"Yes—be careful, divinity," echoed Xia.

Since she was looking at him, Karana winked at the old monk. She winked back, and he laughed in surprise. Then he moved between.

He came out less than ten minutes later in Maoyi, the southernmost city of the continent. The heat swamped him, a fine sheen of sweat appearing instantly on his skin.

Karana appreciated Maoyi, a colorful and energetic city that rolled out before him in low hills (the hills demanded the energy), but he had to admit it was downright unpleasant in the summer. Even up here, on the tallest hill that caught any passing breeze, he felt like he was melting. He took a deep breath and immediately regretted it, for the damp, moist air was suffocating. A valid reason for avoiding Maoyi, but even worse than the humidity were the memories of his lover Santiphaph that came flooding back.

Slowly, he turned around to face her tomb. Made of red carnelian, her likeness smiled at him as perfectly as it had the day he had made it. To either side, the tombs of the Maoyan rulers who had come before and after had crumbled into featureless faces, but they had been made by mortals, not Karana.

He stared into Santiphaph's larger than life eyes for a moment before bowing. "My queen," he said to her.

Santiphaph had been the closest to vain of all his lovers, a symptom of being queen, perhaps, though there had been a trace of humor to her demand that he always address her by her title.

He smiled slightly, thinking that she would be pleased her

monument still remained as a testament to her beauty.

Then he noticed the smoke, drifting slowly and lazily behind her head.

AN NING and Chika stepped into a river; Daichin had already scrambled to shore. He was standing by, well, a tree, for lack of a better term. It looked to be made of yellow topaz, though An Ning supposed that it might be a different material all together. Karana had told them that nothing in the Underworld was the same as Earth, and not to eat anything they found there.

"This doesn't look like any sea I've ever seen," groused Chika. "A forest, maybe."

"Yes," agreed Daichin, unbothered by Chika's bad attitude. "I have studied the zones of the Underworld for some time. Bai calls this the Crystal Forest. He says that he once made a flute from one of these trees, and it gave visions of the past to all who heard it sing."

He touched the topaz tree with his bare hand, and An Ning made an involuntary sound of alarm—Daichin glanced at her but merely smiled. "I wonder what properties a crystalline sword would have." He drew one of his twin swords and sliced at one of the tree's branches.

A sharp ringing shredded the air, and An Ning fell to her knees. Though her hands were pressed as hard as they could be against her ears, the ringing stabbed deep into her brain, into memories long buried.

She remembered a pink silk robe, long out of style and hardly suited to life in Ningjingcun. It had white petals embroidered on it, so delicately that they looked real. She heard a noise, and looked up and saw Karana standing before her, his black lips curved into a mysterious smile. Her heart beat faster.

And then An Ning was back in the Underworld, and she could see Chika doubled over, tears streaking down her face.

An Ning wrapped her arm around Chika's and helped her to her feet.

"Are you a fate-cursed fool?" she demanded of Daichin, angrier than she could ever remember being.

Had that been a memory? Of her as a woman in Xiling, meeting Karana for a tryst?

Had Karana really burned her deliberately, to punish her for her sins? And the rest of the city for good measure?

All of An Ning's fears focused into a glare on Daichin, and he flushed.

He bowed once. "Next time I'll warn you."

That was far from an apology, and An Ning asked, "Is this why you agreed to come with us? To play? If so, perhaps we should travel separately."

"Aren't you called the Peace Bringer?" Daichin was laughing at her. "Rather bellicose, aren't you?" He raised both hands as if to hold her off. "Come now, I promised both Bai and Karana to protect you and help you to the Sea of Souls. I'm sorry to have shocked you, but it was just a little memory now, wasn't it?"

"Some memories hurt worse than others!" hissed Chika.

An Ning glanced at her. What had *she* remembered?

Akemi's death?

An Ning swallowed her anger. "You know where the Sea

of Souls is from here?" She gestured for him to lead the way.

He smirked, and An Ning reflected that he wasn't nearly as nice as she had originally thought.

He pulled a miniscule indigo boat from a bag at his waist and held it out to Chika. "We'll sail this down the river. I think we should only be a week or two from the sea, based on what Jin described."

"Right," said An Ning, "and we will fit on that how?"

Chika plucked the tiny boat out of his hands. She turned it in her hands in awe. "I've never seen anything like this before. Where did you get it?"

"From the Love God's Heart. You know, the being who has nothing to do with your family."

Chika dropped the boat but caught it again before it could hit the ground. For a moment, An Ning thought her stubborn disciple would hand the boat back to Daichin, but then Chika said, "I can grow it."

Chika strode to the river they'd arrived in. She focused intently, and the boat began to grow. Large enough for a child to play with, then big enough for one person to ride, and then all three of them, and on until it was as large as any riverboat that An Ning had seen on the Jingzi.

"Let's go," said Chika.

Daichin said the river would carry them to the sea, eventually, and so the three had little to do.

Daichin liked to talk—more than An Ning or Chika—and he also occasionally insisted on mooring the boat so that he could venture onto the land and retrieve some flower or leaf or stone that he had heard tell of. These little delays, and Daichin's smugness, were like a stone in An Ning's shoe. She held a dozen conversations with him about it in her head, but every time she tried to bring up her concerns, he managed to redirect the conversation or somehow play her (entirely reasonable) requests off as absurd.

But a week after they'd been sailing, while An Ning was gnawing on some of the endless supply of fruit leather they'd brought with them, a flock of black-winged creatures descended on the boat.

Their feet were golden blades, each longer than An Ning's pointer finger and glinting like razors. Daichin leapt into the air, swords swinging. Chika tried to follow, but she was too late.

The boat dripped with a disgusting black ichor, and not a single creature remained. Daichin had his feet planted firmly on the deck again and was cleaning his blades.

And An Ning no longer objected to his self-indulgent side trips.

It was hard to track the passage of time, for there was no sun to mark the hours, but Daichin had taken to carving a mark for each "day" into the boat's deck. Chika protested that it wasn't their boat and he didn't know if a day had actually passed or not, but Daichin said that when he went to sleep, it was a day for him. It set An Ning's teeth on edge; his smugly superior attitude and unrelenting confidence struck her as unbearably male. It made her more eager than ever to become a woman, for she didn't want anyone to liken her to such a being, and yet she wondered that he—who had been raised as a girl by his family—should have so wholly transformed into overbearing masculinity. After three thousand years living as a man, An Ning thought her nature was more mixed than

Daichin's.

After four immortal creature encounters and four interminable stretches between them that Daichin said totaled to ten days, they reached the Sea of Souls. An Ning sighed in relief.

Daichin began explaining that they had to jump into the sea to find Akemi's soul—even though he had been standing next to them as Karana had explained it to all three of them.

Chika climbed onto the boat's rail while he was still expounding. Careless of the resulting rocking, she dove overboard.

An Ning hid a smile at Daichin's shocked and offended face. She lost her smile though when Chika emerged moments later, panicked.

"I can't control the water!"

Her head went under. An Ning had the sudden bizarre thought that Chika might not know how to swim—maybe she was simply accustomed to moving the water around her.

She glanced at Daichin, who sniffed, clearly still miffed that Chika had ignored him so blatantly. An Ning dove in.

But instead of Chika, she found lives.

Her lives.

4,000 years ago

THE sun hung low and golden, coloring the sky red at its edges. That was a good omen—it meant the Sun Emperor was blessing her reign. A relief, since it seemed none of the court officials did.

An Ning adjusted the long run of silk that dangled down her left shoulder, a rich crimson to honor the divine Sun Emperor—or whoever he sent to acknowledge her coronation. The God of War had attended her father's coronation, setting Maoyi on a path of bloodshed for the next fifty years.

All of her brothers had perished in various conflicts with their neighbors, leaving An Ning, a daughter, to ascend the throne for the first time in four generations.

An Ning hoped the Goddess of Justice came today—perhaps that would remind the officials that women could be powerful, too.

And then the god appeared, dripping red silk and with black kohl thicker than her own rimming his eyes. His lips were a matte black, as if ready to bestow the kiss of death.

It was not the Goddess of Justice but her younger brother, the God of Destruction.

No one wished for this particular god's gaze to fall on them. And it was he who would witness her coronation? Would set the tone for her reign?

Perhaps she should cut her throat now and save her people the trouble.

And yet, even as cynical thoughts ran through her head, An Ning could summon no fear. She felt excited. She stepped forward and held out her hand to be kissed.

Belatedly, she remembered that she was supposed to genuflect before him. She froze, her hand still extended.

The God of Destruction narrowed his eyes. Fate weep, his eyes were red. The color of dry blood.

Maybe he'd cut her throat *for* her people, and there'd never be another queen in Maoyi for the rest of time.

He collected her hand and kissed it. Fire seemed to be licking over her skin, and lightning traveled from her knuckles to her toes. She suddenly realized that if he did kill her, he wouldn't use such a plebian tool as a blade.

"My queen?" he asked, ever so slightly mocking.

"Divinity," she murmured. "So good of you to come." She liked the heat that had settled in her core.

He settled her hand on his arm, and she was surprised to feel the play of muscles under her fingers. He was so tall and slim that she hadn't expected the strength as well.

"Do you know who I am?" he asked her. She met those half-thrilling, half-terrifying red eyes and suddenly remembered reading his name. His real name, in a scroll from Jeevanti. Her tutor had slapped her hand when An Ning read it aloud, and begged fate to turn this god's gaze from them.

But An Ning suddenly thought she wanted his gaze on her. Exactly as it was—full of yearning and hope.

Not quite believing her own daring, she said, "You're Karana."

Those black lips parted in surprise, revealing the pink and white within. A moment later, they curled into a smile, and An Ning's felt hers curl in response.

She wasn't scared of him anymore. There was no reason for her confidence, but she had faith he would never hurt her.

To others, he was danger and destruction. But to her...

He was home.

"You're bold for a mortal."

An Ning smiled. "I have to be—how else could I be queen? Besides, for you, I could always be bold."

The yearning in his eyes shifted to something hotter, and

An Ning wanted that too.

He nodded to the door. "Shall we?"

Side by side, they strode down a hall leafed in gold. Soldiers wrapped in red scarves knelt at their passing, their foreheads pressed to the floor. Never had they bowed so quickly before her.

But they always would from now on.

The master of ceremonies stood waiting at the end of the hall, also pressed to the floor.

She stopped before him, and *Karana* (fate love her) stopped at her side. Patient, willing to follow her signal.

"Announce us," she instructed the master of ceremonies.

He rose to his feet and threw open the over-sized doors to the grand hall.

"Queen Santiphaph and her patron, the God of Destruction!"

Santiphaph? Yes, that was my name.

Present Day

KARANA walked around the statue of Santiphaph to find blood-red braziers filled with incense, burned low. The smoke smelled of cardamom and ginger—actually, those scents had always belonged to his older sister's temples, not his own.

That might have led him to assume the worshippers had nothing to do with destruction, but it was even more implausible that they should be worshipping a goddess who hadn't been able to answer prayers in a millennium. It seemed more likely that they were worshipping Guleum; he had always idolized Salaana.

Karana reached out a hand to extinguish the remaining sticks, but then he wondered—would this smoke lead him to Guleum?

Prayers were mortal wishes that were conveyed to gods. Mortals prayed because they wanted something; gods answered prayers because those little extra bits of belief in their power added up. Karana had been taught that a million prayers would double his power.

Of course, answering all those prayers would consume a great deal of power, but the tragedy of prayer is most of them could go unanswered and people would continue to pray. Most mortals thought that the chance of being chosen, of having their deepest desire fulfilled was worth losing a little of their own personal magic.

Karana cradled the red braziers.

He had to focus, for it was not the overwhelming red power from his father that let Karana read the essence of the braziers, but the ephemeral lightning of his mother.

But yes, he was certain. These braziers had been spelled. Somewhere in the world, prayer collectors were tied to these braziers. When the prayer collector was full, Guleum would open it and drink in the prayers, adding them to his pool of power. Maybe he'd even answer a few if it suited him.

Karana couldn't feel exactly where the prayers were going, but he didn't need Bai to tell him it was somewhere in Bando.

As it happened, he had once lost his temper there—it seemed like a good place to start.

He now extinguished the last sticks of incense, without the least bit of guilt. Frankly, he couldn't believe there was a worthy prayer among those sent to the "God of Destruction."

Karana hesitated a moment more though, something teasing along the edge of his thoughts, as if he'd forgotten his fan or something like that.

Ah. Anyone who is praying to the God of Destruction is likely a cultist, and cultists are abhorrent.

Although Karana felt the pressure of time, he also reasoned that he'd be negligent not to look around first. He might save a life.

This time, he did use his red power, to feel the emotion around him. Cultists were ever so predictable; they simmered with anger and resentment.

The city held pockets of acrimony, but it was behind him, in the jungle, that he felt true rancor.

Karana squeezed the hilt of his sword at his waist and descended crumbling stone steps to the jungle.

The air was cooler in the shade, if also damper. The shadows were thick, and Karana went so far as to draw his sword.

He didn't send flames licking down its blade, though it would have served well as a torch, because he didn't want anyone to find him before he found them and because an immortal who wasted their magic was a dead immortal.

Or so he'd heard.

Anyway, it wasn't necessary. The path here was relatively well maintained. After an hour, it led him to a massive pyre, not unlike the one that had been built when Santiphaph died at the ripe old age of ninety, having presided over an era of unprecedented peace.

Though it did occur to him that perhaps the current

Maoyan ruler had died, Karana thought it more likely this pyre was for living mortal women because madmen believed their agonizing deaths would grant eternal life.

Reincarnation. What a ridiculous fantasy.

This pyre seemed fresh—ready for use. He'd wait here for a few hours and see what came of it.

Seeking a decent seat, Karana settled on the pyre itself—that had the added benefit of drama. He was a dramatic fellow after all, and the cultists—even if he'd ignored them for years—still seemed to appreciate it.

He had almost fallen asleep when a low chanting drifted through the jungle.

> *Burn us to ash to live forever,*
> *And our light will never die.*

Those were the fools who idolized him.

Karana leapt to his feet and set the pyre on fire. The chanting abruptly stopped, replaced by shouts of excitement.

Karana didn't have to deal with the cultists himself; they threw themselves on the pyre, tears of happiness streaming down their faces.

Of course, they tried to pull bound and gagged women along with them, but those gags and bindings were conveniently red, so Karana had no problem commanding their fibers and pulling the women to safety.

He jumped down from the pyre and unraveled the ties. Two women turned and ran, but the third curtseyed to him.

"Wait," he bid her, "are there other Sundered here? Can you lead me to their stronghold?"

She winced, then nodded determinedly.

Karana smiled at her. "That's a brave being; I'll be sure to reward you after."

Her eyes widened, but she smiled too.

And she led him into the jungle.

The Pilgrim and the Path of Ash

BURNING cultists was unpleasant work, if necessary. Although he was not eager to face his half-brother, Karana was relieved when he finished incinerating the Sundered in Maoyi. He offered his guide rubies, but she asked for a cure instead.

Karana was surprised that she heard the legends, but he was indeed able to cure the blood sickness of her younger sister. It took more magic than rubies would have, but it also made him feel better too. It was too rare that he got to help people without any destruction tied to it.

And then he went to Bando, in the Byeong Mountains, just a day's walk from the Sanctuary Caves. The most revered holy site in the world, the caves held no attraction for the Sundered, but their vicinity was no coincidence.

Eight-hundred-odd years before Karana met Queen

Santiphaph, a woman named Pyeonghwa had settled in this wilderness because it was close to the caves. She had been seeking enlightenment—the path to eternal peace.

This looked like the right place. The tall cedars filled the air with a crisp sweetness, and wildflowers hid at their feet, little white and blue petals that were all the more charming for their coyness. The woods were dense with animals; even now, birds sang boldly, announcing their territory and looking for mates, though their trills and coos sounded far more innocent to Karana. It was much cooler here than Maoyi—dryer too, arguably the perfect summer clime.

It was unfair that it should be so beautiful. It had been lovely then, but today it ought to be ruined. Stumps and ash should cover the mountainside; the birds should abandon such a cursed land. For Pyeonghwa had been brutally murdered when she was forty years old.

5,000 years ago

A SWEET song drifted to An Ning through the early twilight, and she knew Karana had come again.

She wasn't entirely sure that it was appropriate to let him court her like this—she had intended to be a hermit, to live humbly and alone in order to atone for her failure as a wife.

But when she had met Karana a few months ago, she hadn't been able to refrain from smiling.

Her first smile in what felt like years.

She set down her mending—it was getting too dark to sew anyway—and slipped out the front door of the hut.

He didn't see her, for his eyes were on the branches overhead, and he kept singing "The Monks of the Night and Moon."

An Ning ought to blush at the words—they were full of innuendos. And more than innuendos, now that she thought about it. She wasn't embarrassed though. Maybe if someone else was around, but she was starting to feel that embarrassment couldn't exist between Karana and her.

They were an odd pair, at least so the village thought—a former noblewoman, who had embarked on a religious pilgrimage and ended up settling along in the Byeong Mountains, and a foreigner—Jeevantian, she thought, though Karana had been vague.

She didn't mind. She wasn't eager to talk about her past either. She liked being just *Pyeonghwa* and Karana, two odd souls who somehow fit together.

Pyeonghwa—I was Pyeonghwa.

When An Ning was a few steps from Karana, she said, "Are you trying to suggest something, sir?"

The song cut off abruptly, and his head whipped toward her. "What? Oh, no, I was thinking. One of the farmers was singing it in the village and—it's quite catchy—"

An Ning laughed. "I was teasing!" Her voice deepened as she added, "And I wouldn't mind if you were."

Fate was shocked by her boldness! But they said that fate favored the bold...

An Ning had only ever kissed her former husband. She hadn't liked it much and couldn't understand why everyone made such a fuss over it. She had wondered, between consulting physicians and witch doctors, if her barrenness was due to her "frigidity," as she had heard it called.

Despite that, she wanted to kiss Karana. Sometimes he felt so hot, as if fire were right beneath his skin, that she thought he'd warm even her.

Karana stepped close. "If you *want* me to be implying something..." his voice was huskier than usual, too.

Instead of replying, she stepped forward again, meeting his chest.

One of his large hands slid behind her back, the other cradled the side of her jaw. She tilted her face up, and his lips met hers.

Her veins were full of lightning, and she was ablaze. She finally understood the big deal about kissing, and she understood something that no one had ever told her: kissing someone you really, really like is altogether different from an obligatory kiss.

Oh, how could I have ever forgotten this? I want it again. To stand in Karana's arms and kiss effortlessly and feel totally at ease with myself.

Karana pulled back slightly, and An Ning could just see his smile in the fading light.

"I had come to ask you on a walk, but I think we've already missed the best of the sunset."

She smiled back. "A walk in the twilight has its perks, too."

With great daring (or maybe not, since she had already kissed him), An Ning slid her hand into his and interlaced their fingers.

He gave a happy sigh. "I've missed this."

She stiffened. She had never held his hand before, so whose had he been missing?

She tried to sound nonchalant. "Have you had many lovers?"

"No—" and then he stopped, as if realizing he might have misstepped. He turned to face her, and though his expression was shadowed, she could feel its solemnity. "I have had a few, but it has been many years since I last felt this way." His lips quirked so briefly that it might have been the shadows playing tricks. "I do not wish to mislead you though. I have been in love before."

"What happened to her?'

"She died."

"How?" An Ning didn't mean to interrogate him, and she didn't think she was jealous exactly, but she was curious.

He took so long that she thought he was going to deny her curiosity. "Old age," he said at last.

"Old age? Was she much older than you?"

Again, that heavy pause, that great reluctance. "No. She was younger."

He held up his free hand and a deep red flame appeared on his palm. It was pleasantly warm to her, at a distance of a few feet, and she marveled that his skin did not blister. The rich red light let her at last see Karana clearly—in more ways than one.

"You're immortal."

The flame guttered out.

"Yes," he said regretfully. "Does that bother you?"

It probably should, but, "No, not really. You're still Karana." She squeezed his hand more tightly and they resumed walking.

"Not all immortals are gods," she told him, simply sharing her thoughts aloud.

"They are not," he agreed, "though most mortals don't

realize that."

"The Bandoan court is thorough in its teaching of mythology." Then she blushed, for she had not told him of her old life, that of a nobleman's barren wife, who had been set aside for a younger woman in hopes he might yet produce an heir.

He made an assenting mumble, and she realized he had already suspected her background, despite her silence on the subject. Maybe not her marriage, but her status and education.

"Are you a god?" she persisted.

"Hmmm. Most beings would say that I am," he admitted.

"You don't want to be one."

He laughed. "How is it that you've only known me a few months, and yet you understand me better than my own family?"

It was a rhetorical question, but she responded anyway. "I don't feel as if I've only known you a few months. It feels like I have known you forever. Several lifetimes at least." Then she laughed. "I know, it's an odd fancy." She cleared her throat. "You don't want to tell me your title, do you?"

He lifted their linked hands to his mouth and kissed her knuckles gently—and yet, she could feel flames from his lips.

"I don't, but I will." His hand became tense in her own, and there was a deep mournful note in his voice as he said, "My father named me the God of Destruction."

Her hand jerked involuntarily in his, and he released her.

He started to give her space, but she caught his hand again.

"I was just surprised," she told him. "I'm not afraid of you."

He twisted toward her, but a tree's shadow hid his expression.

"You don't need to fear me," he told her, "but I should tell you that while my last lover died of old age, many others died young. Whether I will it or not, destruction and death seem to go where I do."

An Ning stepped close and hugged him, laying her head on his chest. He smelled wonderful, of some unfamiliar spice that was both hot and sweet at the same time. She fancied that she could hear the strong beat of his heart.

"Thank you for telling me," she said, "but I am not afraid of death. Truthfully, I already narrowly escaped it once, and all the time I have here—with you—is like a gift anyway. I will have no regrets if my association with you sends my soul to the Sea earlier than it would otherwise go."

His hand reached up to stroke the side of her face, tucking a few loose strands of hair behind her ear. His reply danced across her ear and tickled her.

"You might have no regrets, Pyeonghwa, but I would."

But you couldn't leave me, no more than any time we met.

Present Day

IT was here that Pyeonghwa had bled out. There wasn't any visible sign of course, and the terrain was unrecognizable. There'd been a landslide at some point in the past five millennia, and the trees had grown over it, but Karana recognized it with absolute certainty.

At times like this, he hated that little trickle of white magic that ran through his pool of red—he'd rather walk through the woods and pass a place like this by, not recognizing it. Not knowing its history and his intimate connection to it.

The landslide was probably his fault, now that he thought about it. He'd set the entire forest ablaze; without the deep roots to hold the steep mountainside in place, it had probably washed down in the next heavy rain.

He kicked the tall cedar that had the gall to grow exactly where Pyeonghwa's body had lain.

He hurt his toe and regretted his outburst. He'd avenged Pyeonghwa long ago, by killing her murderers. The trees were blameless.

He was confused though, that there was no sign of the cult. He'd been certain that if Guleum had chosen anywhere in Bando as his stronghold, it would be here, where his fire had reshaped the mountain so drastically that it was spoken of in hushed whispers the world over.

He was frustrated to have met a dead end. Should he go to the Ondor Peaks or Jeevanti next? He'd lost a lover—and his temper—in both of those places.

While he stood pondering and pining, his stomach growled.

He pressed a hand to it self-consciously. He'd eaten breakfast with Miho, Chika, An Ning, and Daichin that morning. Then again, that must have been nearly twelve hours ago. Maybe he shouldn't go anywhere tonight—better to find an inn or a farmer who'd put him up for the night and feed him dinner.

He thought suddenly of the black rice that was ubiquitous in Ningjingcun. He could almost taste the thick vegetable congee that Xia served every morning.

Right now though, it was hard to be sure he'd even return to Ningjingcun after this was settled. When it came down to it, An Ning and he hadn't exchanged any promises, and he worried that, if he stayed around her, one day she'd remember her mortal life.

And yet—even knowing the risk—did he have the willpower to stay away?

His thoughts ran in circles as he trudged through the forest. Finally, his musings were shoved aside by the anxiety and fear of a nearby mortal family.

Even after he felt the family's roiling emotions, it took him an hour to reach their small cottage. Honestly, if he had felt a single other being at that time, he probably would have kept walking. He didn't like the emotions leaking out of that house at all. But there was no one else, and he was hungrier than he had been an hour ago.

And maybe, said a voice that sounded an awful lot like An Ning, *you'll be able to settle their worries for them.*

It was late when he knocked on the door; even the long-lasting summer sun was heading to bed. Still, country folks like this tended to live by the sun, so Karana doubted they'd be asleep yet.

No one answered his knock for a minute, and he knocked again, louder.

The cabin remained silent; if it wasn't for his magic telling him three people were inside, Karana would have thought it empty. Their stress had changed into outright terror—surely they couldn't be sleeping in that state?

He started to grow curious. Why did they find his knocking ominous?

Karana tested the door, but something, a bolt at a guess, held it fast.

Karana called through it, "I mean you no harm." Belatedly he wondered if they were cultists, in which case he *would* harm them, but decided that qualification could be overlooked for now. "I'm seeking food, and I might be able to help you if you tell me what's wrong."

Still no answer. Perhaps he should teleport to civilization and choose his next destination in the morning, but he had already wasted more than an hour finding this house. He wanted to know what was going on, and maybe they'd know of a Sundered Temple. One of those in the vicinity would be the sort of thing to make mortals fearful of strangers at the door.

"You can either open the door or I will cut it down," he announced, to be nice. He didn't expect a response and had already unsheathed his red sword when the wooden door swung open.

An middle-aged man stood in the doorway, his feet planted and an axe in his hands. Not a battle axe, but a hefty one for chopping wood that Karana didn't doubt would do a passable job of separating his head from his body, should the opportunity arise.

"Hello," he told the man.

The man eyed him uncertainly, the axe gripped so tightly in his fingers that his knuckles had turned white.

Karana resheathed his sword. "I'm pretty hungry. Why don't you feed me while you tell me what's got you wielding your wood-cutting axe like a murderer?"

The man's eyes widened so that the whites were visible all the way around the iris. Good—the word "murderer" wasn't a comfortable one for him. Not that Karana was scared, but he'd be happier if his host wasn't a psychotic killer. The man lowered the axe. "Come in then."

Karana saw the other two occupants almost immediately—a boy and a girl who hadn't quite reached adolescence.

Karana settled at the table. "Call me Karana. You have trouble with bandits?"

"Not bandits," said the boy, "men of fire."

"Men of fire? Monsters?"

"Monstrous enough, but they're men," said the father—Karana assumed he was the father. "They took my wife and oldest girl a month ago. I was afraid they'd returned for..."

He looked at the girl.

Karana's heart sank. It was stupid—he'd come here looking for the cult and finding them meant he might be able to locate Guleum after all.

But still. It wasn't like the cult was the only bad in the world. He would have liked to come across some immortal creatures, like the Xuezei which were vicious killers and particularly vulnerable to fire. Then not every ill of the world could be laid at his feet.

"Sounds like Sundered Cultists," said Karana. "Men who believe they'll live forever after burning themselves." He almost said, "and women," but he didn't want the children picturing their mother on fire. Karana would guess that it was already too late for her.

The man nodded. "That's what they preach, sure enough. Now, I figure any being has the right to their own crazy, but they shouldn't put their crazy on others. And these pric—men force theirs down your throats." The man paused for a moment. "Don't see what you can do about it though."

"You'd be surprised," said Karana.

The man looked at him uncertainly. Karana smiled, "Any chance I could get some food now though?"

The girl fetched him a bowl of rice, and the boy handed him a jar of pickled roots. Karana supposed they might have harvested the roots themselves, but he hadn't seen any rice paddies.

"Where's this from?" he asked. "Is there a village nearby?"

The man nodded and started describing the surrounding area. Karana listened and asked questions. He did want to learn more about the area to find signs of Guleum, but mostly he was trying to lower the tension in the room.

It worked too; going through the practicalities of their everyday life, the father relaxed.

Eventually he sent his children to bed so they could speak more bluntly, though Karana knew the children were still listening. He could feel their burning curiosity, as their father sat down with great solemnity.

"I see the sword at your side, but the men of fire travel in large groups. If it were a handful of them, we wouldn't let them take our women. They kidnap women from the village too, you know."

Karana nodded. "I am not merely a swordsman, and I came here to deal with them." He was vaguely surprised to find himself explaining even that much—he supposed it came from spending so much time with An Ning and her monks. She had a tendency to treat mortals as peers.

"You don't know where they go?" Karana asked. "The Sundered don't live in the village?"

"No," the man shook his head firmly. "They isolate

themselves from normal folks. It's men only in the cult—I joked with my wife, before they came to our home, that they'd kill themselves off, since you need women to have children. But somehow they don't. There're always angry young men looking to join." He rubbed his forehead and sighed. "What did you ask again? Where they live?"

"Yes."

"Most of us think they live on the mountain east of this one. There is... There's a kind of path. But no one who has followed it has returned home."

Karana asked a few more questions before announcing, "Let's go to bed. You can show me to the path in the morning. Early."

"Fine, fine," said the man, though he looked at Karana like he was saying goodbye. "Let me get you a blanket and a pillow."

Karana laid down his red outer robe and changed it into a mattress after the man went to bed.

He fell into a deep sleep, thanks to the several hours he'd spent hiking the mountains, but his dreams were full of Santiphaph, Pyeonghwa, and An Ning. He was embarrassed when he woke up; he been trying to explain to the three of them that he wasn't disloyal, that they so reminded him of each other that he had fallen in love with all of them.

Birdsong, high-pitched and trilling, woke Karana rather than light. In fact, it still looked like night in the cabin— between the wax paper-windows and the tall trees all around, he supposed it stayed dim even at noon.

He fingered the iron deadbolt that had locked him out last evening before throwing it open and stepping into the early morning air.

The air was cool and damp; dewdrops caught the dawn light as if diamonds had been scattered on the humble wildflowers that hid themselves among the fallen brown needles. He smiled and thought he'd like to show An Ning these mountains, before he remembered his uncomfortable dream where his lovers had discovered one another.

She'd understand though, wouldn't she, that Pyeonghwa had died long before she existed? It wasn't wrong to love more than one being—at least, so he thought. But it felt wrong to him. Maybe because of his father, who had remarried as soon as one wife died—leading to rumors than he had sent his previous spouses to the Sea of Souls himself. Karana tried to shrug off his discomfort, but it settled in his gut.

Needing something to do, he began foraging in the woods for summertime treats that he could contribute to breakfast.

He was lucky enough to find a bees' nest, and he remembered the hive that Pyeonghwa had maintained. This one was uncomfortably high in a cedar hollow, but he lifted himself by his robes and shrank his red sword into a small dagger. He let cool, smoky flames dance its length and held it at the edge of the honeycomb.

When the bees became slow and somnolent, he stopped the fires and used the dagger to free a small chunk of comb. Enough that his hosts would undoubtedly be grateful, but not so much as to harm the bees. He changed a red silk handkerchief that had been tucked at his waist into paper and used it to wrap the dripping comb.

Returning to the ground and sheathing his full-length sword, he started back to the cabin, and he found the mortal man waiting for him in front.

He looked at Karana uncertainly. "I thought maybe you changed your mind and left."

Thought or hoped? Karana held out the wrapped honeycomb. "I found some honey." He offered an easy smile. "You needn't be so worried. Sundered and bees have a nasty sting, but I can handle both."

The man nodded, though Karana could see he still had his doubts.

There were fresh blackberries, more pickles, rice, and the honey for breakfast; then the man gave his children instructions for the day and tied his axe to his belt.

Karana looked at it pointedly and raised his brows.

"Good timber where we're going. I'll cut some after I leave you."

The man kept his face stoic, but Karana could feel his nerves with his magic. He hoped the man didn't intend to do anything stupid, such as use that axe on Karana.

They hiked in silence. It did nothing for the man's nerves, but Karana didn't mind. He enjoyed being in the woods, focusing on the crisp scent of cedar and bird song. At one point, they started following a narrow mountain stream, and the birds' singing was replaced by its pleasant gurgle and the less pleasant buzz of insects.

"There fishing around here?" asked Karana, breaking the tense silence.

The man grunted and shrugged. "Not much of a fisherman, myself."

Another two hours and the man gestured ahead. "That's the Path of Ash."

The man had said it was peculiarly marked; Karana could

make out small urns every ten feet or so lining the path. Cultists? Women? Both?

He felt sick. He could see a dozen just from here. How many people had been murdered to mark this path?

He stepped forward, only to have the ground crumble under his feet.

Karana used his robes to stop his fall, and for a moment he dangled inches above a score of pointed metal stakes, each red and made by an immortal.

It seemed he might find Guleum in these mountains after all.

He twisted to find his guide peering anxiously over the edge of the pit, axe clutched in his hand. Another being might have been grateful to realize the axe was for a mercy killing; if the spikes had left Karana slowly dying in agony, this mortal had intended to cut him down. And conveniently stop him from telling anyone who had led him to this place.

Karana didn't feel gratitude toward beings who led him into traps.

He flipped in the air and pulled the spikes up after him. By the time his feet were on solid ground, the nasty-looking spikes were ringed around his cowardly guide.

He knelt and rubbed his hands together anxiously, begging Karana for his life.

"I'm not a merciful god," Karana told the mortal, "but neither am I a vindictive one. For the sake of your children, I won't kill you today. Tell me, are there more of these delightful little traps along the path?"

Big tears rolled from the mortal's eyes, but Karana couldn't care less. "I think so, divinity. Only the men of fire can walk it safely. They have magic red shoes that allow it."

What, did Guleum float his worshippers above the path's surface? That seemed an incredible power indulgence.

But it didn't faze Karana much—after all, he had only to float himself.

"Run home now," he told the mortal and retracted the spikes.

The man took off like a hare with a dog after it, and Karana wondered that he didn't fall and roll down the mountain. Karana sighed and started flying along the path.

Twenty-one, twenty-two, twenty-three...

Once Karana realized that he was counting urns, he made himself stop.

I can't be everywhere. I can't save everyone.

Fate should curse him. Or maybe it already had—maybe that's why he always fell in love with mortals who were doomed to die.

Or immortals whom he had once burned alive.

Karana heard voices ahead, so he moved higher into the trees, where he was obscured by the branches. (Besides, most people didn't walk looking up).

Five cultists, clearly identifiable by their red tunics emblazoned with flames, soon came into view, joking and laughing. Their conversation had little interest for Karana, revolving around a prank they had played on one of their fellows.

However, he didn't see a reason to let them pass unmolested.

He hauled them up into the treetops by their shirts, which he pinned to the trees using the nasty metal spikes that had almost pierced him earlier.

"Hello," said Karana, "Do you believe in the God of Destruction?"

The Lady-Warrior and the Smoke-filled Dojo

IF Karana had been inclined to give the cultists credit, which he wasn't, he would have been impressed by their lack of fear. Instead, he blamed their calm on their insanity and stupidity.

"The God of Destruction will purge evil so that the sun can return to the world again," howled one man.

Karana couldn't resist glancing at the blinding light that pierced even the dense forest. "Seems like the sun's in the right spot to me."

The cultists looked blank, except for one, who said, "The Sun God. The Sun God will return."

"No, he won't," said Karana. "He quite happily sacrificed himself so he could join his one true love in the Sea of Souls. He has no interest in Earth anymore."

The words were bitter, and Karana was surprised to realize

that it still bothered him that his father had given up his life without so much as a goodbye. He hadn't exactly liked his father, but he had maybe, secretly, loved him.

Karana charged forward, "It's like this: there's a being you've seen who calls himself the God of Destruction, isn't there?"

One of the cultists nodded; the others looked uneasy.

"He's an imposter. I'm the God of Destruction, and I'm pissed off at what he's done in my name. So if you tell me all you can, I will reward you. If you don't, I'll punish you."

No need to explain that the reward and punishment were the same: fulfillment of their greatest dream and an agonizing death.

To be fair, the replies they gave earned both.

"We'd never betray his divinity! He has raised us here!"

"You'll never enter his mountain home! He is the strongest god alive!"

Perhaps they were deliberately hedging their bets. At any rate, when they stopped yelling at him, Karana knew that the Path of Ash led to a temple in the mountainside, and Guleum had been there when these three left.

He incinerated the cultists and continued on his way, faster now, eager to catch his brother and set all of this behind him.

Finally he reached a ruby door set into the mountain. When it refused to open at his touch, he turned to magic. The door dissolved into its original state, and blood soaked the ground.

What a lovely family he had.

Karana stepped into the temple and startled four cultists who were praying to a jasper obelisk. Shocked, Karana realized it was the memorial that he had made for Pyeonghwa—he hadn't wanted to put it at the site of her murder. So many years had passed that the cultists probably believed this was the mountain upon which he had wrecked destruction.

How dare they.

He burned all the Sundered before he could consider other options. Perhaps he had lied to that mortal earlier—maybe he *was* vindictive after all.

"Guleum," he yelled. "Where are you?"

Three more cultists ran into the room, and ever so briefly, Karana spotted Guleum standing behind them. His baby brother, by some standard. He was as tall as Karana now, a disconcerting realization, and he wore his long red hair in imitation of the style Karana had maintained a millennia ago.

He was still skinny; Guleum had always hated any sort of physical exercise, to the exasperation of their older siblings, who had both been warriors.

Guleum stared at him, looking vaguely surprised, but Karana felt no fear in him.

"Shall we talk or fight?" Karana asked Guleum.

But he had forgotten—Guleum's mother was an orange immortal, and the unknowable nature she had gifted her son hid Guleum's feelings from Karana.

A coward always, Guleum teleported away.

He could be anywhere on Earth, fate strike him down.

Karana turned to the three Sundered that Guleum had left behind, each clutching a dagger.

"Your deaths could be painless. If—"

The first one rushed him; the other two ran deeper into the temple.

Oh, Karana didn't like that. Either there was something

they wanted to deal with or an escape route.

Pressed for time, he drew his red sword and cut the first man in half. He followed the runners.

The temple had no windows, but an unnecessary number of torches lined the walls. Apparently, Karana wasn't the only one who liked fire.

He found the first runner in a room full of red cages; he was opening them as quickly as he could, and Bulgae were pouring out of them.

Karana hurried on—the Bulgae could fend for themselves, and they would devour the cultist in moments. However, the other cultist...

Another room and more cages, and inside two women. Girls really—they were only a little older than his guide's daughter. Hearing the Bulgae barking behind him, Karana hesitated to free them. "I'm sorry," he said, "you're safer in than out right now—I will return."

He hoped. The girls screamed and cried as he left.

Karana kept running and practically collided with a dozen Sundered, each carrying a box.

Karana skidded to a stop—Bulgae behind, whatever was in those boxes ahead.

Though the cultists seemed protective of the boxes; they certainly weren't holding them as weapons.

Karana summoned a wall of fire ahead of the cultists, trapping them with him and the approaching Bulgae.

"What do you have there?" asked Karana.

Two of the Sundered ran into the magical fire; Karana didn't mind them catching ablaze, but, as the boxes burned, a thick smoke filled the air. Its cloying aroma turned Karana's stomach. It was like burnt five-spice, with a gamey undertone.

Those boxes are full of mortal dreams! Dreams of the Sundered, at a guess.

Dreams could be collected like prayers, giving deities insight into their worshippers' subconscious desires. Some deities received so many dreams that they captured the dreams in candles; in his father's day, there had been a profitable dream trade in the old Godsmarket. Mortal dreams were more vivid than reality and more intoxicating than alcohol—there were beings who wasted their lives away, seeking the endless high that dreams could provide and willing to pay anything for more of them.

The creation of dream candles was frowned upon by both Karana's niece and the Love God. Karana personally hadn't seen any since his father's death, but he recognized dream smoke readily enough.

As the rich smoke enveloped the other cultists, they sank to the floor, a dreamworld ruled by emotion and impulse overcoming reality. With the Bulgae approaching, the Sundered were as good as dead; if that smoke filled his lungs, Karana would share their fate.

Karana sheathed his sword and covered his face with his sleeve.

He wouldn't mourn the cultists' death—that was the fate he'd planned for them—but it had suddenly become even more pressing that he interrogate them. What were they doing with crates full of mortal dreams?

He would deal with the Bulgae first. Karana ran back the way he came.

The Bulgae were wilder and more aggressive than he'd

expected, probably because of their imprisonment. He drove them back to the room where the girls were by whacking them with his sword.

He could use the cages there to imprison the Bulgae, but how to do that without the girls being eaten?

One Bulgae managed to bite his leg, and Karana let out a howl worthy of his opponents.

Forget cages. He'd chain the creatures.

Six of the cages' bars transformed into chains and flew toward him. They wrapped around the Bulgae necks and through sheer will, Karana pulled those chains back and adhered them to the wall.

The Bulgae continued to scrabble against the stone floor, choking themselves with the chains. Karana knew they wouldn't die, but he couldn't help but think of Ember and Blue, and the rest of the Bulgae in Ningjingcun. He winced.

He turned to the girls.

They were terrified, and Karana realized that he was as intimidating to them as the Bulgae. He tried to soften his expression.

"You can go," he told them. "The men who hurt you are all occupied at present."

Slowly, disbelievingly, they edged out of the cages.

"Wait," Karana called as they reached the door. "Don't take the Path of Ash home. Stick to the woods."

They nodded and ran. Karana rubbed one of his temples. He should escort them home—but there was still so much to do here.

He hauled the Sundered, still caught in the throes of dreams, back to the Bulgae's now empty cages one by one. It would have been faster to carry them all by their red tunics, but Karana had used quite a lot of magic already today. If Guleum came back, he didn't want to be caught unprepared.

They were unwilling to talk at first, but most of the men were cowards. He only had to hurt one of them with his red sword before the others babbled every legend and rumor they had ever heard of their god and the dream candles they'd been carrying.

When Karana had exhausted their knowledge, he burned them and the remaining dreams. He reached the temple's entrance and placed one hand on the jasper monument.

It hurt him to take it down, but he also knew that leaving it here, to be worshipped by kidnappers and murderers, the scum of the Earth, was a greater sin against Pyeonghwa's memory.

He returned the monument to its natural state. Unlike the ruby door, it became red leaves. Pyeonghwa had died in the autumn. He gathered a handful of leaves and whispered, "I'm sorry."

He thought of the Bulgae before he left—it felt cruel to leave them chained—but if he freed them, surely that was the same as killing the girls he had just released. Perhaps later, An Ning would return with him and help them.

With a sigh, Karana teleported to where the majority of the dream candles were shipped.

A dojo in the Crescent Moon.

6,000 years ago

AN NING swung her sword quickly but with control—overcommitting to a swing was a gift to a foe. She finished the defending crane sequence, landing so lightly that the stones under her feet barely shifted. She bowed to a nonexistent opponent.

A slow clap followed, and she turned to find Karana watching her. His hair was braided down his back, and he was wearing a simple black kimono. He was obsessed with black, going so far as to paint his eyelids and lips that color. If his height and blade-like features hadn't already made him look like an outsider, the makeup definitely would have. As it was, he seemed to attract her eye whenever he was in the room.

But that's not because he looks odd, a snarky voice whispered.

An Ning was so glad Karana couldn't hear that voice; he was the dojo's guest after all.

She inclined her head and asked, "Would you care to spar?" She had offered more than a dozen times over the past few months, but he had declined every time.

Predictably, he said, "And embarrass myself?"

She laughed. "It's not embarrassing to lose. It's embarrassing not to try."

He pulled a large fan from his sash and plied it languidly. "Well, then, embarrassment it is."

An Ning shook her head, but she couldn't keep her smile from her eyes. He obviously wasn't the least embarrassed. And despite the role he seemed determined to play, An Ning could tell that Karana was a warrior.

He walked to her now, lightly, nearly soundlessly, and he moved with a grace and fluidity that showed how fit he was. He also watched her and her students with knowing eyes. She wanted to get a sword in his hands and see what he knew.

"If you aren't here to hone your skills, why do you stick around?" she challenged him.

His black-painted lips curled into a smile. "For you, of course, swordsmistress."

The words, combined with his nearness, sent a shiver of awareness down her back. Actually, she shouldn't be surprised by his flirting. He'd been doing it quite determinedly since he had arrived. He'd come with a merchant caravan, and although he looked like a foreigner, he sounded like a native when he spoke the tongue of the Crescent Moon. That name though— she'd never heard of a "Karana" before.

Her students were surprised that she hadn't sent him along his way; she had never had any time for flirting before. But she couldn't.

It felt like fate had brought him here, and she didn't want him to leave. She wanted to flirt back; she would have if she had the least idea how.

Maybe that's why she wanted to spar with him so badly— the intimate play of two swords was the closest to dancing that she knew. She was sure that if she met him blade to blade, she could return his boldness. And then maybe she'd know how they fit together.

Impulsively, she suddenly swung her blade at him. She was ready to pull back, but it wasn't necessary. He sidestepped neatly, evading her blade effortlessly.

It was exciting. She kept going, not intending him any real harm, of course. She began to think she couldn't have hurt him anyway for he was more skilled than she had guessed.

Finally, he caught her wrist, and twisted her arm, forcing

her to drop the sword. They stood chest to chest, both panting so that their breath mixed in the narrow space between their faces, and his hand wrapped around her back like an embrace—if he hadn't been clutching her wrist.

As if he knew her thoughts, he eased his grip, and his fingers traced burning paths along her arms.

There was a question in his eyes, and An Ning knew the answer.

"I want you," she told him. Her voice was low, maybe even a whisper, but she knew he heard her.

"Heiwa—"

An Ning smiled. "That's the first time you called me by my name. Usually you say Nakamura-sensei."

"Your students say that you should marry a man of the Yamada clan. That it would strengthen the dojo."

She hesitated. Should she tell him her desire now had nothing to do with marriage? That wasn't really true. An Ning wasn't a being who could take a lover casually—at least she never had—nor a lover seriously for that matter. She had been content with being chaste before Karana came to the dojo. But now she wanted him. And she'd say anything to get him in her bed, though she was vaguely unnerved by her own determination.

"My dojo will be strong because I am strong," she told him. "No man will have anything to do with it. Now, do you want me, too?"

He was silent for so long that An Ning thought he would refuse to answer—or that he'd lie that he didn't want her.

But his hand cupped her jaw, and he admitted, "I want you."

She trapped his hand with her own and intertwined their

fingers. Then she led him to her room, passing several students.

All bowed, looking curious and possibly shocked.

An Ning didn't care.

She slid open the shoji doors and slipped her feet from her outdoor shoes as she stepped onto the tatami mats of her bedroom.

The small step made her the same height as Karana. She enjoyed that for a moment, their gazes connected by an invisible string as he also slipped off his shoes. He stepped into the room, growing taller than her again, and he slid the shoji doors shut behind him.

Here An Ning grew worried. She had been prepared and trained for every aspect of her life, being the heir of the Nakamura dojo, but no one had trained her for intimate matters between two beings. She had a rough idea of the mechanics—that had been explained—but what did one do first? Should she kiss him? Hug him?

Karana didn't seem to have the same worries. The next moment he had caught her against him, and his lips were blazing a path along her neck.

An Ning wasn't worried about what she should or shouldn't do anymore. She simply was.

Present Day

A BEING could only cremate so many people before starting to question the meaning of it all.

At the ruins of Xiling, when confronted with the kidnapping and imminent murder of nine women, Karana hadn't hesitated to kill all the cultists. He had felt no remorse for their deaths—in fact, the events were covered in such a haze of anger, he didn't really remember them dying.

In Maoyi, when the Sundered—albeit in their lunacy—threw themselves on the pyre, Karana had thought good riddance to bad rubbish. In Bando, the urns of ashes had left his heart hard and cruel, and he had dealt with all of Guleum's followers with efficiency.

And when he had come here, to what was once Heiwa's dojo, he had been so furious at how they had perverted her legacy that it had been easy to call fire.

But now that the men were ash, and he was half choked by smoke of his own making, Karana felt exhausted and nihilistic. The dojo was silent, but Karana's ears were full of screams. It was late in the night, the world given over to blues and grays, but there was a red afterglow everywhere Karana looked, his fires of destruction imprinted on his retinas.

Should he hunt down and exterminate every fate-forsaken murdering prick in the world? Was that his purpose for existing?

He didn't want it. He didn't want to breathe smoke for the rest of his life!

He stumbled from the hazy corridors of the dojo. He stepped down to the wraparound walk along the outer walls, prepared to slip on his shoes, only to discover his feet were covered in ash.

Ash that had once been living mortal beings.

He sat down and cried. No, he *sobbed*, his body shaking uncontrollably, the whole world blurring to incoherence through his tears. He wrapped his arms around his torso, hugging himself, not that he deserved even that comfort.

This was part of the reason he'd stayed in Ningjingcun, ignoring the cult for the past thirty years. He wasn't weary of this battle just from the past few days, horrible as they had been. He had been burning cultists for the past seventeen thousand years, albeit in fits and bursts. And despite having killed, oh, millions of them, they kept coming back.

It made no sense to Karana. The cult itself was based on total fantasy, a promise of eternal life that could never be fulfilled.

There had been many times over the millennia that he had thought he'd gotten all of them. That every last cultist was dead, and that this problem was finished for good. But a few hundred years would pass, and he'd discover a new pocket of Sundered that had sprung up from seemingly nowhere. They always found the magical sites or artifacts that Karana had left behind, rediscovered the old legends, and lashed out at the world with hatred and cruelty all while claiming they were making it better.

Karana wanted to blame his younger brother. To believe that once he had captured Guleum, the cult would fade away.

But he knew better. Guleum hadn't started the cult, hadn't kept it going through the centuries—he wasn't even five thousand years old himself!

No, it seemed that the cult was somehow inextricably tied to Karana himself.

Was there something fundamentally evil about him? Some darkness that had led his parents—when he was a newborn!— to name him the God of Destruction? That caused his first monks to poison the woman who he loved, their supposed leader? That led them to track down and slay half of his lovers over the millennia?

What was wrong with him that he was surrounded by violence and hate?

And why was his only solution to return hate and violence in kind?

Every time he burned a cultist, every single time, he hoped that they would somehow find redemption. That he wasn't really ending them, simply giving them a new beginning.

Maybe that's why he had inspired delusions. He was delusional himself.

There was no fresh start, only an eternity regretting in the Sea of Souls.

The Singer and the Candles

KARANA woke and started coughing.

All the smoke he had inhaled last night seemed to have settled in his lungs. That was odd; usually the smoke from his own fires didn't bother him at all. But this time he felt half-dead, as if killing the cultists-in-training had cost half of his soul as well.

He sat up and winced. He had cried himself to exhaustion last night and passed out on the hardwood boards of the dojo's wraparound walk.

He rose slowly, stretching gingerly, and looked around the courtyard. It wasn't the same as it had been seven millennia ago, but he could almost see Heiwa anyway. The pale gravel matched his memory, and he remembered the way that she had moved over it so lightly that he hadn't even heard the rasp of the stones.

He had thought it wouldn't be as hard to come here as it had been to visit the Byeong Mountains, for Heiwa had lived a long and happy life. Karana had hidden his identity for all of it, though it had eventually become obvious that he was an immortal. After her death, he had cremated her body and made the grandest fireworks display he had ever created.

That display had been his mistake of course—God of Destruction Fireworks, he might as well have called them. The Sundered had not come here immediately, but legends of fireworks were one of the stories they sought. The sparks of his life that they collected and treasured: horrific fires and wondrous fireworks. The only two things he had ever done well.

He shook himself hard. That was enough of that. One night of melancholy was ample. He'd promised Chika that he'd capture Guleum before she returned with Akemi's soul. He had work to do.

He returned to the bleak halls of the dojo to look for dream candles. He had already confirmed that the dreams were used to indoctrinate angry young men (and a few old ones) in the lies of the Sundered, but he hadn't the presence of mind to look for unused candles last night.

He found four crates in total and carried them all to the courtyard.

He paced a circle around them as he thought. The obvious and easiest solution was to burn them, but unlike in the mountain temple, this smoke would not be safely locked inside stone. He could transform them, for the red wax would obey his will, but he worried that the dreams would somehow remain attached to whatever he created, a malaise that could only be cured through destruction.

He'd have to wait until they all burned completely; he didn't want any of these nightmares to be discovered by someone else.

After all, maybe these were the reason the cult had persisted through the millennia.

He set the pile ablaze and retreated a safe distance.

He watched the fire burn for ten minutes or so before he became bored and distracted by his thoughts. By the time he processed the scent that reminded him of rotting barbecue, Karana had already inhaled too much of the smoke to escape the dream.

Karana ran, his hand pressed to his side. He was being chased—they'd kill him if they caught him!

And just because he'd had a bit of fun with a girl.

Cursed prigs: didn't understand that a young man had needs.

The more he thought about it, the angrier he became, and suddenly he was running at his pursuers, rather than from them. He drew his bow and shot arrows at them. As each struck, its target burst into flames, and Karana laughed.

Karana was surrounded by skulls. He was dying, from a venereal disease that was rotting his skin away. It wasn't fair! He had enough money to last three lifetimes, but not one of the quacks he hired could cure him so that he could finish this.

He'd slept with virgins, had salt poured in his open sores, listened to endless chanting, all for naught!

He burst into flame, and he understood—only by dying could he live forever. He opened his mouth to scream but no sound escaped.

That soundless scream woke Karana, and, despite his disorientation, he instinctively rolled several feet away from the bonfire of candles.

Fate slap him, that had been careless. Stupidly risky. He rose slowly, still feeling off-kilter from the adrenaline coursing through him.

He breathed slowly, careful to make sure that the air was clean before pulling it into his lungs. The fire was still burning—nothing had changed. It looked like he was lucky. He wasn't convinced those two had been full dreams—more like snippets.

Now, he had no trouble remaining focused until the candles burned wholly away. And then it was time to move on. The Bandoan Sundered had told him of three other temples. Impulsively, he decided to try one in the Jeevantian wilderness first. Guleum had always been fascinated by Jeevanti, though his mother had come from Bando.

Karana had once been particularly fond of Jeevanti himself. Some seven odd millennia ago, when he had lived with his lover Chain by the Dataa River. She had sung songs of ordinary beauty and everyday joys, and he had thought the area would be imbued forever with her priceless inner peace.

Of course, he'd been wrong. As usual.

7,000 years ago

AN NING stretched, pressing one hand against the small of her back and flinging the other skyward. She'd been weeding all morning. Karana kept saying she should leave such chores for the village girl that came twice a week, but An Ning rather enjoyed weeding. Gardening in general set her at ease—the garden was chaos and order in harmony. She always wrote her best songs when she was weeding.

Something about selecting which plants stayed and which went brought out the philosopher in An Ning, and yet she could let her mind wander as well. She sang as she worked, and by the time she had the hogweed under control, she had a new song about the branching paths of life figured out. She gathered the hogweed carefully and washed it—it might strangle her freesias, but it was quite tasty in lentil curry.

She washed her hands as well, and she started finding the notes she had sung on her sitar. Karana had said he'd be home tomorrow, and she wanted to play it for him. He was pretty much the only being she played for, although sometimes her helper would stay and listen. Oh, and once Karana had brought her to play for his sister.

An Ning hadn't enjoyed that, for though Salaana had been polite, her eyes said an unknown mortal singer was not worthy of her brother.

An Ning knew Karana was a god, of course. Sometimes he performed magic in the house, and he conjured rubies to pay others, but she didn't like to think about it.

When it was just the two of them, it was easy to forget that he was immortal and she wasn't, that he could make a being's blood boil in their veins on whim while she *might* lure them into dancing after hours of effort.

And of course, Karana was convinced that her singing was the most beautiful in the world, but An Ning knew better. He was terribly biased, loving her for no reason. Of course, he was constantly telling her reasons, for he was an affectionate being, but none of them were truly compelling by her judgment. She supposed that's how love was. In the end, it came down to a deep sense of belonging with another being that couldn't be quantified.

There was a noise at the door, and An Ning's fingers silenced the sitar strings. Had she imagined it? Her helper, Laila wasn't supposed to come for three days, and Karana had said he'd be back tomorrow.

But she could definitely hear a scuffling outside the door, and, as she was debating opening it, a knock came.

An Ning carefully set the sitar in its stand and walked placidly to the door. Another knock came, impatient, and An Ning frowned.

She swung open the door and found Laila, looking unwell. Instinctively, An Ning collected Laila's hand in her own.

"Laila? What is wrong? Is everything alright?"

"I'm sorry, Chain-ji. There's—there's a problem at home. Could you..."

Laila barely seemed able to find her words, but An Ning said, "Of course." She stepped out and closed the cottage door behind her.

Even though Laila had asked An Ning to come, she seemed reluctant to lead the way. An Ning ended up tugging the teenager along behind her as they headed toward the village. "Is your mother ill? Or—" She tried to think of a problem that would bring Laila to her door rather than to one of her many aunts. It wasn't as if they'd need her singing urgently or her gardening. Well, she knew a fair amount about poisonous plants, but probably no more than most of the women in the village—truth be told, she wasn't the type of person who would be summoned urgently.

Laila's reluctance seemed ominous in retrospect, and An Ning slowed down.

"Laila, why exactly—"

Something hard and long caught An Ning on the side, and she fell to her knees gasping for air. She managed to twist and saw her attacker was a villager, a man that she recognized but didn't know. He was brandishing a stout stick—a cudgel, even—and he walloped her again.

"You cursed witch," he shouted, "you've brought the plague upon us! Tie her up."

"I'm sorry," cried Laila, "they were going to kill my mother if—"

An Ning lost the rest of Laila's words as angry hands seized her arms and trussed her up like fowl waiting to be roasted.

"I didn't..." she tried, but her voice was weak. Her mouth tasted like metal—that second hit had cut her cheek on her teeth. And her ribs throbbed with an ache that seemed to reverberate through her body. Had they been broken?

"Please, I don't understand," whimpered An Ning but that was a lie.

She understood. Something bad had happened in the village, and she was being blamed for it. Not because it was her fault; likely it was no one's fault, but she was the odd one, the outsider. The singer who paid in rubies, though she never gave a performance. Where did someone even get rubies in a place like this anyway?

She was a fool; she'd occasionally heard whispers of her

own witchcraft, but she'd laughed at them. She'd turned them into a *song*, something to celebrate and be amused by. She hadn't understood the danger they posed.

The villagers brought her before the local magistrate, a small man who compensated for his slightness with anger and force. An Ning didn't for a moment hope that he would be merciful, but she thought perhaps he would have her locked up.

Tomorrow Karana would return, and, while she might not be a witch, he was a god. He would deal with all these men in moments. Normally she would have hoped that his dealings wouldn't be too harsh, but with blood on her teeth and bruises on her body, she didn't worry overly about that.

The magistrate interrogated her with slaps and screaming. An Ning had no answers to give, for she had no magic in her, unless one counted the music, which she certainly wasn't going to mention at present.

She tried to tell the magistrate about Karana, and his name did bring fear, but it seemed rumor had turned him into her conjuring. They couldn't believe a god had walked among them; they thought that killing her would be the end of him as well. They told her that if she ended the curse, they would spare her life.

But she couldn't. She couldn't cure the livestock they brought before her. The goats remained listless and continued to foam at the mouth.

An Ning, desperate and scared, told them that Karana might be able to. He would return the next day. If they waited for him...

But they didn't.

Present Day

A RED brick temple was almost buried beneath the thick green jungle foliage. Karana didn't much care for brick himself, but he hadn't made this temple. Mortals had.

It was placed strangely, like the mountain one. Most deities had their major temples in cities; small shrines were for the remote corners of the world.

But the cult couldn't collect worshippers openly, not with their message of hatred toward the Threefold Goddess. Karana wondered again where it had come from. Surely not Guleum. He had, after all, cursed the Sun Emperor to die, so he shouldn't resent Jin for that death. And yes, he had idolized their sister Salaana, but was it worth throwing his life away?

Why had Guleum glommed on to the Sundered Cult as he had? Just because they were convenient worshippers?

Why would he even want worshippers in the first place? Karana certainly didn't.

Something felt wrong to Karana, so he waited a few minutes. He could feel people inside the temple. A gentle breeze was ruffling the broad green leaves, and a pair of flycatchers were trilling to each other. Nothing to explain his uneasy feeling.

Still he drew his sword before entering the temple.

Too dark to see, he heard a whisper of sound to his right and instinctively brought up his sword. Something slammed into it, and Karana was driven back a few feet.

In a flash, he understood what had felt wrong—if this was really a temple full of cultists, he should have felt their seething, their resentment, their boredom. Instead, the only feeling was fear and worry. The only people in this temple were victims of the Sundered. Guleum had set a trap. Unfortunately, he could still feel the victims—their need stopped him from teleporting away.

Instead, Karana ignited his sword and found himself facing a golem. It had a blank orange face, as if it had been roughly hewn from rock, and an orange sword forged from power. Guleum must have put some effort to using his drop of orange power, inherited from his mother, rather than the pool of red from their father, so that Karana couldn't seize control of the golem.

Karana sent the fire from his blade onto the golem, just because it was what he did best. He wasn't terribly shocked though when the golem didn't burn; Karana's fire wasn't hot enough to ignite stone.

The golem retreated only to attack again. It was a skilled fighter, which suggested that Guleum himself had improved, or perhaps he had found a way to imbue his creation with more skill than he himself had.

Although he'd rather be facing his brother, it was a relief to fight a non-living foe. Almost pleasant after killing so many people.

Possible solutions flashed in his head, and he decided he had to behead it. Assuming its flesh wasn't invulnerable against Karana's sword...

He and the golem danced back and forth, and more than once Karana had to pull himself to safety by his robes. He also managed to slice the golem twice. He was reassured that his sword *could* cut it, though the golem was undeterred by the small lacerations. Maybe if he had managed to slice off a limb...

Finally, with a powerful leap and a little magical boost, he managed to take off the golem's sword arm. He twisted behind the golem with a spin that was flashier than it needed to be and cut off the golem's head.

The stone lost its animation, crumbling into a pile as its head tumbled to the brick floor. Both it and the bricks cracked.

He stood frozen for a few moments, waiting to see if anything would pop out at him and was almost disappointed when nothing did.

He walked cautiously through the temple, feeling his way to the gathering of fear. He passed incense burners that were much like those from Maoyi if perhaps rougher—it seemed this was one of Guleum's earlier sites—and unused prayer collectors.

He found the women, looking like they were on the edge of death.

No one had given them food or water since the temple had been turned into a trap, and Karana's vision went hazy for a moment.

It did the cultists no good to leave these women to die (not that burning them alive did them any good either, but at least they *believed* that it did). The sheer malice it took to abandon other people to starve pushed Karana to the edge of his temper.

He was forced to take deep breaths as he freed the women to keep himself from losing control. Unlike in Bando, he couldn't leave these women to get home on their own. He teleported the lot of them to what had once been Chain's village.

He was vaguely surprised to see it was now a town, and

another time he might have felt irritated that it had thrived, but now he was grateful. A crowd of people all came to help, and Karana left the women in the care of a no-nonsense lady doctor.

He hesitated before returning to the temple, for he was half-convinced there was nothing more to learn there, but then he thought he'd be foolish not to inspect the last few rooms, given he had already dealt with the golem.

In the last, he found a bedroom splattered with wax. The air was sickly sweet with a harsh metallic undertone, cinnamon and cardamom fighting to defeat the tang of blood. Someone had burned thousands of dream candles in this room.

For a moment, Karana thought this was simply where the cultists recruited new members, but words painted on the walls caught his eyes. This had been Guleum's room.

He could almost see Guleum writhing on the floor, wreathed in the scented smoke of the candles, his eyelids flickering as his mind wandered imaginary worlds.

The reek made it hard to breathe, but on top of that, guilt pressed on Karana's chest.

His sister had been a goddess with a surfeit of mortal dreams, and she had sold them to great profit. But she had warned Karana not to partake of them.

He hadn't needed the warning. Karana had a deep distrust of anything that could be more compelling than life.

But it seemed that Guleum hadn't shared that distrust—and maybe Salaana hadn't warned him.

Guleum had always watched Salaana with adoring puppy eyes—maybe he had inhaled a few too many of the dreams she sold at the old Godsmarket. Maybe she had given them to

Guleum herself, easy presents for a younger half-brother.

After the sale of dreams was reduced, after Salaana's worshippers' dreams were no longer available to him, what lengths would an addict go to alleviate his cravings?

The answer was before him, and Karana hated himself for not checking on Guleum. If he had, maybe the cult would never have reached its current heights. Maybe Guleum would have risen above his anger and pain instead of descending to depths that called for his execution.

This sad story was written on the walls in blood. Long rambles in divine characters, nearly incoherent in places, they documented Guleum's descent into madness.

Death to women, betrayers of hope, unclean seducers who ruined the heavens.

I will come again, I will live again, forever, after being cleansed by heavenly fire.

Karana still didn't know how Guleum had found the cultists in the first place, but now he understood why he had stayed.

He had indulged in their dreams until they became his. He believed, as they did, that women were responsible for all the evils of the world and that the red fire of their family brought reincarnation.

Karana quietly left the temple and then turned the red bricks into flames. These burned cleanly away, and when they faded, Karana asked fate, as he always did, why there weren't such things as redemption or second chances.

17

The Mother and the Scorched Graves

AFTER the last traces of the temple had been carried away by the gentle breeze from the Dataa River, Karana followed a deer path to the water rather than teleporting onward. He wanted to bathe. And it wasn't purely an indulgence. Letting his power trickle back, as it always did over the day, seemed wise. He was physically tired from fighting the golem, magically from teleporting the women, and emotionally from realizing how thoroughly he had failed Guleum as a brother.

The Dataa River wasn't anyone's idea of a bath—the water ran slow and brown—but Karana didn't care. He just wanted to wash away his guilt and the past.

A fresh start.

Ha!

Maybe he understood the cultists' desperation for rebirth.

Maybe they realized what horrible people they were and wanted to try again, with a blank slate.

Or maybe they were selfish pricks who burned women because they were delusional.

He stripped off his red and white robes, then stepped into the murky water. He waded until the water reached his chest, then sluiced it over his head.

It was piss warm, but its earthy scent was an improvement over Karana's stale odor and it washed away the uncomfortable stickiness of his skin. Karana scrubbed under the water, and the process calmed him. Nothing existed besides the warm river, the hazy blue sky, and the wildness of the jungle around him.

As clean as muddy water could make him, Karana swam back to shore, and stretched himself out in the sun to dry. He hoped An Ning was safe in the Underworld—no, he wasn't going to think about that right now. Nothing outside this moment and place. He picked up his robes, and his nose wrinkled. He now smelled like dirt and sunshine, and his robes were foul in comparison. After a moment, he changed the red silk to rose petals and then back. He sniffed them cautiously and smirked. They still smelt of roses. He dressed. He was ready for a meal and a nap; the riverbank would do for the latter, and though he wasn't normally too fond of fishing...

The sky turned gold and red as Karana roasted two fish over a fire.

Lacking other dinner companions, he told their lifeless eyes that their deaths might make them famous. "Only for you have I turned the Flaming Sword into a spit. Do you know I once saw it on a list of the ten most wondrous weapons in the world? It was number ten, but still, that puts it above a thousand—no, a million others? Anyway, it's quite fantastic."

The fish didn't reply, which, all things considered, was probably for the best. He ate them shortly after, and then he fell asleep.

Karana sat at a long low table; to his left was Chain, holding her sitar, and to his right was Heiwa, polishing her sword.

"No weapons at the table, please," said Xia as she placed a bowl of black rice before Heiwa.

Karana looked down the table and found An Ning smiling at him. He blushed, thinking she must not yet know who Heiwa and Chain were.

But as he watched, she took the hands of the women on either side of her—Pyeonghwa and Santiphaph. They joined hands with Chain and Heiwa, who in turn held out theirs to him.

"Won't you join us?" asked An Ning. "We'd all be happy together."

Karana bolted upright and was momentarily disoriented by the lack of a table.

Instead there was only the Dataa River, made beautiful by starlight that speckled it with diamonds.

He breathed slowly. His past lovers were long gone. He wasn't being unfaithful.

He'd never get back to sleep now. Karana teleported to another Sundered temple, this one nestled in the foothills of the Great Ladies, where isolated villages depended on the bustling trade of the Kuanbai River and where he had married Santi.

8,000 years ago

"KARANA," An Ning said.

Karana appeared to be sleeping, but after a moment, he mumbled, "Hmmm?"

"I want a child."

It was early, maybe dawn, but An Ning had woken nearly twenty minutes ago from a dream-turned-nightmare. She had focused on Karana's large, warm body tucked close to hers, and tried to let the peaceful sound of his breathing carry away her own sadness. It hadn't worked.

"Karana," she said again when he didn't respond, "I want to be a mother."

He shook himself awake like a dog. And then, "What? A child?"

"Yes," said An Ning decisively. "My sister and my friends all had babies years ago."

Karana was quiet, and the silence stretched between them. "Santi, you and I can't have children."

"I know," she told him. "But there are children who don't have parents. The traders who bring goods up the river told me about it."

Some of the tension went out of him.

"You wish to adopt?"

She couldn't see his face well, but she could hear the surprise in his voice.

"Yes." Under the covers, her hand found his and their fingers interleaved with the ease of long familiarity.

"Yes," he said after a moment. "We could do that. We could

be parents." He spoke slowly, as if the words were foreign. Then he repeated them, with more excitement, "We could be parents!"

An Ning smiled in the dark.

"Yes," she told him, "we could!"

Present Day

THE foothills of the Great Ladies would be called mountains anywhere else in the world, but crouched as they did in the shadow of the Earth's highest peaks, including the White Mountain itself, they were considered "hills."

Thanks to the confessions of the Bandoan cultists, Karana went directly to the gravestone of his wife, Santi. He was prepared for a trap, and he was prepared to have vile men offering up prayers to a being their predecessors had burned alive.

But he had forgotten about the children.

No, not forgotten. Deliberately driven them from his memory.

Santi had been determined to have children; not only was it considered a woman's highest duty among her people, she was particularly fond of children. But of course, Karana couldn't give her a child, for any child of his would cost her life to bear.

So they had adopted. Down the river a few miles, bandits had raided a village, leaving five children without caregivers. Santi and he had adopted all five. They were all within two years of age, and a family like that tended to garner remark.

The next year, two more children arrived by river boat, needing a home. One the next year, and three more the next.

Santi had loved them all; Karana had as well, but he had truly been humbled to see how much of herself she could give to all these little beings just because they craved it.

Before the children had come into their lives, Karana had been careful to keep his immortality and magic quiet. Santi had known, but they lived their lives as mortals.

But it was hard to take care of eleven children, and soon Karana started conjuring food and entertainment for them as a matter of course. The neighbors caught on quickly, and though they believed that Karana and Santi had been blessed by a god rather than one of them being a deity themselves, rumors began to spread on the river.

Karana wasn't afraid. No mortal he had cared about had been killed since his monk Shaanti almost ten millennia earlier. He wasn't a child anymore; he could face any threat.

Word came of a terrible fire across the river that had left many orphans behind. It had seemed so natural that Karana go himself, disguised as a mortal, though he couldn't remember why in hindsight.

The fire had been worse than reports indicated. No survivors.

Karana found the character for destruction carved into trees ringing the village, far too many slashing lines scarring the bark.

He had teleported home immediately, but it had taken a week to travel to the village as a mortal.

His whole family dead, killed by cultists who had been jealous that Karana had committed himself to others while ignoring them.

Never had he let another lover convince him to adopt anything. Sometimes he couldn't believe he had even partially taken responsibility for the Bulgae—but they were immortal and so An Ning was a god.

And not his lover...

18

The Gardener and the Flame Flowers

THE sight of twelve gravestones, each covered with soot, sent Karana to his knees.

He realized, as if Bai were there to explain it to him, that these gravestones were where the Sundered bound women before burning them alive. It was so, so much worse than the Byeong Mountains.

He entered the temple behind the graves, and creatures flew at his head. Karana ended them without even knowing what they were.

The whole world was red, was pain, was fury.

Why did he ruin everything?

Why was he destruction?

Why couldn't he be hope?

12,000 years ago

AN NING stood patiently as Karana fussed over her robes.

They were glorious, a deep red silk covered with silver peonies. An Ning loved them, almost as much as she loved Karana. Because Karana had made them for her, and also because they were beautiful, for she loved beautiful things.

"Don't be nervous," he told her as he knelt before her and adjusted the silver bells at her waist.

"Nervous?" echoed An Ning, "Don't you see my happy smile?"

He looked up at her with a squint, as if searching for her smile.

She laughed, as he intended, and his face relaxed into a grin.

He added, "I do see your happy smile, but I can feel your stress."

He's so at ease—I had thought he was at ease in Ningjingcun, but I never saw him like this.

She reached down and tugged a lock of his hair impudently—he'd spent an hour fussing over it earlier, and he smoothed it after she let go. "Don't worry. I'm not *too* nervous. Tonight just means a lot to me."

An Ning led an unconventional life for a daughter of a wealthy family, starting with her marriage to Karana. In fact, she was fairly confident that her father would have refused to acknowledge the relationship if Karana hadn't taken him aside and given him a private display of his power.

But once An Ning *had* married Karana, it felt like nothing was off limits. So instead of being a socialite or tending house, she grew flowers. Her breeds were popular with the elite families along the Jingzi River, but today was the first time she was holding an exhibition. Karana and she were opening their manor and gardens to strangers—some from far away—to show the flowers that An Ning grew.

She didn't strictly need today to be successful. They didn't need wealth, and fame didn't matter to either of them, but An Ning had poured everything into her plants.

"I hope people like them."

Karana stood, and An Ning had to tilt her head back to keep eye contact.

"I think they will. I have seen many flowers, and the ones you have raised are truly something special."

His hand crept to her neck and his thumb stroked her jaw. An Ning went up on her tip toes and wrapped her own hand around his nape. He obliged her with a kiss.

He always tastes of cinnamon. How is that possible?

Karana pulled back and smiled again, his eyes crinkling provocatively. "I just got you dressed; you aren't going to make me do it again, are you?"

She laughed and released him. "No, but only because I don't want to be late greeting our guests."

She settled her hand on the crook of his arm, and together they walked to the gate of their manor.

A carriage pulled up moments later, and a silk merchant's wife descended with the help of a footman.

She and An Ning exchanged bows.

"Lady Heping, thank you for inviting me," she said, and presented An Ning with a wrapped box. Probably a bolt of silk that was worth three of An Ning's flower bushes.

An Ning accepted the box. "My pleasure, Madam Lin. Do come in!"

Karana had managed to fade back. Other than her father, An Ning doubted anyone around them realized that he was the special one—but she met his eyes and was buoyed up by the love in them.

She was suddenly amused at herself for feeling nervous— why should she care what her guests thought when she had already impressed the only being who mattered?

Present Day

WHEN Karana regained his senses, his face was pressed into the ground. He had destroyed Guleum's temple and whatever immortal creatures he had trapped there to attack Karana.

Like a young hooligan (or like An Ning), he had expended his power until he had fainted. If Guleum had found him in that state...

Karana tried to sit up, only to discover his hands were bound.

"You're awake," said a strange-yet-familiar voice.

Karana twisted his head uncomfortably, scraping his cheek on the ground, but he managed to see the speaker.

Okay, Guleum *had* found him in that state.

Karana stared at him a minute. He was surprised that he was still alive, and it made him think that perhaps Guleum wasn't as far gone as he'd thought.

Karana tried to burn the bindings on his wrists to no affect.

"I made them from orange peels," Guleum said. "The fruit

was quite tasty."

Karana didn't know what to say to that, so he looked around, as best as he was able. They weren't in the foothills of the Great Ladies any longer.

Red flowers bloomed everywhere. Memory stirred but did not settle.

"Where are we?" he asked Guleum.

Guleum smiled. "The locals call these flame flowers. Supposedly, long ago, a god lived here and grew red flowers that sold for their weight in gold."

Despite the exaggeration, there was enough truth in the legend that Karana recognized it.

Heping. Our garden on the Jingzi.

"Why did you bring me here?"

Guleum gestured to the flowers carelessly. "I like to be surrounded by the flowers that my brother planted. I never even knew you liked gardening until I found this place."

Karana was shocked. "That *I* planted?"

"You didn't? Then who did? There's an arch nearby that one of our family made."

Karana tried to sit up; Guleum watched but didn't offer any help. Frustrated, he gave up. "I made the arch, but my wife planted the flowers."

"Your wife?" echoed Guleum. "You've never been married."

"I've never wed an immortal," Karana said. "But I have been married a few times. Are you really going to talk to me while I am tied up?"

"Is there a better way to talk to you?" asked Guleum. "If I untie you, won't you attack me?"

Not immediately, thought Karana. "Guleum, I'm your

brother. Can't—"

"Not a good one though," countered Guleum. "I haven't seen you since Father died. Doesn't seem very loving."

"You weren't alone," protested Karana, to cover his guilt, "You had your mother. Where is Teodolda anyway?"

Guleum scoffed. "A *woman*."

Truthfully, it was hard for Karana to call his young stepmother's face to mind—just a vague impression of dark hair and bronzed prettiness—but he had always seen how deeply she loved her son. He had thought Guleum was devoted to her as well—after all, Guleum had justified his attempted patricide for his mother's sake. To hear Guleum dismiss her with such vitriol...

Karana was shocked.

"Didn't you live with your mother?" What had Bai said at his wedding? "She and you wanted to escape the pressure of being in our family—"

"I never wanted that!" hissed Guleum. "I am stronger than any of you realized! I wouldn't let her hold me back."

"Then—why didn't you come to Jin's wedding? Or any of the other dozen parties there have been?"

"And why would I celebrate with someone who tried to kill me?" snarled Guleum.

Karana asked carefully, "Who tried to kill you? Surely not Jin."

Guleum abruptly stood and started disrobing. Karana would have looked away, but he didn't want to scrape his face again.

When Guleum peeled back his undertunic, leaving him in nothing but orange breeches, he stretched out his arms and showed Karana his chest.

Guleum was quite a bit paler than Karana, peachy rather than brown, and in stark contrast to the pallor of his skin was a black tattoo of a peony. But at several points, the design was ruined by bubbling scar tissue. Karana had never seen that before, but what had it to do with Jin?

"I don't understand," he admitted.

"This! This is what happened when she broke the death curse! It rebounded on me. One moment I was drinking tea in my room, the next it was like someone was carving my chest with a knife! When the pain stopped, the black peony was here."

That sounded horrible, but not deadly. And, to be fair, Guleum had tried to *murder* his own father, so...

"I'm sorry for the pain, but—"

"Not just pain, Karana! It was killing me! Slowly poisoning me! Luckily, I discovered it in time. I had to travel to the Underworld myself. I have to eat a black peony petal every day or I will die."

Karana stared at him. "Jin doesn't know this though. And she isn't the one who broke the death curse anyway."

Guleum stared at Karana in confusion. "You broke the curse?"

"No. Bai. Her husband."

Guleum snorted. "He's lying to protect her. The curse can only be broken by a blood relative."

Karana was taken aback. There was no reason for Jin and Bai to lie—as far as they knew, no one blamed them for breaking the death curse.

"Bai explained it to me," Karana said. "Our father was once a drop of his blood—"

Gu snorted. "I'm sure he wants you to believe that."

"Well, I know Father formed from a drop of blood, and Bai was the only other being at the time—"

"Who told you that? *Bai*? How can we even be sure he's the oldest immortal? It was Father who became Sun Emperor."

Even Chika didn't interrupt Karana as ruthlessly as Guleum. "Father told me that Bai is older. And so did Gang. It was—"

"And isn't it convenient that both of them are dead, so I can't verify it?"

"You could go to the Sea of Souls—"

"I'm not going to fall for that! I know Jin healed Father and set the curse upon me!"

And Karana suddenly realized there was no point to arguing. Evidence, objective truth, didn't matter to Guleum. Everything that contradicted his own thoughts had to be deliberate deception by outsiders.

Karana sighed. "Why did you bring me here? What do you want from me?"

Guleum knelt before him.

"Your power, Karana."

"My power?"

"How do you bring beings back to life?"

Karana searched Guleum's red eyes for any sign that this was a joke. That he was mocking Karana.

"I've never brought anyone back to life. Jin—"

"I'm not talking about her perverted ability to resurrect the dead!" Guleum spoke so forcefully that spittle flew from his lips to land on Karana's face. Karana stiffened and held still.

"I mean, reincarnation," said Guleum, eerily recomposed. "How do you reincarnate beings?"

Karana felt sad. "I can't, Gu. That's just a story the cultists tell. It's wishful thinking—"

"No!" Guleum abruptly slapped him. Karana's cheek burned as blood rushed to the handprint Guleum had left behind. "Don't lie to me!"

"I can't—"

Guleum pulled a dagger and pressed it to Karana's throat.

As fitting as it would be to die here, where his third love had passed on gently, Karana wasn't ready for death. He swallowed his denials.

He wished that he could feel Guleum's emotions or read his essence with his white magic. If only Guleum wasn't orange. *Guleum was orange.*

Karana usually knew when someone was lying because of his white magic. He avoided lying himself because of it, preferring to skirt around topics he wished to avoid. But Guleum had none; he was orange instead. Karana could lie to him.

"Okay," he said slowly, feeling like the lie must be written on his face. "You're right. I can reincarnate beings. And I will teach you. You are after all my brother."

The twisted anger on Guleum's face eased. "Yes. Teach me the power of reincarnation."

The Khan's Daughter and Karana's Bluff

"I NEED my hands free to demonstrate," Karana tried.

Guleum's glower returned. "As if I'd fall for that," he told Karana. "Explain it instead."

At least his throat hadn't been cut. If he couldn't get Guleum to free his hands, he'd have to figure out how to turn the tables on him while tied up. He had sixteen millennia on his brother, after all. Surely he could figure something out.

Unfortunately, he had never tried to defeat someone as powerful as himself. And most of his strategies had rather fatal consequences.

"Well. You know it has to do with fire." For the next half hour, he didn't understand half the things that came out of his mouth. If a tangent came up, he took it. A philosophical ramble? Perfect.

Guleum didn't think so though. "Is all of this really relevant?"

"Oh, yes," said Karana. "Reincarnation is highly dependent on your understanding of the usual death cycle. Only by thoroughly mastering it can you circumvent it. You see," and he was off again.

It felt like he talked for hours, but that might have simply been the cramp forming in his shoulders from having his hands tied behind his back. Guleum did prop Karana up so he wasn't talking to the ground, but that was the only concession that he would allow.

Suddenly, Guleum cut off Karana's nonsense with a sharp hand motion. Karana used the opportunity to catch his breath.

"You knew all of this the first time?"

"Sorry?" said Karana.

"The first time you reincarnated your monks, when you sacrificed the one who held you back. You knew this?"

Karana had never reincarnated any monk, and he found Guleum's conversation as confusing as his own rambling had been, but he definitively said, "Absolutely. I can't remember not knowing it."

At least that covered *when* he had learned it.

"Still, it must have to do with her sacrifice," Guleum murmured.

Her? "What sacrifice?" Karana asked.

"The monk! The one that coddled you. It was when you burned her that you ascended to greatness and realized the depths of your powers! So why didn't it work for me?"

Karana blinked. "Who did you sacrifice?" Dread filled Karana.

Guleum waved his hand. "That's not—"

"Did you burn your mother alive?"

"She's just a woman. She didn't have power like we do!"

"You're the reason the cult started burning women. Sacrificing them," Karana realized. The timeline fit. He thought that the cult had poisoned Guleum's mind, but he had poisoned theirs... No, it was more than that. They had poisoned each other, their hatreds and prejudices merging to form a more toxic and abominable delusion.

"All those minor goddesses the cult burned—you must have been the one to capture them. But you cannot be everywhere, so the cultists turned to mortal women..."

Karana felt like he was choking. Karana himself had executed far too many mortals to count and had caused the death of his infant brother, but Guleum's villainy had exceeded Karana's expectation.

"You murdered your mother to try to get more power," Karana repeated. "Not by accident or in a moment of terrible emotion, but a calculated decision to make yourself more powerful."

But Guleum was pacing, oblivious to Karana's horror. "Since it's so tied to the location and the atmosphere—" Had Karana said that? He must have. "—why don't we go to where it all began?"

Karana just wanted to find a way to bind Guleum. To get this over with.

Of course, getting Guleum to drain his magic would help achieve that goal.

Karana summoned the façade he had cultivated since childhood. He drawled, "That might help, but I'm not going to teleport you."

Guleum rolled his eyes. "I never thought you would."

His hand settled on Karana's shoulder, bony fingers digging in. He pulled them both between.

14,000 *years ago*

THE horse quickened its pace, and An Ning automatically tightened her grip on Karana's waist. She snuggled her head against his back, too. He laughed, from pure happiness, and it reverberated through her. Right in front of her eyes was his dark red hair. It wasn't the same as when they met—then he had dyed it black, but it had grown out, and it had been this lustrous auburn ever since.

An Ning couldn't see her own hair, but it was more gray than black now. Having the evidence of Karana's unchanging form before her reminded her that she had promised her father to ask him about it.

They were alone here, riding the edge of the tribe's territory in an ostensible patrol. The Eagle Tribe didn't really need to patrol anymore—shortly after Karana had married her, his skill as a warrior had become legend. No one wanted to make an enemy of such a fearsome warrior.

An Ning hadn't married him for that, but she was glad of it. His fame had soothed her father when they failed to have any children.

"Karana," she said softly. He didn't respond—the wind had carried away her voice.

She lifted her head and said more forcefully, "Karana! I

have something to talk to you about."

He glanced back at her in mild surprise and used his legs to stop the horse.

"Shall we walk a ways?" he asked her.

She nodded.

He slid down first, then lifted her to the ground. She was not a slight woman, and she had thickened after reaching forty, but he was a big man, and, as everyone had begun to notice, hadn't aged a day since he'd come to the tribe.

The horse whinnied, and Karana turned from her to pet its neck. He gathered her hand in one of his, and the horse's reins in his other.

His red eyes smiled down at her—he was almost too pretty for a man. The other warriors of the tribe had adopted his habit of lining his eyes with kohl to reduce sun glare on the plains, though when they'd first seen it, they thought it vanity.

To be frank, An Ning believed that it was. She saw how many hours Karana spent on his hair and face every morning—and he'd redraw those lines five times if the flick at the end wasn't just right.

"Amalgan, my love?" he asked curiously, and An Ning realized that she'd been staring at him.

She blushed and said, "You're as handsome as the day we met."

He raised her hand to his lips and brushed a kiss over her knuckles. "And you are even more beautiful."

An Ning snorted but smiled. The smile faded quickly though. "I also look twenty-six years older, but you look the same age."

He didn't immediately speak.

"You must remember how uncertain my father was to let me marry a man who was a decade older. But now you look a decade or more younger."

He started to make a token protest, but An Ning pressed her free hand to his mouth.

"Karana," she said, "people are wondering if you are a god."

His hand tightened on hers, and he wouldn't meet her eyes.

Finally, he nodded, sharp and short.

She thought about that a moment, and then asked, because she'd wondered for some years now, "Is that why we never had a child?"

His eyes raised to hers, stricken with guilt. "I know you wanted..."

She had been quite cursed when it came to children, hadn't she? And now that she was immortal, her body couldn't bear them...

She smiled. "Not instead of you. I was just curious."

He sighed. "It's not impossible for a mortal woman to bear an immortal child. But a normal immortal pregnancy takes a thousand years. The cost of making an immortal in only nine months is always the mother's life—if she is able to carry the babe to term. Usually, both die."

An Ning felt a little sad, but not too sad. She had come to terms with not having a child a decade ago, and she had thrown herself into being the best aunt in the tribe.

"I see," An Ning said. "Thank you for valuing me over a son." Most men of her tribe would not have. "Though..."

He cocked his head, his eyes still worried.

"I worry that you will be alone when I die."

"Ah." He leaned forward and kissed her. "I have a family of my own."

God or not, An Ning twisted his wrist behind his back.

"An immortal wife?" she demanded.

He burst into shocked laughter. "No! Parents, a sister, and a brother."

"Oh." She released his wrist and felt embarrassed for her burst of jealousy.

He turned to her and pulled her tight against him with one arm.

"For me, there is only you," he told her. Not for the first time, An Ning thought she might combust as she gazed into his red eyes.

His lips met hers, oh-so-familiar in taste and texture, and yet as thrilling as the first time.

"I love you," An Ning told him, between kisses.

"And I love you," he rejoined, the words tumbling into her own mouth and heating her whole body.

Present Day

SUNLIGHT filtered down into the dank room through holes in the ceiling. Stale earth and damp filled Karana's nostrils, though at least he had arrived on his knees, rather than his face against the dirty floor.

Moments after arriving, Guleum threw fire around the room, lighting several torches, all of which looked far newer than the ruins themselves.

Karana didn't need the light to know where they were though.

It was his first temple. His only temple, actually. The

wooden doors had long since rotted, and once-vibrant red murals had faded into brown blurs, but Karana could see them as if they were new.

The portrait directly ahead remained pristine—Salaana had made it herself. It wasn't quite accurate—he had been a gangly teenager when it was done, and not sufficiently godlike, so Salaana had embellished a little.

Still, it was his rusty red eyes that met his own. Long auburn hair spilled over bare shoulders (those were too muscular at the time, but not broad enough now), and fire filled his hands and encircled the whole mural.

Shaanti had loved that portrait, though it had embarrassed Karana terribly. She had said it wasn't quite as handsome as the real thing, but it would do nicely.

Karana had been both mortified and gratified by her words.

Though he usually remembered Shaanti as she had been near her death, he could now see her as a young woman, with her long braid and smooth dark skin. She had been so beautiful that it had hurt Karana to look at her. How he had wished and wished to mature faster himself, so that he did not look like a child at her side!

Guleum's fingers snapped directly in front of Karana's eyes, and Karana lifted his head to glare at him.

He wished he could stand, but with the bindings on his feet, he'd make a fool of himself.

"Tell me about burning the Sundered here," Guleum ordered. "How did you know they'd come back?"

Karana couldn't quite keep himself from laughing, though the half-stifled gurgles made him sound like a madman. If they had come back—well, he probably would have killed himself!

He had destroyed them in a blind rage, avenging Shaanti's murder.

"Guleum," he said, "you think the cult persisted because they came back to life?"

"Of course."

"I let the children go. The children lived and kept the cult going."

Guleum shook his head. "You really don't know?"

"Know what?" Karana snapped. Trying to get comfortable, he sat back on his heels. It wasn't much of an improvement.

"They found the children."

"Who?"

"The cultists! The ones that were reborn! Their past lives came back to them, and they found the children that you had spared. That was why the cult persisted."

Lunatics, thought Karana. "Oh?" asked Karana dryly. "If all the cultists remember their past lives, why do you have to inculcate them with mortal dreams?"

"They don't now! And of course we are recruiting new members as well, but back then they used to."

"Why? What changed?"

"Father closed the Underworld."

Karana raised his eyebrows.

"The Sea of Souls," Guleum persisted. "One of the men you reincarnated travelled to the sea, and when he entered it, he remembered his past life. He brought back jugs of it, and gave it to strangers, looking for others like him. Eventually, ten men all found each other, and restarted the cult."

"Then why don't you feed your followers some sea water now?"

Guleum's face flushed and he pressed his lips into a hard line.

Surprised by the reaction, Karana mulled over Guleum's possible reasons and burst out laughing. "What, are you afraid they'd remember what I looked like and realize you aren't the God of Destruction after all?"

Guleum grabbed the front of Karana's robes, but he wasn't strong enough to move Karana much.

"Stop laughing!"

Again, spittle landed on Karana's face, and he did in fact oblige Guleum. It's hard to be amused when someone else's saliva is decorating your cheek.

"You don't deserve worshippers," continued Guleum, "while I—I have increased them a thousand-fold!"

"And made the world a worse place while you were at it," said Karana.

Guleum shoved Karana backward, and, unable to move his arms or feet, Karana tumbled into a heap. Curse it, but the dirt smelled worse up close and personal.

Guleum put his muddy slipper on Karana's chest, and though Karana struggled to knock it off, he couldn't manage it.

"You're wasting my time," said Guleum. "Tell me—what was special about the fire you used here? Why did the men reincarnate? What's different about my fire?"

Karana was exhausted. He was sick of bluffing, and he still hadn't come up with a plan. "Why are you so sure your fire doesn't lead to reincarnation while mine does?"

"I checked," said Guleum. "The men I burned—I looked for them in the Sea of Souls, and they were there."

"And mine aren't?" Karana snorted.

Guleum shook his head. "I went after you killed my men at the ruins of Xiling. Not one of them was in the sea."

"You couldn't find them."

"No, they weren't there."

Karana closed his eyes. Guleum craved this special power so badly that his mind had warped to believe in it. But Karana had to humor Guleum. What did he do when He burned people that Guleum didn't? "Maybe you didn't care enough," suggested Karana.

"Care about what?"

"The men," said Karana. "Maybe when you burned them, you didn't care whether or not they came back."

Guleum took his foot off Karana's chest. "And you did?"

Karana shrugged—well, he tried to. It's a tricky maneuver when you've been stomped into the ground. "I hate killing. I didn't want them to die."

Guleum crossed his arms, as if seriously considering Karana's idea. "But they're mortals. Why would you care about them?"

Karana thought of his nine loves. "They're beings. Mortal or immortal—we're not so different. We have hopes and ambitions, weaknesses and foibles. We love the same." He cut himself off, not wanting to share anymore with Guleum, who was once again shaking his head.

Guleum said, "And you think I'm the crazy one."

20

The Monk and the Sundered Temple

19,000 years ago

AN NING lay on her bed, both of Karana's hands clutching her own.

He looks even younger than Chika now.

Karana looked fifteen, maybe sixteen years old. He had a small flick of kohl at the edge of both his eyes, but his lips were bare.

They're pink, after all.

His long hair was a beautiful dark red, and silver clasps kept it out of his face.

"Shaanti," he breathed, and fat tears escaped his eyes. "Shaanti, you have to live. I can't do this without you."

Her chest hurt, and her legs were tingling.

"Divinity," she said, "even if it weren't for the poison, I would have died soon anyway. I am eighty years old."

"No! You might pass a hundred."

She wanted to lift her hand and stroke his hair, but she didn't have the strength. She did manage to shake her head.

"It already hurts to have you look at me when I am so old, while you are as young as the day we met. I don't want you to care for me when I am infirm. I want you to remember me—"

She started coughing.

"Shaanti!" More tears spilled over. "I love you. I have always loved you."

An Ning met his eyes. "I know that. I love you, too. You've been like a son to me—"

"No! No! Not like a mother. Like…. Like…"

She knew the words he wanted to say. *Like a lover.* She didn't want to hear it. She didn't want his first confession to be to an old woman on her death bed. She wanted him to forget her and, when he was a little older, to fall in love with a woman who was young and beautiful.

"Don't say it," she practically choked. "Save it for the next."

His shoulders began to shake, and his face crumpled. He pressed his head to her shoulder, and the tremors of his grief shook her body. She at last managed to tug one hand free from his and place it on his crown. His free hand snuck around her waist in a hug.

She remembered the first time she had seen him. A beautiful boy who looked about her own age. He was shy and gawky; not how a god should look. But those red eyes met hers, and she had stepped forward. Pledged herself to his service.

If she was totally honest, she had already had an epic love story unfolding in her head. But he had only returned once a year to the temple she built for him, and each time she was a year older, while he seemed caught in eternal youth.

He had told her that he would eventually become an adult—but not until she was nine hundred years dead. She had realized then that they couldn't be lovers. Even though he was the god, he was also a child. It would have been wrong to seduce, as she instinctively felt that she could have.

And it would have been cruel to take his heart when she couldn't offer hers for the rest of his life.

But she knew he had given his to her anyway, and he was left with her paltry mortal one.

"I'm sorry," An Ning said.

And then her body died.

Almost immediately she felt the call of the Sea of Souls. It would be warm there, and she would drift content, the pain of leaving Karana blunted by the presence of every soul that had come before her.

She fought the call.

She might find peace, but she would leave Karana in torment. She couldn't. She loved him. He needed her.

So she held onto her corpse, listening to the being she loved mourn her death.

He kissed both her lids, her own thick kohl painting his lips black. Then he surprised her by starting a fire.

"Come back to me," he told her. "Come back."

He couldn't hear her, but she answered anyway. *I will.*

I always will.

Present Day

AN NING sat up and gasped for air. Both Daichin and Chika were looking at her with concern, their brows furrowed. Chika was holding her hand.

"Sensei?" she asked. "Are you alright?"

An Ning squeezed Chika's hand, though part of her wished it were Karana's. She wanted to see him so badly; she had abandoned him so many times over the years! How had he borne it?

And all those years when he hadn't even known she was there!

For though she always dodged the Sea of Souls, tethered to Earth by Karana's red fire and his will, she wasn't always reborn as a mortal. Sometimes she had been a flower or a butterfly or a tree or a cat. Those lives were foggy, but she knew they were there just the same.

Poor Karana.

She wanted to hug him, but he wasn't here, so she pulled Chika into her arms instead.

Chika was surprised but hugged An Ning back.

"Is everything okay?" she whispered.

An Ning found her voice. "Yes. Or—it will be. Chika—I remembered!"

Chika pulled back and looked at her. "You remembered what? Your life as a mortal? The Knowing God was right?"

That pulled An Ning up short. "No, I didn't remember that," she admitted. Her fears that Karana had hated the woman she had been returned, though they were muted. They had shared eight of her lives. An Ning didn't know what had gone wrong in Xiling, but she was sure they could overcome it.

Karana was the only one for her in this world, and she was the only one for him, though he didn't know it yet.

And he should be the first to know, she realized belatedly. She couldn't tell Chika before Karana, though she really wanted to tell someone.

She rose shakily to her feet. "I'll tell you everything later," An Ning promised. She looked around. The indigo boat was still drifting on the cerulean blue sea.

She smiled fondly at the water. She didn't think the sea was alive, but it was nice of it to have kept her memories all this time, even though she hadn't let it keep her soul.

"Did you find Akemi's soul?" she asked Chika.

"She refused to look until you woke up," griped Daichin.

"Oh," said An Ning and blushed. Then, "How long was I out?"

"Several hours," said Chika.

Hours. It seemed incredible that she had revisited two-hundred odd lives in that time, but somehow she had. The memories were shockingly clear, for her immortal mind seemed to have no trouble recalling thousands of years.

"I will help you look now," An Ning announced.

"No!" exclaimed Chika. "What if you faint in the water again? If Daichin hadn't pulled you out—"

"Hadn't pulled *both* of you out," corrected Daichin, and Chika's cheeks mottled.

"If Daichin hadn't pulled *us* out, we would have drowned," Chika amended.

An Ning smiled and squeezed Chika's shoulder. "Don't

worry. It won't happen again." And then, though it was worse than picking up Bulgae poop, she said, "Thank you, Daichin."

He gave a sort of half-nod in acknowledgment.

She looked back at Chika. "Can you swim?"

Chika's cheek mottling worsened.

"Let me go in first," An Ning said.

Daichin put a hand on her arm to stop her. "I'll go in, and the girl can hold on to me."

The girl? Surely he knows her name is Chika.

And in that little moment, when nothing special was happening, An Ning had a life-changing epiphany.

Daichin had to be a man because he had grown up in Ehkoron, where men and women were divided by personality, expectations, dress, and futures. She understood; she had lived in Ehkoron herself, albeit several generations before Daichin did. But the pressure she had felt to have children, the way her worth had been measured by her husband's skill as a warrior—those things didn't disappear from a culture overnight.

An Ning—the An Ning she had been, before she became an immortal and adopted a male form—must have had a similar experience. She had been taught that sexual relationships only occurred between men and women. She thought women were supposed to dress prettily and speak softly; that they were to stay pure and chaste.

But she wasn't just An Ning. She was Shaanti, the first mortal to follow Karana who had recruited a hundred men. She was Amalgan, a woman of the plains who had loved a god. She was Heping and Santi, Chain and Heiwa, Pyeonghwa and Santiphaph. A gardener, a mother, a singer, a warrior, a pilgrim, and a queen. She knew power; she knew war; she knew nine different cultures and nine different views of womanhood.

And none of them was the right one. None of them was the definitive way of being.

There wasn't one way to be a man or to be a woman. And if she wanted to be a woman because that felt right to her, well, she could be.

For most beings, epiphanies were personal things. The being who had it would be forever changed, but no one else could see it.

An Ning wasn't most beings though; she was a god. Her epiphany manifested itself in her body, and it felt wonderful, like stretching after a deep sleep.

Chika gasped, and Daichin blinked.

"I've never seen that before," he admitted, and he eyed her nervously.

An Ning wasn't bothered. She at last felt completely at ease in the body she had shaped when she ascended. Whether certain parts were curved or flat, inverted or hanging free, didn't make her less herself. She turned to Chika, whose mouth was still agape, and clasped her shoulders.

"Come, let's find Akemi."

Chika snapped her mouth shut and nodded firmly—that was Chika. Down to business, no matter what happened.

An Ning tugged her to the water, and Daichin followed. With Chika supported between the two of them, it didn't take long to find Akemi's soul. Or perhaps it would be more accurate to say Akemi's soul found them.

The soul, a ball of indigo light with thin threads of white and green, pressed itself to Chika's chest. Chika grimaced, her brow furrowing and deep lines bracketing her mouth.

Unnerved, An Ning reached for the ball, intending to dislodge it, but Daichin caught her hand.

"Don't! That's her cousin. They are communing."

"How do you know?" asked An Ning.

"I've been here before. After I ascended to immortality, I came to the sea to tell my mother and father. The dead you seek always find you and then you... It's hard to describe, but it's like talking to them in a dream." His eyes moved to Chika's face. "Or a nightmare. She must not like what her cousin is saying."

"Maybe Akemi doesn't want to be resurrected," An Ning worried.

"I wouldn't," agreed Daichin. "To age as a mortal, forgetting your immortal life? Sounds terrible."

An Ning was surprised. "Forget? How much will she forget?"

"Pretty much everything, I've heard," said Daichin. "After all, how can a mortal mind retain millennia of memories?"

An Ning was troubled. She knew that Akemi and Chika were close, closer than either was to Miho, but was it right to bring Akemi back? Against her own inclination?

But at that moment, Chika broke into a wide smile. "She'll come! She says she'll come!"

An Ning felt torn. Was Akemi only coming for Chika?

But if Akemi had agreed...

"Does she understand that she'll be mortal?" asked An Ning.

Chika's eyes shuttered, but she nodded. "That's why she didn't want to come. But... I convinced her that sixty years are better than nothing. And she can still live with us, can't she? There's usually a monk or two who stays at the house—"

An Ning nodded. "Yes, of course, she's always welcome at home." She glanced at the ball of light that had attached itself to Chika. "Can she hear me?"

Chika nodded.

"Thank you, Akemi. We all love and miss you."

Daichin cleared his throat, managing to convey his boredom quite eloquently. "Time to get back to Earth then. Souls can only last a few weeks out of the sea. We should find the nearest portal and teleport to the White Mountain."

"No," protested Chika, "we need to stop at home first. Miho will want to come."

"Fine," snapped Daichin, as if he had any say over the matter—it was Chika who'd do the teleporting. "Ningjingcun, then the White Mountain."

He pulled out a colorful metal ornament. "You can put her in this."

"What is it?" demanded Chika suspiciously.

He rolled his eyes. "A gift from the Threefold Goddess."

An Ning didn't miss how it was always "Jin" when Daichin referred to her in relation to himself, and "Threefold Goddess" when he talked to them, but she wouldn't have to deal with him much longer.

Even better, whatever whims of fate ruled the Underworld seemed to want to speed them on their way. No sooner were the three of them back on board the indigo boat and coursing over the bright blue sea than Daichin spotted an iridescent patch of air.

"Look!" he called. "A portal to Earth!"

Chika steered the boat through, and moments later the boat slid smoothly over earthly waters, familiar green trees on a nearby shore.

"Why, it's the Lake of Reflection," Chika said in surprise.

An Ning nodded—she could see the green copper roofs ahead.

"Shall we dock first?" suggested An Ning. "It might be easier to shrink the boat when we're not on it."

Chika smiled. "Someday I'd like to be able to shrink a boat and teleport at the same time. But yes, for now, let's dock first."

While she and Chika—well, mostly Chika—focused on reaching a dock, Daichin busied himself with packing all his mementos just so.

"It occurs to me that you don't need me any longer," he told the two of them as they disembarked at the algae-coated docks of the Wood Pavilions. "I'll head home without you."

He barely waited for their farewells before disappearing.

"And good riddance," An Ning muttered to Chika, who laughed.

An Ning smiled. Chika hadn't laughed in quite some time. For that alone, she couldn't help but be grateful that Akemi had come with them. "I honestly don't know why he accompanied us in the first place, though I'll admit his skills were useful."

"I think he was interested in you," said Chika. "He asked Miho and I a lot of questions that first night that made us think he saw you as a potential partner. But I think he realized what you thought of him on the boat."

"You're kidding!" said An Ning.

Chika giggled. "No, really!"

She turned to the boat and got busy shrinking it. "We should have sent this with him. I'm sure that—the Love God's

Heart—must want it back."

An Ning looked at Chika closely. "Who is the 'Love God's Heart' anyway?"

Chika bit her lip. "Ojichan disowned her. You shouldn't mention it to any of my family that we used something she made."

An Ning nodded. "Not even Miho?"

Chika smiled. "Well, I'll tell Miho. But other than that..." She pressed a finger to her lips.

Then she took An Ning's hand, and they were in between.

An hour later, An Ning and Chika had both been licked "clean" by eight rambunctious Bulgae only to seek a more standard cleanliness in respective baths. The warm water and rose-scented soap were wonderful, but An Ning was also impatient to find Karana again.

A little nervous, too, but mostly impatient.

So instead of soaking, as she half-wanted to, An Ning dried off as soon as she was clean and dressed quickly.

Miho was waiting in the courtyard with a pot of tea on the stone picnic table. "Chika's still bathing."

An Ning took the seat opposite her disciple, taking in the rather pretty eye patch that covered her empty socket. "It's good to be home. Have you heard anything from Karana?"

Miho shook her head. "He left right after you did, so a little over a week ago."

"A week?" echoed An Ning in surprise. So Daichin's day count hadn't been right. As for herself, having several lifetimes return to her at once had totally skewed her sense of time. She frowned. "I wish there was a way to check on him."

"There is." Miho held out her wrist and unwound a

peculiar bracelet.

"What's that?" asked An Ning.

"Uncle's hair. He said to use it to find him if we needed."

An Ning must have looked puzzled for Miho elaborated, "The hair will pull you to him if you focus on it while teleporting. Blood—or any part of their body, I suppose—and magical items can serve the same purpose."

An Ning took it gently. "Should we all go together then?"

"I think you and Chika should go," said Miho. "The sooner the murderer is captured, the sooner Akemi can be restored. But I will stay here."

An Ning hesitated. "You really don't want to ask the Threefold Goddess for a new eye?"

Miho touched the embroidery of her eye patch lightly. "No, I don't think so. Maybe if I had lost both eyes... but right now, this feels like a lesson to be learned."

An Ning wouldn't have understood before her memories had returned, but now she thought of all the suffering she had undergone. It had been horrible, of course, and she wouldn't wish it on anyone, but it was also important. It wasn't right to rob someone of their challenges for that was what made them stronger. Of course, sometimes a challenge was so overwhelming that a being would be crushed under its weight, but she would respect Miho's decision that this wasn't one of those times.

It didn't look like one of those times.

So An Ning took the hair. When Chika emerged, clean, armored, and looking closer to her old self than she had since Akemi's death, they teleported to Karana.

ONCE Guleum backed off and began pacing, trying to parse the only true things Karana had said all day, Karana looked around the room.

Despite having once been his temple, there wasn't much red or white left in the ruins. Only the mural made by Salaana. He had no compunction about destroying it to take down Guleum, but what could he do? Make manacles so that they were both bound?

But making white manacles would take time and Guleum could destroy red ones. Plus, although Karana was reluctant to lose Guleum after having spent a week trying to find him, Guleum might very well teleport away. He seemed to have realized that Karana didn't have much to offer about reincarnation.

Maybe Karana couldn't deal with this.

He could teleport to the White Mountain. Guleum's orange manacles would be gone with a blink from Jin. Bai could find Guleum again and undoubtedly deal with him in minutes.

Though he had said that Karana and Chika had to produce Guleum themselves as the price for resurrecting Akemi.

He deserved this. He had failed to protect An Ning and his nieces from the cult, so now he had to lie in the dirt at Guleum's whim.

He had to overpower Guleum himself! But how?

Two sets of feet, one in black cloth boots and the other in indigo sandals, suddenly appeared so close to Karana's face that it was a wonder they didn't step on his nose. He jerked his eyes up in surprise.

An Ning smiled down at him like he was the best sight

she'd ever had; Chika eyed him like he'd forgotten to put on pants.

Karana struggled to look past them to see Guleum, but the skirts of their robes blocked his view. Of course, there wasn't shouting and fire everywhere, so maybe—

"What cursed fate do you have to come here?" asked Guleum. An Ning and Chika each spun to face his voice, conveniently parting so that Karana had an unimpeded view of a flaming red sword that looked ridiculously like his own. (It wasn't though—it was too thin and had rubies, of all things, set in the hilt).

Guleum raised his sword to strike An Ning.

Karana pressed it against his throat.

Yes, he pressed Guleum's sword against Guleum's throat through will alone.

And Guleum's hand was still wrapped on the hilt, but he couldn't move it because Karana was using the blood in his body to hold him still. He hadn't known he could do that.

He probably couldn't for long.

So curse pride—it had never done him any good anyway.

Unfortunately, he couldn't teleport Guleum without touching him. So he dragged Guleum across the room by his blood, even as he rolled forward into An Ning and Chika's ankles.

He teleported all four of them to the White Mountain.

He'd beg Bai before he let anyone hurt An Ning ever again.

The Soul's House

AN NING steadied herself against a painted rock wall as they came out of between. She blinked at the bright orange, oversized lily, trying to figure out where Karana had brought them.

"Help," Karana growled from the floor, and An Ning jerked her head to find him still bound by orange chains.

She opened her mouth to ask how she could help, when the chains flaked apart, leaving a pile of orange chicken feathers behind as Karana leapt to his feet.

She had barely processed this when an angry roar pulled

her attention to the left, and she found the man who'd charged them—Karana's brother Guleum—bound by chains of his own. These were a silver so light they seemed to glow.

An unfamiliar, heavily pregnant woman was stepping toward him.

The Threefold Goddess, An Ning realized.

"Gu?" the goddess asked. "Is that you? I—"

A wad of spit hit the goddess on the cheek.

Her golden eyes widened, and An Ning's heart ached for the woman. It seemed a sin that anyone should spit at such a beautiful, innocent being.

And the Knowing God agreed with her—he backhanded Guleum, sending him tumbling to the ground.

Except the floor, which was a coarse white stone, moved to meet him. It made a chair, but a chair with shackles, and a gag wrapped itself around Guleum's mouth.

Guleum twisted and contorted.

"Don't hurt yourself!" pleaded the Threefold Goddess. "I can't let you teleport away and—"

Flames, orange and red, shot from Guleum's fingers.

They were instantly extinguished, but the Threefold Goddess burst into tears. An Ning realized that the goddess had not been hurt; she was overcome by the stress of the situation. The Knowing God was too busy coating Guleum with stone to soothe his wife, but she was crying so hard that

An Ning feared for her health. Was it alright for the baby to be shaking like that?

Although she felt rather overwhelmed herself, An Ning stepped forward to fold the goddess into a hug.

She wiped the spit from the woman's cheek with her sleeve and promised, "It will be alright." She then flushed, realizing her words were hasty. Guleum was the Threefold Goddess's relative—he had committed heinous crimes, and now it was her duty to execute him and resurrect Akemi.

If An Ning were her, would it be "alright"?

The Threefold Goddess hugged her back briefly and whispered, "Thank you, Peace Bringer." Then the goddess pulled away and addressed her husband. "Bai, I know what he did is horrible—but he's in so much pain! I should have looked harder for him. Maybe if I found him earlier..."

Uncomfortable, An Ning looked at Chika, whose face was mottled with embarrassment again, and then at Karana.

Only Karana wasn't there. Where had he gone?

An Ning looked around their surroundings more carefully and realized they were in a cave. A very nice cave, to be sure, but still a cave, and the room they were in obviously did triple duty as a kitchen, dining room, and study. Through a half-open curtain she could see a wooden bed, and she realized that the two most famous deities in the world lived in a two-room cave.

She remembered the vast Immortal Grounds with its multicolored pavilions and endless bureaucracy.

Well, whatever worked for them.

Where had Karana gone? Not into the bedroom—that left only the other door, which presumably led outside the mountain.

Fate mock her, that was an appealing idea. To escape this room of sorrow and anger for a few minutes...

She hesitated, then squeezed Chika's arm in reassurance and slipped out the door. Chika made a half-hearted attempt to grab her arm, but An Ning murmured, "Karana."

Chika let her go, though she pouted.

An Ning stepped out of the cave into a garden. The air smelled of jasmine and columbine, a heady combination, and she was overwhelmed by color. She immediately understood that this was where the two deities spent most of their time, not the humble cave.

She also spotted Karana, sitting by a small waterfall. She sat down next to him. His eyes slid right, noticing her, but his jaw stayed set. He didn't acknowledge her presence in any other way.

"Hard day? Probably a hard week?"

He shrugged. "I'm sorry."

"What for?" asked An Ning.

"I was supposed to have Guleum restrained before you returned from the Underworld."

"Seemed to me that you managed well enough."

He shrugged.

An Ning worried her bottom lip between her teeth, not sure how to comfort him. She felt so close to him right now— closer than they'd ever been in Ningjingcun, but he was more distant than ever. How could she bring them into alignment?

Surely she just needed to reveal their shared past. She began badly though, blurting awkwardly, "How many times have you been in love?"

She felt Karana stiffen beside her, and she was trying to figure out how to erase her words when he said, curtly, "Before we met—nine times."

That answer surprised her; she had truly expected him to say eight. But no matter—in seventeen millennia, he had fallen in love with her eight times. What did it matter if he once loved someone else?

She reached for his hand, but instead of interleaving his fingers with hers, he kept his palm pressed against his leg. His knuckles were raised and rigid.

"I want to show you something," she said with a smile.

Just as she had at the Sea of Souls, when she understood that her soul wasn't the body that housed it, she let her essence shift.

From queen to monk, she shrank and grew, her form slowly sliding from each. She was sure it must seem strange, but it felt so right to her, like knots in her muscles releasing after a long time.

She stopped in Shaanti's body. Her original form. Short and curvy, with long black hair.

She had never kissed Karana in this form, and she wanted to. She was sure he would want to as well. She slid her hand up his arm to his shoulder and leaned forward.

STRAIGHT from his nightmares, An Ning shifted before his eyes into every lover he'd ever had, every lover that he'd failed to protect.

Every lover but one. The one he'd failed the worst. But he couldn't fool himself that wasn't part of her past, too.

She was his petite but regal queen; the soft and reserved hermit. The fierce clan leader and the day-dreaming singer. A mother, a gardener, a daughter, and, at last, a monk.

His monk. His Shaanti.

He didn't want it to be true. He couldn't have set Shaanti on a path of perpetual reincarnation because if his fire brought eternal life...

There was some other explanation. Some unfamiliar magic.

"I don't understand," he said aloud.

She smiled, brilliantly. "When I entered the Sea of Souls, all my memories returned. Karana, you asked me to come back to you, so I did. Your fire tethered my soul to Earth. I reincarnated over and over, until I eventually ascended to immortality in Xiling."

Guleum's story was true. Karana's wish to save those he killed had manifested this paradox.

The reason the cult persisted, rose over and over again, was he, Karana, had truly granted never-ending life to the worst narcissists, rapists, and murderers that he had ever encountered.

To those who deserved death, he had granted eternity.

No. No. It can't be true.

An Ning said her memories returned in the Sea of Souls. Maybe his lovers had simply found her there. Not her memories at all, just memories that she had gathered.

These weren't her forms; they were dead women who had been drawn to her.

He would go to the sea himself and prove it.

KARANA'S face shifted even as An Ning leaned forward. When she answered his query, confusion turned to horror and hatred. And then, like he had a few weeks ago, after she had kicked him, Karana disappeared.

An Ning froze, her hand suspended in the air where it had been resting on his shoulder.

What happened? How had she driven him away?

She knew there was something fraught between them—some unresolved tension from before they went on their separate quests. But she had thought their history would wipe all of that away.

Slowly she lowered her hand, and then leaned forward to look at the water.

Black eyes, not so different from the ones she'd had for the past three thousand years, looked back. Her face was as dark as Karana's own; her lips were wider, plumper. Had this face somehow offended him?

But she remembered how, in his youth, he had watched her with open admiration. The tenderness as he had pressed his lips against her lids as she lay dying.

To this day, he painted his lips black, as they had become in that moment! Didn't that mean he cared about her?

An Ning briefly wondered if her shapeshifting had disturbed him. There were beings who'd be uncomfortable partnering someone who was roughly three-quarters female and one quarter male.

But she was sure Karana wasn't one of them. She'd be hard-pressed to find someone who had embraced a greater sense of individuality, completely disregarding other beings' expectations of gender and behavior. She had worried, before her memories returned, that he might not have been truthful when he claimed to find her attractive regardless of her physical form, but after remembering how he made love to her when the beauty of her youth was long gone, she now believed it.

Her memories didn't lie.

Except for maybe the ones she was still missing.

An Ning thought again about Karana's claim to have loved nine beings. What if that ninth being *was* her? The mortal woman from Xiling.

Something terrible had happened then; why else would Karana have burned Xiling?

Was his hatred for that being so great that revealing herself to be all of his lovers contaminated those past loves as well?

She had to know what happened in Xiling.

She sat in silence and fought tears. When she judged that she had defeated them, she rose and returned to the cave. Her stride was shaky, but no one was there to see anyway.

When she re-entered the all-purpose room, not much had changed. The wicked Guleum was still bound to the floor, Chika had caved in on herself in discomfort, and the Threefold Goddess was crying again.

But when the goddess's eyes fell on An Ning, they widened in surprise and the tears halted. "Who are you?"

An Ning was taken aback. She knew she wasn't an important deity and obviously there was a lot going on, but they had just hugged! The goddess had addressed her by her title!

"I am An Ning," she said clearly and politely, "called the Peace-Bringer."

"You are? But—I thought... You can change your form? Bai said that you wanted me to make your body female, but..."

An Ning pressed her hands to her cheeks. She had forgotten that she was presenting herself as Shaanti!

"Oh! I—well, I discovered that my form really is my choice, as your husband said. This was what I looked like in my first life. I thought Karana would be happy to see it, but..."

Seeking a familiar face, An Ning twisted to look at Chika. Her face remained mottled, but she was also smirking. An Ning knew her disciple well enough to realize that she felt they had pulled one over on the Knowing God.

"So reincarnation is possible," he mused now. "You pass through the Sea of Souls every time you die, washing away your memories, but remain the same soul. And you haven't always been a mortal being, have you?"

An Ning found herself interrogated by the Knowing God for the next few hours—well, it felt like an interrogation, but she thought he answered more questions than she did. It was rather surreal, especially when he suggested they go to the garden—leaving Guleum alone in the cave. An Ning almost objected, but she saw how he looked at his wife when he made the suggestion.

She realized the Knowing God might not be as fascinated by reincarnation as he was acting. He wanted to let his wife adjust to the idea of executing Guleum.

So An Ning obliged and squeezed Chika's hand when the girl tried to interject.

The Threefold Goddess clearly felt certain behavior was expected of a hostess, and she became quite calm once they were outside. She settled them into chairs An Ning hadn't noticed earlier (maybe they really hadn't been there? These beings seemed to make magical artifacts as easily as she breathed).

The Threefold Goddess brewed jasmine tea right there in the garden, all while smoothly redirecting the Knowing God's more intrusive questions. An Ning was awed by and envious of their ease with each other—although she had experienced something similar in previous lives, it seemed the true partnership she wanted might be denied to her.

And then the Threefold Goddess said, "Wait, your name is An Ning? And you are from Xiling? So you are the woman that Karana avenged? But—you didn't die after all! How wonderful! Where is Karana anyway? You said he wasn't pleased?"

"No, he wasn't pleased. He left—but wait—the woman he avenged? What do you mean?"

"I—" The Goddess was flustered, but she cleared her throat and said, "Uncle Karana told me that he fell in love with a mortal in Xiling. But she was, um, brutally murdered. So he burned the city to punish the crime."

"But then—wasn't he mad at me?"

"Mad at *you*? No, never!" The Threefold Goddess's perfect cherry lips quirked softly at the corners. "How could he be mad at you, the love of his life?" She sighed. "It's a terribly romantic story, isn't it?"

"I thought so," admitted An Ning, "but I don't think Karana agrees. There must be something I am forgetting. If only I could remember what happened in Xiling myself."

"What about Daichin's branch?" suggested Chika.

An Ning frowned. "His branch?" If that was a euphemism...

"You know, the one he cut in the Underworld? You said that the memory it recalled was strange."

"Oh, yes, the topaz branch! You are right, Chika! I think that must have been a mortal memory." An Ning stood in her excitement. "If I can find Daichin—"

"That isn't necessary," said the Knowing God. "If you are referring to the Crystal Forest, I have a flute made of the same material. If you would wait a few minutes..."

Even as he spoke, he passed through what looked like a solid stone side of the mountain.

The Threefold Goddess looked at An Ning, clearly unphased by this remarkable feat. "It will take him a little time—there's quite a few artifacts to dig through."

So maybe the cave wasn't as small as it looked.

The Threefold Goddess continued, "Are you sure you want to remember? I—I read Karana's thoughts when he told me... I'm sorry, sometimes I have nightmares from that. You might be traumatized."

An Ning slowly sat down again. "This might sound strange, but I think I already am. Sometimes I remember... I've always been afraid of intimacy. Of men. I'm sure some people would want to forget, but I think that I need to remember to move on."

The Threefold Goddess nodded. "I admire your courage."

THE gentle blue waves lapped against Karana's face as he

drifted aimlessly in the Sea of Souls.

They really weren't here. That annoying sixth sense—the one that let him pinpoint the exact spot Pyeonghwa had died and understand that An Ning was a woman regardless of the form she wore—was telling him that they weren't here.

Not one of the cultists that he had incinerated in the past few weeks was in the Sea of Souls. None of the people he had burned over a score of millennia had stayed in the sea to reflect on their sins. Instead, his wish for them to live, to try again, had been fulfilled. Like Shaanti, he had tethered those souls to Earth—maybe to *him*—so that they reincarnated every time they died. He hadn't made them immortals, but he had granted them eternal life.

Guleum was the one that was right; Karana was the one that was delusional. Denying reality to make his own existence more bearable.

Karana had despaired that the only way he could help was to harm, but now it seemed that he couldn't even do that right.

The one thing he had thought he could do, the one thing he had been good at, executing selfish pricks that hurt the world—well, he'd failed.

He was no use to anyone.

3,000 years ago

AN NING lay in the intricately carved bed, a diaphanous red canopy hanging overhead, still turning the world a merry red thanks to the many candles that were burning in her bridal chamber.

Next to her, her new husband lay in quiescent satisfaction, though An Ning thought he did not yet sleep.

She hated him.

And she hated herself.

She had been passive, submissive, as she had been instructed, while he used her body for his pleasure.

It had been fairly brief, very uncomfortable, and in utter contrast to everything that had passed between Karana and her.

She was so upset that she had agreed to this, that she had gone along with this marriage to please her father! She couldn't bear to do this every night for the rest of her life, she just couldn't!

And so she said so aloud.

She, for the first time in her seventeen-odd years, felt rebellious and angry, and because hating herself and her decisions was uncomfortable, she released her wrath on her husband.

She nitpicked over his bedroom skills, a scathing analysis that turned his cheeks red with fury and embarrassment.

He grabbed her wrist.

"And what fate-curse brings me a bride that knows such things?" he hissed at her.

"One who slept with a god!" she told him.

His face reddened. "A god, you call him? You whore!"

He threw her from the bed and punched her in the face.

Her cheek throbbed; no one had ever hurt her like that. An Ning was suddenly very, very scared. She realized that her husband didn't realize she meant a literal god—instead, he had viewed the epithet as an insult to his own manhood. She tried to apologize. To explain. He didn't listen.

He dragged her by her hair to a storage room near the back of the mansion.

He locked her there, and An Ning breathed easier.

Their marriage would be set aside; her reputation would be ruined, but she would escape this future that she couldn't tolerate.

Karana would come for her, she was sure. And somehow it would all work out.

Except it didn't.

Present Day

AFTER not having been here for years, it was strange that Karana had come back again, but as soon as he had emerged on Earth, he had teleported directly to his mother's grave.

Though the sun had set and it was too dark to see color, Karana knew exactly what he was looking at. He touched the stone gently, his fingers tracing the delicate white swirls surrounded by deep red. It was cool and hard to his touch; almost soothing.

Well, it probably was soothing, but Karana was in no mood to be soothed.

"I always despised you for killing yourself," he told his mother. It was a nonsensical thing to do; he could probably have communed with his mother's soul, but he hadn't cared to seek it out in the Sea of Souls. He didn't want to hear what she had to say for herself; he just wanted to unburden himself.

"I really, really hated it. But right now, I feel like maybe you knew something I'm learning. If—if you are bad for the world, is the best thing you can do to exit it?"

Karana hadn't expected an answer, but he got one anyway.

"No. The best thing you can do is change."

AN NING was gasping for breath as tears streamed down her face.

Oh, she had been wrong. She hadn't needed to remember any of that. She didn't want to face it.

Slowly her breathing settled, and she realized Chika was holding one of her hands and the Threefold Goddess the other.

She was alright. She was a god.

All of those men had died a long time ago.

She had remembered a lot of wretchedness in the Sea of Souls. Judgments, violence, and the not-quite-rape-but-downright-unpleasant marital relations with her husband at the Bandoan court. For fate's sake, she had remembered being murdered four different times in four different ways!

She had overcome all of those memories. She would overcome this one, too.

It might not have been possible for her as she had been—a seventeen-year-old girl who had led a sheltered life—but she was a god with the experiences of eight different mortal lives. She squeezed the hands in hers and looked at the Knowing God. His hands no longer touched the magnificent topaz flute that had brought horror to An Ning.

Not just horror, she realized slowly.

She also remembered growing up in Xiling, the spoiled daughter of a wealthy merchant. She remembered the rules of etiquette that had given her such a clear sense of male and female.

Truth be told, although she had known girls who had chafed at those rules, who had dressed as boys to sneak out of their homes, An Ning hadn't minded them so much. She had fit well into the definition of "feminine" that her family had taught. She had been quiet; she liked pretty things. She was eager to please, to make life easier for others. It was only now, when she also had the memory of Heiwa's strength and Santiphaph's audacity that she found the definition ridiculous and limiting.

Even if she still liked pretty things and taking care of others.

And she remembered falling in love with Karana. The overwhelming delight they had found with each other, though she'd been ludicrously young and naïve.

"The Threefold Goddess is right. Karana never hated me."

She remembered his tears; his promise to destroy everything.

"He hated himself," she murmured.

Unable to catch the inaudible words, Chika said, "What?"

An Ning shook her head.

She still felt a bit shaken, but she was going to move on. To heal rather than forget.

And she was going to do it with Karana. He'd been avoiding her ever since he had realized who she'd been. He probably blamed himself for her rape—well, he wasn't perfectly blameless. He was an old and powerful god; he could have handled the situation better.

But he wasn't perfect—he was the being she loved.

The being she knew almost as well as herself. She

remembered the way he had cried when she died, and how he always begged fate to bring her back to him.

She had to go to him now.

"I will fetch Karana back," An Ning announced. "Chika, I supposed you are waiting for the resurrection—" she bit her lip.

The Threefold Goddess hadn't yet said she would do it.

But there was a new serenity on the goddess's face.

"The resurrection will wait for Karana," the goddess declared. "I thought it over while you were remembering. If he wants to restore your disciple, he will have to burn Guleum himself."

An Ning was confused. "But why?" Didn't the Goddess understand how hurting others was akin to hurting himself for Karana?

"Because," said the Goddess, "then Guleum can have a chance at redemption. An opportunity to start again. Like you did."

An Ning's eyes widened. She looked at Chika and the Knowing God.

She saw resignation on their faces rather than the peace that was in the Threefold Goddess, but neither objected.

In fact, the Knowing God said, "Go."

And, though it took most of her power, An Ning followed the hair wrapped around her wrist to Karana.

22

The God of Rebirth

AN NING came out of between in an unfamiliar place. Dark sky surrounded her, white stars the only specks of light. She must have come many leagues east of the mountains.

She peered through the darkness but saw nothing but rough shapes and blurry mounds. But Karana must be nearby, since last time they had followed Karana's hair to him, she and Chika had practically landed on his nose.

Suddenly, Karana spoke. "I always despised you for killing yourself."

An Ning was confused—she had never committed suicide, not in all her lives, though she supposed her defeat as the mortal An Ning had been close. Still, it had been the beating that killed her.

"I really, really hated it," Karana went on, and she realized he wasn't speaking to her. Who else was standing in the darkness? "But right now, I feel like maybe you knew something I'm learning. If—if you are bad for the world, is the best thing you can do to exit it?"

What nonsense! Whomever he was talking to should be slapped for not objecting earlier.

"No," declared An Ning. "The best thing you can do is change."

A block directly in front of her shifted, and then fire cast a blood-red glow over the scene. Karana himself looked haggard, his thin cheeks edging into hollow and his hair a damp tangle around his shoulders. An Ning looked past him but saw nothing but overgrown brush and a large stone.

To whom had he been talking?

Puzzled, An Ning refocused on Karana. She wanted to hug him, but, afraid that would make him run again, she settled for wrapping her arms around herself.

"Why did you leave earlier?" she asked. "Who were you talking to?"

He didn't answer, and, in the face of his silence, her insecurities echoed in her mind. Even though she was nearly certain it was self-disgust she had seen in his eyes when he teleported away, An Ning asked, "Does my shifting bother you? It's unusual. Freakish, even."

She thought Karana's eyes widened, though the flickering firelight made it hard to be certain.

"No, it's not that at all. It's not freakish. It's right. It's natural. And I'm happy for you. Your reincarnation might be the only good thing I've accomplished in my life. I'm—I'm glad you found yourself. That you are whole."

An Ning took a tentative step closer. "Offhand, I can think

of at least fifty good things you've done."

"Can you?" said Karana, his voice wistful and soft. "That is because I have always shown you the best side of myself. Hidden my failures."

An Ning considered his words. "Why don't you tell me about your failures then?"

Even in the weak red light, she saw him flinch. She thought he might run again, but instead he spoke.

"Where to start? At Xiling, when I burned the cultists who kidnapped you. I thought I was punishing them, but instead I fulfilled their deepest dreams instead."

"I don't understand," admitted An Ning.

"But you're the one who told me."

An Ning shook her head, completely lost.

"They were right all along. My fire brings rebirth, not death."

An Ning remembered the slow chant of the cultists.

> *The immortal blaze will save us*
> *From drowning in the Sea of Souls.*
> *Seared by the gaze of Destruction,*
> *We can see the infinite life.*

They were right? Yes, Karana had given her the gift of rebirth but...

"I'm not the only being you set on a cycle of reincarnation," An Ning said aloud. "The other monks—the ones who killed me. Everyone that you've burned over the millennia? Surely not..."

"I searched the Sea of Souls," said Karana. "No one I burned was in there."

If An Ning hadn't seen the sea for herself, she might have

let this pass unchallenged. As it was, "How could you know that? The Sea is immense—"

"It's vast, yes, but my mother's magic gives me a glimpse into the essence of things like Bai's. I'm certain, An Ning. All of them—the worst scum I've encountered in my life—were reborn. That's why the Sundered Cult never dies. They aren't the ones denying reality after all—it was me all along."

"That's simply untrue." Karana started to argue, but An Ning held up a hand. "So what if your fire brings rebirth? The cultists still made up the nonsense of killing women and themselves. That has no basis."

"It's wrong, but it's my fault," Karana whispered. "The legend started after my first monks returned to Earth and recovered their memories from the Sea of Souls. And then, Guleum believed your death was what caused the reincarnation. He murdered so many women trying to replicate it..."

An Ning tsked, a little impatient with him. "So you're going to blame yourself for a selfish prick," she couldn't believe she said that word, "murdering people? That was his choice. Sure, maybe bad things had happened to him, but you know what? Bad things have happened to you. To me. We don't go around twisting reality to suit ourselves, hurting people to try to make our lives better. They are the ones who were delusional and used their delusions as an excuse to inflict death and horror."

"I—yes, but I should have realized—"

"Yes," agreed An Ning abruptly, shocking Karana into silence. "You should have. I told you before, you shouldn't have abandoned them." She shrugged. "But Karana, don't you see? You have a second chance. And so do they. A chance you gave them."

KARANA had been avoiding Shaanti's—An Ning's—eyes, for he was afraid of seeing disappointment in them, but he glanced at them now.

If it was anyone else, he'd be sure they were mocking him. But An Ning would never tease about something as important as this. "I don't follow."

Was there even anything to follow? An Ning was undoubtedly trying to comfort him, whether or not there was actually any bright side to this situation.

An Ning spoke with confidence though. "I'm saying that what you always wished for—it's been true all along." She took several steps toward him, though she stopped too far away to touch.

"And what have I always wished for?" His question came out as a whine, and Karana felt vaguely embarrassed, but he let it stand.

Before his eyes, An Ning shifted again, into the Maoyan queen Santiphaph.

"You once told me that you hated being the God of Destruction. That you wanted to create, to redeem, rather than destroy."

Karana remembered. It had been in the third year of her reign, when a group of nobles had tried to plan a coup. He had ended up annihilating them and their armies. A few hundred beings dead by his hand—he had felt awful. Santiphaph—An Ning—had held him as he cried, and he had confessed his secret wish.

"How does granting the condemned reincarnation accomplish that?"

"Because you are giving them a chance to be better!"

He snorted and turned away from her. "I wish I could believe that, but it seems clear that they follow the same violent path every time."

"No," said An Ning. "For one, you don't know whether current cultists are those who've been reborn. It's a continuous cycle, you know—so I doubt they are mortals every time. They might have reincarnated as plants or animals. And—look at my lives. They were so different!"

Karana shook his head. "You were always you. Gentle and kind."

"I was always me, but I led vastly different lives," corrected An Ning. "As a queen, I never let anyone tell me what to do. I made my own rules. I challenged history. Because I had been raised to do so—my father had taught me what I needed to run a country. Compared to my last life—I daresay all my other incarnations would have cringed to meet An Ning! Even now I am mortified by my extreme passivity and subservience! The way we are raised, what we are taught, matters!"

Karana stiffened, not fully hearing what she was saying, except for one detail.

"You remembered your life as a mortal? In—in Xiling?" His voice quavered; *he* was quavering. He tried to block the images that came to him. Her bloodied and bruised face. The way she had begged for it all to end...

"I'm so sorry," he whispered and turned away from her, back to his mother's grave. "I failed you..."

And then her arms slid around his waist. He was surprised

to realize she was no longer in Santiphaph's body though—she was taller, and he could feel the muscles of her chest pressed against his back. He looked at the pale hands that now held his own.

It was the form he had loved for the past thirty years.

"You didn't fail me," An Ning said. "You could never have conceived of what would happen because you are too kind and good. I couldn't have conceived of it—if I had, I would never have taunted him."

"Taunted who?"

An Ning sighed and pressed her face against Karana's back.

"My husband. I was angry and upset about the marriage. I felt uncomfortable and unhappy. I realized I had to escape, to return to you. And I was stupid and seventeen, so I taunted him. That's how he realized I wasn't a virgin."

Karana found himself turning in her arms and hugging her back. He was still shaking. "It's still his—taunt or not—no one deserves—you—you—"

She nuzzled his chest. "I know that. If I could do it over again, I would be more cautious, but I know that I'm not to blame. And neither are you."

"An Ning, I thought you had died. You were so badly beaten, and I burned you, but you became an immortal. Doesn't that mean..."

Karana was surprised when An Ning freed a hand to wipe his face. He was crying.

"The first time I died, I lingered too," she said. She stroked a thumb over his lower lip. "I saw you kiss me and burn the other monks. I heard you ask me to come back. Karana, please don't hate your power. It is the greatest gift of my life."

"But An Ning—your husband in Xiling—even he has been reborn. He might be on Earth right now, as a man, hurting others!"

"He might," agreed An Ning. "Or he might be a flower bringing joy or an ox plowing a field or a mother raising her children well. We don't know.

"But," she continued, "if you're so worried about it, there's an easy answer."

"What?"

"Find him. Find all of them. Make sure they are on the right path. Guide them if they're not. It's not like we don't have enough time. Karana, you don't have to be the God of Destruction any longer. You can be the God of Rebirth."

Karana wrapped his hand around her jaw and tilted her face up to his. "You believe that? You really think this is a blessing rather than a curse?"

"Yes," An Ning said. Then she twined her arms behind his neck and kissed him.

"Don't run away from me again," she warned him.

"Never," he agreed. "You always find me anyway."

"That's right." She smirked at him before clearing her throat. "Who were you talking to?"

Karana stiffened, but a moment later, he relaxed.

"My mother's gravestone. She killed herself about ten millennia ago."

An Ning had been so focused on her revelations, that she hadn't completely understood everything she now knew about Karana. But the realization hit like a deluge of rain, and she blurted, "Salaana—your sister—she was imprisoned after the Sun Emperor—your father died. And your other brother died then too. Only you and...and Guleum are left."

She recalled how nonchalantly Karana had declared his intention of finding Guleum and punishing him for Akemi's death. Oh, how that calm must have cost him! How hard he worked, every day, to present to her a calm and loving harbor when he had faced so much anguish in his life.

No wonder he had been horrified to see her past faces. All that pain that he had tried to forget, that he had tried to bury, brought to the forefront with no warning.

"Oh, Karana, I'm so sorry." She hugged him even more tightly.

"You don't have to be sorry, anymore," he said, "because it's going to get better. Together, we will make it better."

"Yes." And then, because she couldn't hide it, "The Threefold Goddess is waiting for your return. She wants you to burn Guleum so that he will reincarnate like I did."

"GIVE Guleum a second chance?" Karana echoed. "But—yes, but—no! Oh, An Ning, he doesn't deserve it. The things he has done..." Karana thought of his stepmother, of Akemi, of countless mortal women and none too few immortals either.

He had shifted the blame for those deaths off of himself for so long, but now they felt like his as well. Why would he give Gu, their murderer, a second chance?

"I don't know if I *can*."

"What do you mean?" asked An Ning.

"With you—I truly wanted you to live, more desperately

than I have wanted anything maybe. Maybe as desperately as you yearned for life in Xiling, to elevate yourself to immortality. I think I matched that yearning when you died as Shaanti. And then, I sort of applied that yearning to everyone else. All these years, I've recalled that feeling whenever I burned someone and prayed for redemption.

"But, now that I *know*... I am not sure I can summon that desperation again. I am afraid of it."

"It's a frightening power," mused An Ning. "I can't really understand it. I mean, I make rice and food, and not much beyond that. But there is someone who could."

"Who?" asked Karana, though he thought he already knew the answer.

"Your niece. The Threefold Goddess. She can bring beings back to life, can't she? It's rather similar."

Karana dropped a kiss on An Ning's black locks. "Alright. Are you ready to go?"

An Ning smiled up at him, and he moved them between.

Jin was waiting for them in the garden when they arrived. She was lounging on a chair that resembled a massive peacock, but she looked far from relaxed.

She sat up when she saw them, and Karana let An Ning slide away.

This was a conversation for Jin and him.

Karana held his arm out to Jin, and she took it. Briefly, she pressed her head against his arm, and it reminded him of when she was a child, living in her grandmother's caravan.

She had always been so sad, and Karana had known why. She had yearned for her family, but only he had visited her. At that time, he had thought she was his baby sister—he hadn't been aware of the affair between his elder brother and their stepmother—and he had lavished affection and care on her, trying to redeem himself for killing her mother's other baby.

"You're upset about Gu?" he asked.

"Yes. And all the others." It was a strange thing to say, but Karana knew exactly what she meant. Didn't he feel the loss as keenly as Jin, though he tried to hide it? The emptiness where their family members should be?

"I'm sorry, Jin. I wish I could make it up to you."

"What," laughed Jin, "be my father and brother and grandfather all in one?" Then her open face settled in long lines. "Does Gu have to die, Karana? He was our baby brother—don't we bear responsibility for his crimes?"

Karana didn't need his red magic to feel her regret.

"I tried to find him," she added. "Even though his mother said that she wanted to be forgotten. I went everywhere I could think off. But he wasn't there."

"It's I who needed to look for him, Jin. He was with the Sundered Cult, the Cult of Alag Karana. They give their followers mortal dreams—the dreams that should come to me, but that I ignored. He..."

He trailed off, for Jin had paled.

"Xiao told me that Gu was addicted to dreams," she admitted. "I wanted to believe that it was just Salaana..."

And now it was her turn to drop a painful line of thought.

"I have gone to see her, you know. I keep trying."

Karana could imagine the scene. Wrath was their family's besetting sin, and Salaana never forgot a grudge for all of time.

"Maybe you should let it go, Jin," he told her.

"And maybe you have let go too much!" she snapped. Then she flushed. "It's just, I think you should visit her, Karana. She misses you. She loves you."

"What, did she accuse you of stealing me?" Karana meant the words to be mocking, but they came out sincere.

Jin nodded.

Karana rubbed his forehead. "I'll try visiting again, but she turned me away last time."

"Several hundred years ago?" Jin mocked.

"Exactly," grinned Karana, though it wasn't funny. He tapped her on the forehead. "You're avoiding the issue at hand."

"Yes." She cleared her throat. "You said Gu was feeling the cult's dreams. But then, are his actions his fault? Can't he be forgiven? I could imprison him like Salaana."

"Jin, he killed Teodolda."

Jin recoiled, as if Karana had confessed to the murder himself. "What?"

"He burned her, trying to figure out the trick to reincarnation. He thought I had sacrificed An Ning, so he sacrificed her. He's irredeemable."

"You just want me to bring back An Ning's disciple. The Sea Dragon's granddaughter."

"No," Karana said. "She was a nice child, but I wouldn't bring her back to live out a mortal life. I don't mind using Guleum's life for the purpose, if we are taking it anyway, but I truly believe that Guleum is too far gone and too powerful to be allowed to live."

Jin tried one last argument. "We forgave him for cursing Papa because Salaana admitted she had manipulated him with dreams. Maybe..." Jin still called Karana's father "papa," for she had believed him that for five thousand years.

"Jin, it's different. He was a child then, now he's an adult. As much as the cult poisoned him, he also poisoned the cult. He taught them to sacrifice living beings. You could feel his anger when we arrived. It's too much."

She leaned her head against his arm again, but this time Karana felt it grow damp. She was crying. Good thing he didn't cry as easily as she did, or he wouldn't be able to wear kohl.

"Okay," she said. "But won't you burn him, Karana? So that he can be born to a new family? One that won't neglect him, and he can be the person he should have been?"

"Oh, Jin," he groaned. He thought of what An Ning said. If he set Gu on the path to reincarnation, he'd be one more being that Karana would have to track. To ensure that he was redeemed.

The weight of that was almost too much. But maybe Karana needed that—he needed so much weight that he was nearly crushed beneath it because that was the only way to earn his own redemption.

"I will burn Guleum."

AN NING felt quite small as she hovered in the corner, watching the Threefold Goddess and the Knowing God build a body that matched Chika's memories.

"Yes," Chika breathed. "It's Akemi. It's Akemi exactly." She held the orange and blue vessel that contained Akemi's soul next to the body. "See, love? You're going to live again."

The Threefold Goddess set a hand over the ornament. "You know she is doing this for you, don't you?" she asked Chika, and An Ning froze. She had suspected as much, but to hear it said so baldly!

"She is willing," the Threefold Goddess went on, "but I worry that you will come to regret it, and it can never be undone."

"Why would I regret having my best friend back?" scoffed Chika.

"She'll be mortal. She will forget what it was to live as the Sea Dragon's granddaughter," mused the Knowing God.

"But she'll still be Akemi," insisted Chika. "She will still like to play pranks and be bold and laugh. We will make new memories together.

Jin shrugged, then looked at Karana. "It's your turn."

Karana approached Guleum, still chained to the stone chair, and kissed his forehead once, though Guleum's eyes spit fire— literal fire, that singed Karana's hair.

And then he was ablaze.

A moment later, Akemi sat up with a gasp. She looked at Chika; they hugged and laughed and cried.

She looked at An Ning, and her face broke into a smile. "Sensei, you look beautiful."

An Ning was surprised, for she wore the male form that Akemi was familiar with. But then she smiled, too—she did look beautiful.

SOME things are easier said than done, and tracking down a few thousand reincarnated beings was one of them.

An Ning wasn't troubled by the slow progress, though Karana obviously was. Especially whenever they found a reincarnated sinner who had fulfilled his worst fears, for many of them had indeed joined the cult. An Ning theorized that Karana had tied these beings to himself and not just to Earth, which is why the cult appealed to them.

But for every failure, there were three successes. Beings who were living perfectly unobjectionable lives or ones of great kindness and utility.

Regardless of what they were or how they were living, Karana wanted to keep track of them all. At first, this seemed an impossible task, but An Ning had an idea that made it manageable.

"Karana," she said as they sat down to breakfast one morning with their disciples and monks, "Can you find this hair the same way I can use it to find you?"

Karana stopped filling bowls with Xia's thick black rice congee to look at An Ning's wrist. His hand wrapped around it, hiding the red hair that now resembled a jasper bracelet. "Yes," he agreed and smiled.

"Why don't you tie a hair around the souls who are reincarnating?"

Chika snorted. "Sensei, do you want to make Uncle bald so

that he can't cheat on you?"

"He doesn't need one hair per soul," Miho pointed out. "He could stretch one to any length he needed."

Karana's fingers turned An Ning's bracelet slowly.

"That could work. That will work. An Ning, have I mentioned how much I love you?"

An Ning smiled. "It could bear mentioning again."

However, her idea wasn't enough to soothe Karana's biggest worry.

"I still haven't found Guleum's soul," he lamented, as they lay in bed that night.

"Perhaps he's still in a womb," An Ning suggested. "You weren't able to identify the others until after they were born."

"It's been over nine months," Karana pointed out.

She stroked his red hair back from his temples. "Maybe he's becoming an animal with a longer gestation time. Or— you said you weren't confident that it worked."

"I wasn't, but I've searched the Sea of Souls at least five times now. He's not there. He's not anywhere!"

An Ning leaned forward and kissed him.

"You'll find him eventually," she promised.

"EMBER! Blue! Get back here!" The Bulgae were making off with two of the chickens that had been roasting for dinner. The two firedogs continued cheerfully on their way, guilt-free. If An Ning were the one scolding them, Karana was sure they'd both have come back with their tails between their legs.

Karana glanced at the five chickens still roasting over the

fire and sighed. Today was the opening of the Temple of Rebirth and Inner Peace—they'd promised dinner to everyone, and now they were going to be short two chickens. He could get two more, but they wouldn't finish cooking in time. Maybe it would be faster to teleport to Maoyi or Daedo and buy chicken from one of the restaurants there.

"They stole the chicken?" called Chika.

Karana turned to see her and Miho running up—Miho pointed at the disappearing Bulgae, and Karana nodded. Miho kept running to fetch them home, but Chika stopped by his side. "I'm sorry, I accidentally let the Bulgae get out. Why don't I get more meat?"

Karana turned to her and shuffled his feet. He wasn't quite sure where the two of them stood—as far as he knew, she still hadn't forgiven him for not being home when they went after the cult. Yes, Akemi had been resurrected, but already she was losing her memories.

"You don't have to. I can..."

"Don't be silly," said Chika. "I'm happy to." She bit her lip. "Uncle Karana, I'm sorry. What you and sensei have been doing these past few weeks—I should never have accused you of evading your responsibilities."

"I'm grateful that you did," Karana said. It was strange how an immortal being could stay stagnant for a thousand years, and then suddenly mature in just a few weeks. Looking at Chika now, even though she was still short and slim enough to be mistaken for a child, he realized she was ready for her adulthood ceremony. Though they'd wait another twenty years so that it aligned with her four thousandth birthday. "I was neglecting my responsibilities. I thought I couldn't do this, so

I didn't dare try, but now..." He shrugged. "Instead of a Sundered Cult, we hope to create temples that offer second chances to those who want them."

"I was wondering—will you continue to grant rebirth only to those you execute? What if someone petitions you? Or—?"

Karana snorted and cut her off. "I haven't figured out all the answers yet. I also feel odd that executions result in rebirth—perhaps it's possible to end the cycle of reincarnation once a soul has been redeemed. But we don't have time to discuss this now. Or have you forgotten about the chicken?"

"Oh! Yes! Right away—don't worry, I'll be back before dinner!" And Chika disappeared.

A few minutes later, Miho came back, leading both Ember and Blue by newly made indigo leashes. It was a lot easier to catch Bulgae with leashes that flew themselves around their necks.

"Sorry, about that, Uncle Karana," said Miho. "Sensei wants you to join her in the temple—two mortals want to pledge themselves to the God of Rebirth."

"But the chicken—"

"Xia was on her way when I left—I'll stay until she comes."

"Alright," agreed Karana, and he headed for the temple.

The temple was a deep red stone—an auspicious color, even after the Sun Emperor's passing—and black and white roses filled the gardens in front. Karana found the scent strong but soothing—hopefully petitioners would feel the same way.

As soon as he passed through the red pillars that framed the door, he spotted An Ning. She looked like the Peace Bringer that the villagers knew. Karana had initially worried that she felt obliged to present herself as male, but she insisted that wasn't the case. It was that she felt like a woman, or more precisely, like herself, regardless of the form she adopted.

She said this body was a part of her now, and it was the one that felt the most natural in Ningjingcun.

"An Ning?" he said as he approached. She turned to him and smiled.

Karana took a deep breath. This path he and she had chosen would not always be easy, but that was okay because they had chosen it together.

The Courage of Love

300 years later

As if the sky itself were subject to the whims of Karana's niece and nephew-by-marriage, the sun was a rich red on the horizon, spreading into a pale gold and pure cerulean, while startlingly white clouds clustered around the Immortal Grounds.

Far less crowded than the last time he and An Ning had been here, the air was redolent with floral sweetness, and flowers bloomed everywhere, with no regard to season. Karana supposed that the Koch-ssi, an immortal creature that seemed to be made of flowers itself, had been prevailed upon to help with decorations.

An Ning's hand tightened on Karana's arm, but in excitement rather than nerves. Over the last few centuries, she had grown accustomed to mingling with the most famous deities of the world, and Karana knew that she was thrilled to be an aunt.

Technically, she had Jin as well as a few dozen nieces and nephews through his connection to the Sea Clan, but she kept saying that Jin's baby was different—because it *would* be a baby rather than an immortal who might look younger than An Ning but had been alive for more millennia.

"Oh, Karana, it's so beautiful!"

She looked almost exactly the way she had in the royal hall of Maoyi when he had arrived for her coronation.

"Yes," he agreed, keeping his gaze fixedly on her.

"Oh, stop that," she laughed. "You can only use that indirect compliment so many times before it becomes trite."

Karana widened his eyes and furrowed his brow. "Already bored of me, my love?"

She gently tapped his chest. "You know I'm not!"

He attempted to look even more pathetic and hid his mouth behind an oversized crimson fan. "Then where's my compliment?"

"I already told you how handsome you look! As if you needed me to—you are well aware of the impression you make!"

An Ning seized his hand so that the fan sheltered both of them. She planted a kiss on his cheek. "You are the handsomest being in the world."

"You only say that because you haven't met the Love God yet," Karana bemoaned.

She laughed. "Then I will meet him tonight and repeat the compliment to you in the morning!"

Karana smirked. "Your confidence in me is moving."

Her dark eyes became briefly solemn. She whispered, "No one will ever outshine you in my eyes because I will never love anyone more than I love you."

Karana was glad that his dark cheeks didn't show his flushes. An Ning might say his compliments were trite—and yes, he did tend to rely on the same bag of tricks—but her confessions had yet to lose their power over him.

"I love you, too."

She smiled and moved away, releasing his hand that held the fan. "Now, are we supposed to find seats? Speeches or food first?"

It was speeches and food simultaneously, a sumptuous banquet that had undoubtedly taken multiple days of preparation. Pastries so buttery that they melted in the mouth, and bottle after bottle of sugary grape juice that could only have been provided by Xiao—the Love God himself.

He was also the first one to give a speech; Karana was hardly surprised to learn that Xiao and his "Heart" were helping the new parents host, for Jin and Xiao had more or less grown up together. That did mean there'd be no celebratory wine served, but Karana had no objection. From mortal dreams to wine, he'd never been overly fond of anything that warped a person's sense of reality, and with his ongoing struggle to reform the cult...

Well.

After Xiao welcomed the guests, Bai and Jin appeared, a bundle in Jin's arms, and Bai's around Jin. It was a little much, but Karana thought he'd do the exact same thing if An Ning was holding their child.

Not that that would ever happen. Karana stifled a pang of regret.

"Thank you so much for joining us," said Jin. "We are delighted to introduce our daughter to all of you—Light-catching Lotus. Lian."

Karana didn't quite suppress a groan.

"What does that mean? She has two names?" whispered An Ning.

"No—it was an affectation of my father. My brother was Sunlight Glints on Steel, and my sister was Sunlight's Allure. Jin herself is Sunlight Turns Petals Gold. And then we were all given nicknames because those mouthfuls are too ridiculous for everyday use."

"Oh. What's your name?"

"Sorry?"

"Karana must be a nickname. What's your full name?"

"I think Bai has something else to say—"

The speeches continued, and soon Jin and Bai (and Lian, too, though she was asleep) were in front of Karana and An Ning.

"Oh, she's lovely!" said An Ning.

"Thank you!" Jin's smile rivaled the sun in brightness. "Will you have one soon? Lian needs a playmate, and I don't think Xiao and Nanami will have children."

Karana gaped. How could his usually tactful niece be so unsensitive?

"I hope so, if Karana agrees," said An Ning, not missing a beat. "Things have settled down around the temple, and now that Karana accepted some disciples, we have more time on our hands."

"Oh, I'm so glad to hear that!" said Jin. "You'll both be wonderful parents. Did I ever tell you—"

Cue way too many saccharine anecdotes about how Karana had spoiled her as a child. He would have objected, but An Ning kept casting him approving glances, and her smile was nearly as bright as Jin's.

Bai finally released Jin's shoulder (for a moment) to step closer to Karana.

"I'm impressed, Uncle." He managed to imbue that appellation with so much irony that it was amazing it didn't land with a clang. "You've done excellent work these past few decades."

"It wasn't so you'd approve of me," Karana told him, more annoyed with his own pleasure in Bai's praise than the condescension itself.

"I know," Bai said with a smirk. "That's why I bothered to compliment you. Because you're sincere."

Jin beamed at her husband like he was the cleverest being in the world. Unfortunately, he probably was.

"I have a proposition for you," Bai went on. "For both of you. My school will open soon, and I need teachers."

"It will?" Karana asked skeptically. "The construction still looks half-finished to me."

Bai waved a careless hand. "I was busy helping Jin, but now that Lian is born—"

"You'll have even less time," mused An Ning.

Bai stared at her.

Jin pressed a hand to her mouth to keep in her amusement and met Karana's eyes.

Bai opened his mouth to say something, but Jin pressed the

baby into his arms.

Taking An Ning's hands in her own, Jin beamed, "Thank you for making Karana so happy."

An Ning laughed. "It's easy to do, for he makes me happy, too!"

An Ning's laugh woke the baby. She fluttered one tiny hand and twisted her head, ever so slightly, in her father's arms.

Her still unfocused baby eyes met Karana's, and he was surprised to see that one eye was orange and one eye was red.

And inside was a soul he recognized, a soul he had tethered to Earth himself.

Guleum.

AN NING was filling the bath with warm water when Karana slipped into the room.

He hovered behind her and said, "An Ning, I need to talk to you about something."

The baby. Maybe I should have checked with Karana before answering Jin. Karana had been odd for the rest of the celebration, after she had talked to Jin about babies.

"You don't want children?" she asked, trying to hide the tremor in her voice. He might still be scarred from when their foster children died several millennia ago. It scared her too, but she was a god now.

"What? Oh, um," said Karana. "I *was* thinking about babies. Yes, about babies, and what happens to the souls that I tether to Earth." He laughed, but it was pitchy and fake. "I never thought about it before, but do you know—do you remember—every time you passed through the Sea of Souls, you returned to Earth as a baby or a seed, and... Did you oust the soul that was already there?"

"Excuse me?" She felt mildly offended. "Are you asking me if I kicked out baby's souls?"

"Ah, no, you wouldn't do that. You would never do that."

"Thank you."

"But," Karana persisted, "you're nice and some of the beings I reincarnated aren't. So, I'm trying to understand, when does a soul form? Is it at conception or birth or..."

An Ning rubbed her brow. "I don't know the answer to that."

"But you've experienced passing through the sea and returning to Earth. You said you remembered it." His hands were suddenly wrapped around her upper arms, and An Ning realized that as bizarre as this questioning was, it mattered to him.

She considered his words carefully, and she thought she saw the problem. He was genuinely concerned that he was somehow hurting new, fresh souls by letting reincarnated ones take their physical forms. An Ning closed her eyes and tried to remember.

"You have to understand," she said, "even though the memories of passing through the sea and returning to Earth came back to me, they are very vague. Like I experienced them as a baby myself. But... I suppose, if I had to describe it, it's more like I was floating, lost, and then someone embraced me, and I was where I was supposed to be. Maybe—you realize I am not one to dwell on such things, but maybe every time I reincarnated, I joined a like-minded soul."

"A like-minded soul?" he echoed. "But then, wouldn't evil

beings stay evil, and our whole mission be doomed?"

An Ning flicked him on the forehead. He winced, but those red eyes became a little less wild. A little closer to rust, a little farther from blood.

"You know that's not true. The souls we have tracked over the past three hundred years have not gone down the cult's route of anger and violence.

"When I said like-minded... Remember, returning to Earth, the soul is practically a blank slate. None of them are evil. But I suppose we still have some affinities, some natural inclinations. You say mine is peace. I like making things, growing things. And being quiet and careful. So souls like that would call to me, and we would join, I think. Becoming a new, bigger soul, maybe."

"Hmmm." Karana released her arms and rubbed his lips. "So you believe in our mission? You believe that no one is inherently evil, and that reincarnation truly allows someone a fresh start?

She pounded on his chest for being obtuse. "Yes, of course!"

"Okay. Okay. Good." He shook his head. "That's all I needed to talk about, thank you." He started to walk away, even though she had thought he was going to join her in the bath.

An Ning put her hands on her hips. "You didn't answer *my* question."

Karana stopped and blinked. "Which was?

"Do you not want children?"

"Oh!" He returned to her and caressed her cheek. "After what happened in the foothills—our adopted children—"

An Ning nodded once, to let him know he didn't have to

detail it.

"I thought I would never take responsibility for a child again. When you adopted the Bulgae, I was terrified. And then I realized that you've been caring for your disciples like they are your children too. And now—well, the challenges we've overcome together have given me courage. I do want children.

"But I thought—you like to change your shape. Including your male form. Maybe a baby could be alright inside you while you cycle through the others, but I don't think the pregnancy would last through that."

"Oh. Yes. But for the sake of baby, I could keep one." An Ning licked her lips nervously. "Actually, there is one form that is more comfortable to me than the others, but I have hesitated to show it to you."

Karana released her. "Why?"

"I thought it might bring back bad memories."

He tilted his head, confused.

An Ning shifted. When she finished, she had combined her favorite parts of her male-An Ning form (the height and strength) and her female-An Ning form (the curves and her face). She had looked in the mirror and knew, despite being taller and more muscular, she closely resembled the seventeen-year-old who had been beaten to death.

For her, it was empowering. It said that she was her, and her body was hers, no matter how anyone else violated it. She couldn't always control what happened to her—or how others saw her—but she always had autonomy over who she was.

She was afraid Karana wouldn't see it that way though. She was afraid he would see a victim, a woman he had failed to protect.

He looked shocked, and An Ning was about to shift again when he set his hand on either side of her face and kissed her deeply.

It was a little aggressive—not too long ago, a kiss like this would have scared An Ning. Not any longer though: after three centuries together, she had confidence in herself and trust in Karana.

She kissed him back, and Karana untied and discarded her robes. She returned the favor.

He gathered her in his arms and lowered her into the bath, then joined her in the water.

For a moment, he stared at her in silence. "You always look beautiful, and I love you in all your forms, but..." His brow wrinkled, and An Ning grinned.

"I know," she said. "I feel this one is the truest expression of me as well. Though sometimes I still enjoy the shifting, adopting the attitude of a different version of myself...this is the one I could hold for a thousand years."

His eyes flickered over her body, and his lips spread in a wide smile. "Then I think we should get started on our goals right away."

"I couldn't agree more," she purred, and slid against him, heedless of the water that sloshed out of the bath. Soon she didn't know where she ended and he began.

Which was just how she liked it.

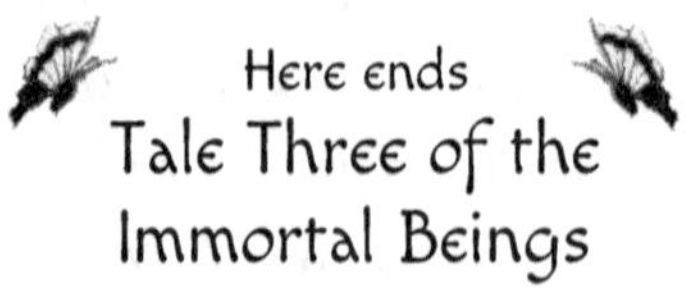

Here ends
Tale Three of the
Immortal Beings

Glossary

Amalgan – Karana's first mortal lover; a woman of the Eagle Tribe in Ehkoron who lived 87 millennia after creation.

Akemi – one of the Sea Dragon's granddaughters and a disciple of An Ning.

An Ning – a young immortal.

Bando – the peninsula separated from the Zhongtu region by the Byeong Mountains. Bando is a mortal nation as well as an immortal region and claims an unbroken line of rulers for 40,000 years.

Bai – see Knowing God.

between – how immortals refer to the time lost during teleportation; between is remembered only by the sense of time passing.

black – the ninth color, black magic changes the essence of things.

blue – the sixth color, blue magic reads thoughts.

Bulgae – immortal creatures that resemble dogs made of fire.

Byeong Mountains – mountain range that forms the border between Zhongtu and Bando.

Chain – Karana's fourth mortal lover; a singer who lived in Jeevanti 94 millennia after creation.

Chika – one of the Sea Dragon's granddaughters and disciple of An Ning.

Colors – how the first nine immortals are known collectively. Also, the way the essential natures of immortals are categorized. All immortals can identify their natures by a set color, though it is only obvious in the appearances of the Nine Colors and their offspring.

Crescent Moon – a long island east of Bando; the Moon Deer lives here.

Cult of Alag Karana – see Sundered Cult.

Daichin – the God of Swordsmanship.

Dalagoi – Immortal creatures that a resemble a fusion of serpents and eagles, they are native to Ehkoron.

deity – an immortal who has mortal worshippers. The beliefs of those worshippers amplify the power of the deity but can also limit their abilities if the mortals specifically believe a deity cannot do something. Disciples of a deity thus spend much time ensuring the worshippers' beliefs align with their deity's goals. Deities are properly addressed as "divinity."

disciple – immortals who follow and learn from another immortal are called disciples; most deities have disciples.

Earth – one of the three realms in the world, the others being the Heavens and the Underworld.

Ehkoron – the northernmost region of Earth, north of the Cold Peaks.

golem – a magical construct that has a singular purpose.

god/goddess – see deity.

Godsmarket – a marketplace in the former Sun Palace where immortals sold and traded goods.

green – the fifth color, green magic heals. See Haraa.

Guiying – a common name among An Ning's worshippers; also the courtesan who became her first monk.

Guleum – The youngest son of the Sun Emperor and the Goddess of Flight, Guleum was named the God of Wind at his birth 97,000 years after creation, but he had no established temples at the Sun Emperor's death. His full name is Sunlight through the Clouds. A mostly red with some orange immortal.

Haraa – Once a leaf, Haraa became the first green immortal 29,000 years after creation. Haraa is known as the Warden and is the ultimate doctor for all immortals. She is the mistress of the Wood Pavilions.

Heping – Karana's second mortal lover, a gardener who lived in Zhongtu 89 millennia after creation.

Heaven – one of the three realms in the world, the others being Earth and the Underworld. Currently it holds the Immortal Meeting Grounds, Salaana's prison, and the ruins of the Sun Palace.

Heiwa – Karana's fifth mortal lover, a leader of a warrior clan in the Crescent Moon who lived 95 millennia after creation.

immortal being – a being that will not (it is believed) die of old age; the oldest immortal being is Bai, who is 78,000 years old as of this tale. Immortals can be formed spontaneously, from anything, when they persevere in existing. The oldest nine immortals (the Colors) each formed 1000 years apart; after that, an immortal appeared spontaneously each year. It is commonly believed that this change accounts for the dramatic decrease in power between the first nine and all subsequent immortals. All power an immortal has can be categorized as one or more colors. Immortals can also be born if at least one of their parents is an immortal. In this case, the born immortal gains access to their parent's power pool. If the family members compete for their pool of power, it comes down to will and need. Immortal pregnancies last 1000 years and born immortals reach adulthood after 4-6,000 years. As adults, immortals age due to trauma, stress, or grief.

immortal creature – creatures that live forever. Like beings, each has innate colors.

indigo – the seventh color, indigo magic nullifies yellow (influence thoughts), violet (influence emotion), and black (influence essence).

Jeevanti – The westernmost region of the world, it is known for a colorful aesthetic and rich, spicy food.

Jin – see Threefold Goddess.

Karana – a red and white immortal; the former God of Destruction. His full name is Sundered by Sunlight, and he is the son of the deceased Sun Emperor and the uncle of the Threefold Goddess.

Knowing God – Bai, the husband of Karana's niece (the Threefold Goddess). A main character of Tales 1 and 2 of the Immortal Beings.

Koch-ssi – an immortal creature with an affinity for plants.

Love God – Xiao, a violet and black immortal whom Karana has known since he was born. A main character of Tales 1 and 2 of the Immortal Beings.

Love God's Heart – Nanami, a disowned daughter of the Sea Dragon and the wife of the Love God. A main character of Tales 1 and 2 of the Immortal Beings.

magic – the word immortals use for their associated powers. All magic is categorized by the color over which it has dominion and comes with an associated ability. The first nine immortals—originally known as the Colors—have significantly more magic than all other immortal beings, but all immortals have some magic.

Maoyi – city on the southern tip of Zhongtu region famous for its street food.

Miho – one of the Sea Dragon's granddaughters and disciple of An Ning.

Moon Deer - a white immortal who will remember and keep all secrets told to him. His home in Tsuku also houses an extensive collection of maps and research on immortal creatures. His wife died long ago; he has three daughters, notably Atsuko, who runs his household, and Miko, who married the Sea Dragon, and many grandchildren.

Moon Goddess – Once twilight, the Moon Goddess became the first violet immortal 32,000 years after creation. She was married to the Night God and had one child, the Love God.

Night God - Once a shadow, the Night God became the first black immortal 33,000 years after creation. He was married to the Moon Goddess, and they had one child, the Love God.

Nine Colors – see Color.

Ningjingcun – a "peaceful village," where An Ning is the patron god. They prosper through their unusual crops, including black rice and black roses, all created by An Ning.

Ojichan – the Sea Dragon (as called by his grandchildren).

orange – the third color, it nullifies the powers of white (knowing the essence), red (feeling emotion), and blue (reading thoughts).

Po – a large island south of Ni.

Pyeonghwa – Karana's sixth mortal lover, a pilgrim who settled in the Byeong Mountains of Bando 96 millennia after creation.

red – the second color, red magic feels emotion.

Ruins of the Sun Palace – once a city in the Heavens from which the Sun Emperor ruled, it was laid to waste by the immortal creatures upon their escape from the Underworld. It remains suspended in the Heavens by the will of the Threefold Goddess.

Salaana – Karana's full sister. Once known as the Goddess of Justice, she is currently imprisoned by her niece (the Threefold Goddess).

Santi – Karana's third mortal lover, who lived in the Great Ladies 93 millennia after creation.

Santiphaph – Karana's seventh mortal lover, a queen of

Maoyi who lived 97 millennia after creation.

Sanctuary Caves – these caves are worshipped by mortals for restoring things to their natural state, including curing most diseases as long as the ill remain inside.

Sea Dragon – Ao, the Color Indigo, and the grandfather of An Ning's three disciples.

Sea Palace – the underwater residence of the Sea Dragon, the Sea Palace is contained within a magical dome of air.

Shaanti – Karana's head monk, who lived 82 millennia after creation.

Sun Emperor – the father of Karana and the former ruler of all immortals. The Sun Emperor was the Color Red; his power was inherited by his descendants, Karana, Salaana, Guleum, and the Threefold Goddess.

Sundered Cult – a cult that arose out of Karana's first temple. Despite being eradicated multiple times, the Cult always seems to rise again.

teleport – the word immortals use when they magically move from one place in the world to another. Teleporting takes a great deal of power; the average immortal can only teleport once a day and it takes them about an hour.

Threefold Goddess – a red, orange, yellow, and blue immortal, she is Karana's niece, Jin, and a main character of

Tales 1 and 2 of the Immortal Beings.

Underworld – one of the three realms in the world, the others being the Heavens and Earth.

violet – the eighth color, violet magic influences emotion.

white – the first color, white magic knows the essence of things.

White Mountain – Bai's origin and home, the White Mountain is the tallest mountain on Earth and is perpetually snow-capped. It is on the border of Ehkoron and Zhongtu.

Wood Pavilions – The home of Haraa, the Wood Pavilions are a section of forest with twenty-odd copper-roofed buildings. They are known for wild parties and hedonistic living but are also the best place to go for healing.

Xiao – see Love God.

Xiling – a city burned by Karana 98,000 years after creation.

Xuezei – immortal creatures that drink blood.

yellow – the fourth color, yellow magic influences thoughts.

Zhongtu – the largest region on Earth, to the east of the Great Ladies and the south of the Cold Peaks; the Wood Pavilions are here as well as Ningjingcun.

Author's Note

Many readers will recognize An Ning's internal struggle as gender and body dysphoria. Given its magical cause and solution, her journey cannot be equated to those of real humans whose bodies do not align with their self-image, but hopefully An Ning's questions and epiphanies have some relevancy to the real world. I believe that most adults today (including me) feel some body dysphoria (which can be exclusive of gender identity) because we receive so much external input about how our bodies "should" be and many of us are seeking to be more ourselves. If this book happened to introduce you to concepts that you haven't considered before, please know that An Ning's journey and happy ending is unique to her—everyone's experience is different—and consider checking out GLAAD.org to learn more about the variety of ways gender dysphoria manifests, how to be an ally, or how to find support for yourself.

A Note About Language

Because I am more interested in studying existing languages than creating my own, I drew names from the real-world languages whose cultures and myths inspired elements of this world.

Just like in our languages, the words of Immortal Beings shift and change. When I write a name in English—such as the White Mountain—the characters know what it means (just like the name Joy has a clear meaning in English). When I use a different language—such as Ningjingcun—it represents a meaning that has shifted or is no longer used, and the characters may or may not be aware of its roots (just as only linguists and history buffs will know a town called Chester was probably once a fort). Some names I took wholly from a language (An Ning/ 安宁 means peaceful in Chinese; in fact all of her names mean peace), while others are variations I created (Karana is derived from the Hindi phrase अलग करना/alag karana meaning "to sunder," and I have since learned is the "to" part). And a few names I created without regard to their meaning—the city Xiling could have a few meanings in Chinese, but I choose it for its sound rather than its possible definitions.

If I have made a mistake in my use of various languages, please forgive me, and know my intent was to celebrate and reference the inspirations for this book.

Acknowledgments

Thank you to my beloved partner Joshua who—though he never aspired to it—has become my most trusted editor and sounding-board.

So much gratitude to my alpha readers who found errors and improved character arcs. Each brought their own strengths to hopefully make this book better rounded: James Zola (who is upright and analytical), Hwona (who is curious and subversive), Helen Luk (who is artistic and efficient), and Ashley Hanson (who is compassionate and enthusiastic). Your encouragement and criticisms are equally appreciated!

Just as essential are my beta-readers, who do all the same things for the second draft! So much gratitude to Matilda Pilch Williamson (who's keen in sights immediately resonated, though I never would have thought of them myself) and Genevieve Zola (who told me not to settle with the ending). You both brought this book closer to the story I wanted to write, and I was honored to have your help. And a big thank you to Margaret Ball (who said it's heartbreaking), Faith Enuol (who said everyone can be more themself), Gail Hanson (who said it's terribly romantic), Cheryl Chudyk (who whipped my verbs into shape *and* wondered if Bai realized what would happen to An Ning at the Sea of Souls), Amena Jamali (who reminded me that I have to deal with whatever ending I chose) and Daryl Leonardo (who read the whole book aloud). Both Amena and Daryl are authors—epic fantasy fans should check out Amena's series *The Lord of Freedom* and YA readers will love Daryl's novels, *drown* and *silver boy.*

Lastly, shoutout to Steven J. Morris, author of the marvelous urban-space-fantasy *The Guardian League,* and Beth and Nicole of ByTheBookVBP, who have given me so many flotation devices as I doggy-paddle in the murky waters of self-promotion.

About the Author

Edith Pawlicki lives in Connecticut with her husband, twin sons, dog, and two rabbits. She fell in love with words in fourth grade and finds writing necessary to free the worlds and characters in her head. When she isn't busy being a mom and author, she enjoys cooking and crafts. In addition to the Immortal Beings series, she has also written a YA science fiction novel, Minerva. Find her and her books at edithpawlicki.com or on Instagram @edithpawlicki.

Book Design

This book features two open-source fonts: Macondo Swash Caps by John Vargas Beltran for chapter titles and Amiri Khaled Hosny and Sebastian Kosch. The images surrounding each chapter number are edited photographs from public domain images of tsubas (Japanese sword guards) from the Met Online Collection. The six butterflies at each scene break were scanned and cut from the same handmade origami paper featured on the front cover. Behind the maps and diagrams is more handmade origami paper. All layout and image edits were done by Edith Pawlicki.